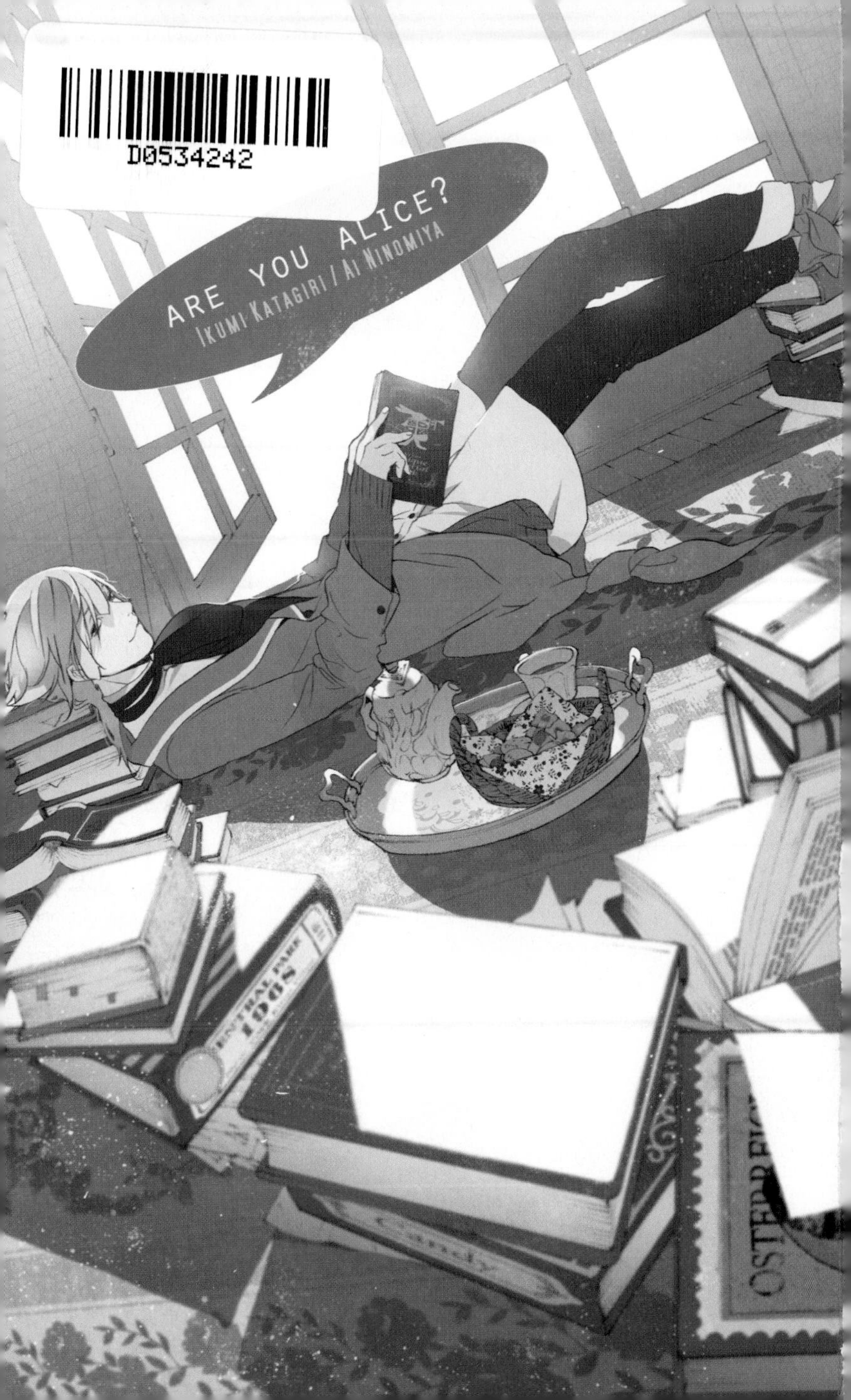
ARE YOU ALICE?
IKUMI KATAGIRI / AI NINOMIYA

Are You Alice?
11
CONTENTS!

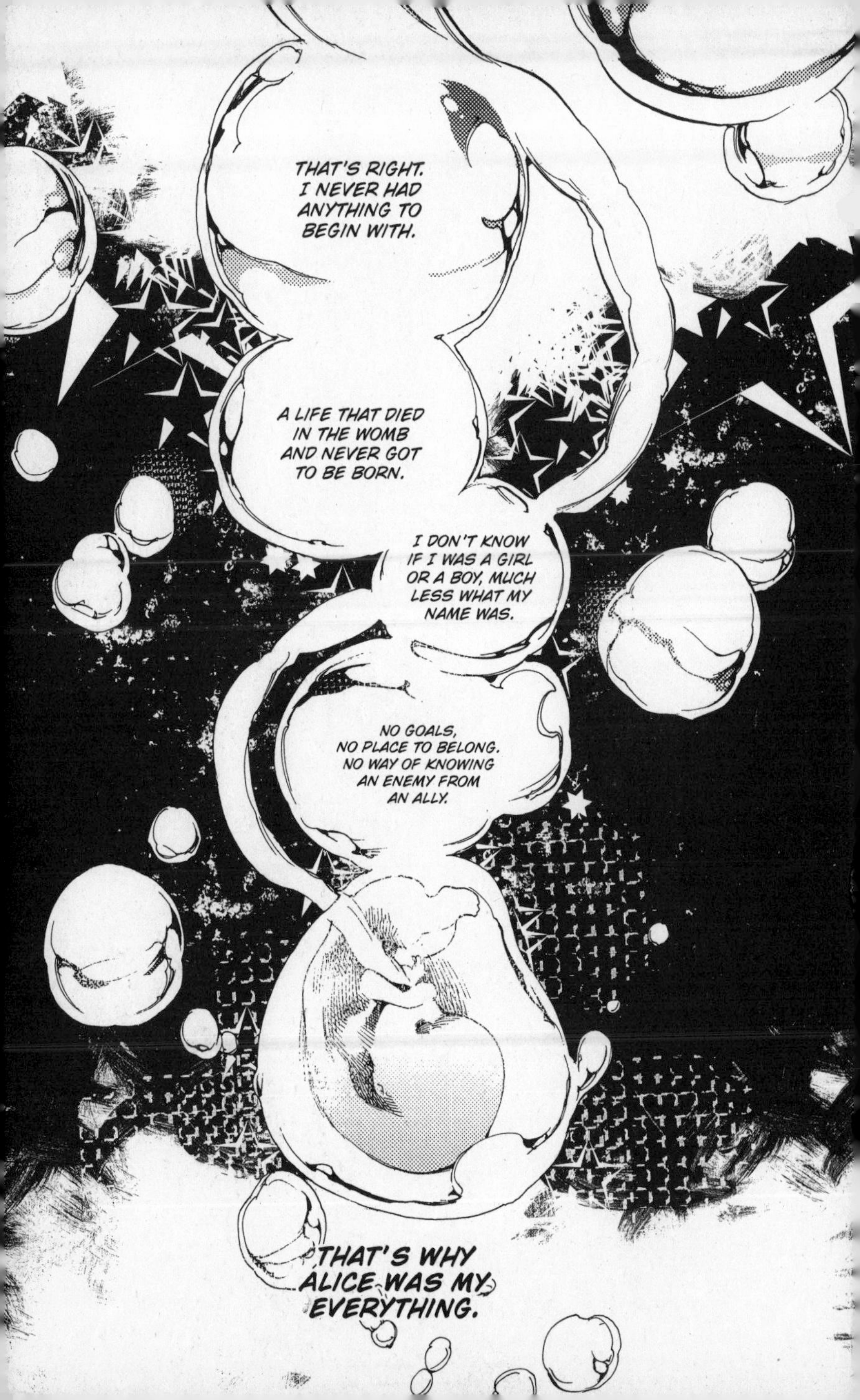
THAT'S RIGHT. I NEVER HAD ANYTHING TO BEGIN WITH.
A LIFE THAT DIED IN THE WOMB AND NEVER GOT TO BE BORN.
I DON'T KNOW IF I WAS A GIRL OR A BOY, MUCH LESS WHAT MY NAME WAS.
NO GOALS, NO PLACE TO BELONG. NO WAY OF KNOWING AN ENEMY FROM AN ALLY.
THAT'S WHY ALICE WAS MY EVERYTHING.

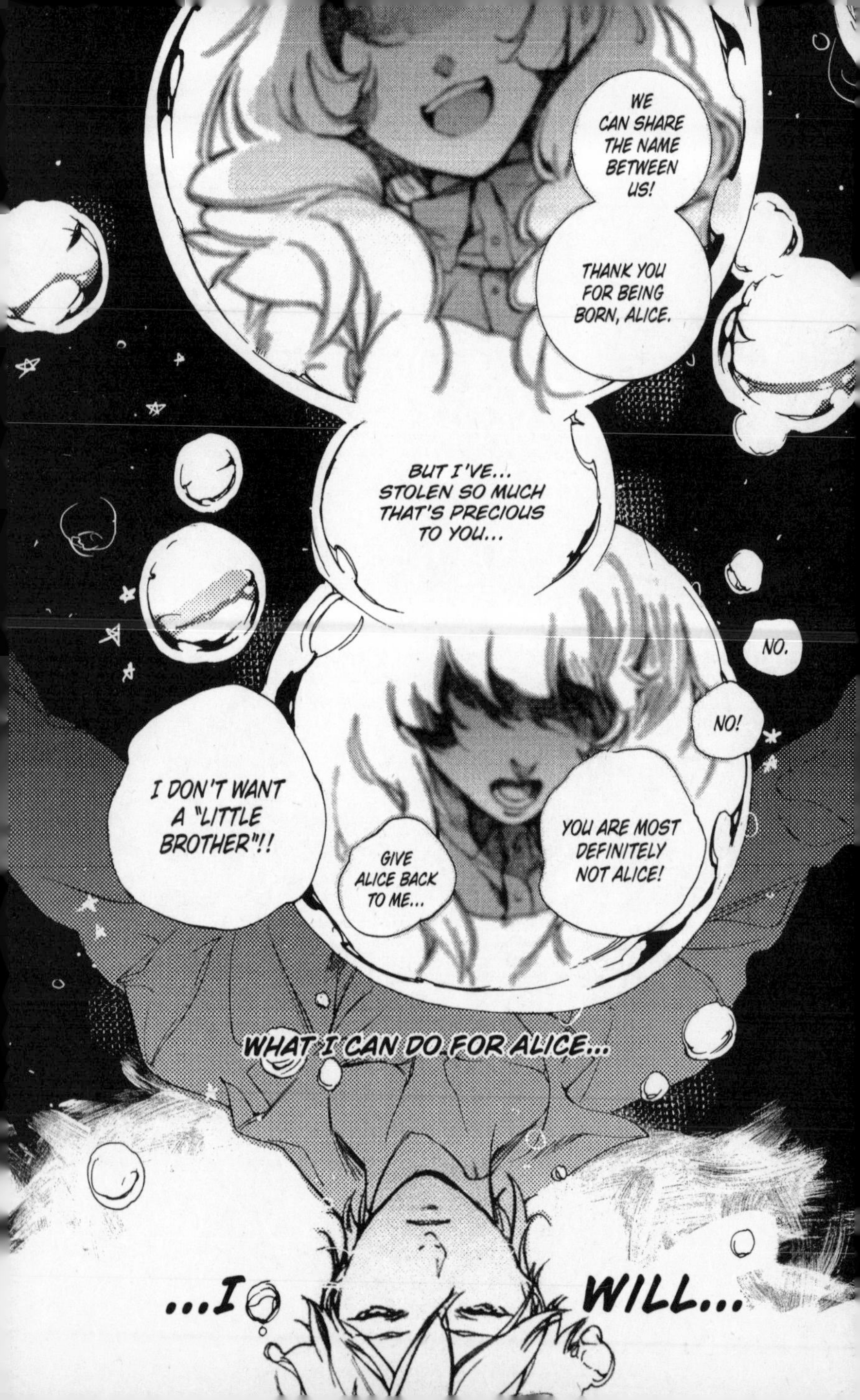
WE CAN SHARE THE NAME BETWEEN US!
THANK YOU FOR BEING BORN, ALICE.
BUT I'VE... STOLEN SO MUCH THAT'S PRECIOUS TO YOU...
NO.
NO!
YOU ARE MOST DEFINITELY NOT ALICE!
GIVE ALICE BACK TO ME...
I DON'T WANT A "LITTLE BROTHER"!!
WHAT I CAN DO FOR ALICE...
...I WILL...

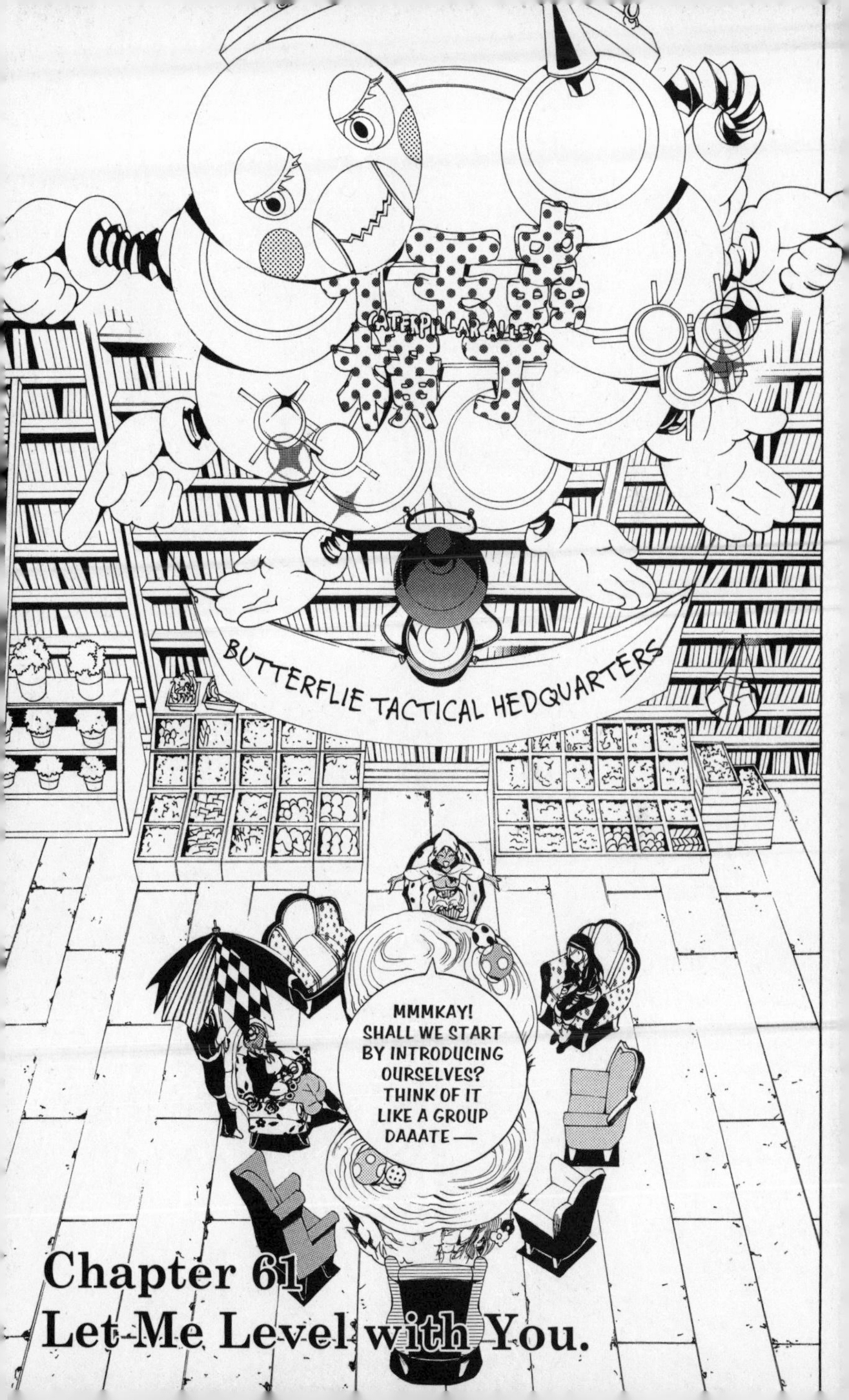
CATERPILLAR ALLEY
BUTTERFLIE TACTICAL HEDQUARTERS
MMMKAY! SHALL WE START BY INTRODUCING OURSELVES? THINK OF IT LIKE A GROUP DAAATE —

Chapter 61
Let Me Level with You.

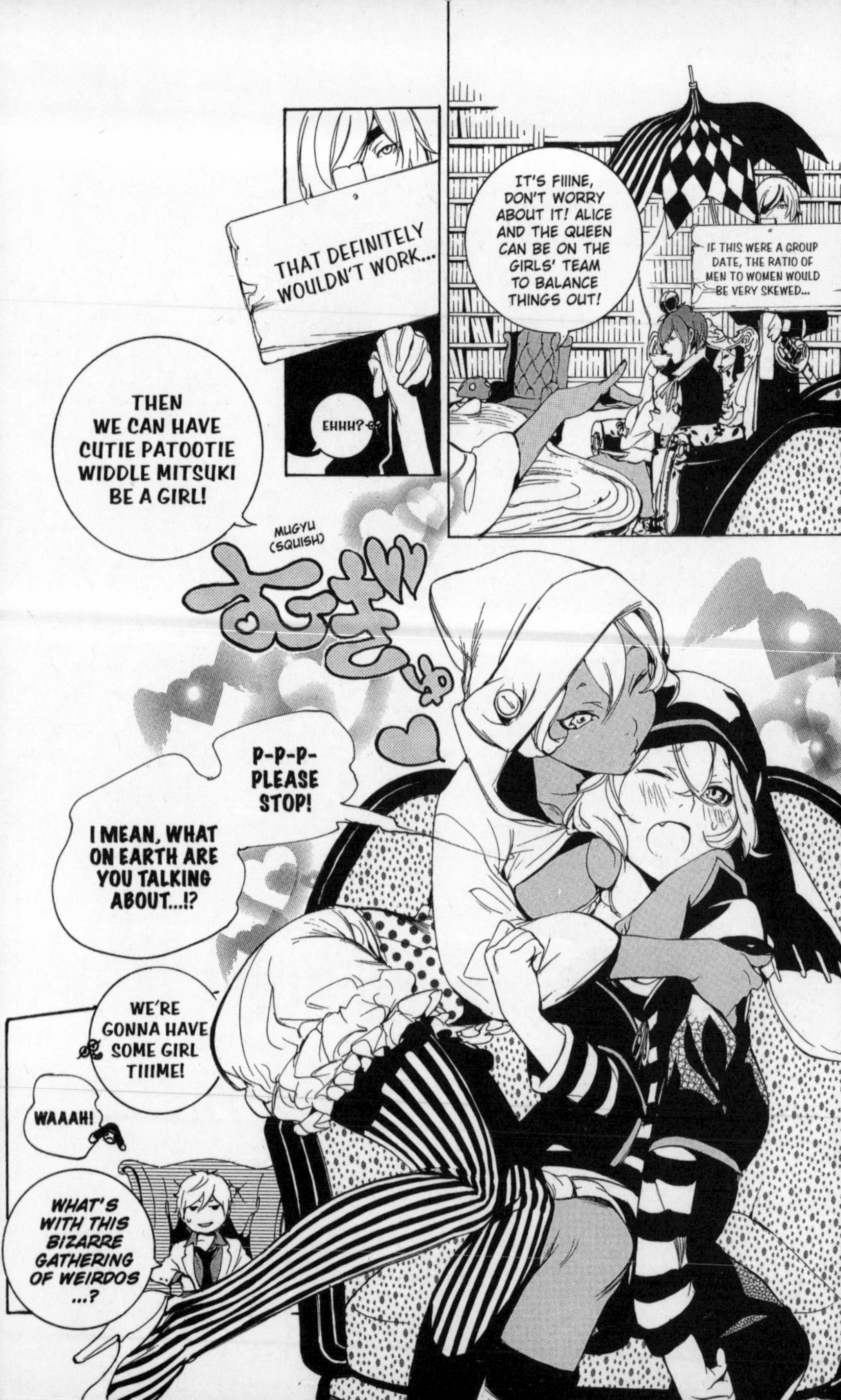
IF THIS WERE A GROUP DATE, THE RATIO OF MEN TO WOMEN WOULD BE VERY SKEWED...
IT'S FIIINE, DON'T WORRY ABOUT IT! ALICE AND THE QUEEN CAN BE ON THE GIRLS' TEAM TO BALANCE THINGS OUT!
THAT DEFINITELY WOULDN'T WORK...
EHHH?
THEN WE CAN HAVE CUTIE PATOOTIE WIDDLE MITSUKI BE A GIRL!
MUGYU (SQUISH)
むぎゅ
P-P-P-PLEASE STOP!
I MEAN, WHAT ON EARTH ARE YOU TALKING ABOUT...!?
WE'RE GONNA HAVE SOME GIRL TIIIME!
WAAAH!
WHAT'S WITH THIS BIZARRE GATHERING OF WEIRDOS ...?

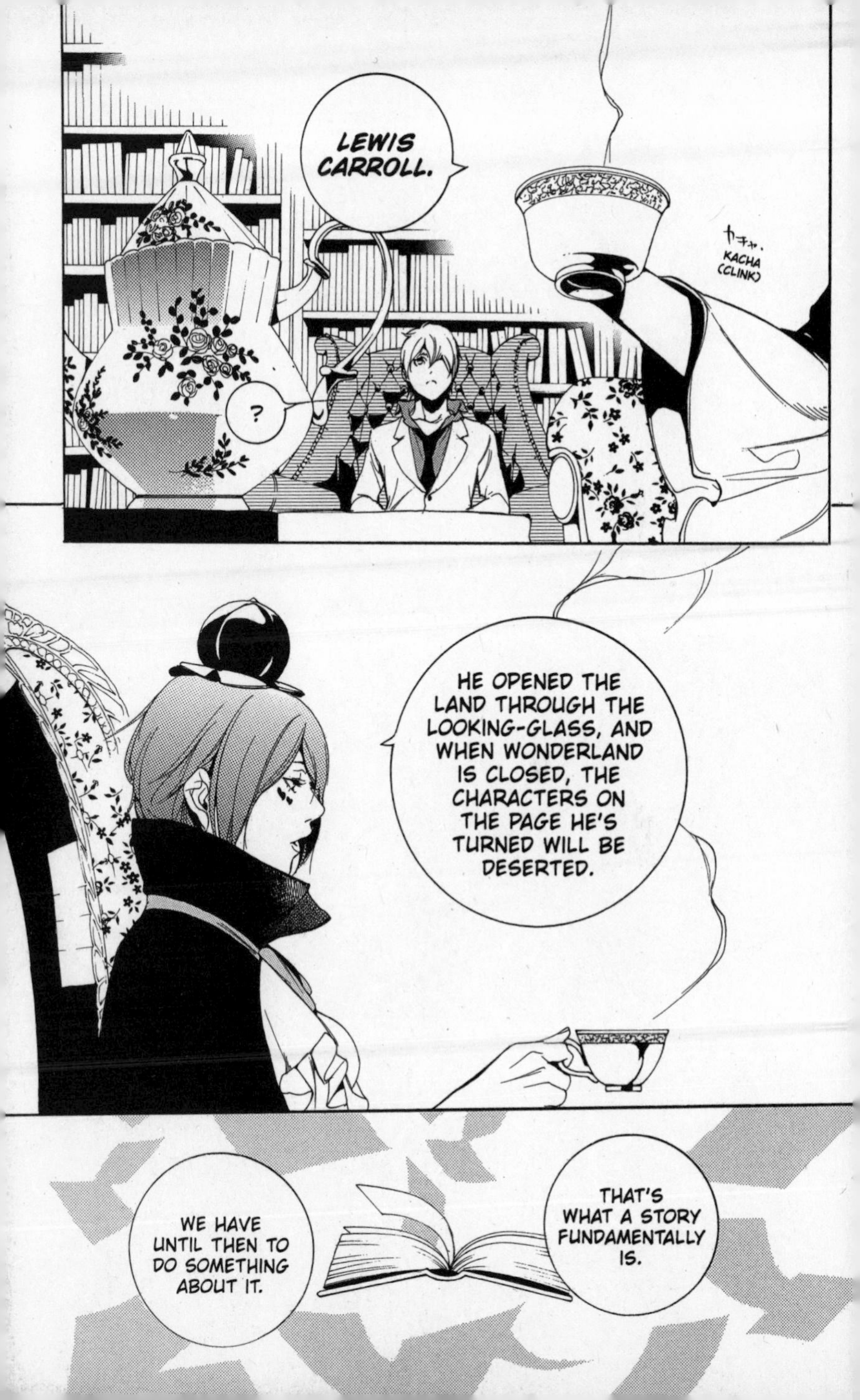
カチャ.
KACHA (CLINK)
LEWIS CARROLL.
?
HE OPENED THE LAND THROUGH THE LOOKING-GLASS, AND WHEN WONDERLAND IS CLOSED, THE CHARACTERS ON THE PAGE HE'S TURNED WILL BE DESERTED.
THAT'S WHAT A STORY FUNDAMENTALLY IS.
WE HAVE UNTIL THEN TO DO SOMETHING ABOUT IT.

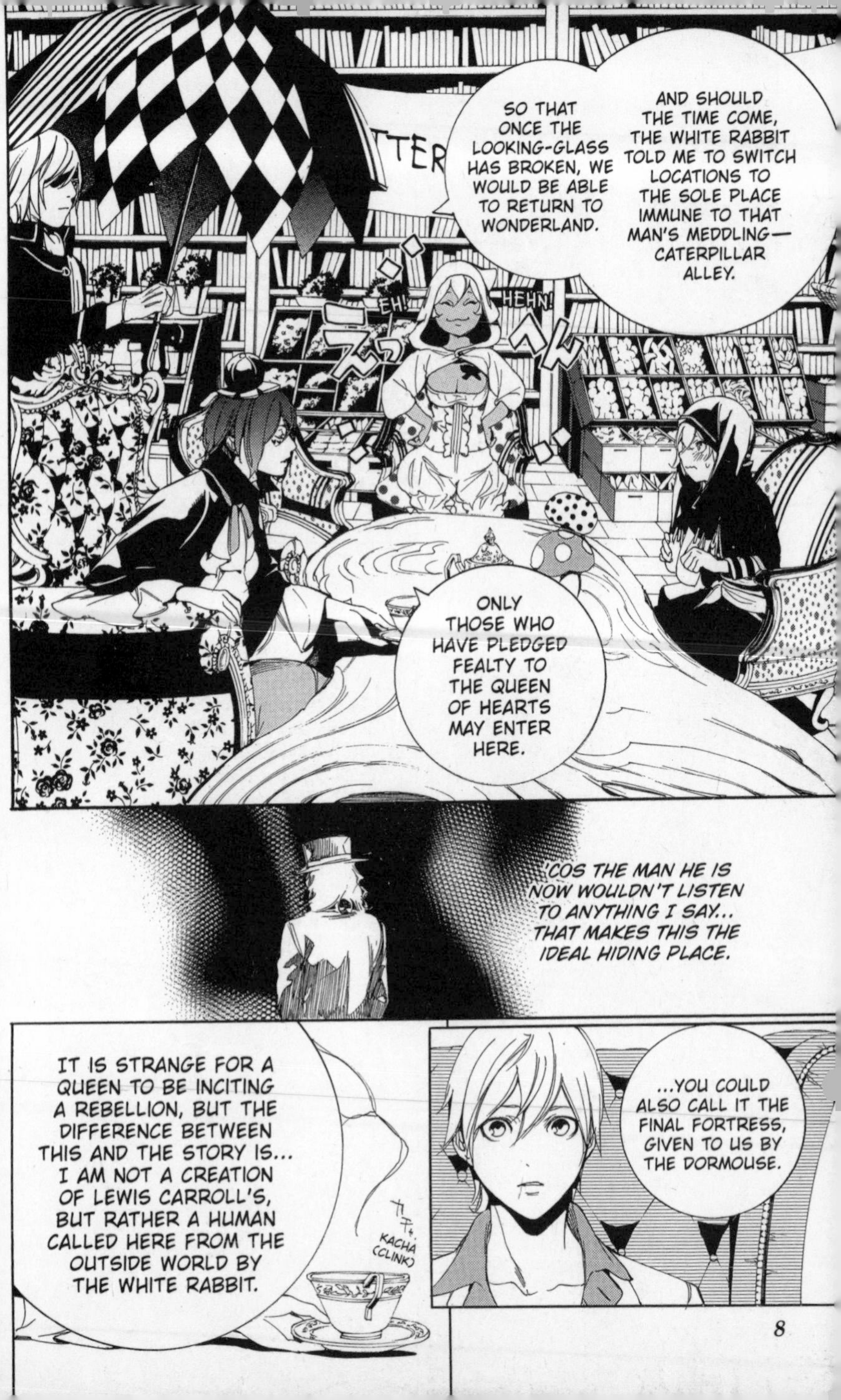

AND SHOULD THE TIME COME, THE WHITE RABBIT TOLD ME TO SWITCH LOCATIONS TO THE SOLE PLACE IMMUNE TO THAT MAN'S MEDDLING—CATERPILLAR ALLEY.
SO THAT ONCE THE LOOKING-GLASS HAS BROKEN, WE WOULD BE ABLE TO RETURN TO WONDERLAND.
HEHN!
EH!
ONLY THOSE WHO HAVE PLEDGED FEALTY TO THE QUEEN OF HEARTS MAY ENTER HERE.
'COS THE MAN HE IS NOW WOULDN'T LISTEN TO ANYTHING I SAY... THAT MAKES THIS THE IDEAL HIDING PLACE.
...YOU COULD ALSO CALL IT THE FINAL FORTRESS, GIVEN TO US BY THE DORMOUSE.
IT IS STRANGE FOR A QUEEN TO BE INCITING A REBELLION, BUT THE DIFFERENCE BETWEEN THIS AND THE STORY IS... I AM NOT A CREATION OF LEWIS CARROLL'S, BUT RATHER A HUMAN CALLED HERE FROM THE OUTSIDE WORLD BY THE WHITE RABBIT.
KACHA (CLINK)

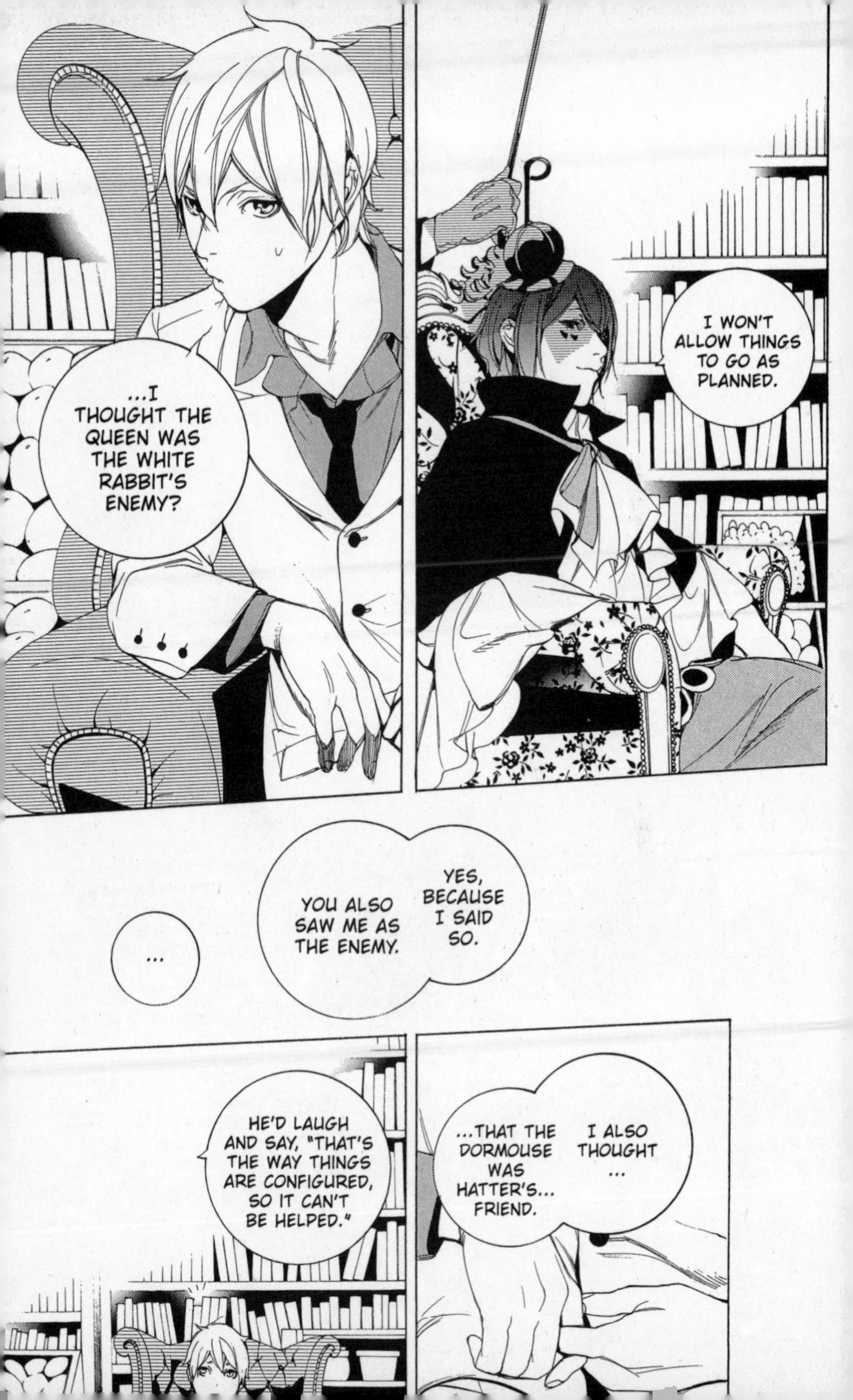
I WON'T ALLOW THINGS TO GO AS PLANNED.
...I THOUGHT THE QUEEN WAS THE WHITE RABBIT'S ENEMY?
YES, BECAUSE I SAID SO.
YOU ALSO SAW ME AS THE ENEMY.
...
I ALSO THOUGHT ...
...THAT THE DORMOUSE WAS HATTER'S... FRIEND.
HE'D LAUGH AND SAY, "THAT'S THE WAY THINGS ARE CONFIGURED, SO IT CAN'T BE HELPED."

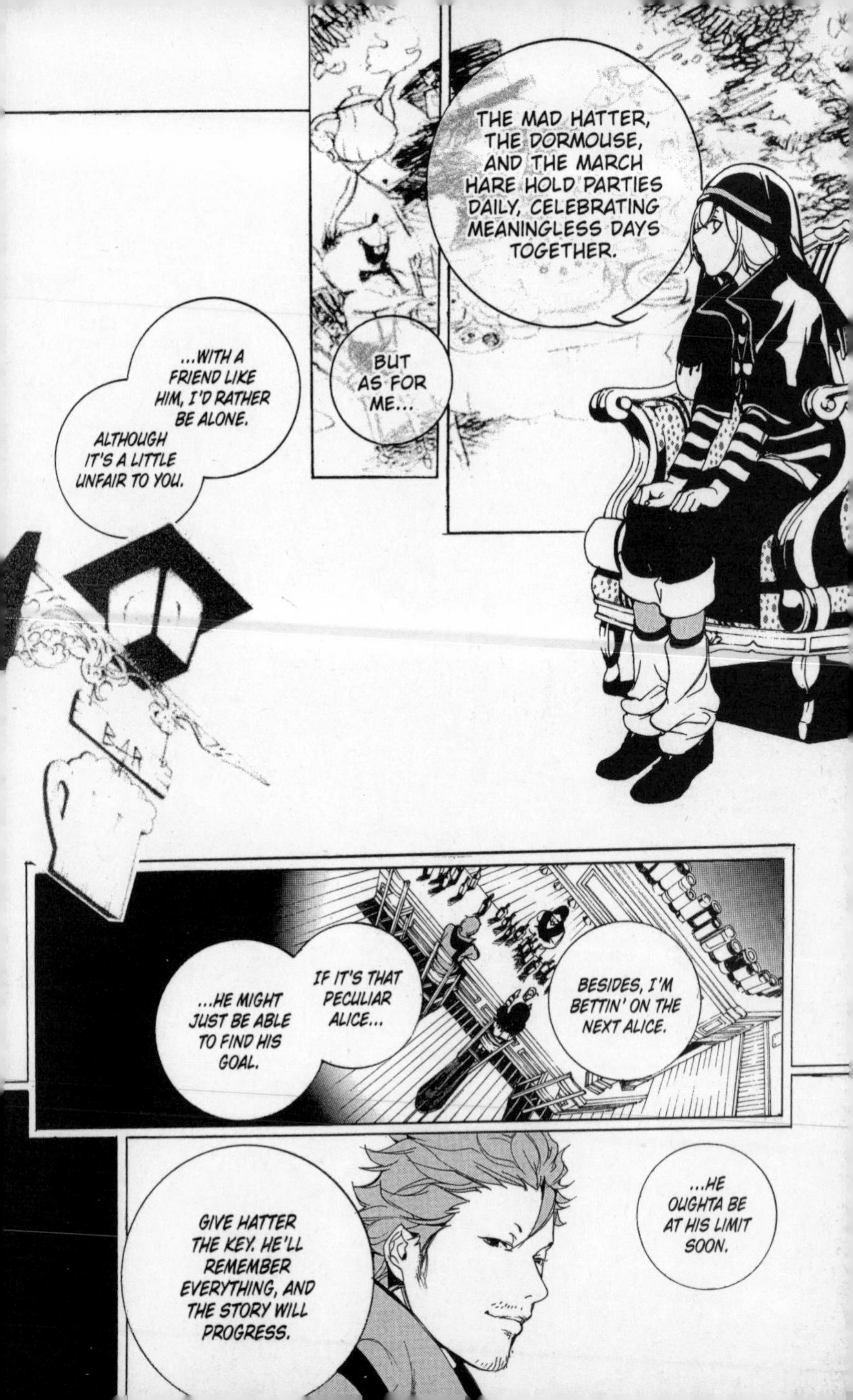
THE MAD HATTER, THE DORMOUSE, AND THE MARCH HARE HOLD PARTIES DAILY, CELEBRATING MEANINGLESS DAYS TOGETHER.
BUT AS FOR ME...
...WITH A FRIEND LIKE HIM, I'D RATHER BE ALONE.
ALTHOUGH IT'S A LITTLE UNFAIR TO YOU.
BAR
BESIDES, I'M BETTIN' ON THE NEXT ALICE.
IF IT'S THAT PECULIAR ALICE...
...HE MIGHT JUST BE ABLE TO FIND HIS GOAL.
...HE OUGHTA BE AT HIS LIMIT SOON.
GIVE HATTER THE KEY. HE'LL REMEMBER EVERYTHING, AND THE STORY WILL PROGRESS.

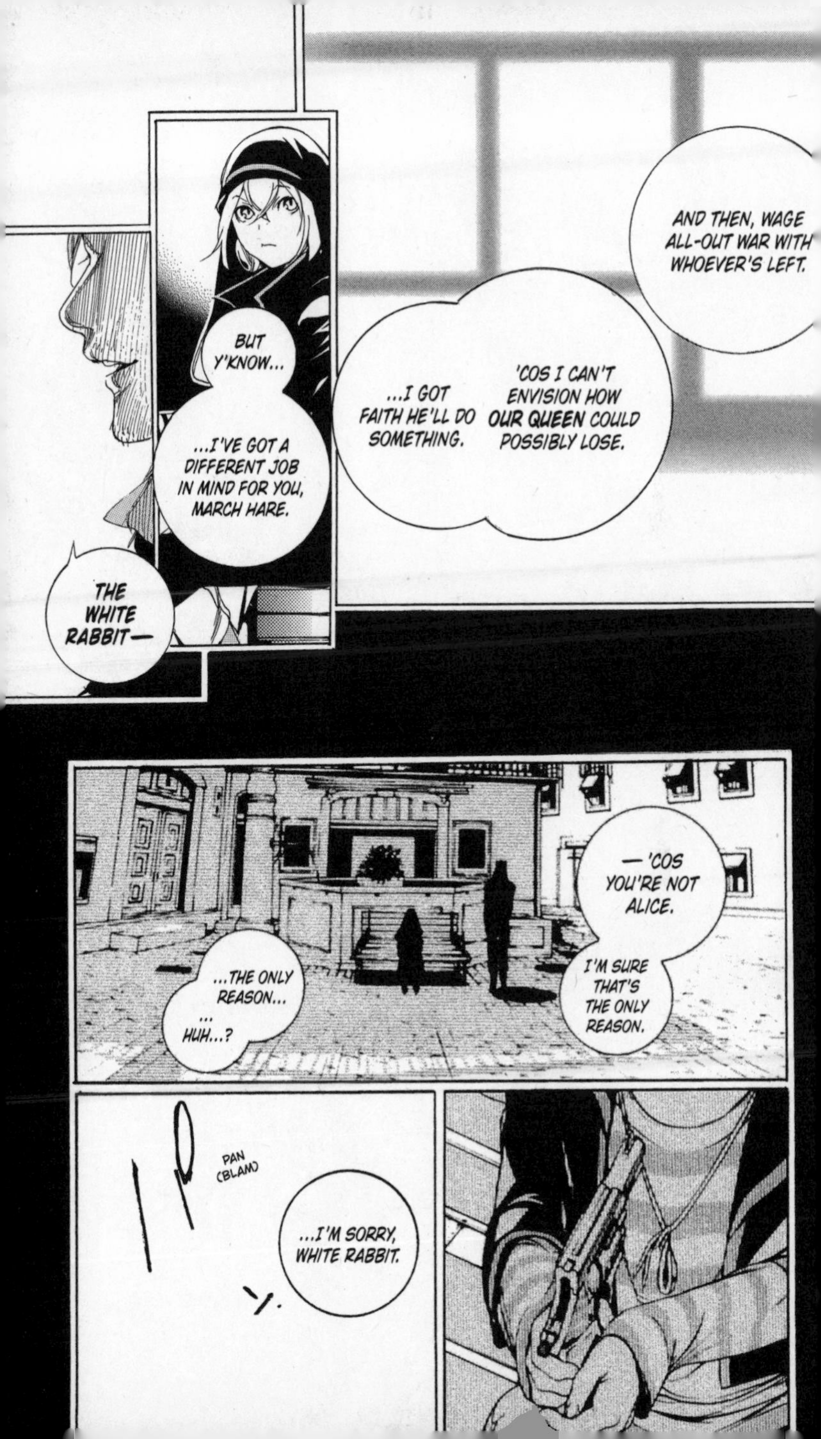
AND THEN, WAGE ALL-OUT WAR WITH WHOEVER'S LEFT.
'COS I CAN'T ENVISION HOW OUR QUEEN COULD POSSIBLY LOSE.
...I GOT FAITH HE'LL DO SOMETHING.
BUT Y'KNOW...
...I'VE GOT A DIFFERENT JOB IN MIND FOR YOU, MARCH HARE.
THE WHITE RABBIT—
— 'COS YOU'RE NOT ALICE.
I'M SURE THAT'S THE ONLY REASON.
...THE ONLY REASON...
... HUH...?
PAN (BLAM)
...I'M SORRY, WHITE RABBIT.

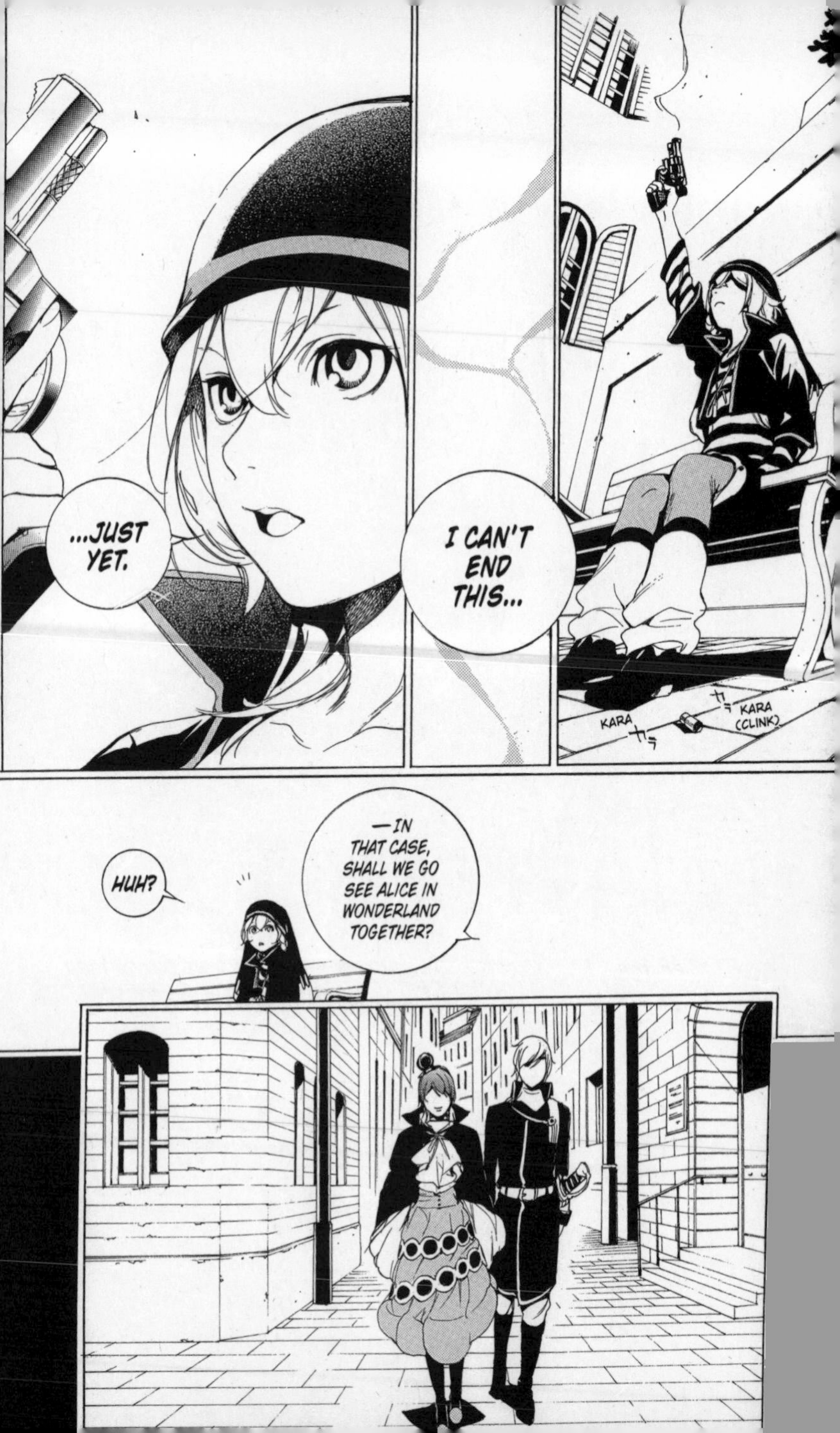
KARA (CLINK)
KARA
I CAN'T END THIS...
...JUST YET.
—IN THAT CASE, SHALL WE GO SEE ALICE IN WONDERLAND TOGETHER?
HUH?

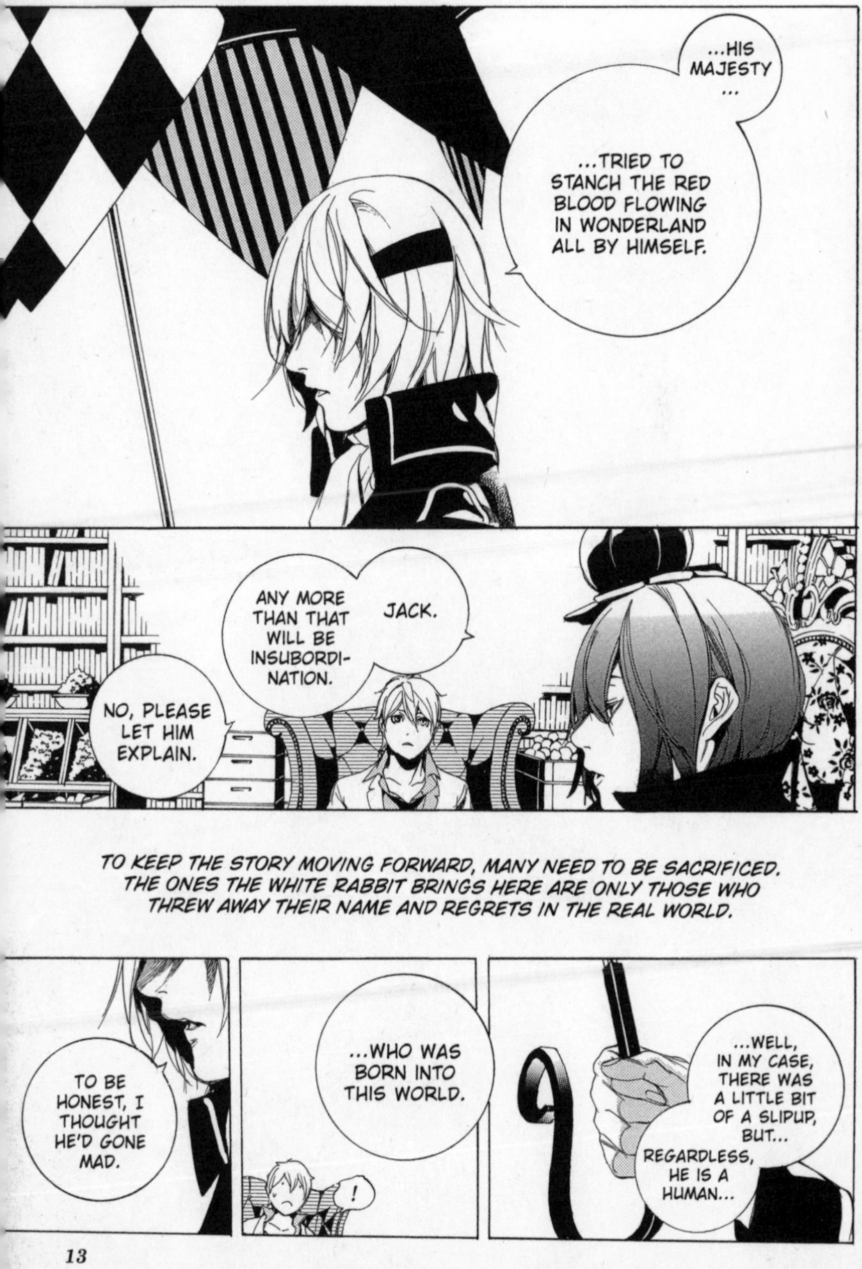
...HIS MAJESTY ...
...TRIED TO STANCH THE RED BLOOD FLOWING IN WONDERLAND ALL BY HIMSELF.
JACK.
ANY MORE THAN THAT WILL BE INSUBORDI- NATION.
NO, PLEASE LET HIM EXPLAIN.
TO KEEP THE STORY MOVING FORWARD, MANY NEED TO BE SACRIFICED. THE ONES THE WHITE RABBIT BRINGS HERE ARE ONLY THOSE WHO THREW AWAY THEIR NAME AND REGRETS IN THE REAL WORLD.
...WELL, IN MY CASE, THERE WAS A LITTLE BIT OF A SLIPUP, BUT...
REGARDLESS, HE IS A HUMAN...
...WHO WAS BORN INTO THIS WORLD.
!
TO BE HONEST, I THOUGHT HE'D GONE MAD.

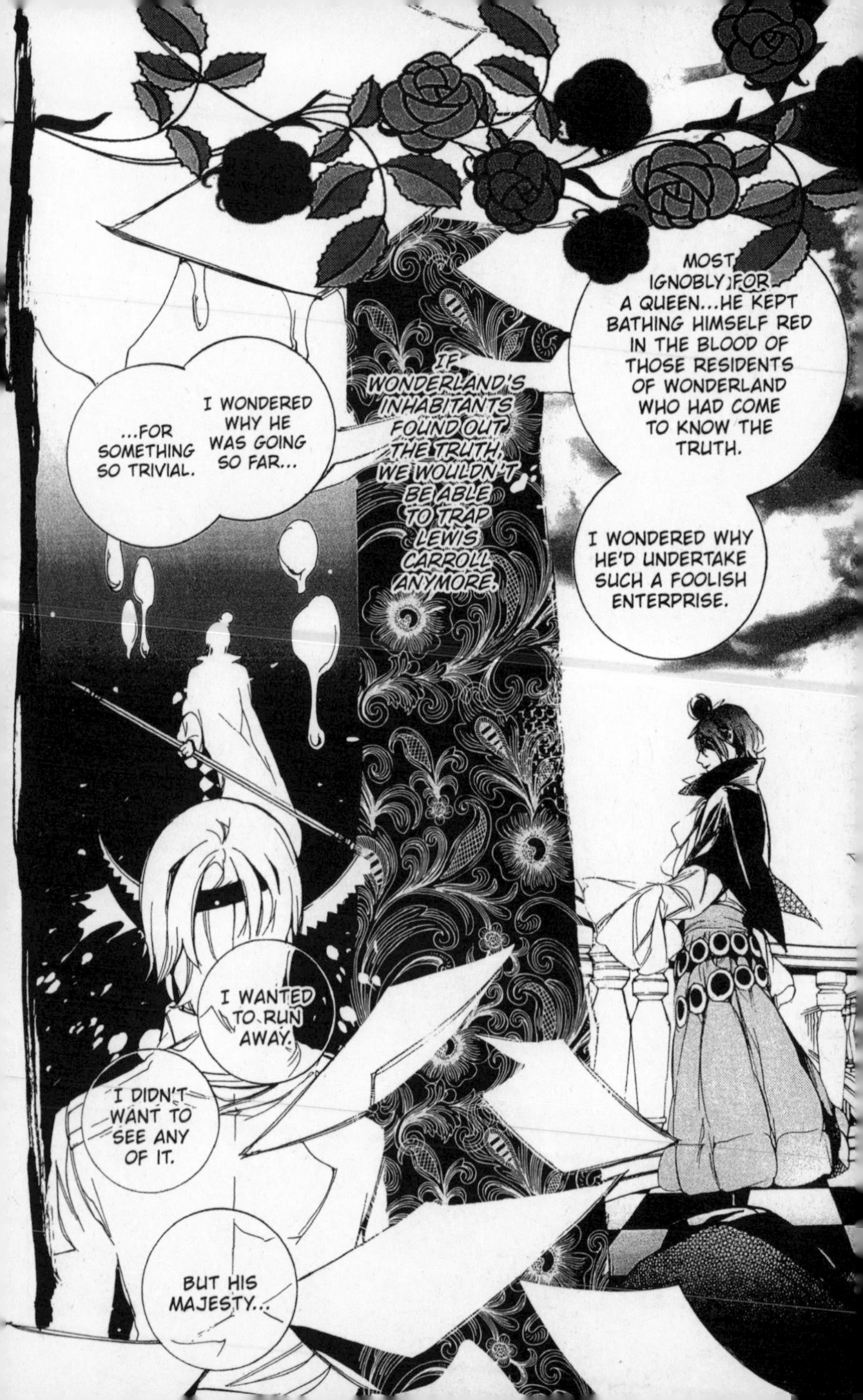
MOST IGNOBLY FOR A QUEEN...HE KEPT BATHING HIMSELF RED IN THE BLOOD OF THOSE RESIDENTS OF WONDERLAND WHO HAD COME TO KNOW THE TRUTH.
I WONDERED WHY HE'D UNDERTAKE SUCH A FOOLISH ENTERPRISE.
IF WONDERLAND'S INHABITANTS FOUND OUT THE TRUTH, WE WOULDN'T BE ABLE TO TRAP LEWIS CARROLL ANYMORE.
I WONDERED WHY HE WAS GOING SO FAR...
...FOR SOMETHING SO TRIVIAL.
I WANTED TO RUN AWAY.
I DIDN'T WANT TO SEE ANY OF IT.
BUT HIS MAJESTY...

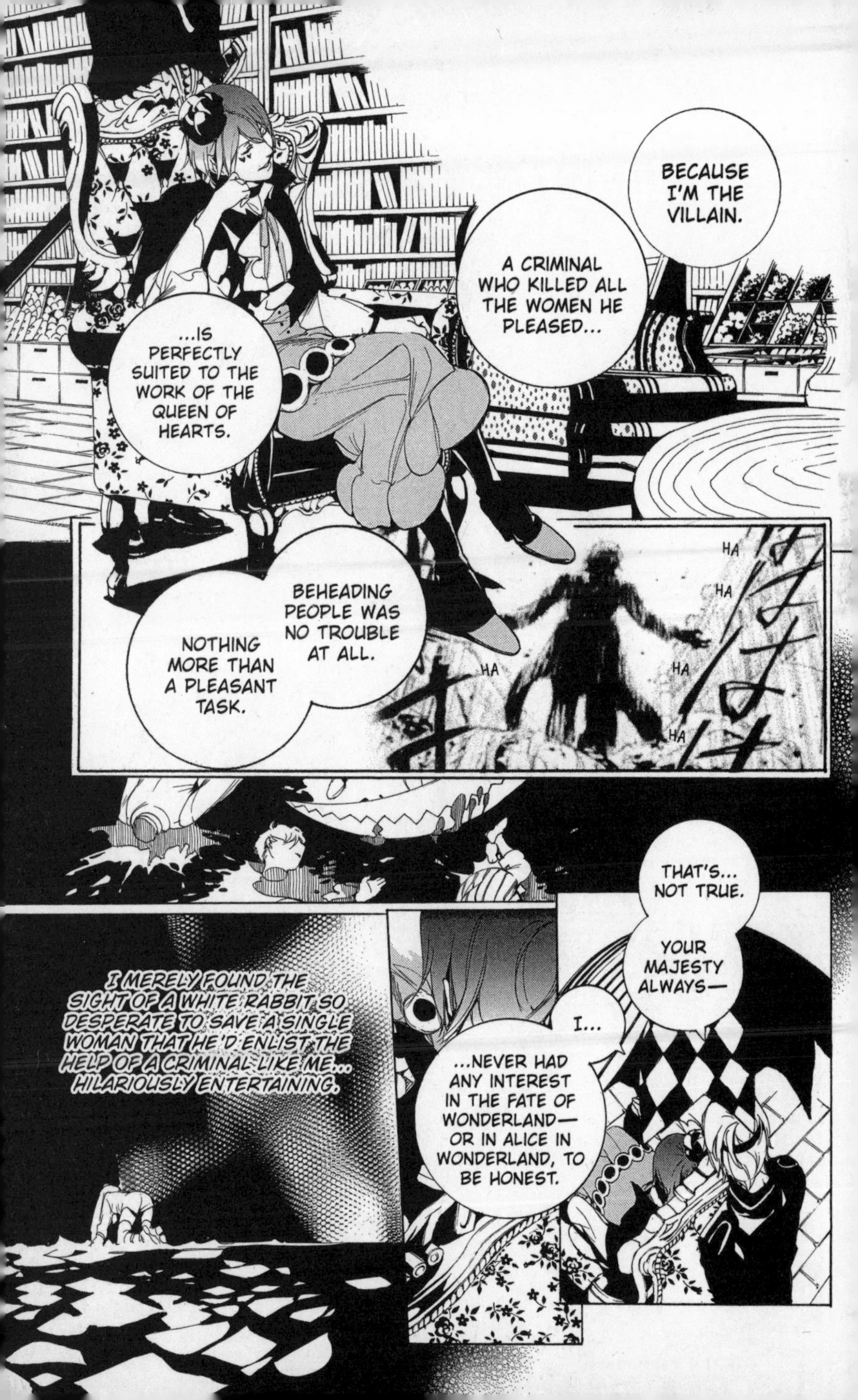
BECAUSE I'M THE VILLAIN.
A CRIMINAL WHO KILLED ALL THE WOMEN HE PLEASED...
...IS PERFECTLY SUITED TO THE WORK OF THE QUEEN OF HEARTS.
HA HA HA HA HA
BEHEADING PEOPLE WAS NO TROUBLE AT ALL.
NOTHING MORE THAN A PLEASANT TASK.
THAT'S... NOT TRUE.
YOUR MAJESTY ALWAYS—
I...
...NEVER HAD ANY INTEREST IN THE FATE OF WONDERLAND—OR IN ALICE IN WONDERLAND, TO BE HONEST.
I MERELY FOUND THE SIGHT OF A WHITE RABBIT SO DESPERATE TO SAVE A SINGLE WOMAN THAT HE'D ENLIST THE HELP OF A CRIMINAL LIKE ME... HILARIOUSLY ENTERTAINING.

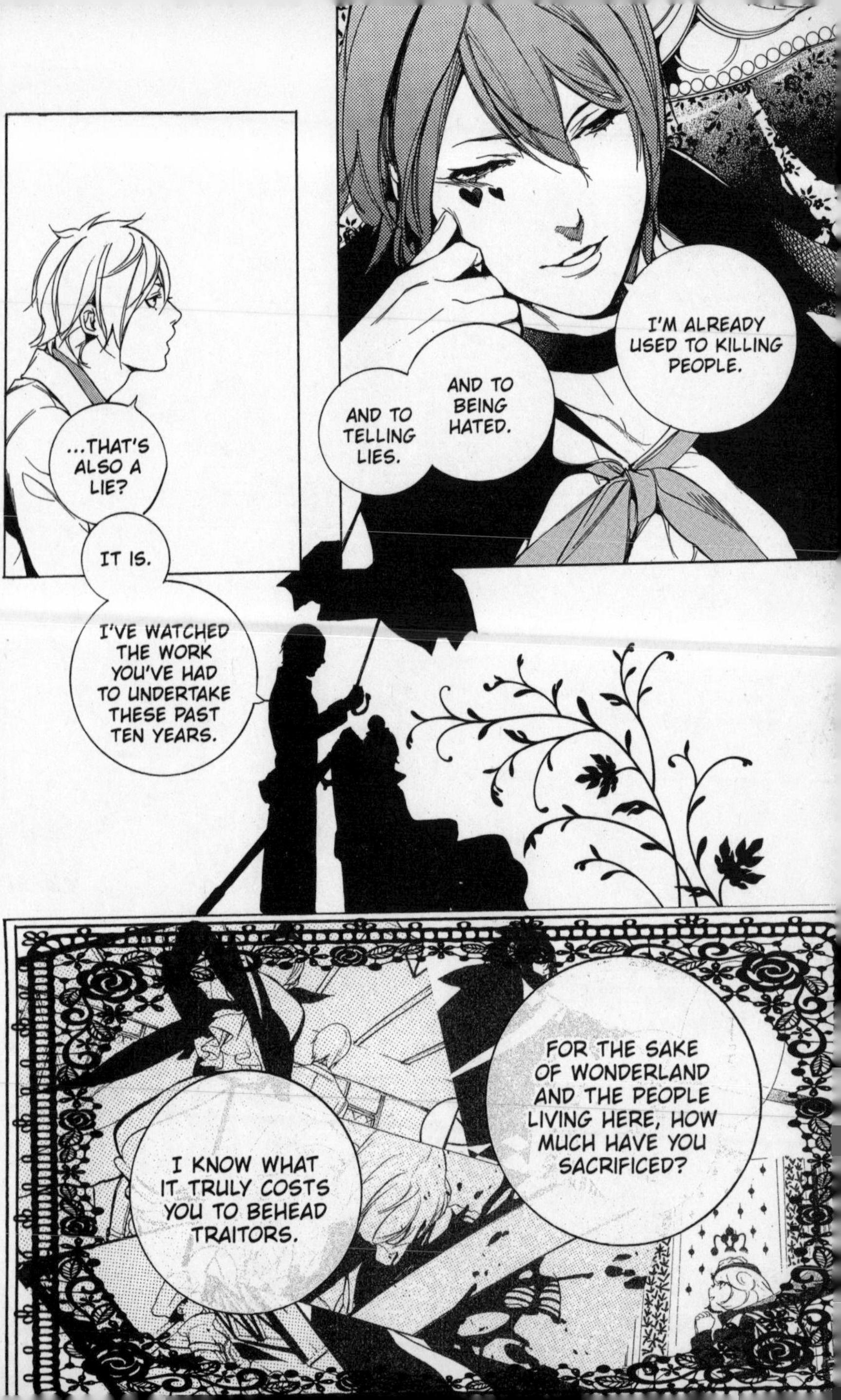
I'M ALREADY USED TO KILLING PEOPLE.
AND TO BEING HATED.
AND TO TELLING LIES.
...THAT'S ALSO A LIE?
IT IS.
I'VE WATCHED THE WORK YOU'VE HAD TO UNDERTAKE THESE PAST TEN YEARS.
FOR THE SAKE OF WONDERLAND AND THE PEOPLE LIVING HERE, HOW MUCH HAVE YOU SACRIFICED?
I KNOW WHAT IT TRULY COSTS YOU TO BEHEAD TRAITORS.

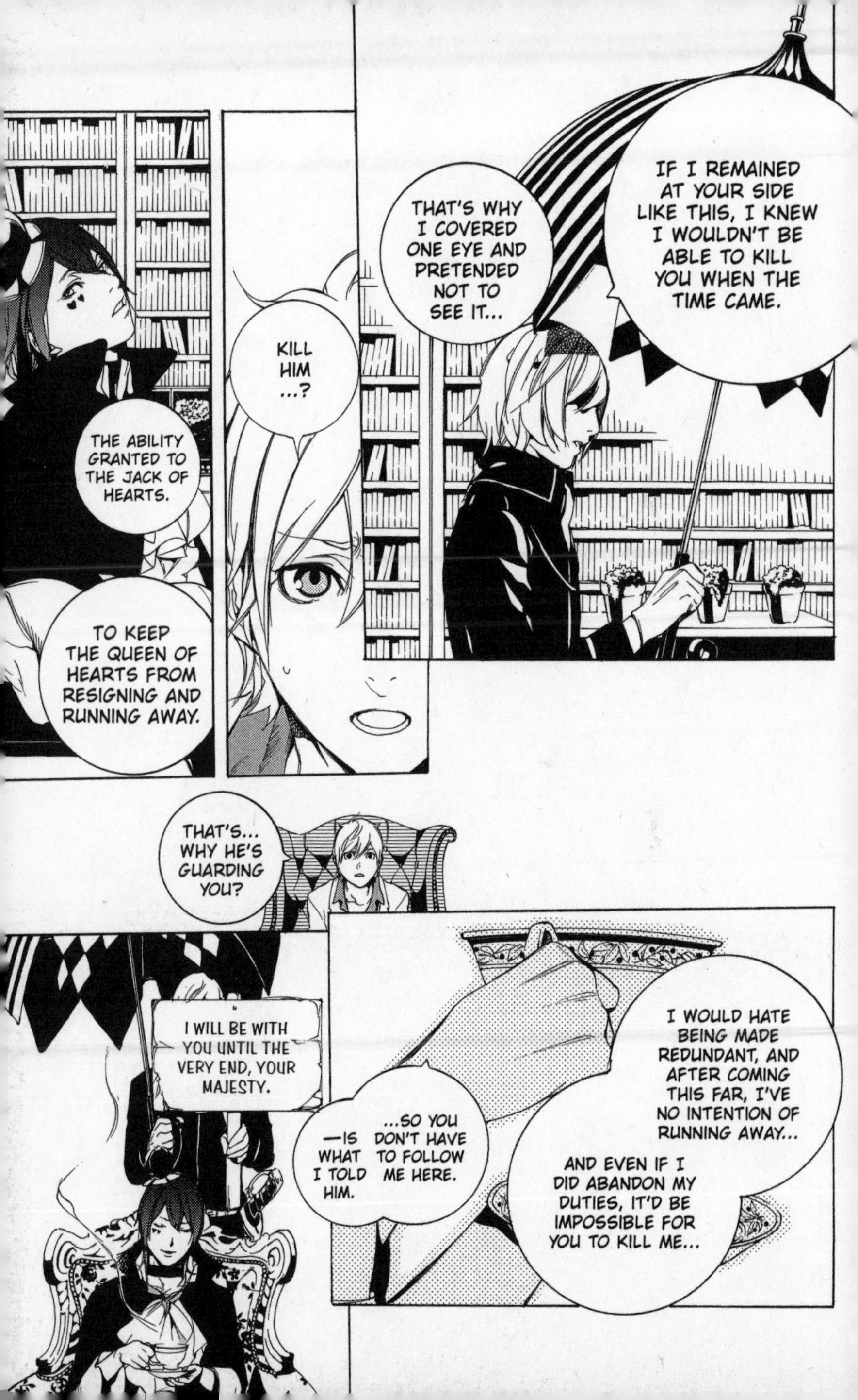
IF I REMAINED AT YOUR SIDE LIKE THIS, I KNEW I WOULDN'T BE ABLE TO KILL YOU WHEN THE TIME CAME.
THAT'S WHY I COVERED ONE EYE AND PRETENDED NOT TO SEE IT...
KILL HIM ...?
THE ABILITY GRANTED TO THE JACK OF HEARTS.
TO KEEP THE QUEEN OF HEARTS FROM RESIGNING AND RUNNING AWAY.
THAT'S... WHY HE'S GUARDING YOU?
I WOULD HATE BEING MADE REDUNDANT, AND AFTER COMING THIS FAR, I'VE NO INTENTION OF RUNNING AWAY...
AND EVEN IF I DID ABANDON MY DUTIES, IT'D BE IMPOSSIBLE FOR YOU TO KILL ME...
...SO YOU DON'T HAVE TO FOLLOW ME HERE.
—IS WHAT I TOLD HIM.
I WILL BE WITH YOU UNTIL THE VERY END, YOUR MAJESTY.

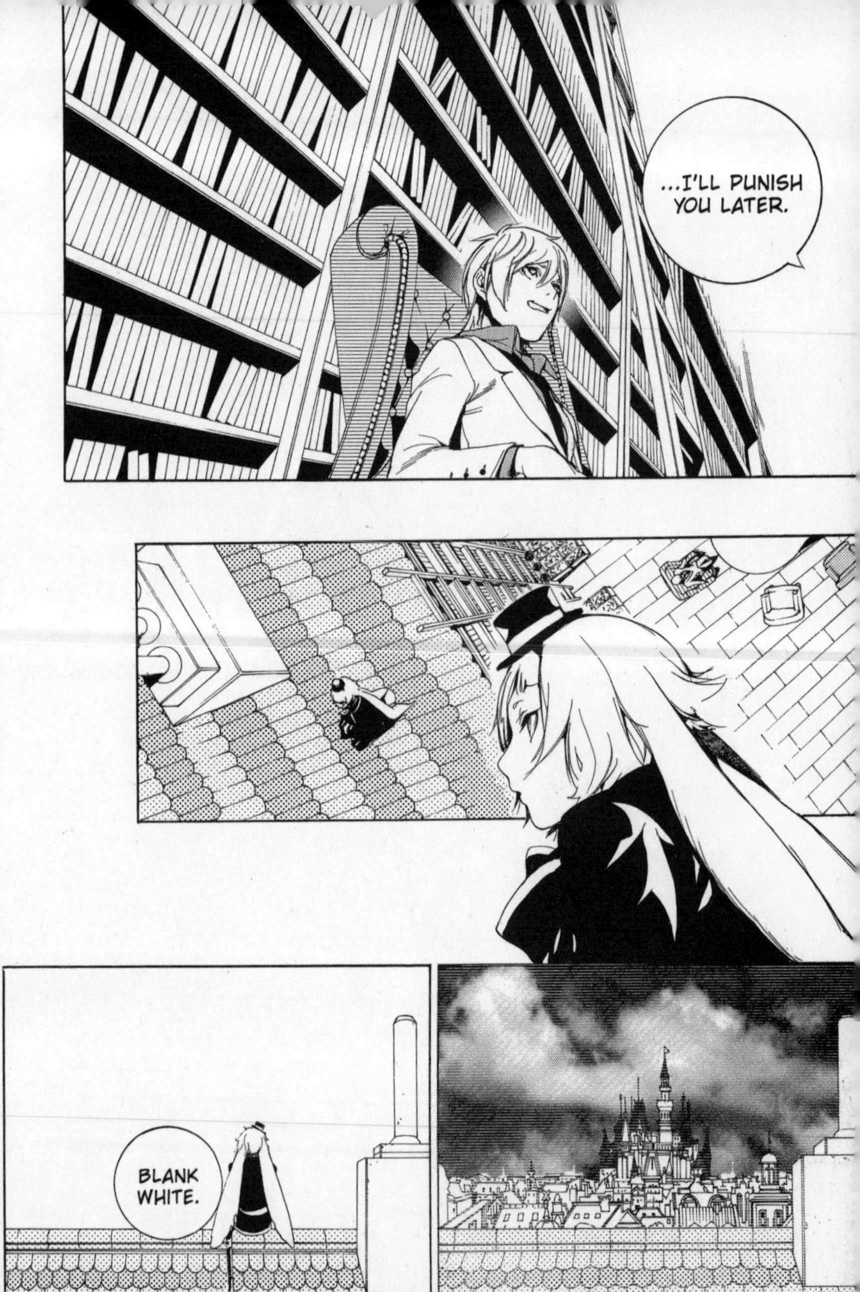
...I'LL PUNISH YOU LATER.
BLANK WHITE.

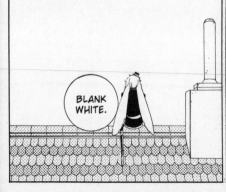

A STORY WITH A NONEXISTENT CONTINUATION.
...I THOUGHT WONDERLAND WAS DIFFERENT.
WONDERLAND... AND ALICE IN WONDERLAND...
...I THOUGHT I COULD PROTECT THEM...
WHAT CAN YOU DO FOR ALICE?

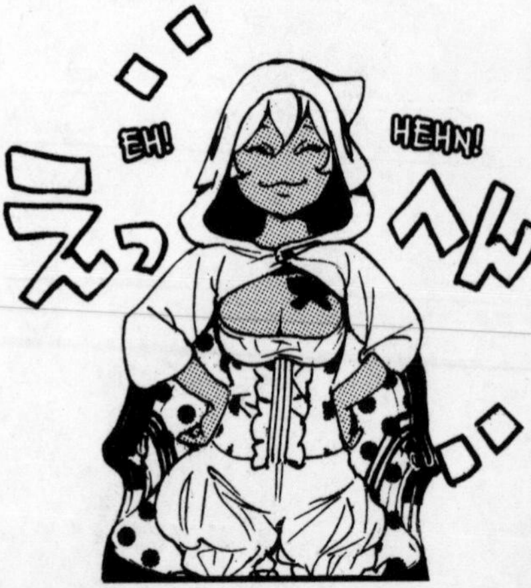
えっ
EH!
へん
HEHN!

Chapter 62

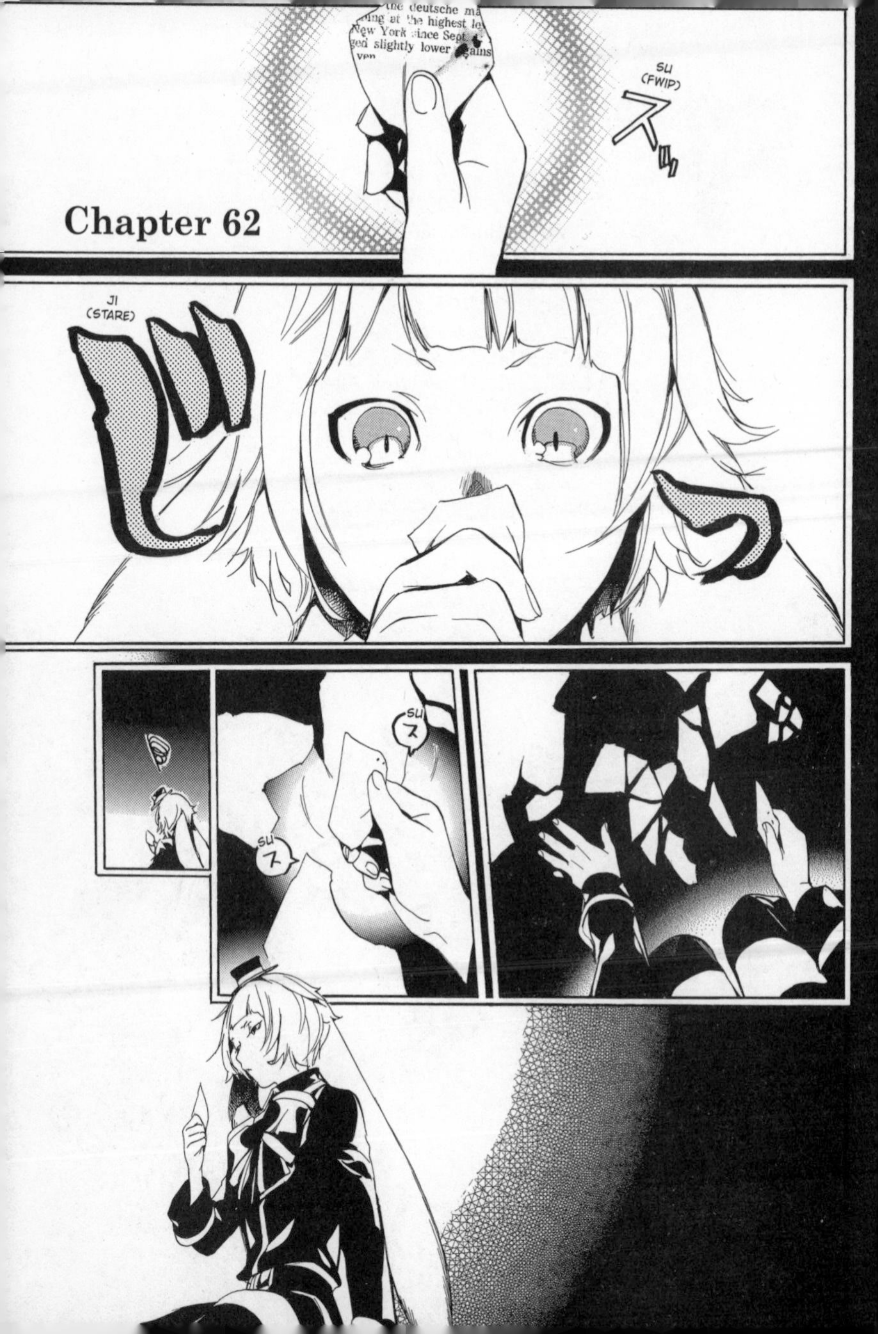

the deutsche ma
ding at the highest le
New York since Sept
ged slightly lower agains
SU (FWIP)
スッ
JI (STARE)
SU
ス
SU
ス

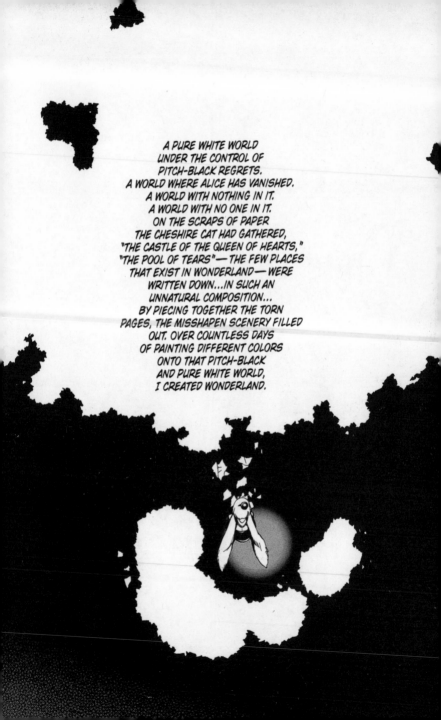

A PURE WHITE WORLD
UNDER THE CONTROL OF
PITCH-BLACK REGRETS.
A WORLD WHERE ALICE HAS VANISHED.
A WORLD WITH NOTHING IN IT.
A WORLD WITH NO ONE IN IT.
ON THE SCRAPS OF PAPER
THE CHESHIRE CAT HAD GATHERED,
"THE CASTLE OF THE QUEEN OF HEARTS,"
"THE POOL OF TEARS"— THE FEW PLACES
THAT EXIST IN WONDERLAND— WERE
WRITTEN DOWN...IN SUCH AN
UNNATURAL COMPOSITION...
BY PIECING TOGETHER THE TORN
PAGES, THE MISSHAPEN SCENERY FILLED
OUT. OVER COUNTLESS DAYS
OF PAINTING DIFFERENT COLORS
ONTO THAT PITCH-BLACK
AND PURE WHITE WORLD,
I CREATED WONDERLAND.

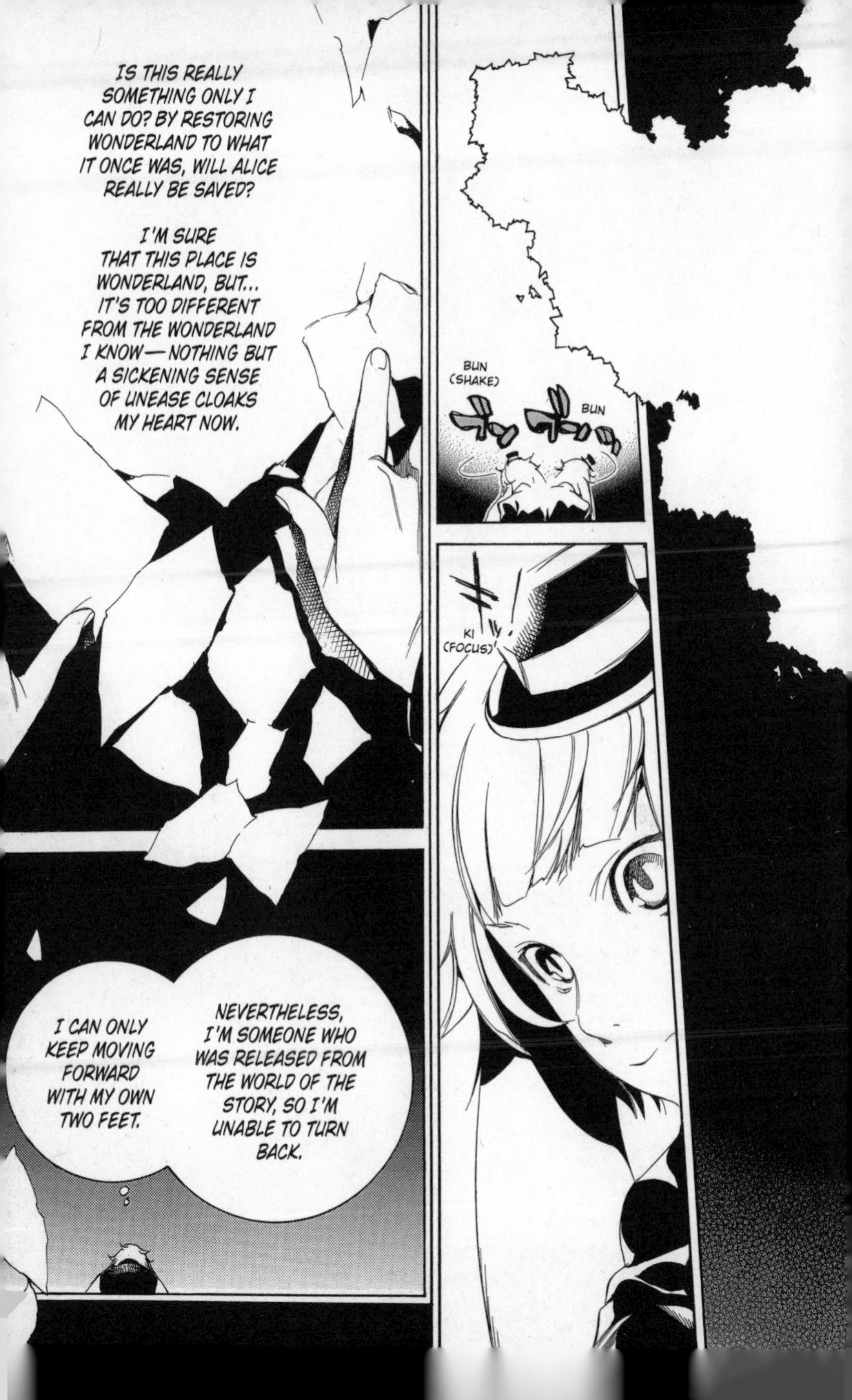
BUN (SHAKE)
BUN
KI (FOCUS)
IS THIS REALLY SOMETHING ONLY I CAN DO? BY RESTORING WONDERLAND TO WHAT IT ONCE WAS, WILL ALICE REALLY BE SAVED?
I'M SURE THAT THIS PLACE IS WONDERLAND, BUT... IT'S TOO DIFFERENT FROM THE WONDERLAND I KNOW—NOTHING BUT A SICKENING SENSE OF UNEASE CLOAKS MY HEART NOW.
NEVERTHELESS, I'M SOMEONE WHO WAS RELEASED FROM THE WORLD OF THE STORY, SO I'M UNABLE TO TURN BACK.
I CAN ONLY KEEP MOVING FORWARD WITH MY OWN TWO FEET.

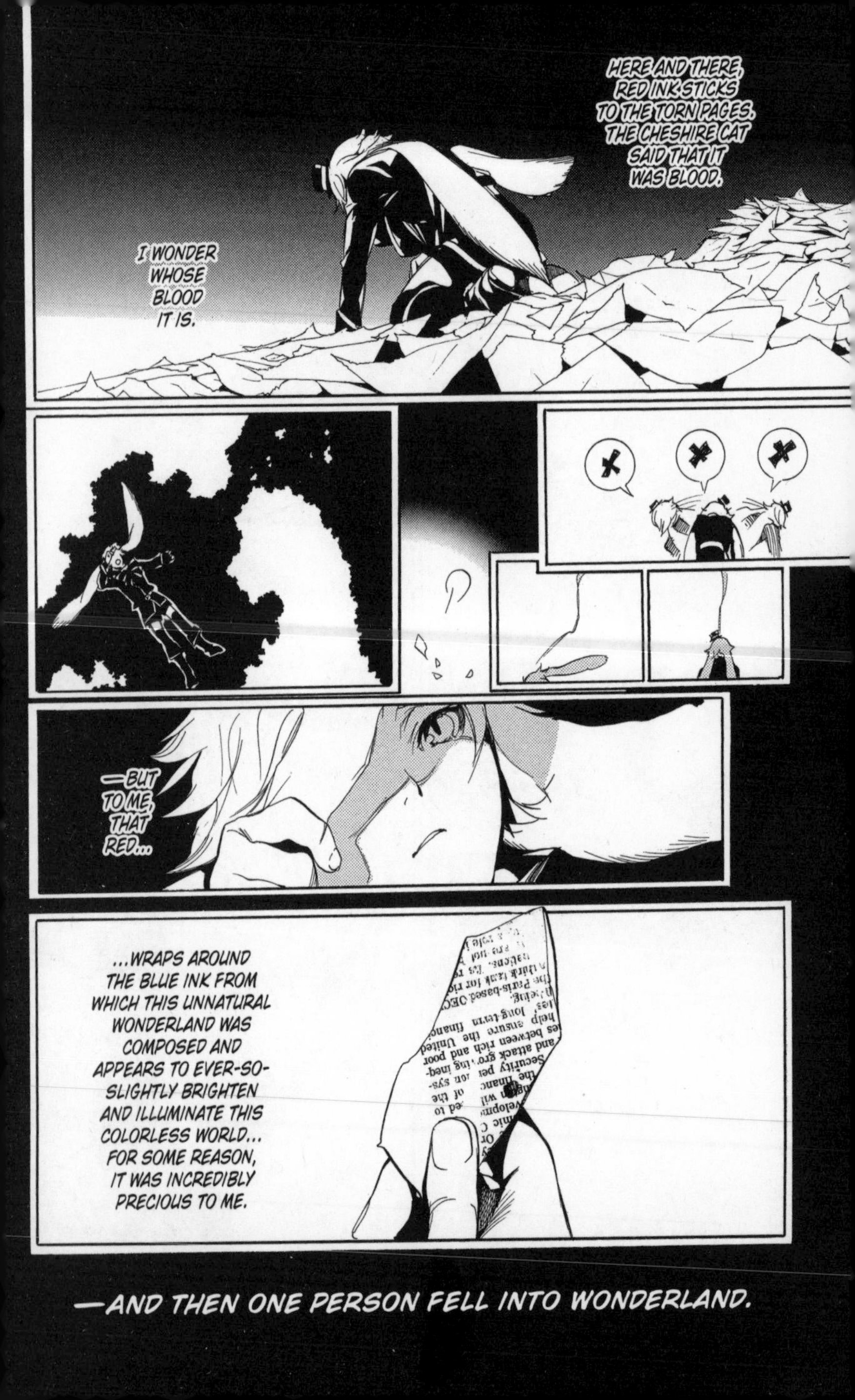
HERE AND THERE, RED INK STICKS TO THE TORN PAGES. THE CHESHIRE CAT SAID THAT IT WAS BLOOD.
I WONDER WHOSE BLOOD IT IS.
—BUT TO ME, THAT RED...
...WRAPS AROUND THE BLUE INK FROM WHICH THIS UNNATURAL WONDERLAND WAS COMPOSED AND APPEARS TO EVER-SO-SLIGHTLY BRIGHTEN AND ILLUMINATE THIS COLORLESS WORLD... FOR SOME REASON, IT WAS INCREDIBLY PRECIOUS TO ME.

—AND THEN ONE PERSON FELL INTO WONDERLAND.

Alice was
get very
by her s...
and of th...
do - one
had pe...
her ...
but ...
conversa...
...y the...

Alice, without pictures or conversations?...

...ery in her own mind, (as well as the...

...day made her feel very...

...trouble of getting up and pick...

...abbit with pink eyes ran close by her...

Chapter 62 WHITE RABBIT.

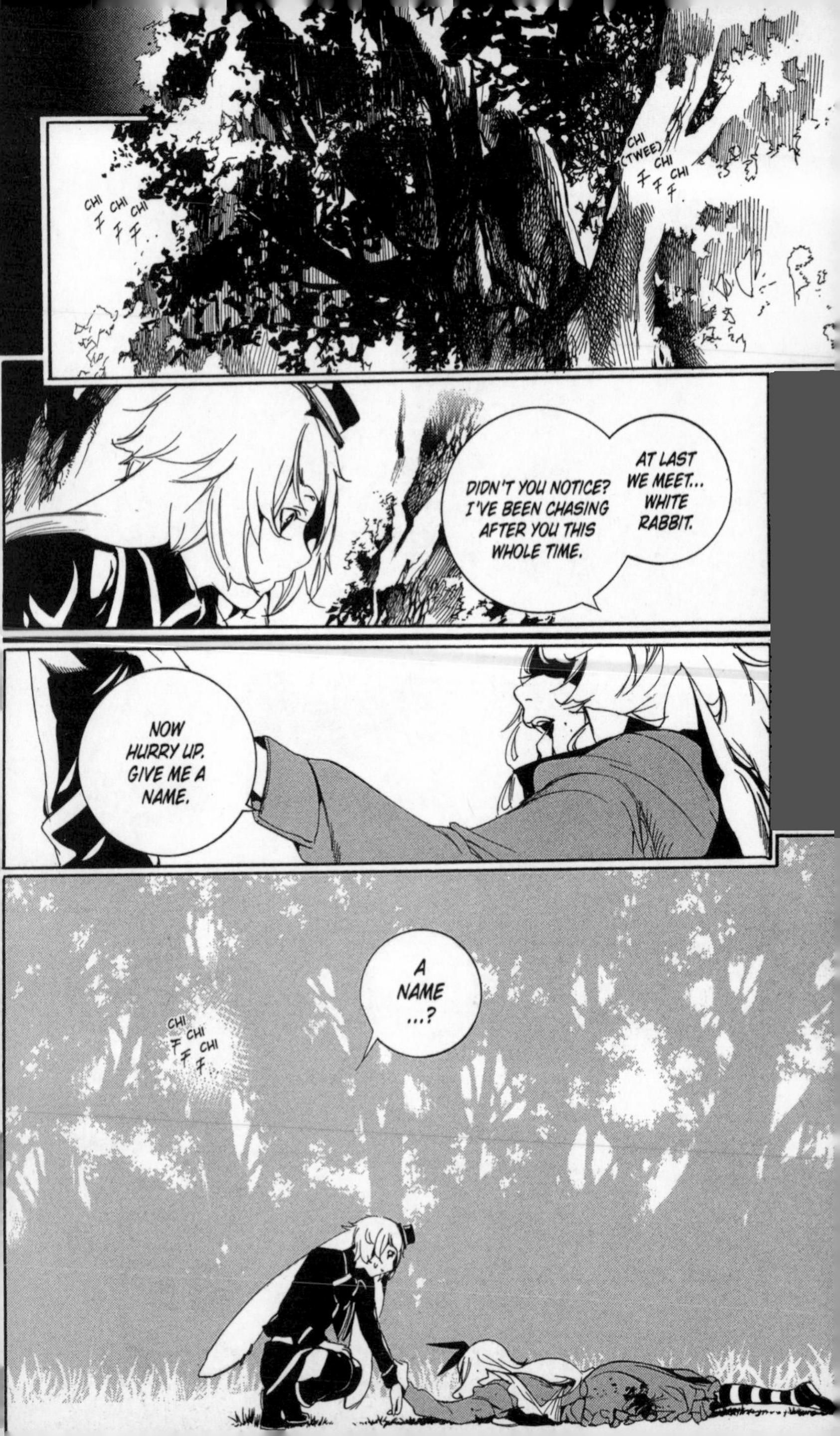
CHI (TWEE) CHI CHI
CHI CHI CHI
AT LAST WE MEET... WHITE RABBIT.
DIDN'T YOU NOTICE? I'VE BEEN CHASING AFTER YOU THIS WHOLE TIME.
NOW HURRY UP. GIVE ME A NAME.
A NAME ...?
CHI CHI CHI

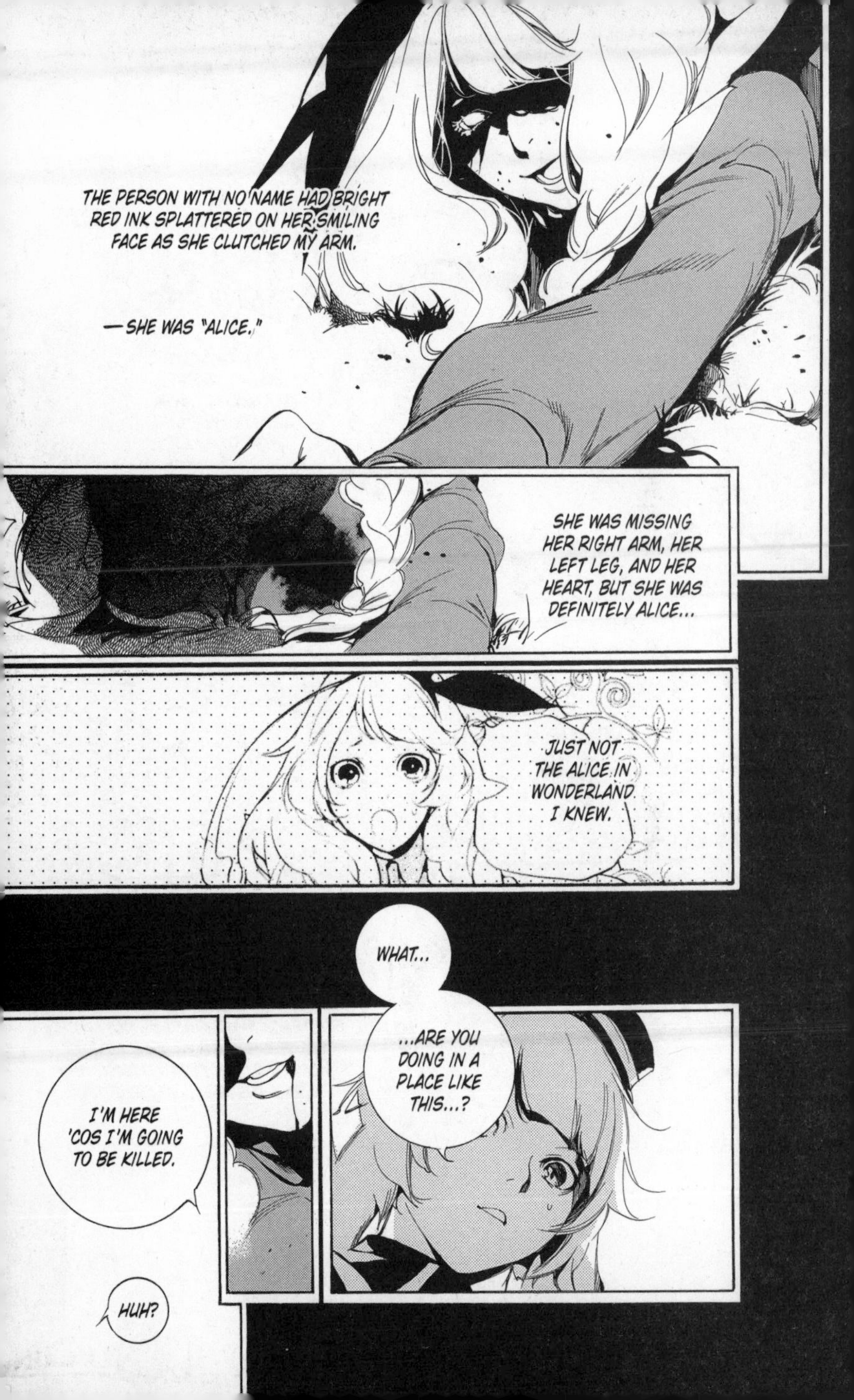
THE PERSON WITH NO NAME HAD BRIGHT RED INK SPLATTERED ON HER SMILING FACE AS SHE CLUTCHED MY ARM.
—SHE WAS "ALICE."
SHE WAS MISSING HER RIGHT ARM, HER LEFT LEG, AND HER HEART, BUT SHE WAS DEFINITELY ALICE...
JUST NOT THE ALICE IN WONDERLAND I KNEW.
WHAT...
...ARE YOU DOING IN A PLACE LIKE THIS...?
I'M HERE 'COS I'M GOING TO BE KILLED.
HUH?

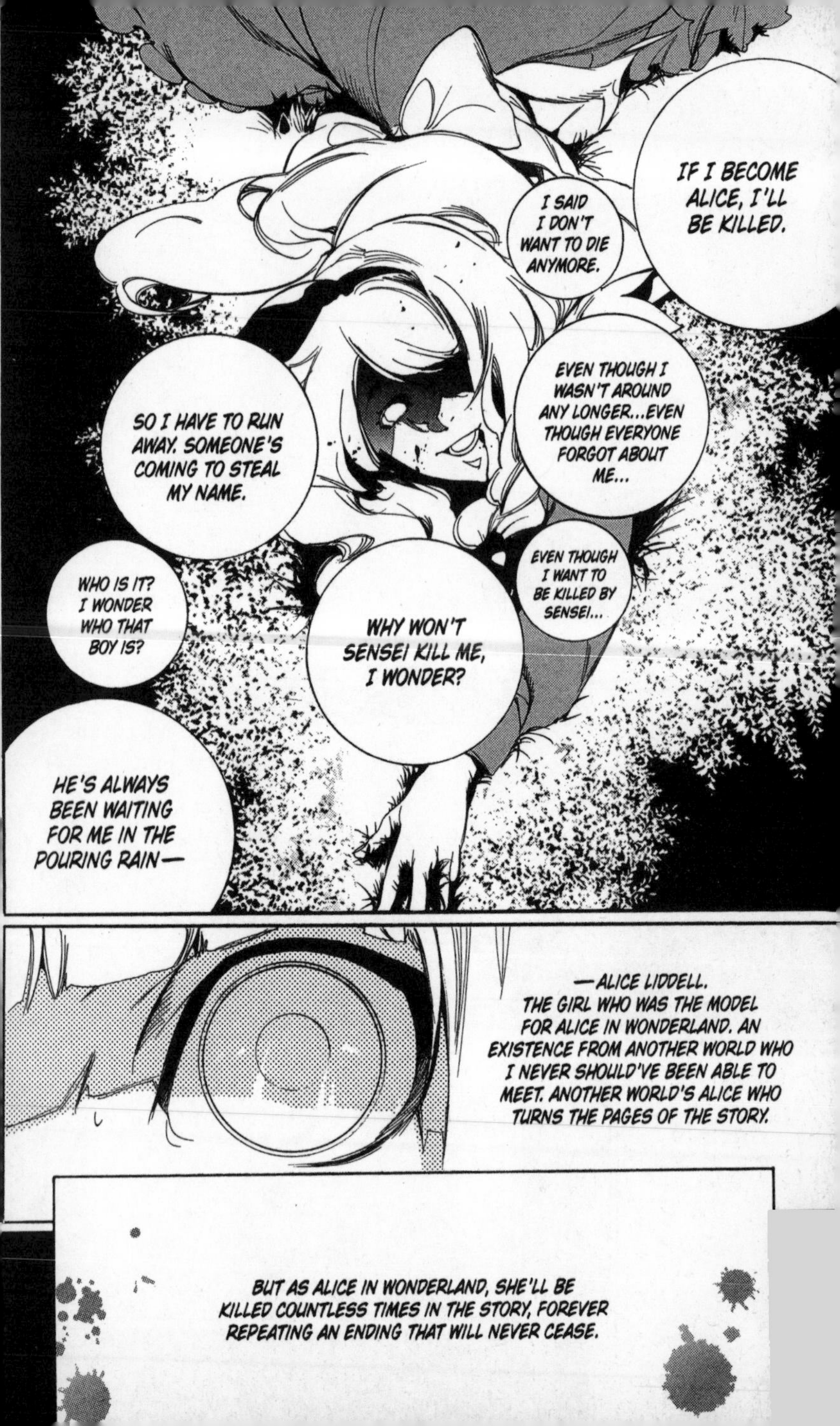
IF I BECOME ALICE, I'LL BE KILLED.
I SAID I DON'T WANT TO DIE ANYMORE.
EVEN THOUGH I WASN'T AROUND ANY LONGER...EVEN THOUGH EVERYONE FORGOT ABOUT ME...
SO I HAVE TO RUN AWAY. SOMEONE'S COMING TO STEAL MY NAME.
EVEN THOUGH I WANT TO BE KILLED BY SENSEI...
WHY WON'T SENSEI KILL ME, I WONDER?
WHO IS IT? I WONDER WHO THAT BOY IS?
HE'S ALWAYS BEEN WAITING FOR ME IN THE POURING RAIN—
—ALICE LIDDELL. THE GIRL WHO WAS THE MODEL FOR ALICE IN WONDERLAND. AN EXISTENCE FROM ANOTHER WORLD WHO I NEVER SHOULD'VE BEEN ABLE TO MEET. ANOTHER WORLD'S ALICE WHO TURNS THE PAGES OF THE STORY.
BUT AS ALICE IN WONDERLAND, SHE'LL BE KILLED COUNTLESS TIMES IN THE STORY, FOREVER REPEATING AN ENDING THAT WILL NEVER CEASE.

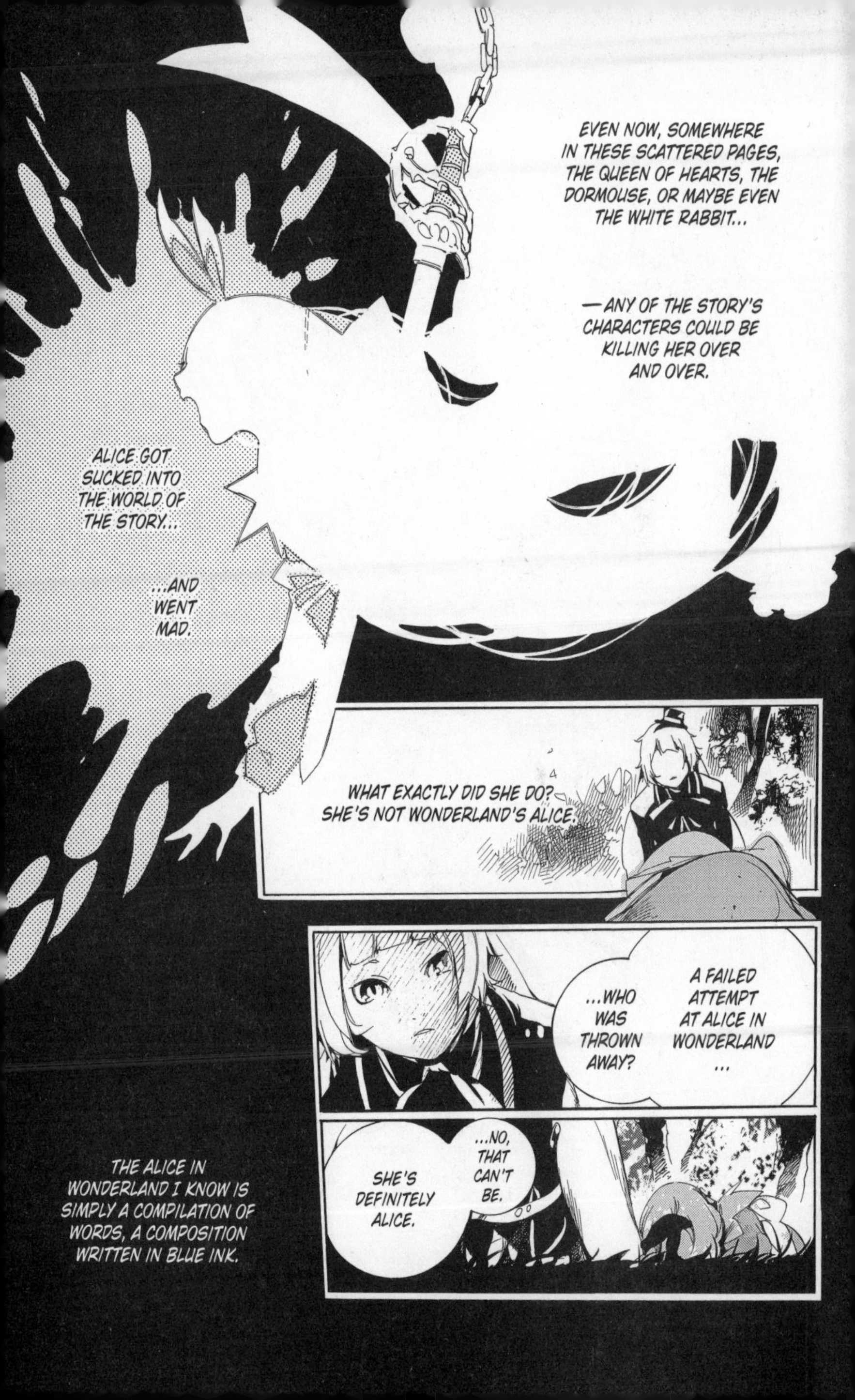
EVEN NOW, SOMEWHERE IN THESE SCATTERED PAGES, THE QUEEN OF HEARTS, THE DORMOUSE, OR MAYBE EVEN THE WHITE RABBIT...
—ANY OF THE STORY'S CHARACTERS COULD BE KILLING HER OVER AND OVER.
ALICE GOT SUCKED INTO THE WORLD OF THE STORY...
...AND WENT MAD.
WHAT EXACTLY DID SHE DO? SHE'S NOT WONDERLAND'S ALICE.
A FAILED ATTEMPT AT ALICE IN WONDERLAND ...
...WHO WAS THROWN AWAY?
...NO, THAT CAN'T BE.
SHE'S DEFINITELY ALICE.
THE ALICE IN WONDERLAND I KNOW IS SIMPLY A COMPILATION OF WORDS, A COMPOSITION WRITTEN IN BLUE INK.

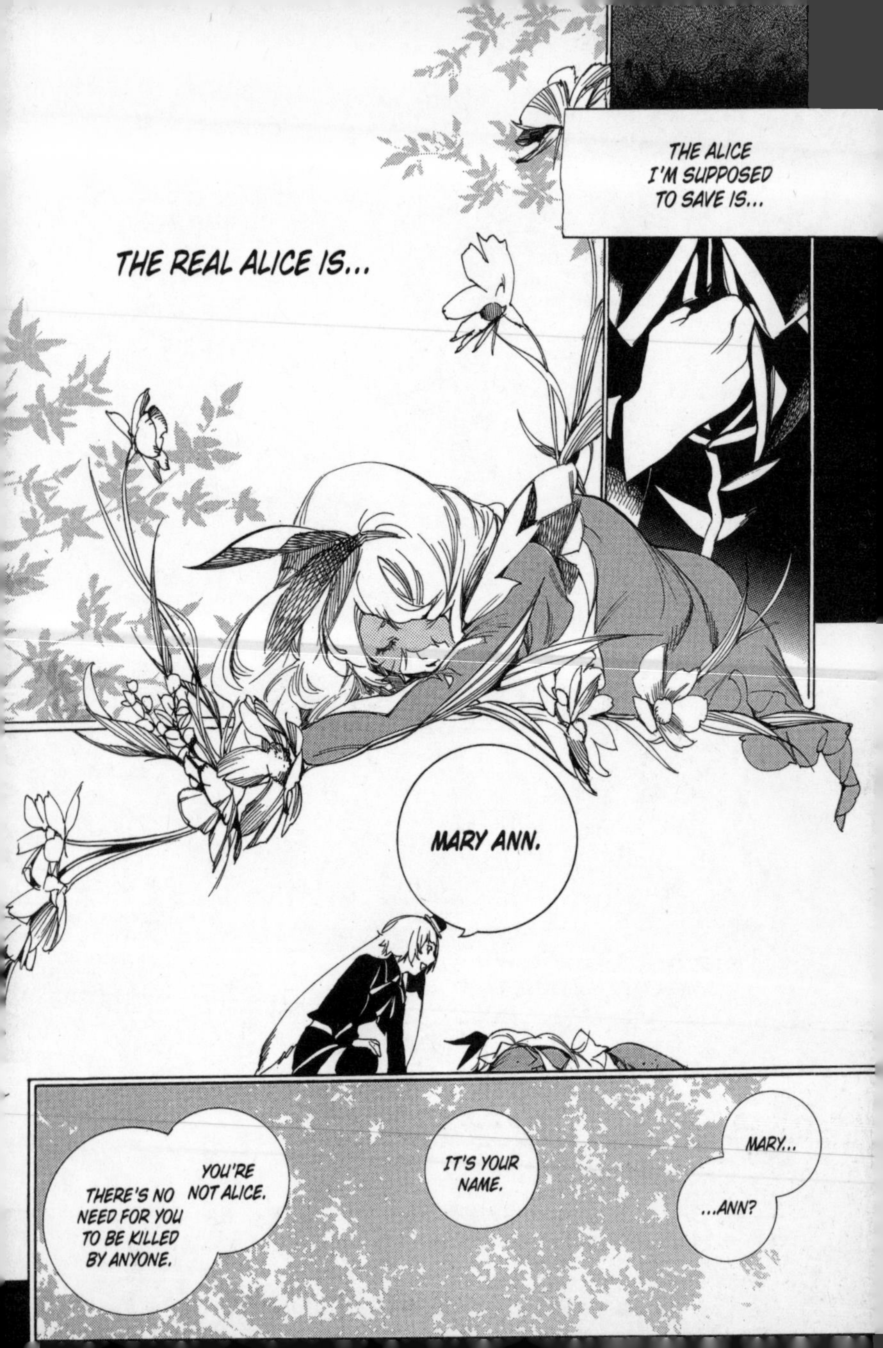
THE ALICE I'M SUPPOSED TO SAVE IS...
THE REAL ALICE IS...
MARY ANN.
MARY...
...ANN?
IT'S YOUR NAME.
YOU'RE NOT ALICE.
THERE'S NO NEED FOR YOU TO BE KILLED BY ANYONE.

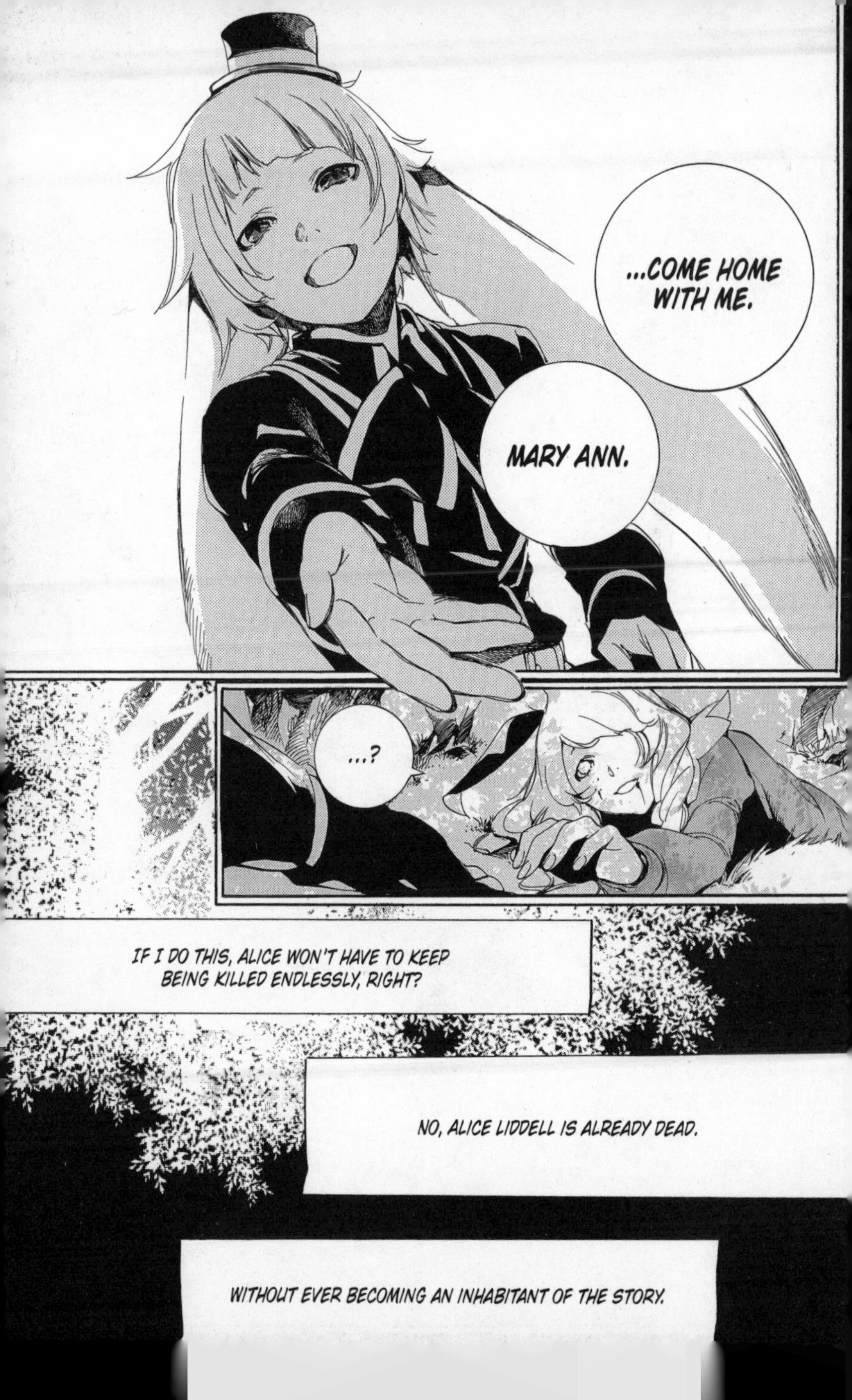
...COME HOME WITH ME.
MARY ANN.
...?
IF I DO THIS, ALICE WON'T HAVE TO KEEP BEING KILLED ENDLESSLY, RIGHT?
NO, ALICE LIDDELL IS ALREADY DEAD.
WITHOUT EVER BECOMING AN INHABITANT OF THE STORY.

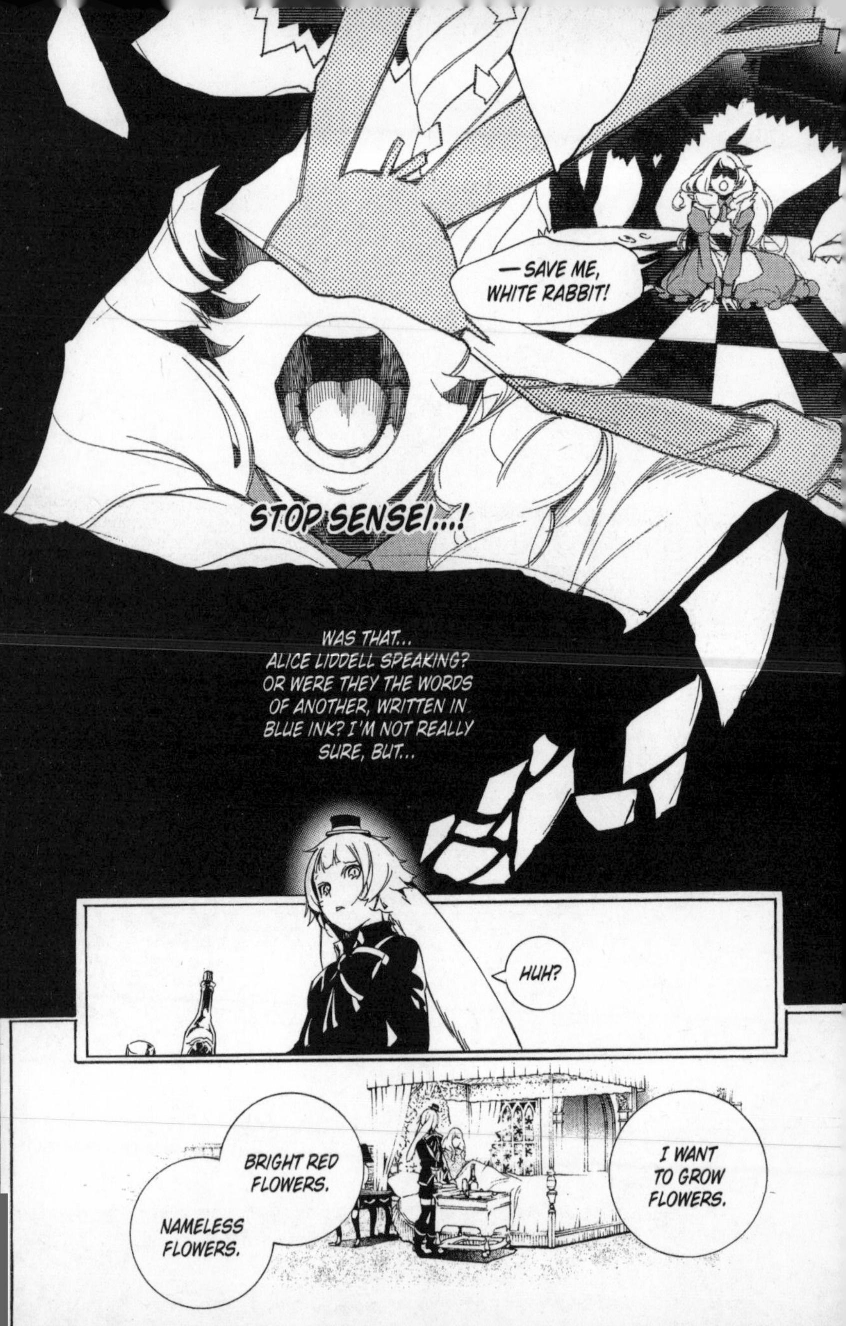
—SAVE ME, WHITE RABBIT!
STOP SENSEI...!
WAS THAT... ALICE LIDDELL SPEAKING? OR WERE THEY THE WORDS OF ANOTHER, WRITTEN IN BLUE INK? I'M NOT REALLY SURE, BUT...
HUH?
I WANT TO GROW FLOWERS.
BRIGHT RED FLOWERS.
NAMELESS FLOWERS.

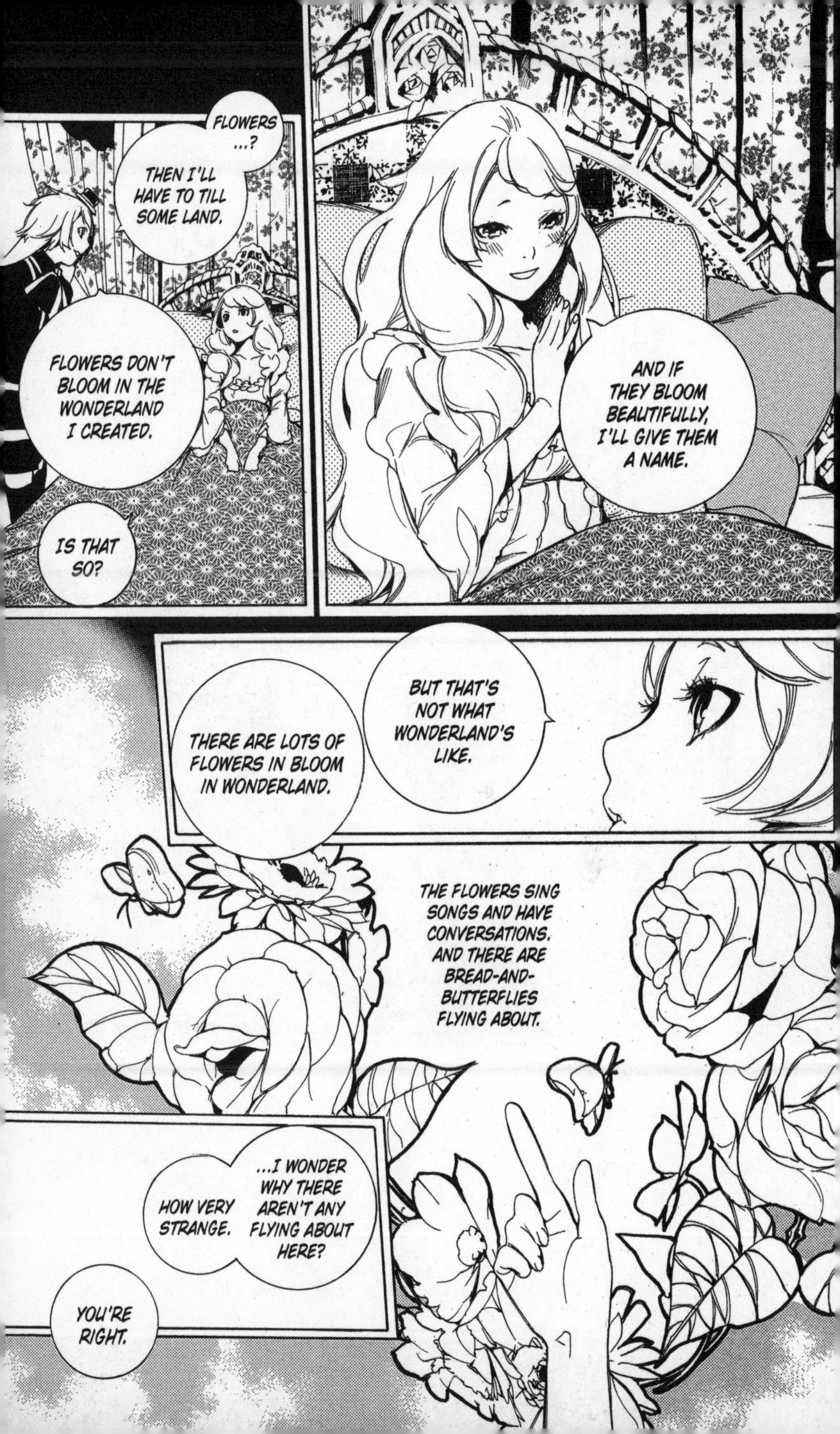
AND IF THEY BLOOM BEAUTIFULLY, I'LL GIVE THEM A NAME.
FLOWERS ...?
THEN I'LL HAVE TO TILL SOME LAND.
FLOWERS DON'T BLOOM IN THE WONDERLAND I CREATED.
IS THAT SO?
BUT THAT'S NOT WHAT WONDERLAND'S LIKE.
THERE ARE LOTS OF FLOWERS IN BLOOM IN WONDERLAND.
THE FLOWERS SING SONGS AND HAVE CONVERSATIONS. AND THERE ARE BREAD-AND-BUTTERFLIES FLYING ABOUT.
...I WONDER WHY THERE AREN'T ANY FLYING ABOUT HERE?
HOW VERY STRANGE.
YOU'RE RIGHT.

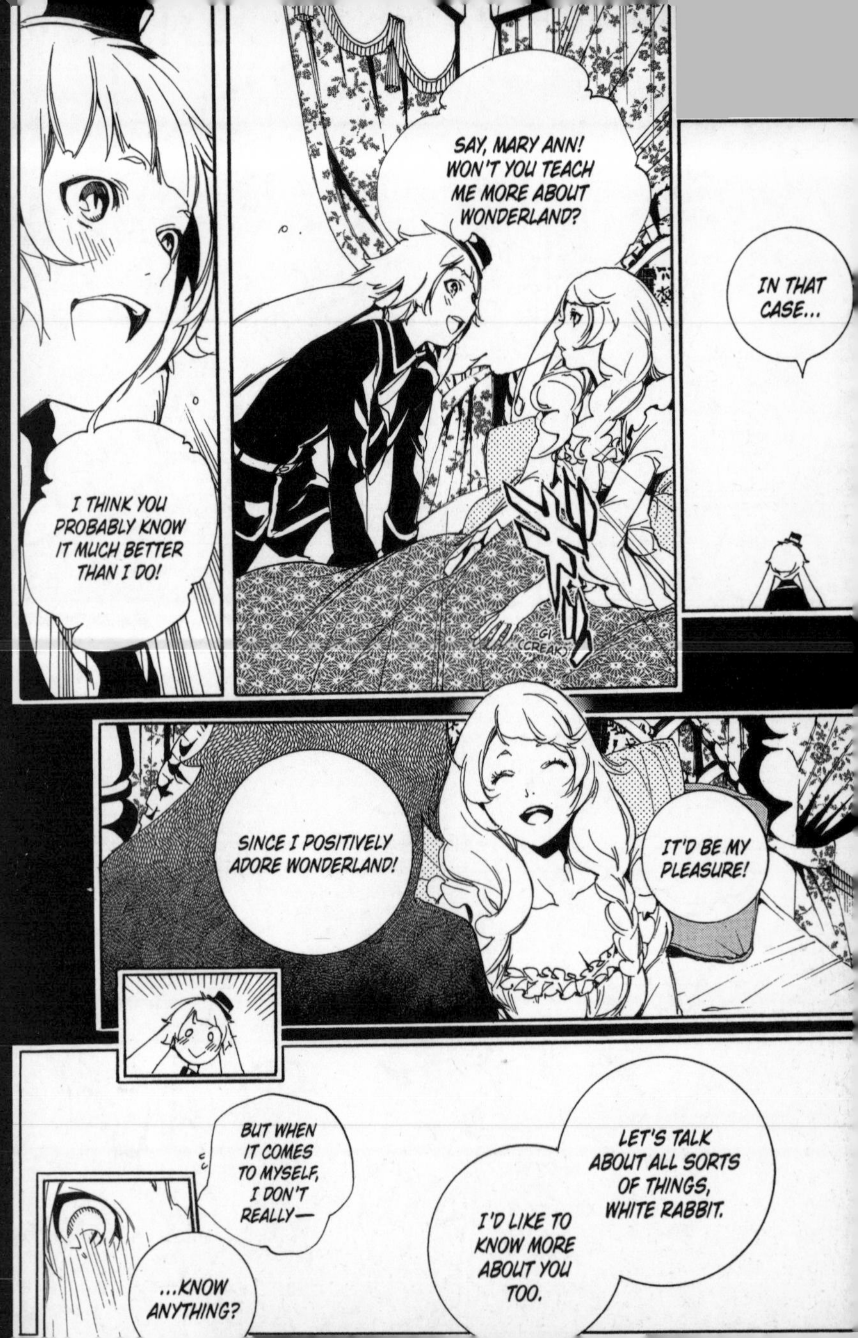
IN THAT CASE...
SAY, MARY ANN! WON'T YOU TEACH ME MORE ABOUT WONDERLAND?
GI (CREAK)
I THINK YOU PROBABLY KNOW IT MUCH BETTER THAN I DO!
IT'D BE MY PLEASURE!
SINCE I POSITIVELY ADORE WONDERLAND!
LET'S TALK ABOUT ALL SORTS OF THINGS, WHITE RABBIT.
I'D LIKE TO KNOW MORE ABOUT YOU TOO.
BUT WHEN IT COMES TO MYSELF, I DON'T REALLY—
...KNOW ANYTHING?

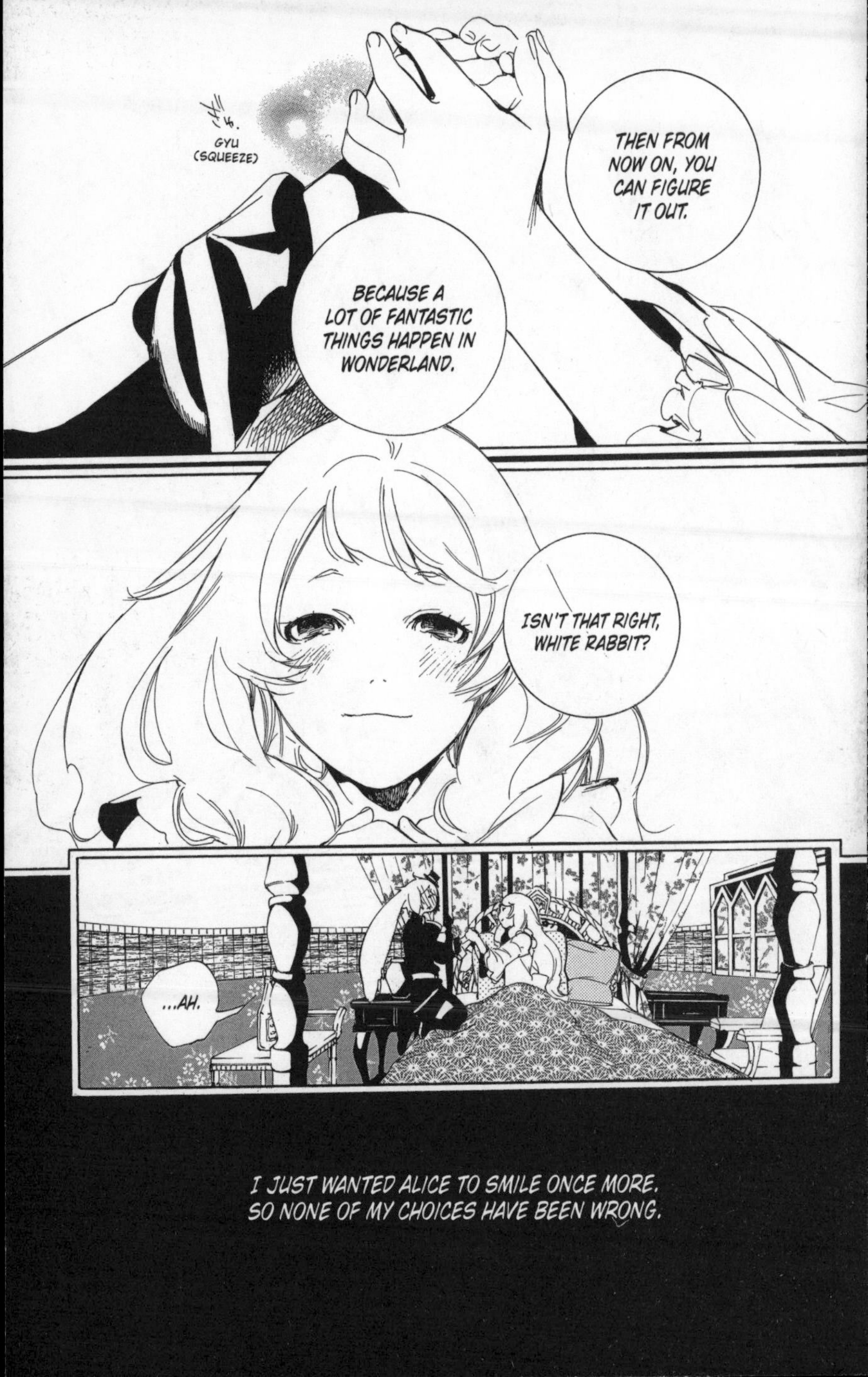
THEN FROM NOW ON, YOU CAN FIGURE IT OUT.
GYU (SQUEEZE)
BECAUSE A LOT OF FANTASTIC THINGS HAPPEN IN WONDERLAND.
ISN'T THAT RIGHT, WHITE RABBIT?
...AH.
I JUST WANTED ALICE TO SMILE ONCE MORE.
SO NONE OF MY CHOICES HAVE BEEN WRONG.

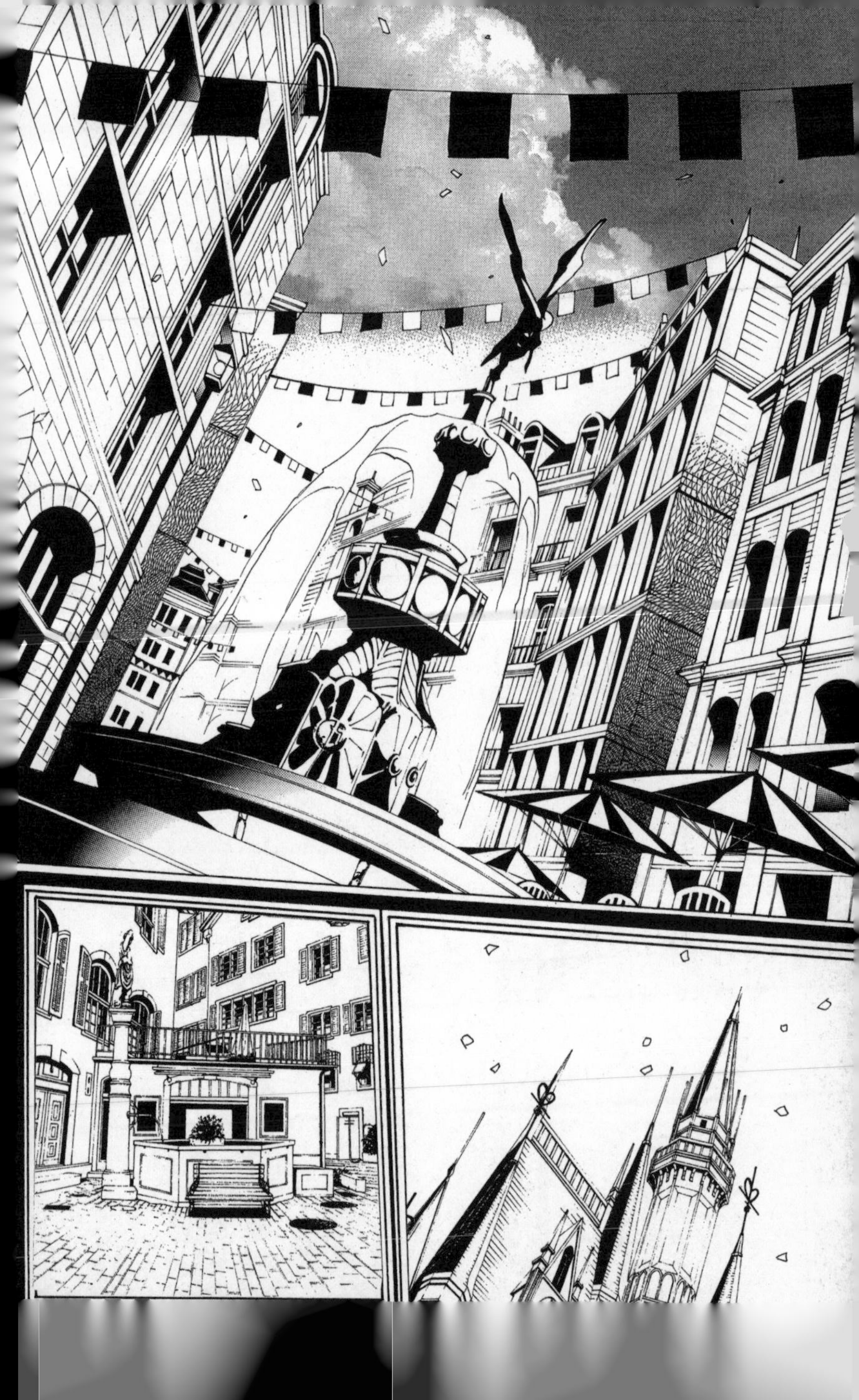

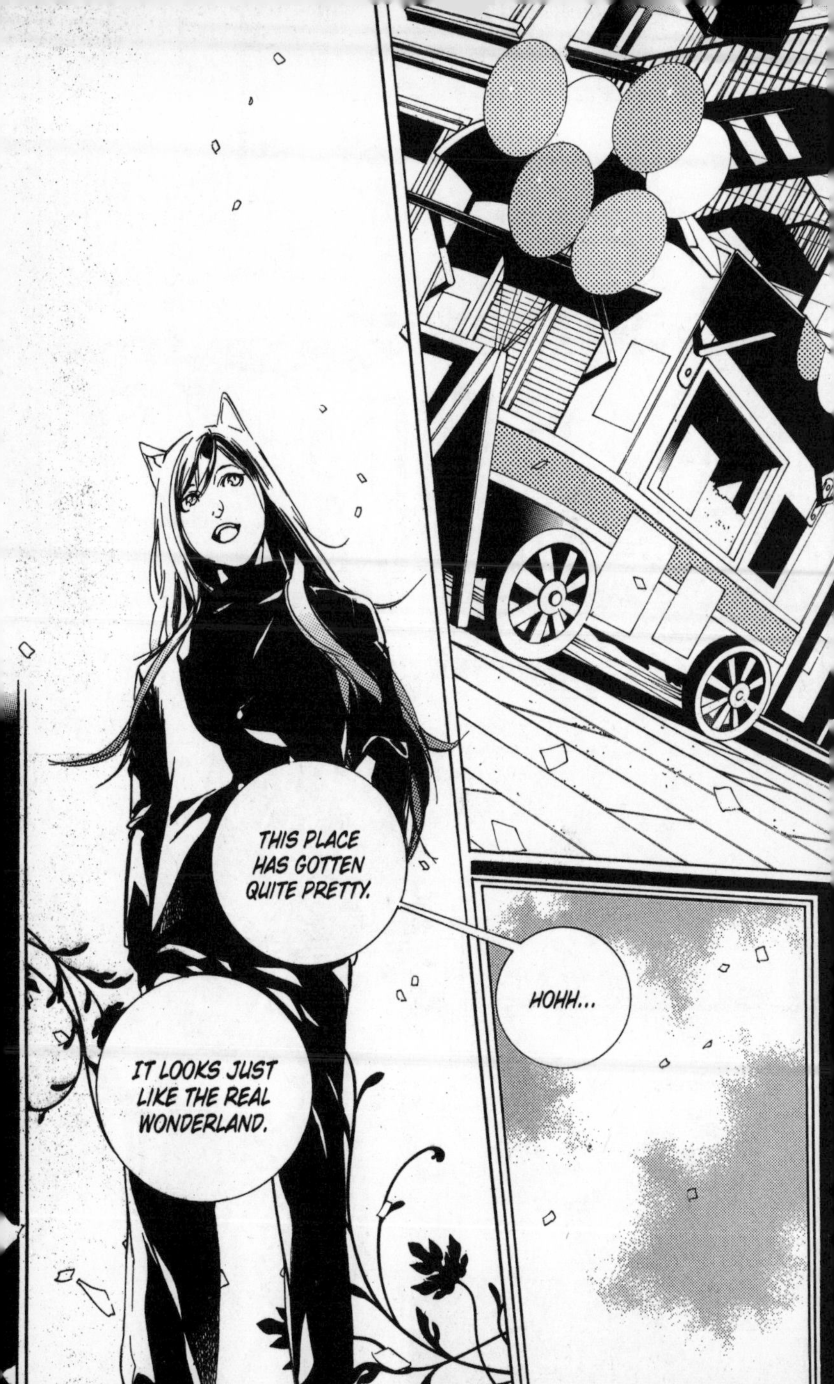
HOHH...
THIS PLACE HAS GOTTEN QUITE PRETTY.
IT LOOKS JUST LIKE THE REAL WONDERLAND.

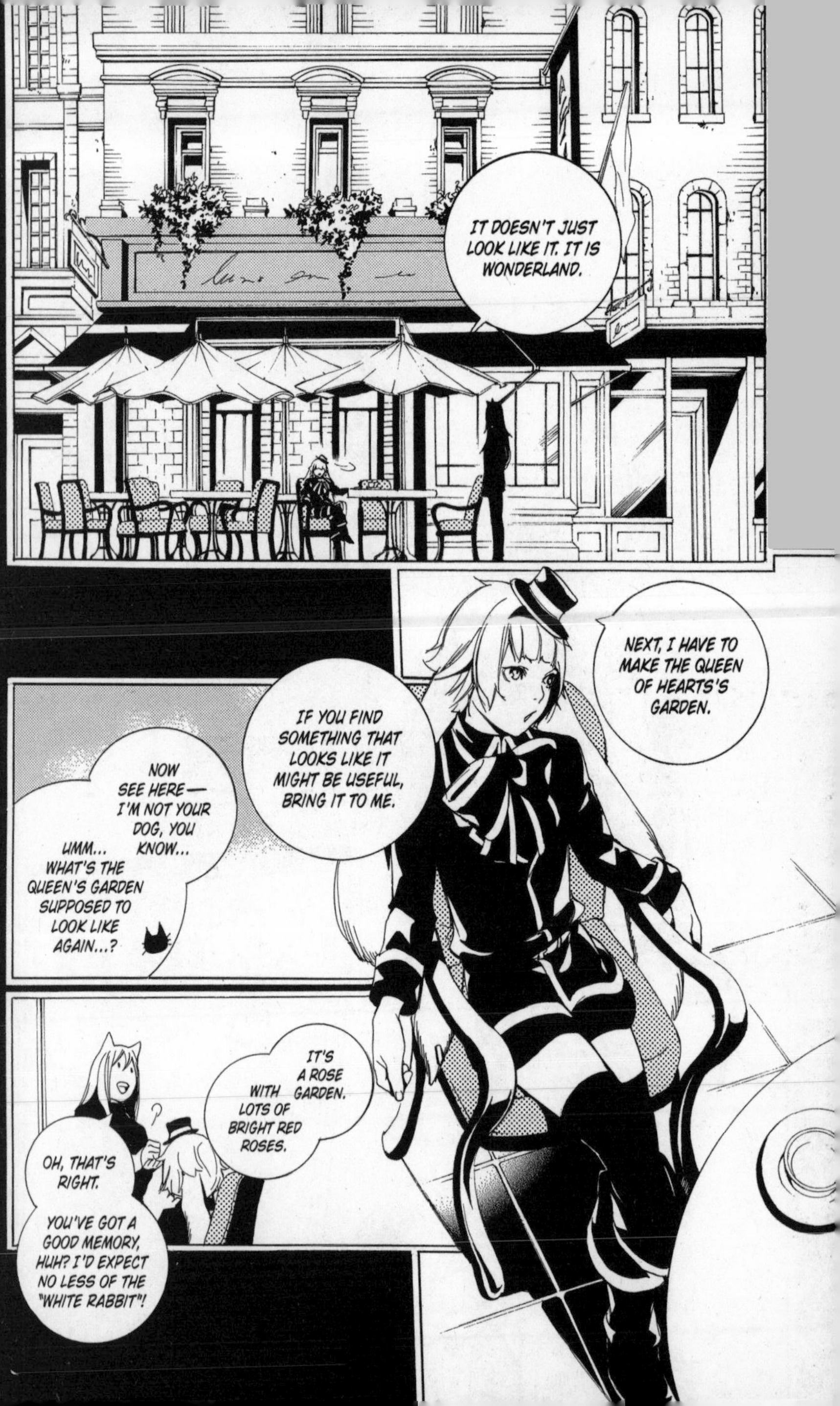
IT DOESN'T JUST LOOK LIKE IT. IT IS WONDERLAND.
NEXT, I HAVE TO MAKE THE QUEEN OF HEARTS'S GARDEN.
IF YOU FIND SOMETHING THAT LOOKS LIKE IT MIGHT BE USEFUL, BRING IT TO ME.
NOW SEE HERE— I'M NOT YOUR DOG, YOU KNOW...
UMM... WHAT'S THE QUEEN'S GARDEN SUPPOSED TO LOOK LIKE AGAIN...?
IT'S A ROSE GARDEN.
WITH LOTS OF BRIGHT RED ROSES.
OH, THAT'S RIGHT.
YOU'VE GOT A GOOD MEMORY, HUH? I'D EXPECT NO LESS OF THE "WHITE RABBIT"!

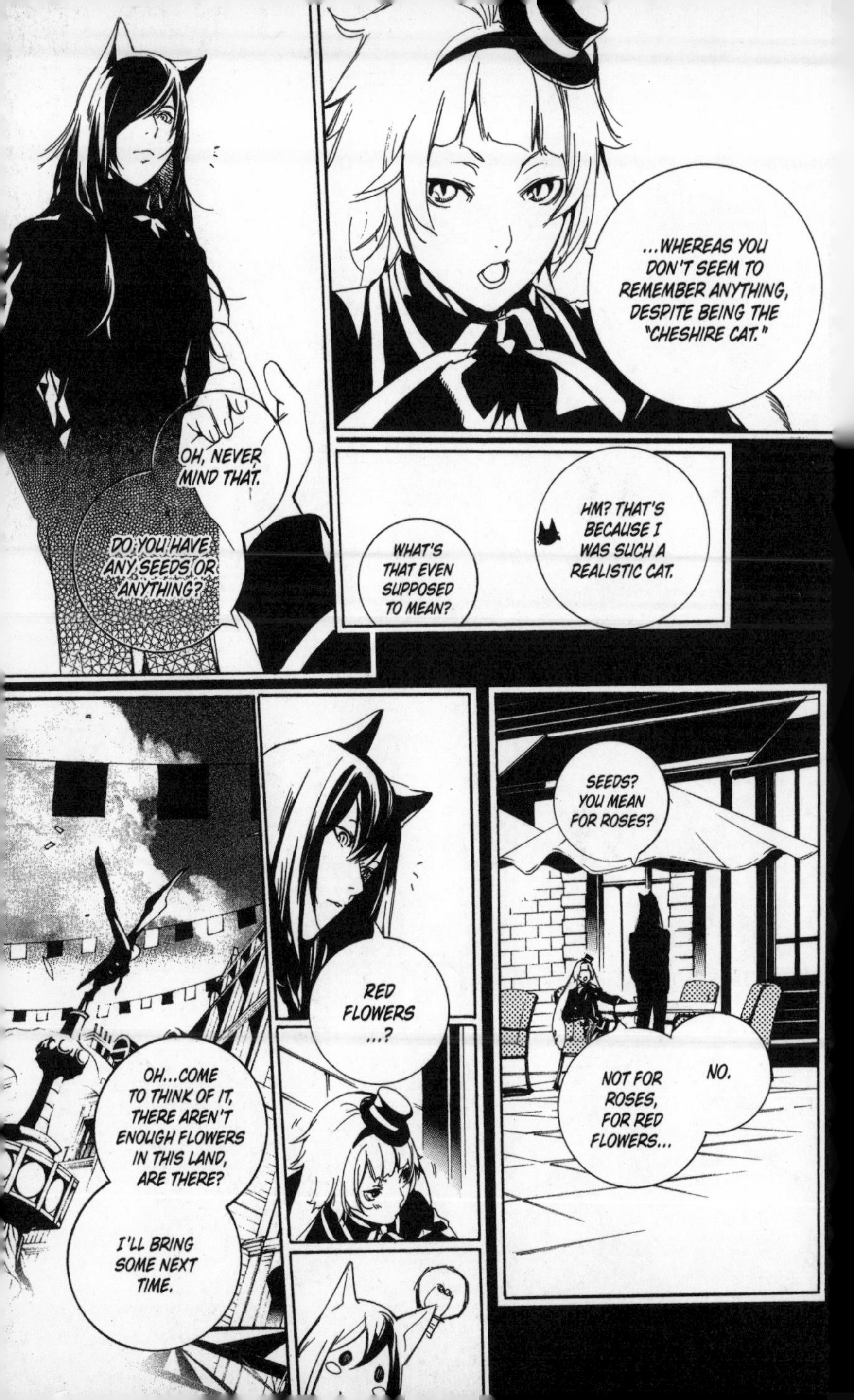
...WHEREAS YOU DON'T SEEM TO REMEMBER ANYTHING, DESPITE BEING THE "CHESHIRE CAT."
HM? THAT'S BECAUSE I WAS SUCH A REALISTIC CAT.
WHAT'S THAT EVEN SUPPOSED TO MEAN?
OH, NEVER MIND THAT.
DO YOU HAVE ANY SEEDS OR ANYTHING?
SEEDS? YOU MEAN FOR ROSES?
NO.
NOT FOR ROSES, FOR RED FLOWERS...
RED FLOWERS ...?
OH...COME TO THINK OF IT, THERE AREN'T ENOUGH FLOWERS IN THIS LAND, ARE THERE?
I'LL BRING SOME NEXT TIME.

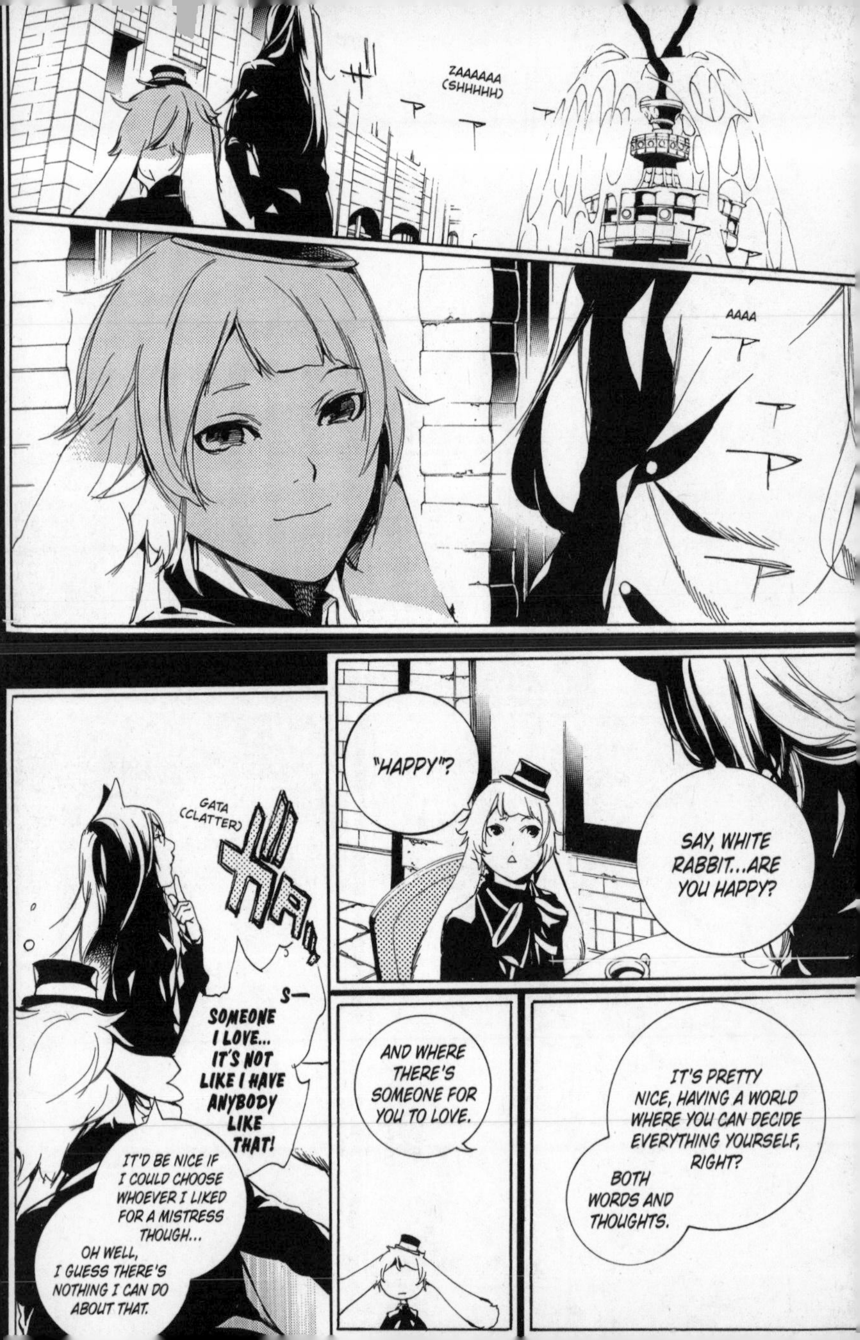
ZAAAAAA (SHHHHH)
AAAA
SAY, WHITE RABBIT...ARE YOU HAPPY?
"HAPPY"?
GATA (CLATTER)
S—
SOMEONE I LOVE... IT'S NOT LIKE I HAVE ANYBODY LIKE THAT!
IT'D BE NICE IF I COULD CHOOSE WHOEVER I LIKED FOR A MISTRESS THOUGH...
OH WELL, I GUESS THERE'S NOTHING I CAN DO ABOUT THAT.
IT'S PRETTY NICE, HAVING A WORLD WHERE YOU CAN DECIDE EVERYTHING YOURSELF, RIGHT?
BOTH WORDS AND THOUGHTS.
AND WHERE THERE'S SOMEONE FOR YOU TO LOVE.

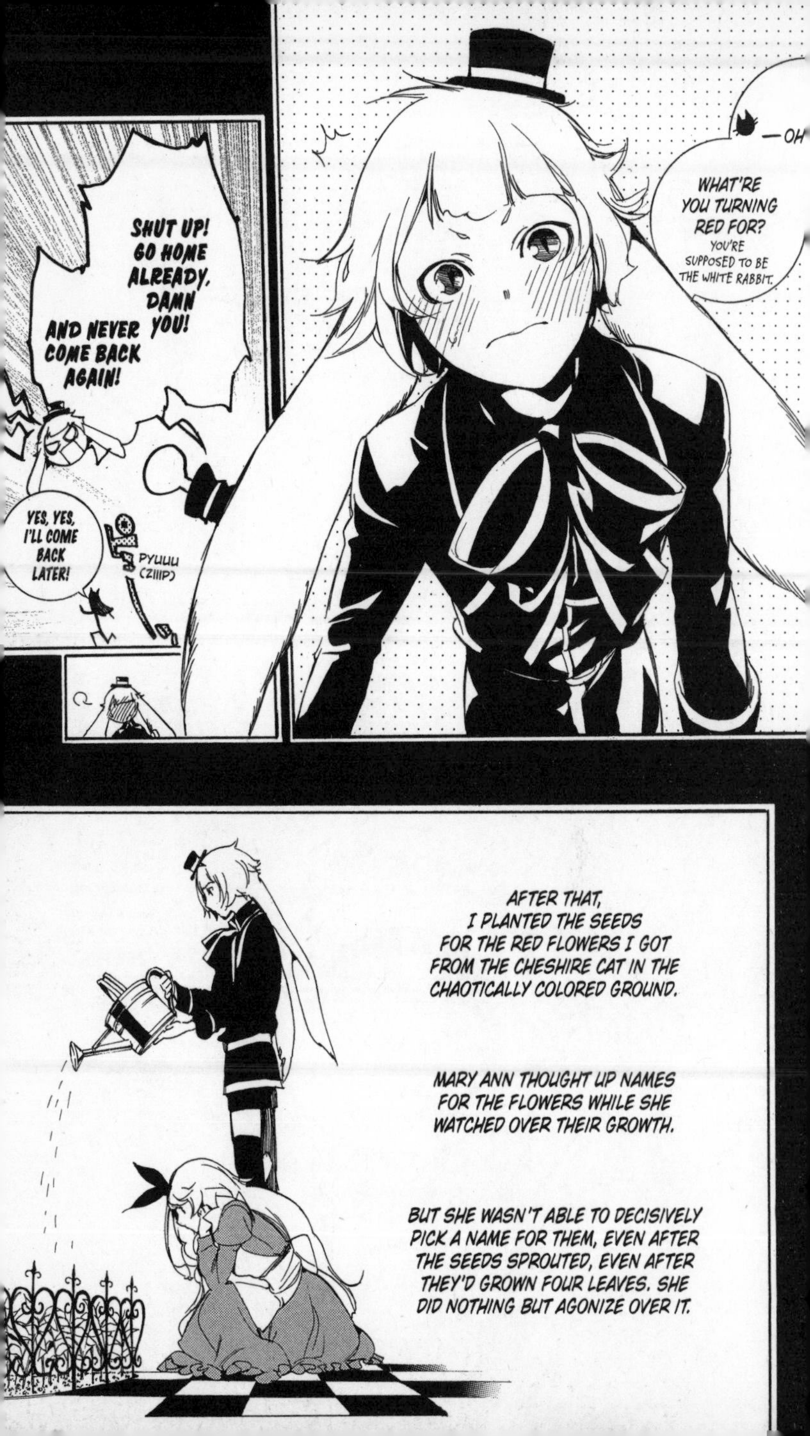
—OH
WHAT'RE YOU TURNING RED FOR? YOU'RE SUPPOSED TO BE THE WHITE RABBIT.
SHUT UP! GO HOME ALREADY, DAMN YOU!
AND NEVER COME BACK AGAIN!
YES, YES, I'LL COME BACK LATER!
PYUUU (ZIIIP)
AFTER THAT, I PLANTED THE SEEDS FOR THE RED FLOWERS I GOT FROM THE CHESHIRE CAT IN THE CHAOTICALLY COLORED GROUND.
MARY ANN THOUGHT UP NAMES FOR THE FLOWERS WHILE SHE WATCHED OVER THEIR GROWTH.
BUT SHE WASN'T ABLE TO DECISIVELY PICK A NAME FOR THEM, EVEN AFTER THE SEEDS SPROUTED, EVEN AFTER THEY'D GROWN FOUR LEAVES. SHE DID NOTHING BUT AGONIZE OVER IT.

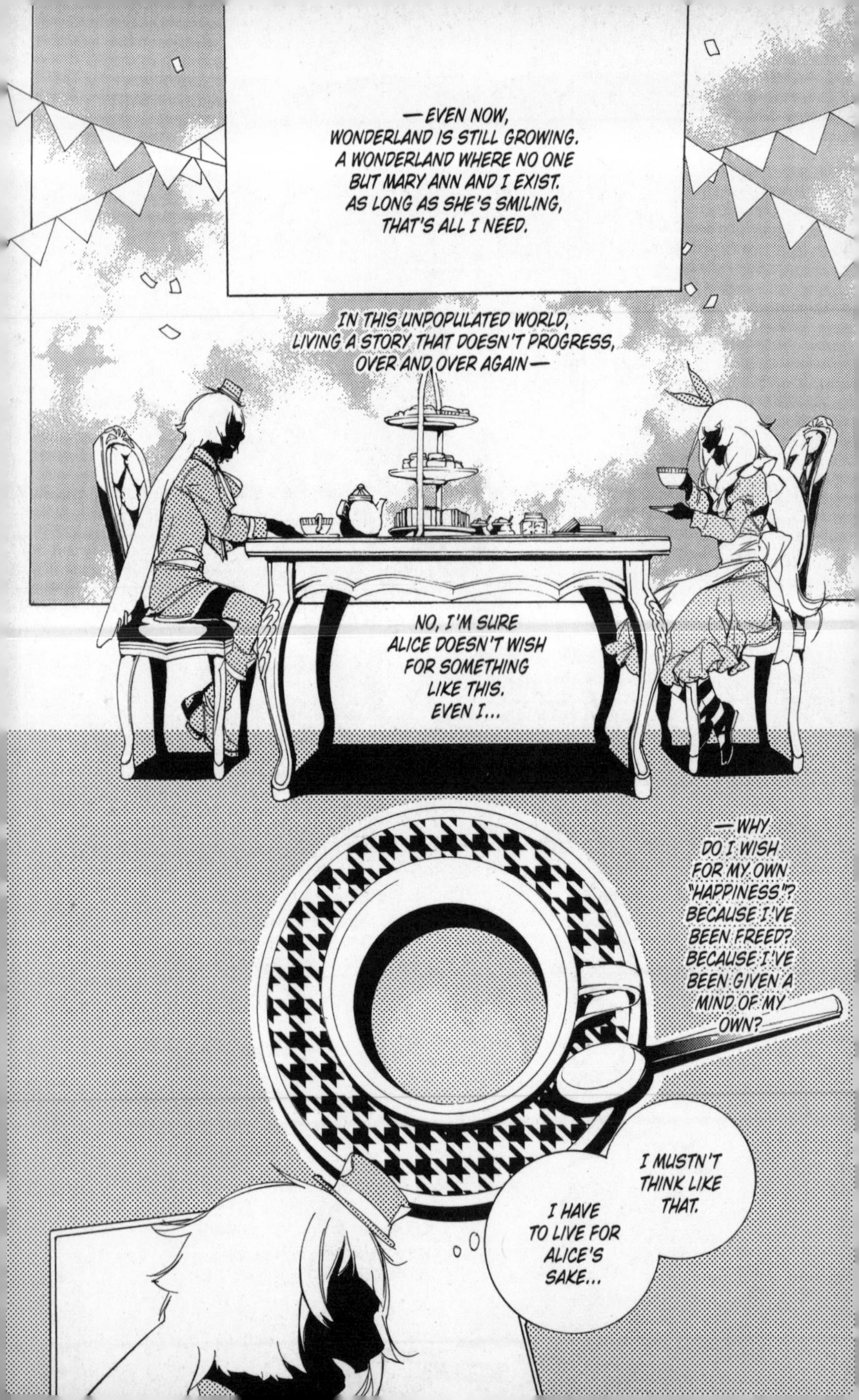
—EVEN NOW, WONDERLAND IS STILL GROWING. A WONDERLAND WHERE NO ONE BUT MARY ANN AND I EXIST. AS LONG AS SHE'S SMILING, THAT'S ALL I NEED.
IN THIS UNPOPULATED WORLD, LIVING A STORY THAT DOESN'T PROGRESS, OVER AND OVER AGAIN—
NO, I'M SURE ALICE DOESN'T WISH FOR SOMETHING LIKE THIS. EVEN I...
—WHY DO I WISH FOR MY OWN "HAPPINESS"? BECAUSE I'VE BEEN FREED? BECAUSE I'VE BEEN GIVEN A MIND OF MY OWN?
I MUSTN'T THINK LIKE THAT.
I HAVE TO LIVE FOR ALICE'S SAKE...

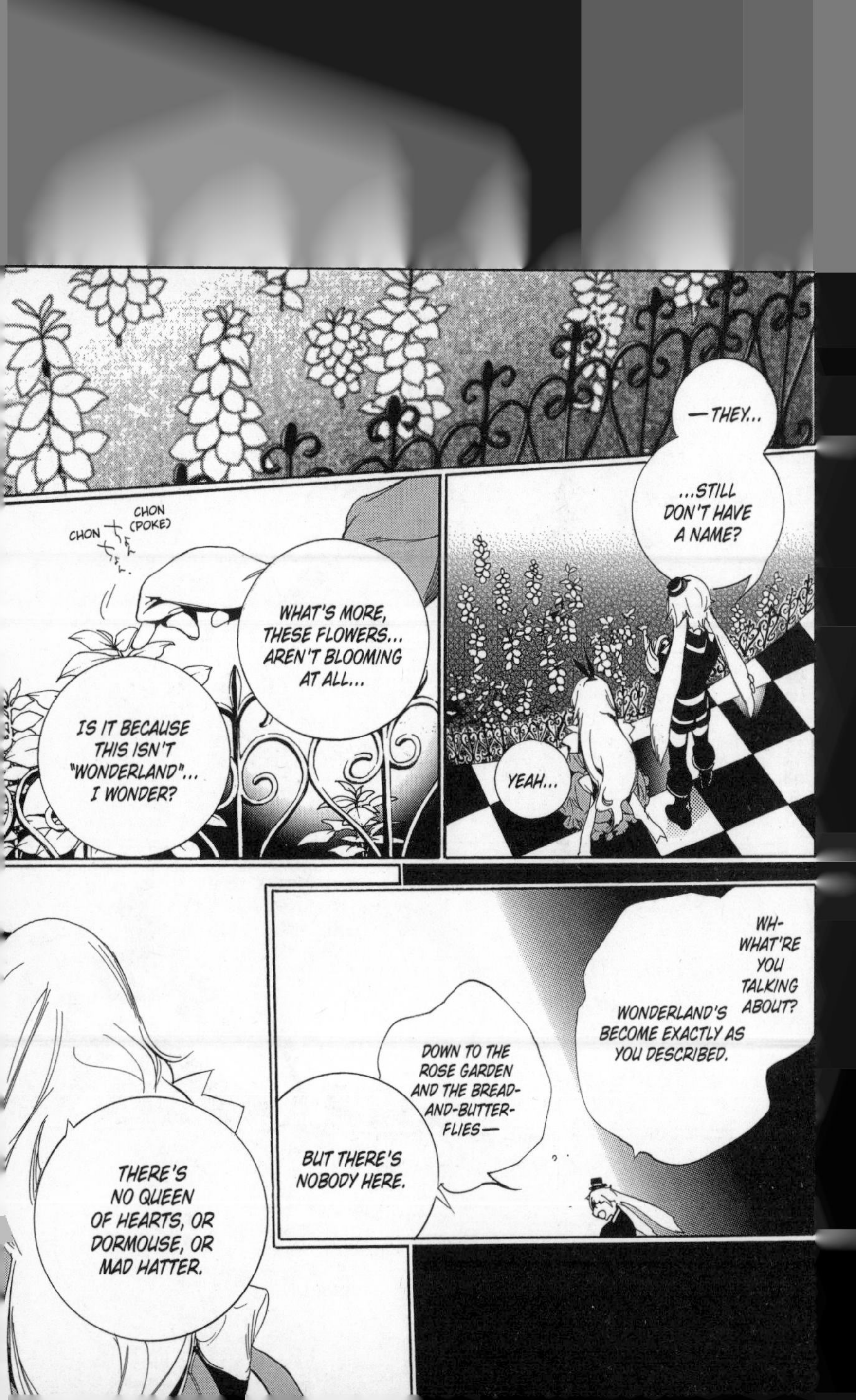
—THEY...
...STILL DON'T HAVE A NAME?
YEAH...
CHON CHON (POKE)
WHAT'S MORE, THESE FLOWERS... AREN'T BLOOMING AT ALL...
IS IT BECAUSE THIS ISN'T "WONDERLAND"... I WONDER?
WH- WHAT'RE YOU TALKING ABOUT?
WONDERLAND'S BECOME EXACTLY AS YOU DESCRIBED.
DOWN TO THE ROSE GARDEN AND THE BREAD-AND-BUTTER-FLIES—
BUT THERE'S NOBODY HERE.
THERE'S NO QUEEN OF HEARTS, OR DORMOUSE, OR MAD HATTER.

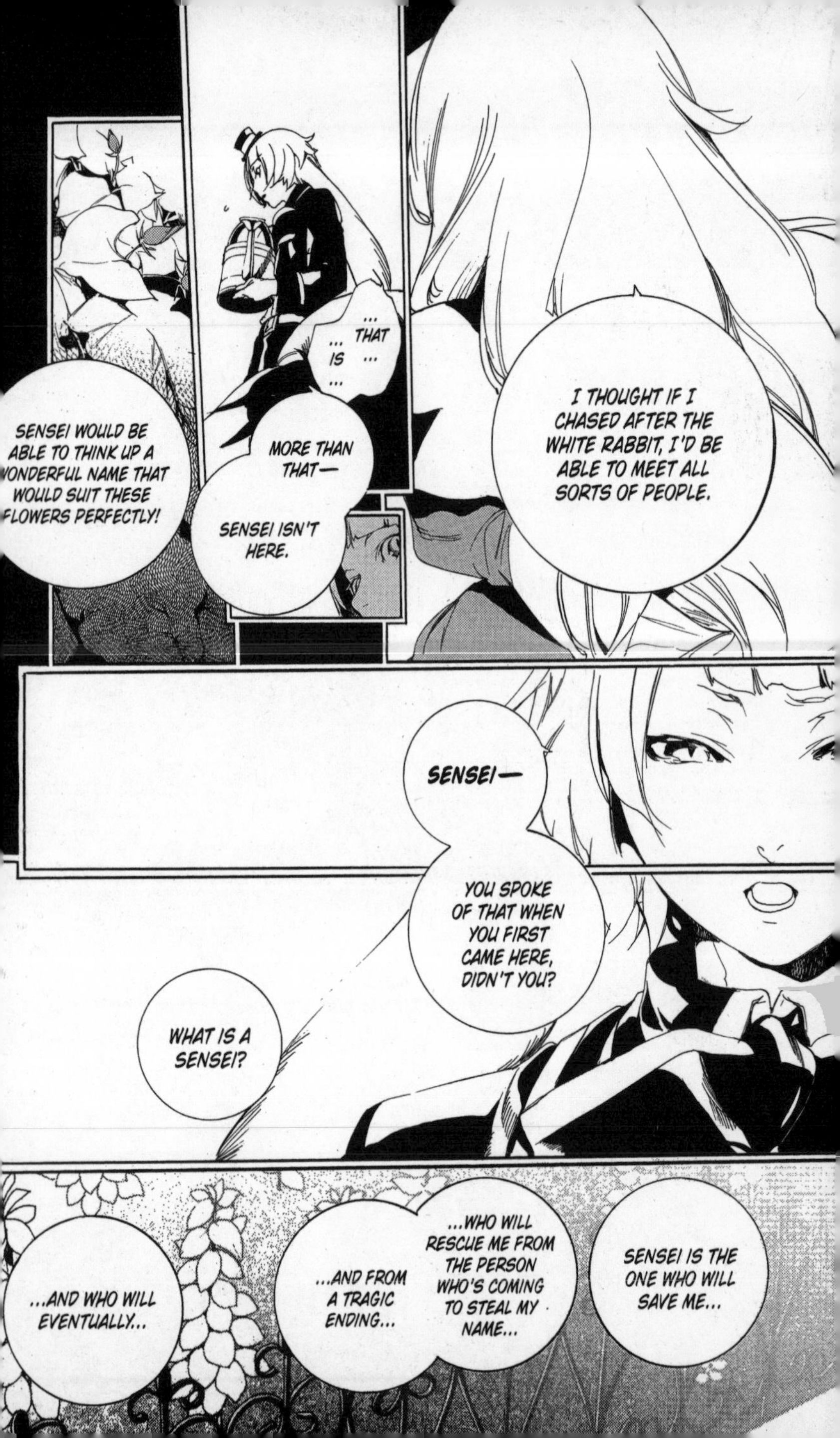
I THOUGHT IF I CHASED AFTER THE WHITE RABBIT, I'D BE ABLE TO MEET ALL SORTS OF PEOPLE.
...THAT... IS...
MORE THAN THAT—
SENSEI ISN'T HERE.
SENSEI WOULD BE ABLE TO THINK UP A WONDERFUL NAME THAT WOULD SUIT THESE FLOWERS PERFECTLY!
SENSEI—
YOU SPOKE OF THAT WHEN YOU FIRST CAME HERE, DIDN'T YOU?
WHAT IS A SENSEI?
SENSEI IS THE ONE WHO WILL SAVE ME...
...WHO WILL RESCUE ME FROM THE PERSON WHO'S COMING TO STEAL MY NAME...
...AND FROM A TRAGIC ENDING...
...AND WHO WILL EVENTUALLY...

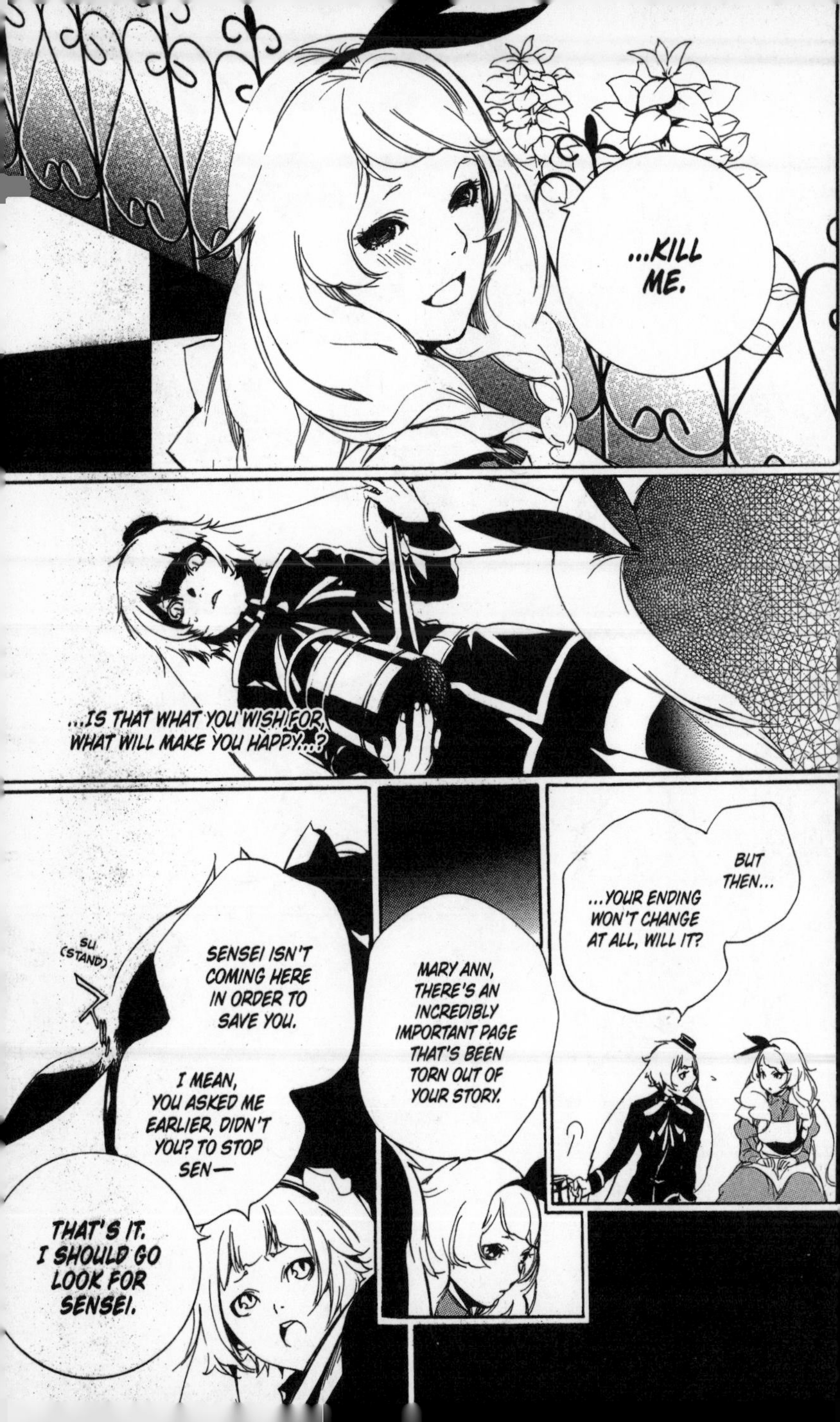
...KILL ME.
...IS THAT WHAT YOU WISH FOR, WHAT WILL MAKE YOU HAPPY...?
BUT THEN...
...YOUR ENDING WON'T CHANGE AT ALL, WILL IT?
MARY ANN, THERE'S AN INCREDIBLY IMPORTANT PAGE THAT'S BEEN TORN OUT OF YOUR STORY.
SENSEI ISN'T COMING HERE IN ORDER TO SAVE YOU.
I MEAN, YOU ASKED ME EARLIER, DIDN'T YOU? TO STOP SEN—
SU (STAND)
THAT'S IT. I SHOULD GO LOOK FOR SENSEI.

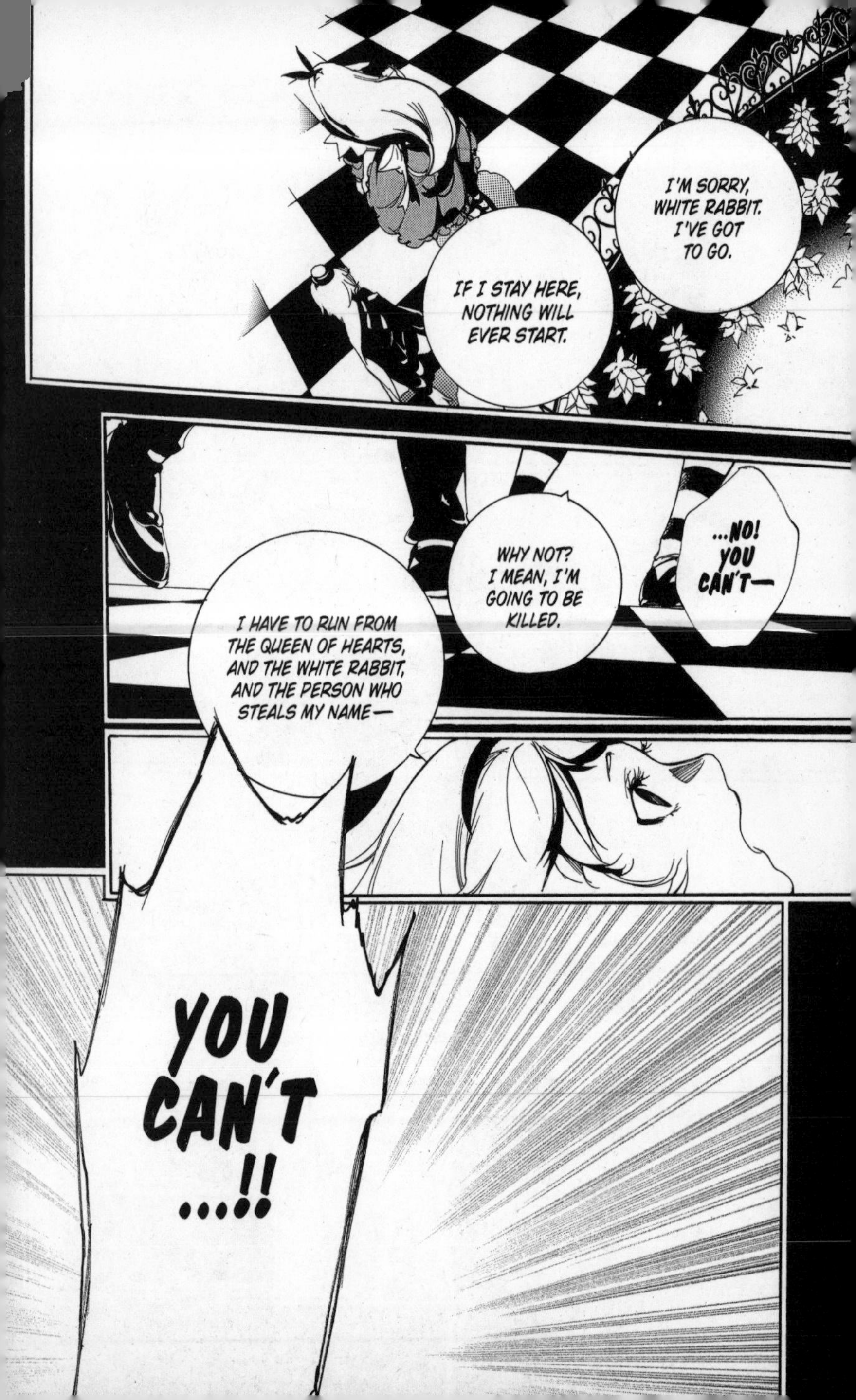
I'M SORRY, WHITE RABBIT. I'VE GOT TO GO.
IF I STAY HERE, NOTHING WILL EVER START.
...NO! YOU CAN'T—
WHY NOT? I MEAN, I'M GOING TO BE KILLED.
I HAVE TO RUN FROM THE QUEEN OF HEARTS, AND THE WHITE RABBIT, AND THE PERSON WHO STEALS MY NAME—
YOU CAN'T ...!!

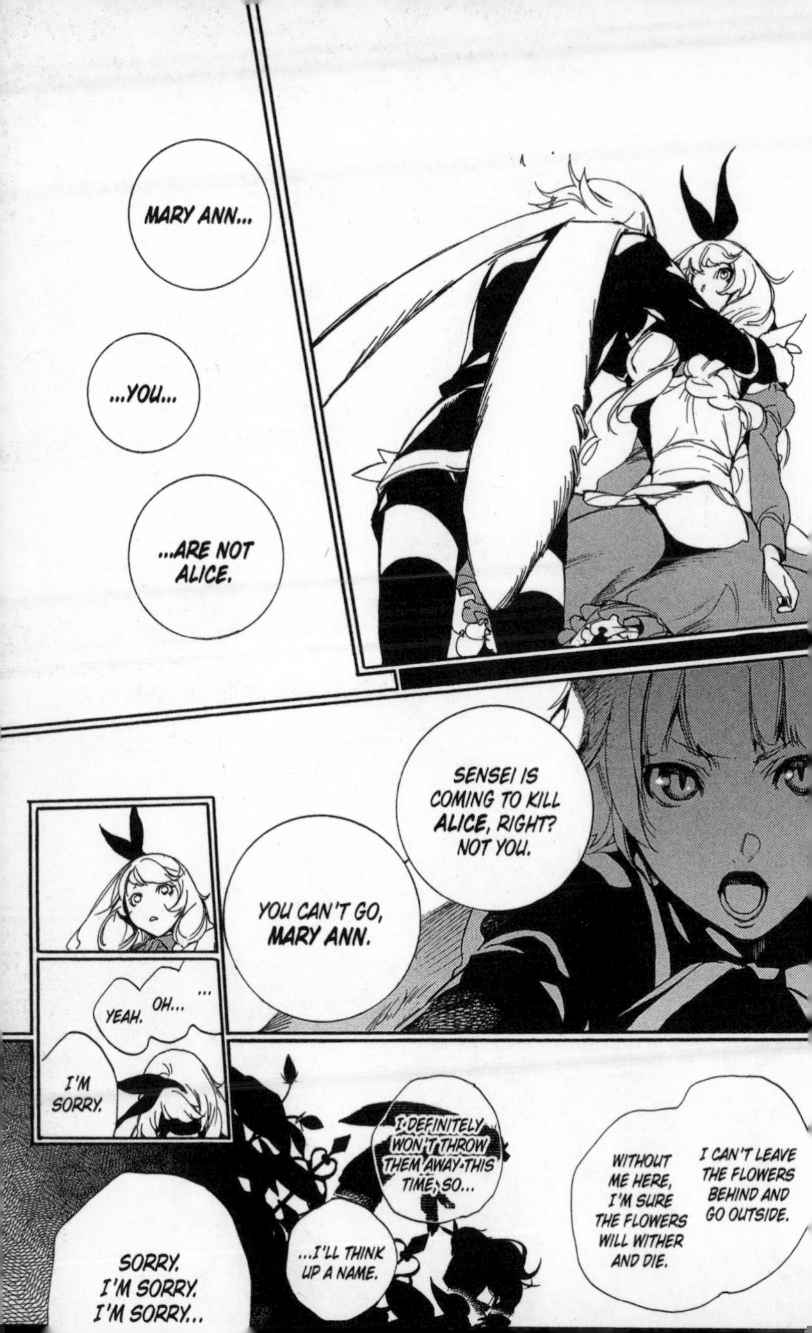
MARY ANN...
...YOU...
...ARE NOT ALICE.
SENSEI IS COMING TO KILL ALICE, RIGHT? NOT YOU.
YOU CAN'T GO, MARY ANN.
...
OH...
YEAH.
I'M SORRY.
I CAN'T LEAVE THE FLOWERS BEHIND AND GO OUTSIDE.
WITHOUT ME HERE, I'M SURE THE FLOWERS WILL WITHER AND DIE.
I DEFINITELY WON'T THROW THEM AWAY THIS TIME, SO...
...I'LL THINK UP A NAME.
SORRY. I'M SORRY. I'M SORRY...

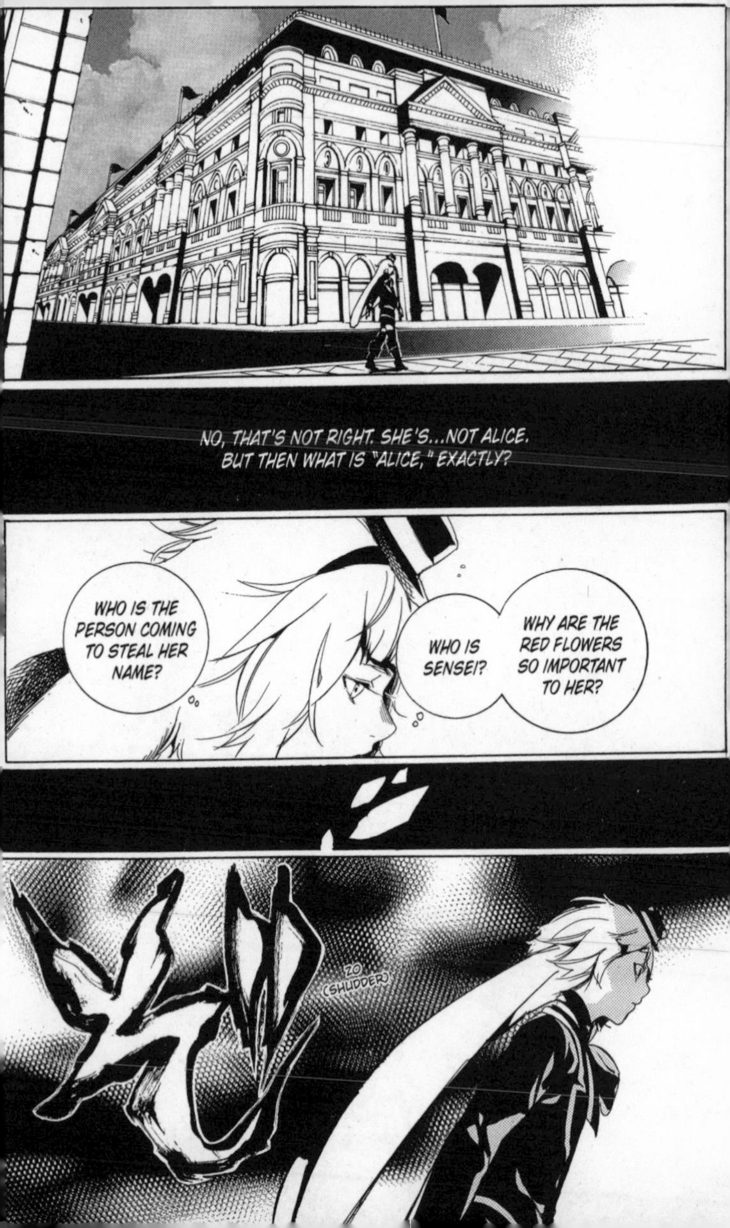
NO, THAT'S NOT RIGHT. SHE'S...NOT ALICE. BUT THEN WHAT IS "ALICE," EXACTLY?
WHY ARE THE RED FLOWERS SO IMPORTANT TO HER?
WHO IS SENSEI?
WHO IS THE PERSON COMING TO STEAL HER NAME?
ZO (SHUDDER)

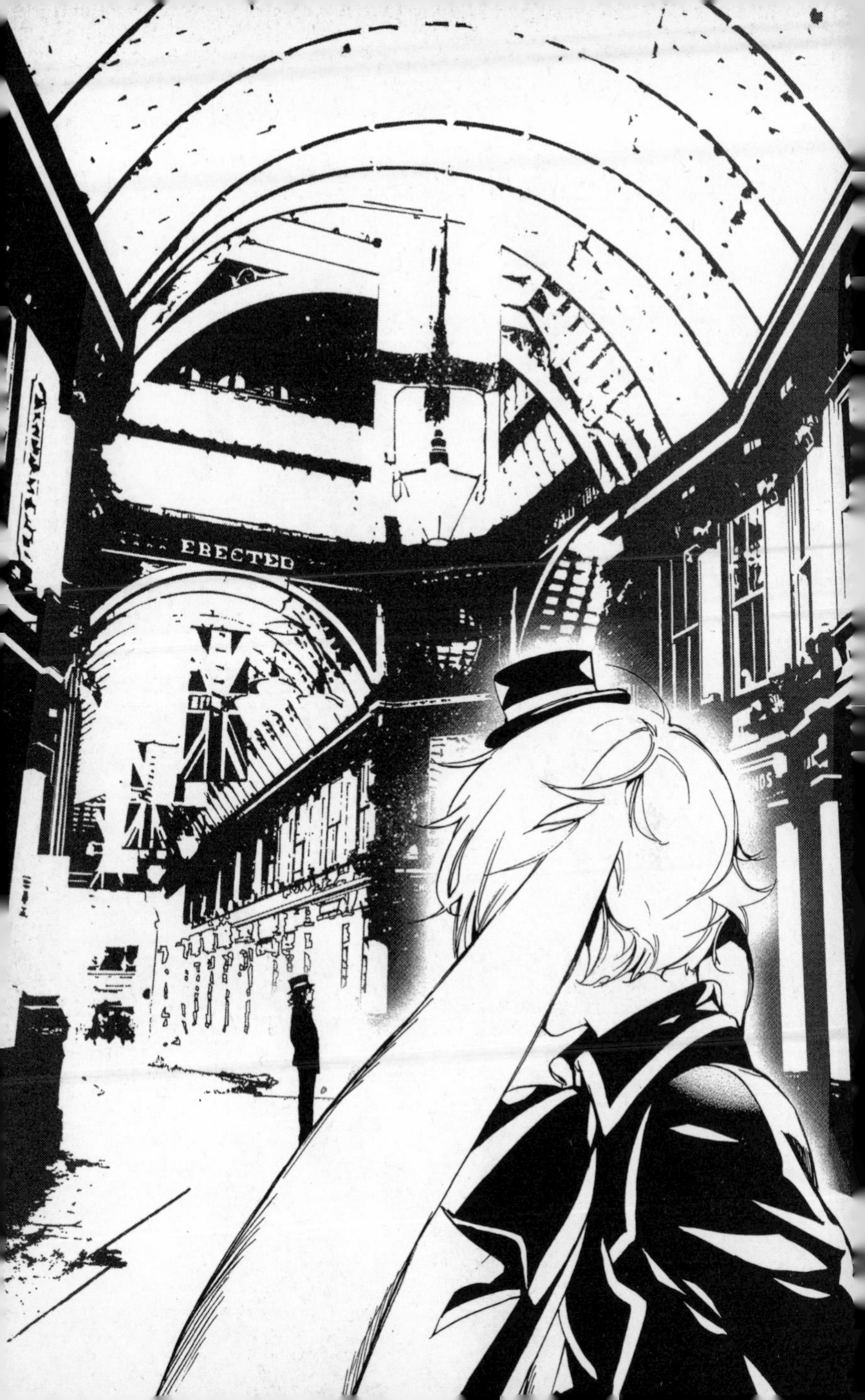
ERECTED

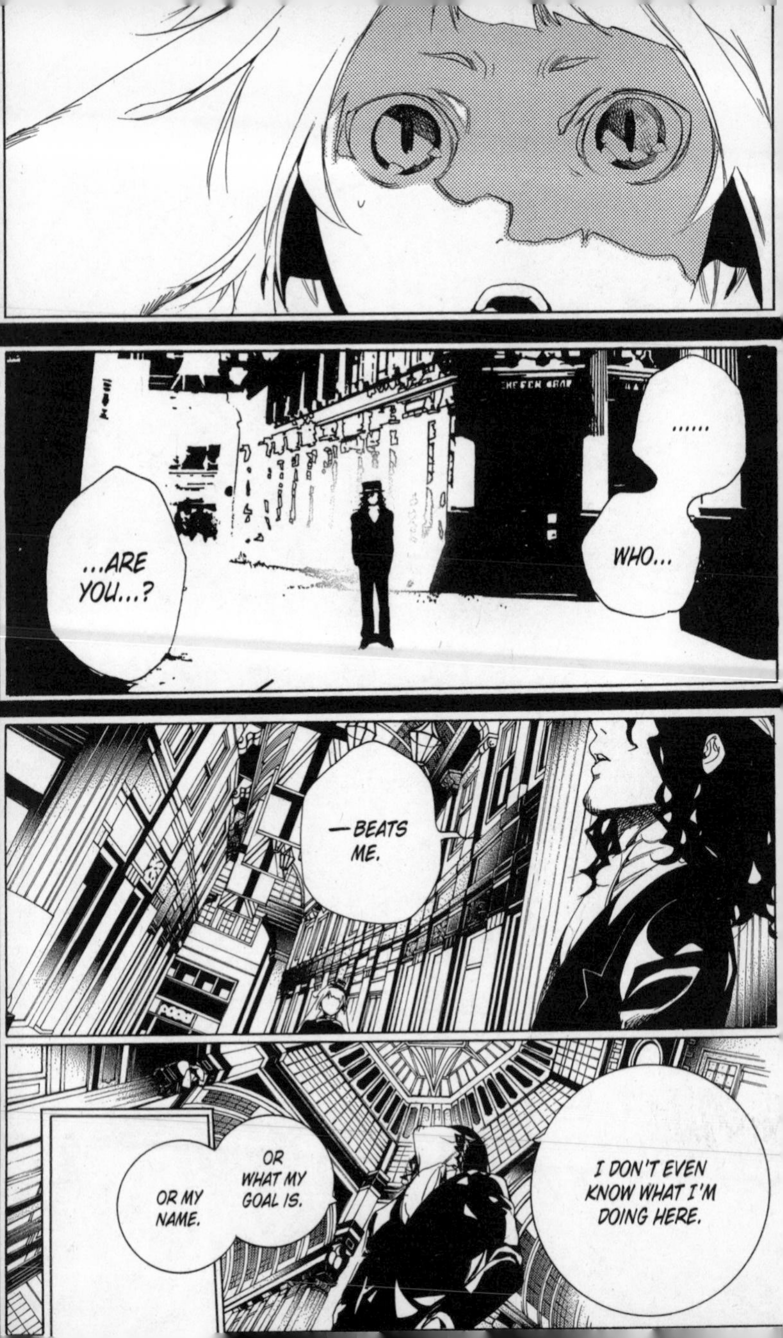
......
WHO...
...ARE YOU...?
—BEATS ME.
I DON'T EVEN KNOW WHAT I'M DOING HERE.
OR WHAT MY GOAL IS.
OR MY NAME.

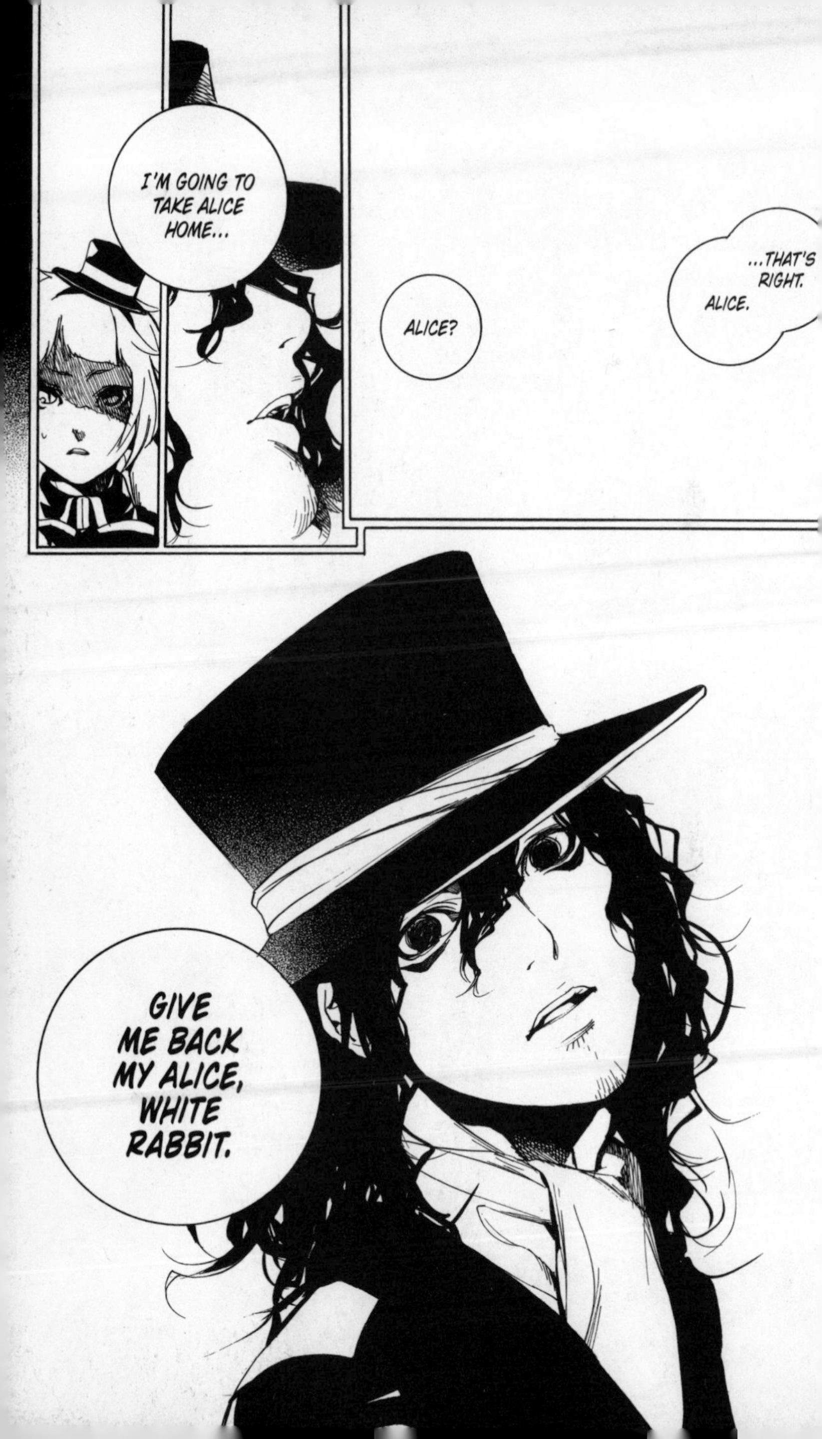
...THAT'S RIGHT. ALICE.
ALICE?
I'M GOING TO TAKE ALICE HOME...
GIVE ME BACK MY ALICE, WHITE RABBIT.

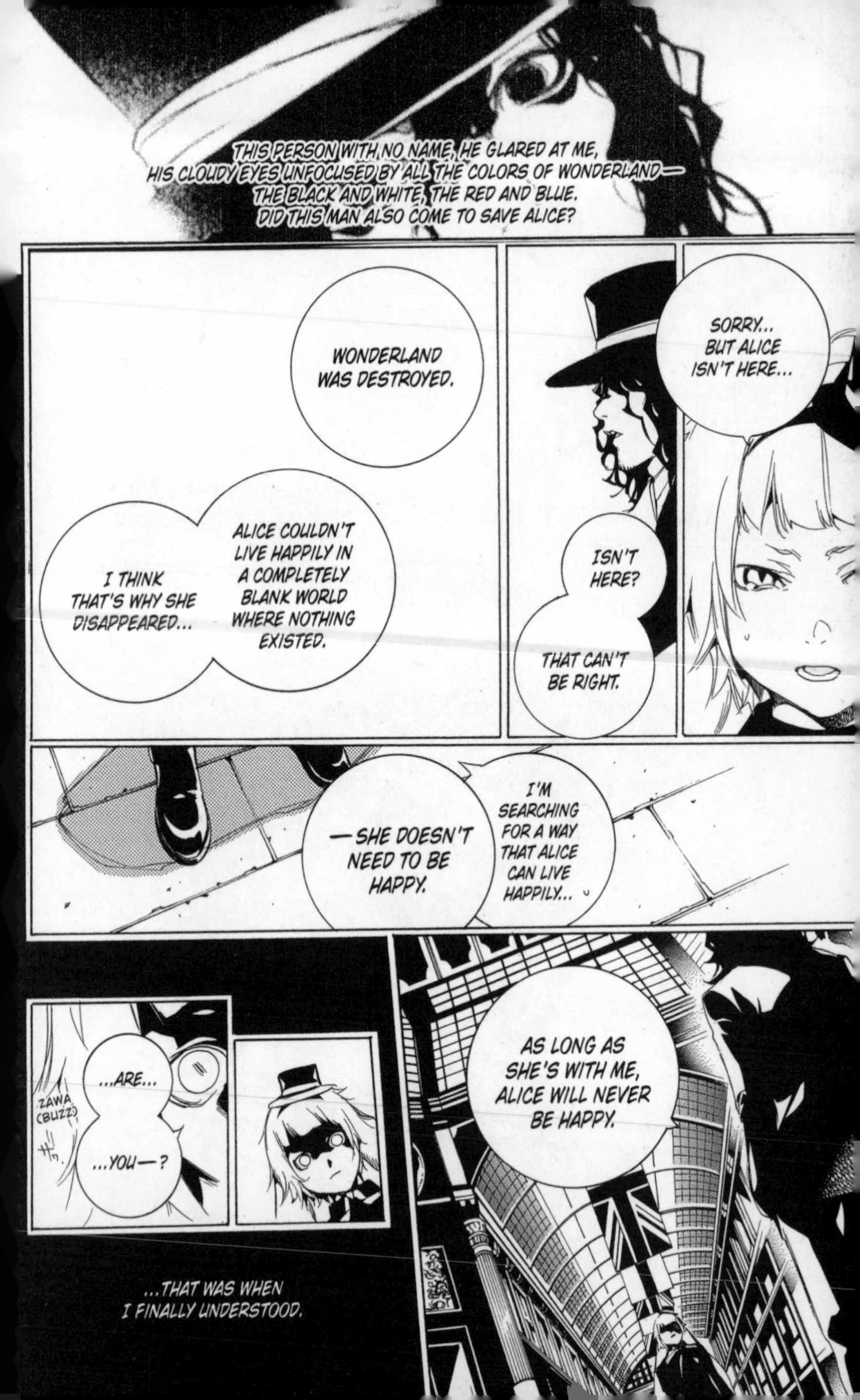
THIS PERSON WITH NO NAME, HE GLARED AT ME, HIS CLOUDY EYES UNFOCUSED BY ALL THE COLORS OF WONDERLAND— THE BLACK AND WHITE, THE RED AND BLUE. DID THIS MAN ALSO COME TO SAVE ALICE?
SORRY... BUT ALICE ISN'T HERE...
ISN'T HERE?
THAT CAN'T BE RIGHT.
WONDERLAND WAS DESTROYED.
ALICE COULDN'T LIVE HAPPILY IN A COMPLETELY BLANK WORLD WHERE NOTHING EXISTED.
I THINK THAT'S WHY SHE DISAPPEARED...
I'M SEARCHING FOR A WAY THAT ALICE CAN LIVE HAPPILY...
—SHE DOESN'T NEED TO BE HAPPY.
AS LONG AS SHE'S WITH ME, ALICE WILL NEVER BE HAPPY.
...ARE...
...YOU—?
ZAWA (BUZZ)
...THAT WAS WHEN I FINALLY UNDERSTOOD.

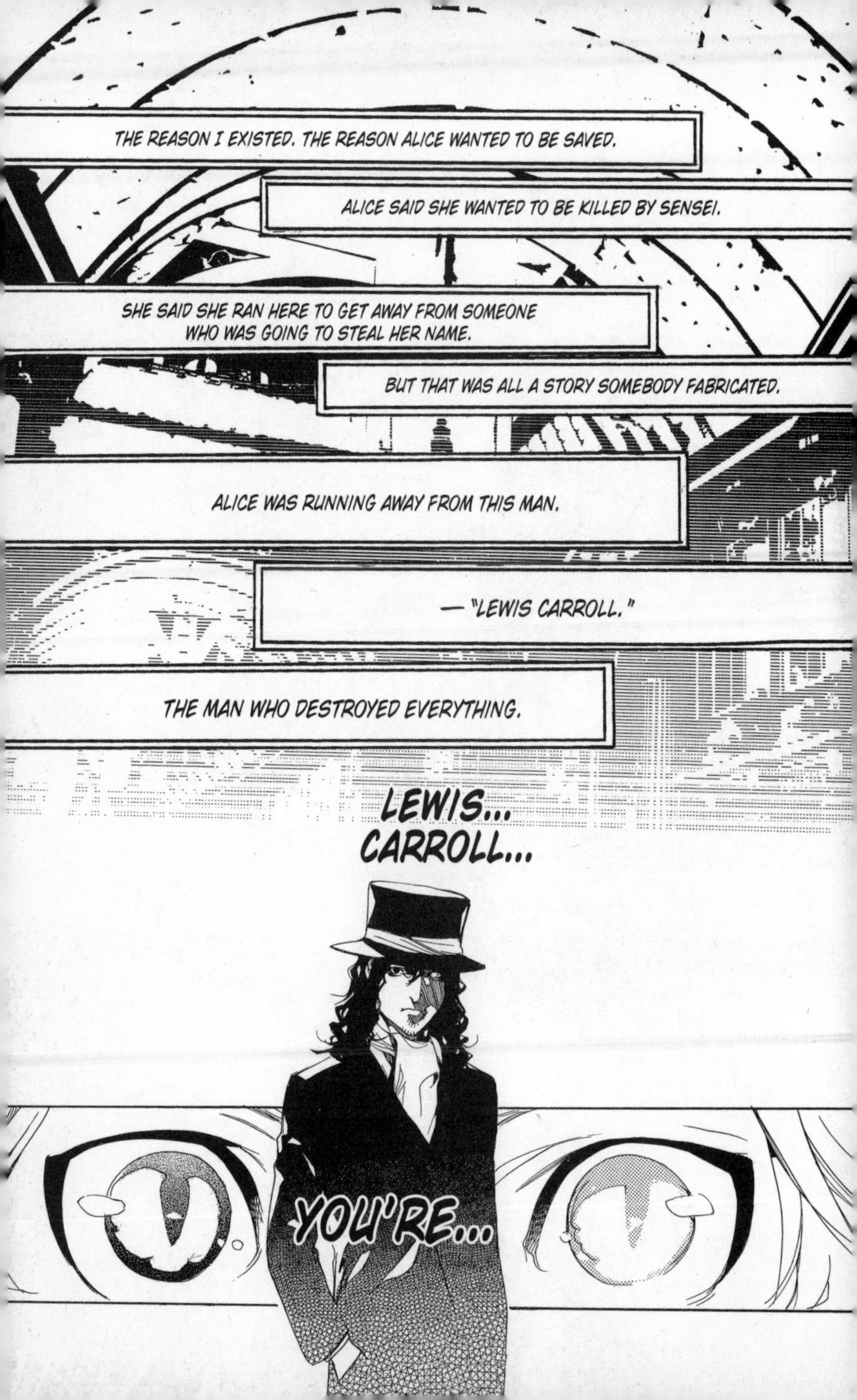
THE REASON I EXISTED. THE REASON ALICE WANTED TO BE SAVED.
ALICE SAID SHE WANTED TO BE KILLED BY SENSEI.
SHE SAID SHE RAN HERE TO GET AWAY FROM SOMEONE WHO WAS GOING TO STEAL HER NAME.
BUT THAT WAS ALL A STORY SOMEBODY FABRICATED.
ALICE WAS RUNNING AWAY FROM THIS MAN.
— "LEWIS CARROLL."
THE MAN WHO DESTROYED EVERYTHING.
LEWIS... CARROLL...
YOU'RE...

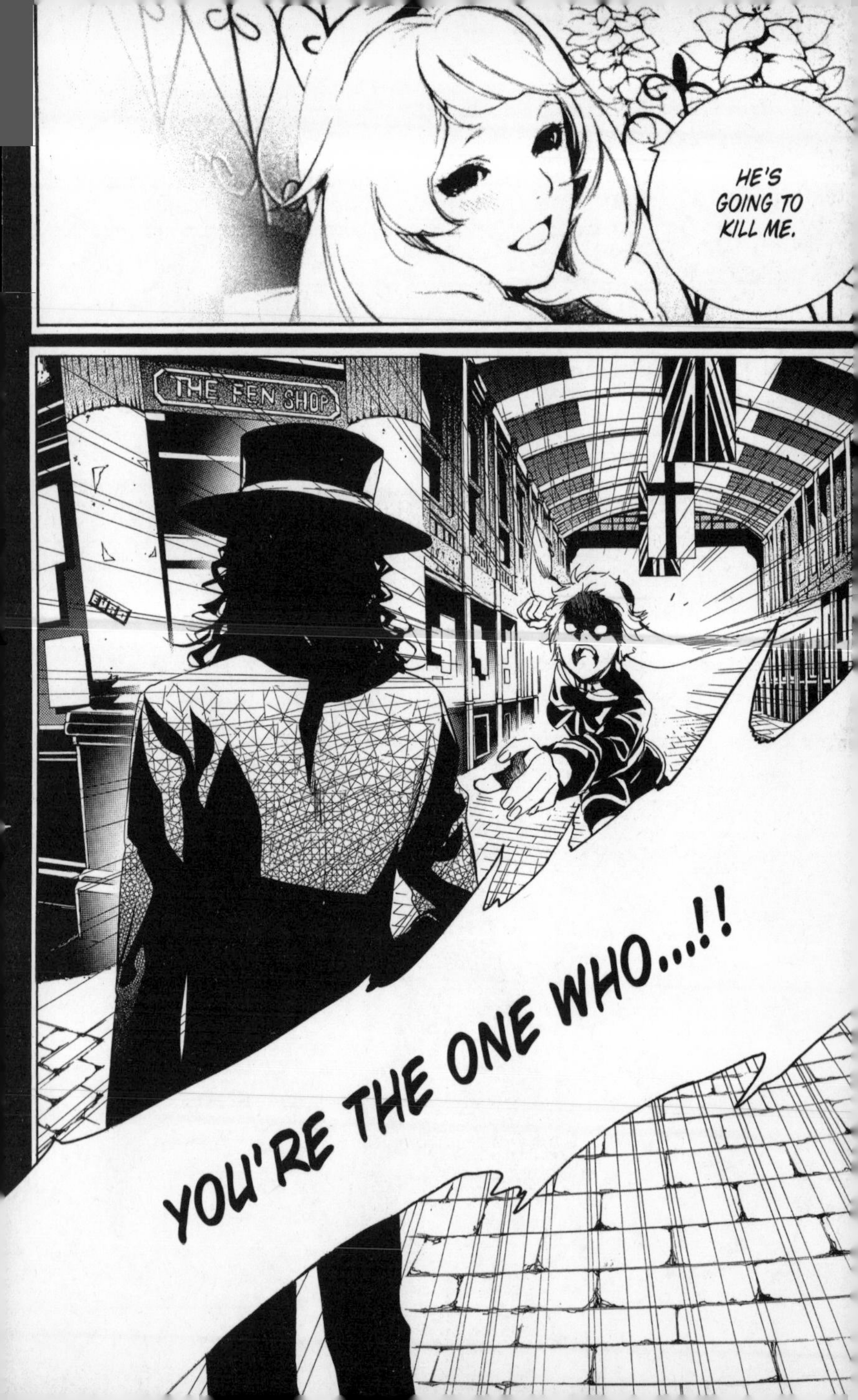
HE'S GOING TO KILL ME.
THE FEN SHOP
YOU'RE THE ONE WHO...!!

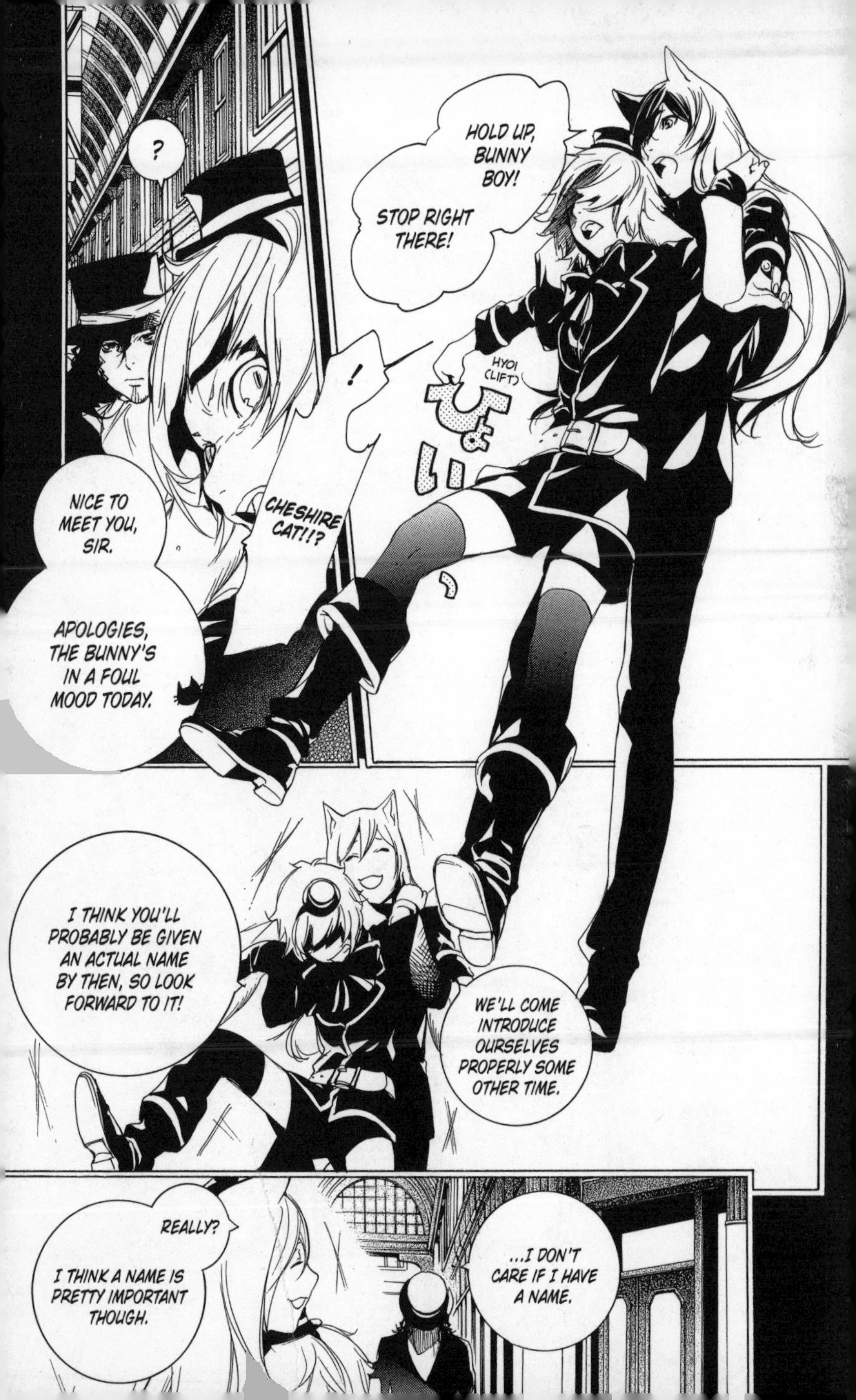
HOLD UP, BUNNY BOY!
STOP RIGHT THERE!
HYOI (LIFT)
?
!
CHESHIRE CAT!!?
NICE TO MEET YOU, SIR.
APOLOGIES, THE BUNNY'S IN A FOUL MOOD TODAY.
WE'LL COME INTRODUCE OURSELVES PROPERLY SOME OTHER TIME.
I THINK YOU'LL PROBABLY BE GIVEN AN ACTUAL NAME BY THEN, SO LOOK FORWARD TO IT!
...I DON'T CARE IF I HAVE A NAME.
REALLY?
I THINK A NAME IS PRETTY IMPORTANT THOUGH.

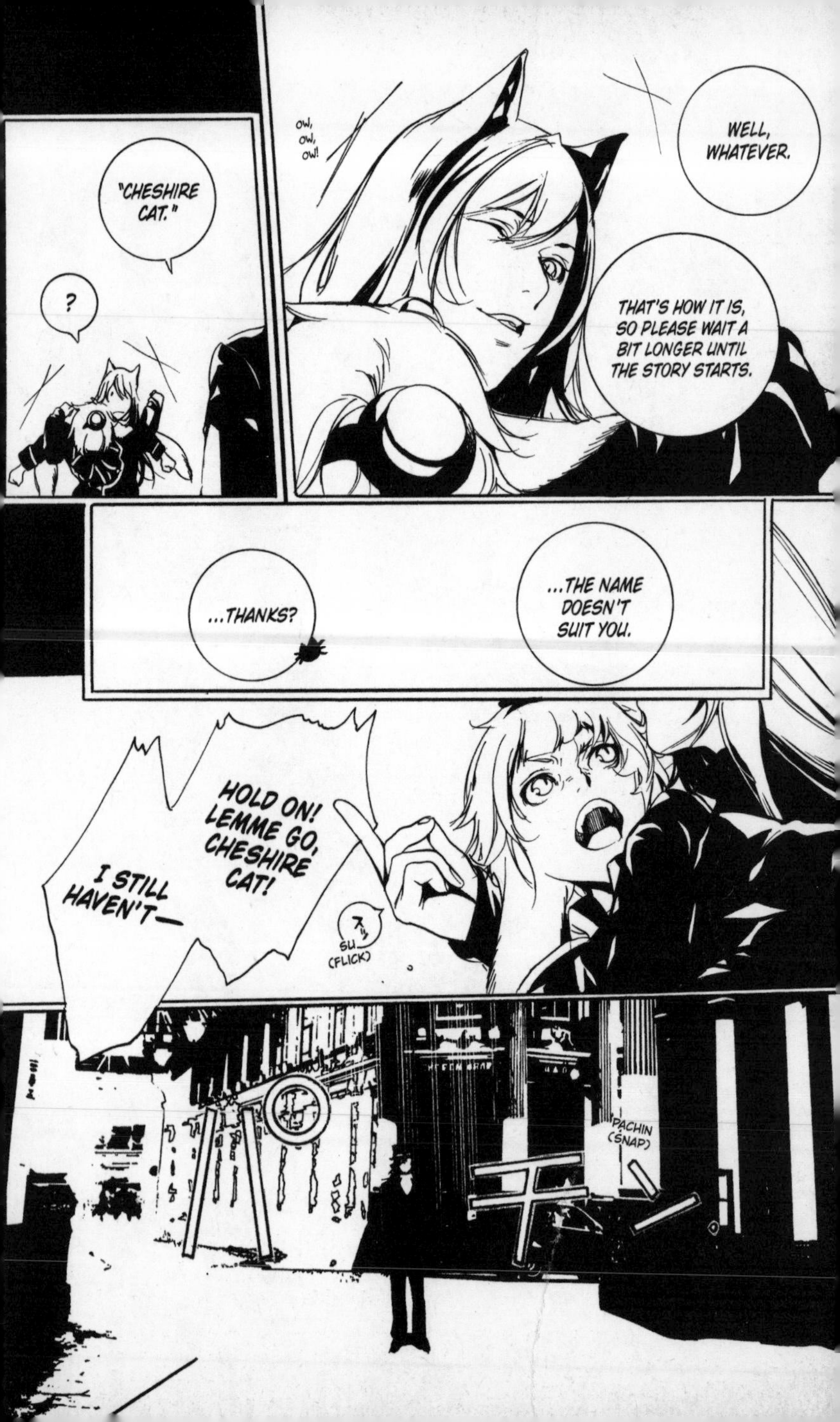
WELL, WHATEVER.
OW, OW, OW!
THAT'S HOW IT IS, SO PLEASE WAIT A BIT LONGER UNTIL THE STORY STARTS.
"CHESHIRE CAT."
?
...THE NAME DOESN'T SUIT YOU.
...THANKS?
HOLD ON! LEMME GO, CHESHIRE CAT!
I STILL HAVEN'T—
スッ
SU (FLICK)
PACHIN (SNAP)

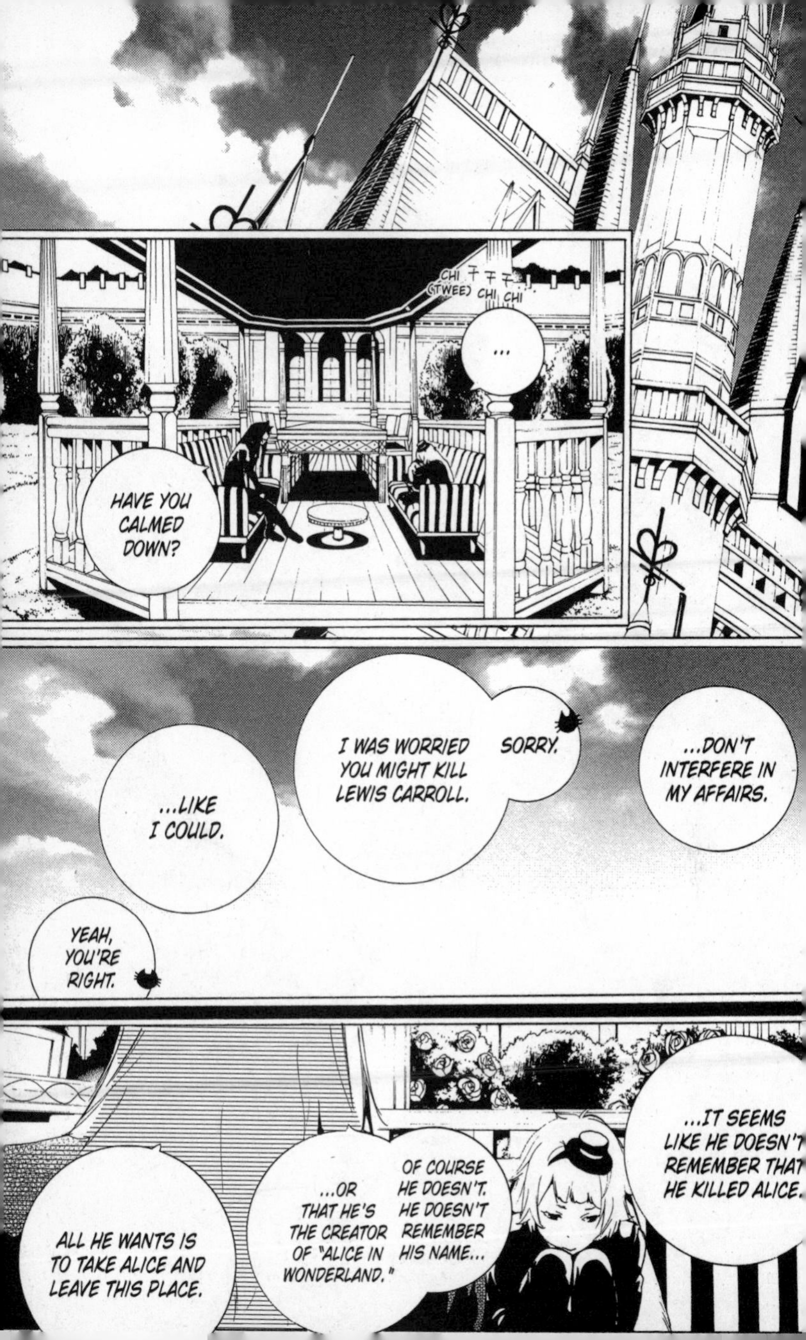
CHI チチチ (TWEE) CHI CHI
...
HAVE YOU CALMED DOWN?
...DON'T INTERFERE IN MY AFFAIRS.
SORRY.
I WAS WORRIED YOU MIGHT KILL LEWIS CARROLL.
...LIKE I COULD.
YEAH, YOU'RE RIGHT.
...IT SEEMS LIKE HE DOESN'T REMEMBER THAT HE KILLED ALICE.
OF COURSE HE DOESN'T. HE DOESN'T REMEMBER HIS NAME...
...OR THAT HE'S THE CREATOR OF "ALICE IN WONDERLAND."
ALL HE WANTS IS TO TAKE ALICE AND LEAVE THIS PLACE.

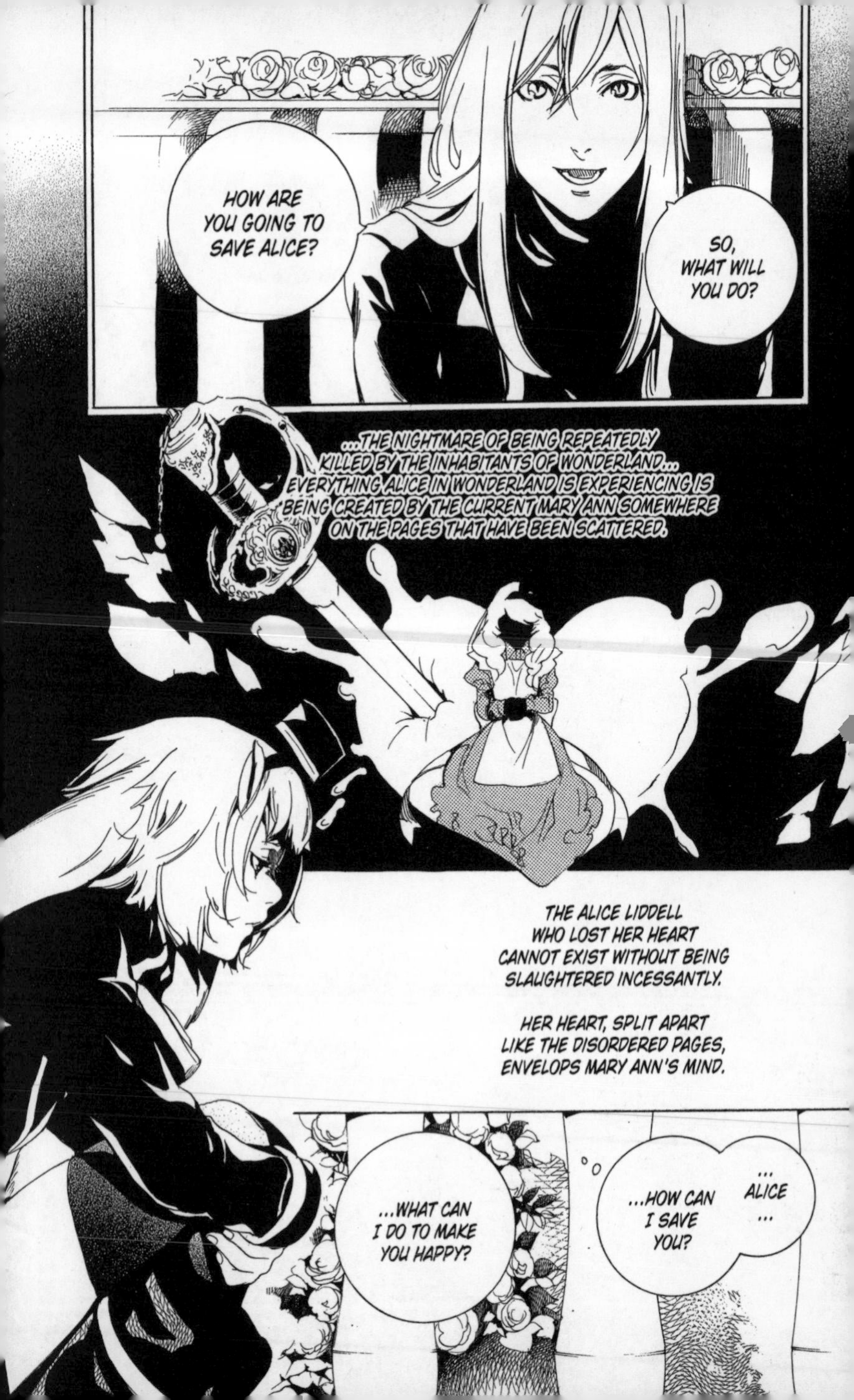
SO, WHAT WILL YOU DO?
HOW ARE YOU GOING TO SAVE ALICE?
...THE NIGHTMARE OF BEING REPEATEDLY KILLED BY THE INHABITANTS OF WONDERLAND... EVERYTHING ALICE IN WONDERLAND IS EXPERIENCING IS BEING CREATED BY THE CURRENT MARY ANN SOMEWHERE ON THE PAGES THAT HAVE BEEN SCATTERED.
THE ALICE LIDDELL WHO LOST HER HEART CANNOT EXIST WITHOUT BEING SLAUGHTERED INCESSANTLY.
HER HEART, SPLIT APART LIKE THE DISORDERED PAGES, ENVELOPS MARY ANN'S MIND.
...ALICE...
...HOW CAN I SAVE YOU?
...WHAT CAN I DO TO MAKE YOU HAPPY?

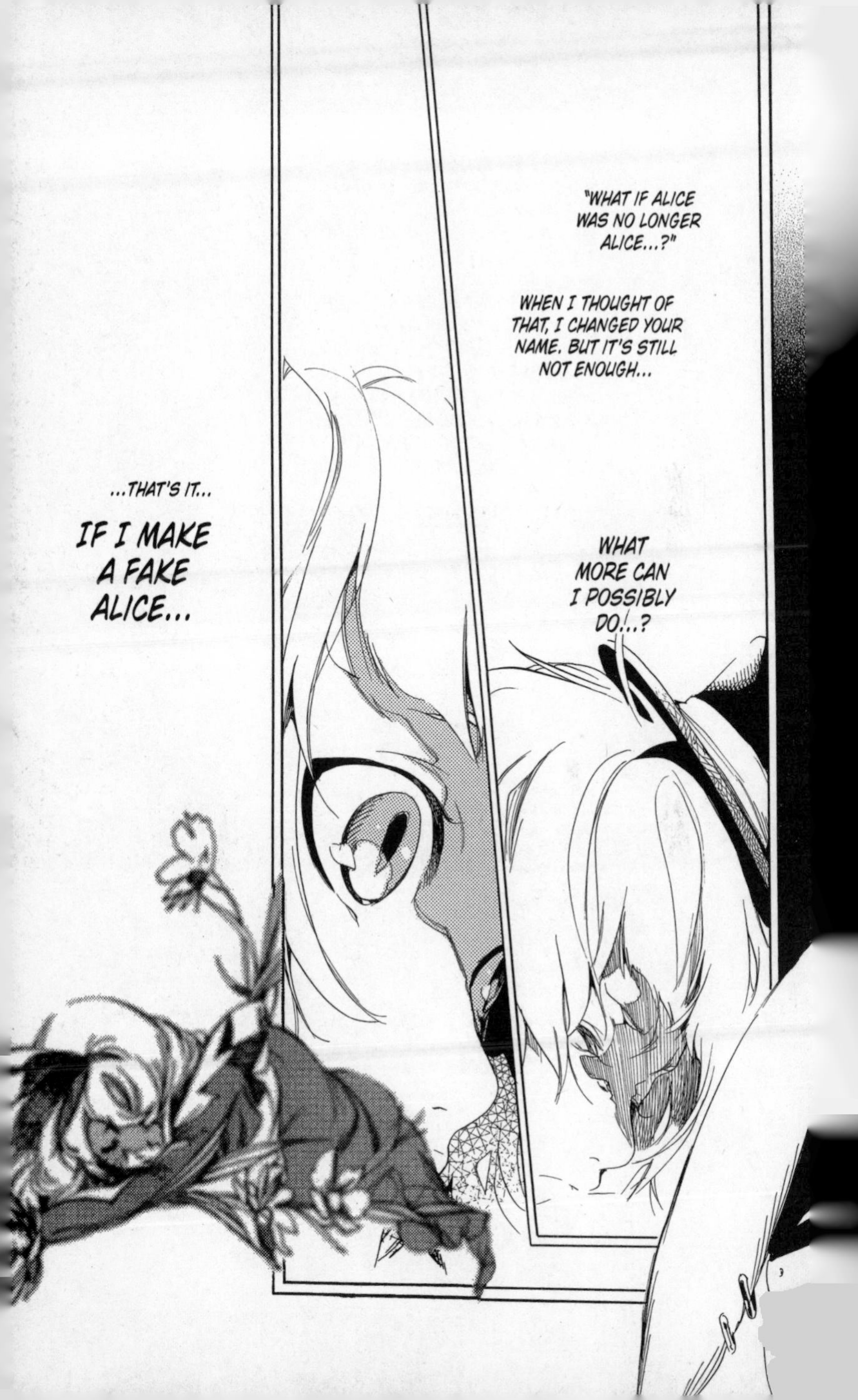
"WHAT IF ALICE WAS NO LONGER ALICE...?"
WHEN I THOUGHT OF THAT, I CHANGED YOUR NAME. BUT IT'S STILL NOT ENOUGH...
WHAT MORE CAN I POSSIBLY DO!...?
...THAT'S IT...
IF I MAKE A FAKE ALICE...

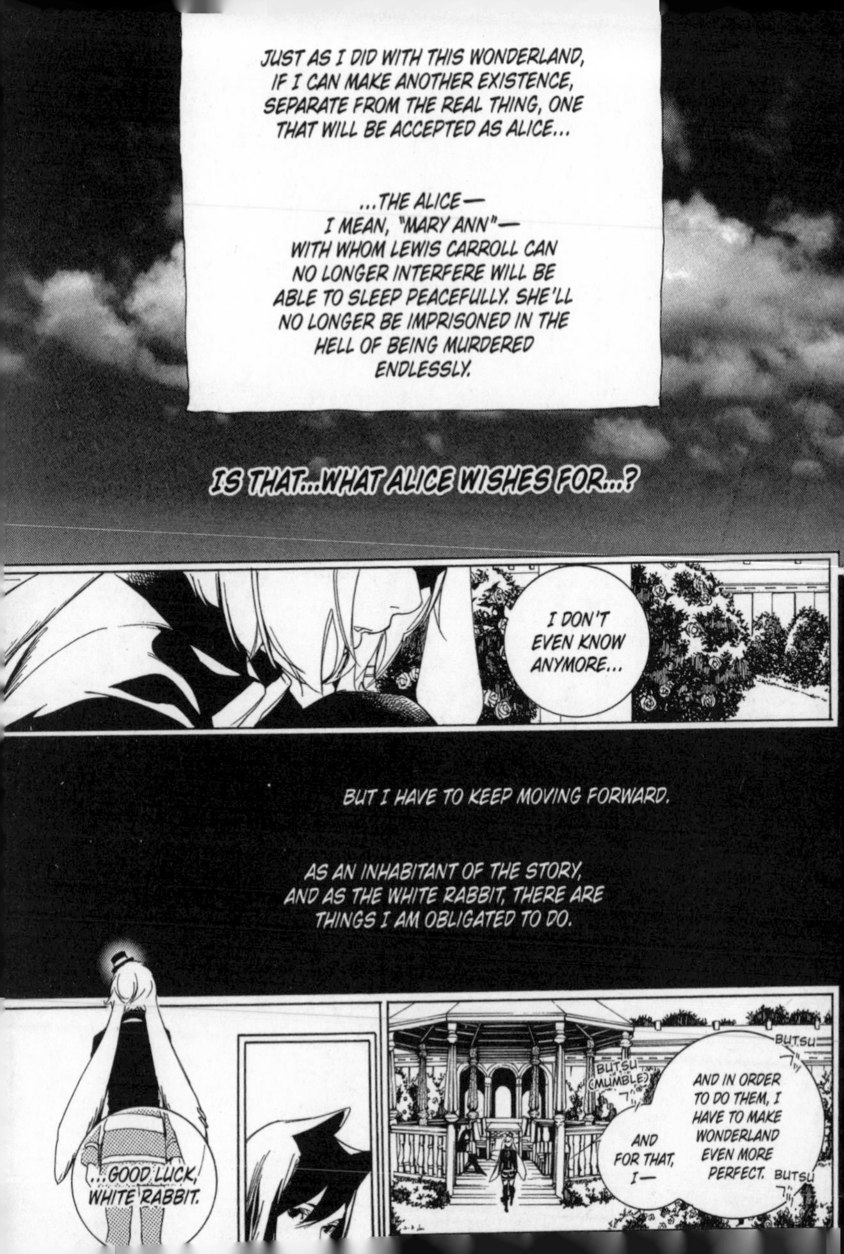
JUST AS I DID WITH THIS WONDERLAND, IF I CAN MAKE ANOTHER EXISTENCE, SEPARATE FROM THE REAL THING, ONE THAT WILL BE ACCEPTED AS ALICE...
...THE ALICE— I MEAN, "MARY ANN"— WITH WHOM LEWIS CARROLL CAN NO LONGER INTERFERE WILL BE ABLE TO SLEEP PEACEFULLY. SHE'LL NO LONGER BE IMPRISONED IN THE HELL OF BEING MURDERED ENDLESSLY.
IS THAT...WHAT ALICE WISHES FOR...?
I DON'T EVEN KNOW ANYMORE...
BUT I HAVE TO KEEP MOVING FORWARD.
AS AN INHABITANT OF THE STORY, AND AS THE WHITE RABBIT, THERE ARE THINGS I AM OBLIGATED TO DO.
BUTSU
AND IN ORDER TO DO THEM, I HAVE TO MAKE WONDERLAND EVEN MORE PERFECT.
BUTSU (MUMBLE)
AND FOR THAT, I—
BUTSU
...GOOD LUCK, WHITE RABBIT.

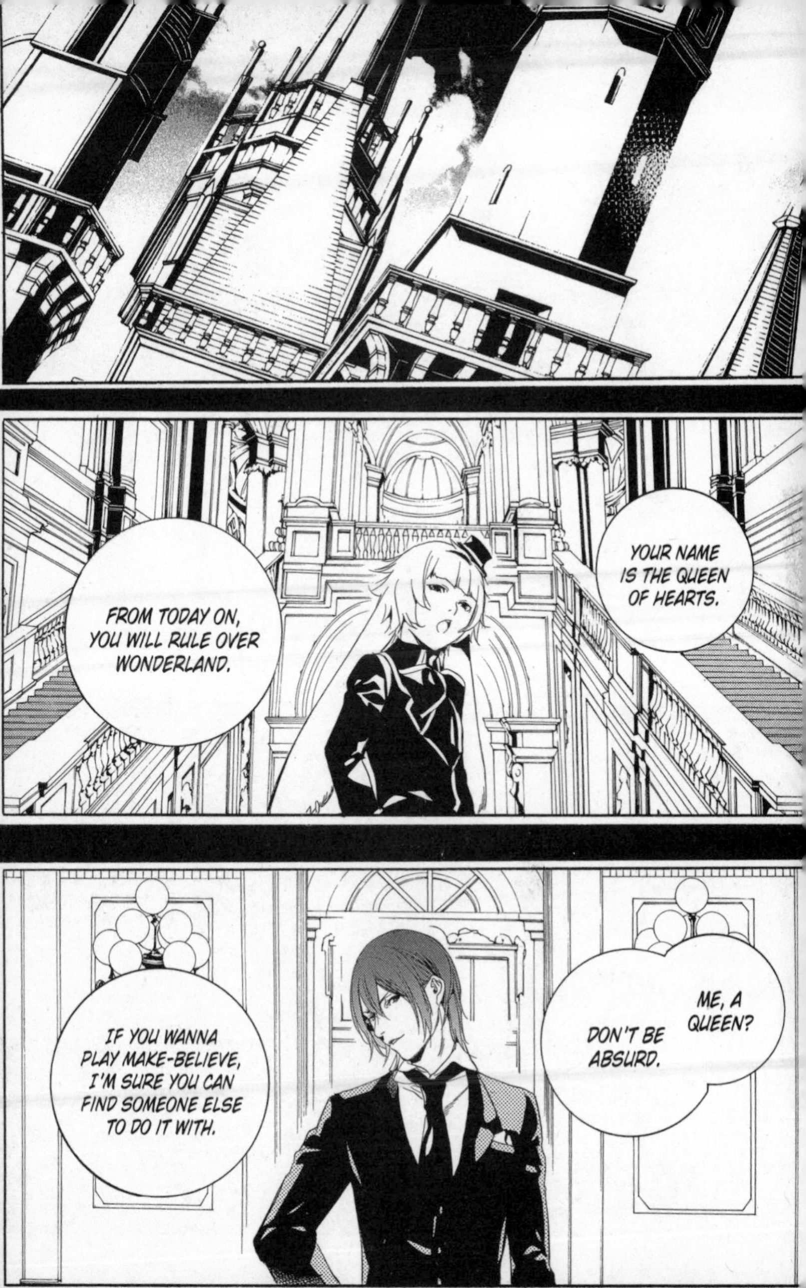
YOUR NAME IS THE QUEEN OF HEARTS.
FROM TODAY ON, YOU WILL RULE OVER WONDERLAND.
ME, A QUEEN?
DON'T BE ABSURD.
IF YOU WANNA PLAY MAKE-BELIEVE, I'M SURE YOU CAN FIND SOMEONE ELSE TO DO IT WITH.

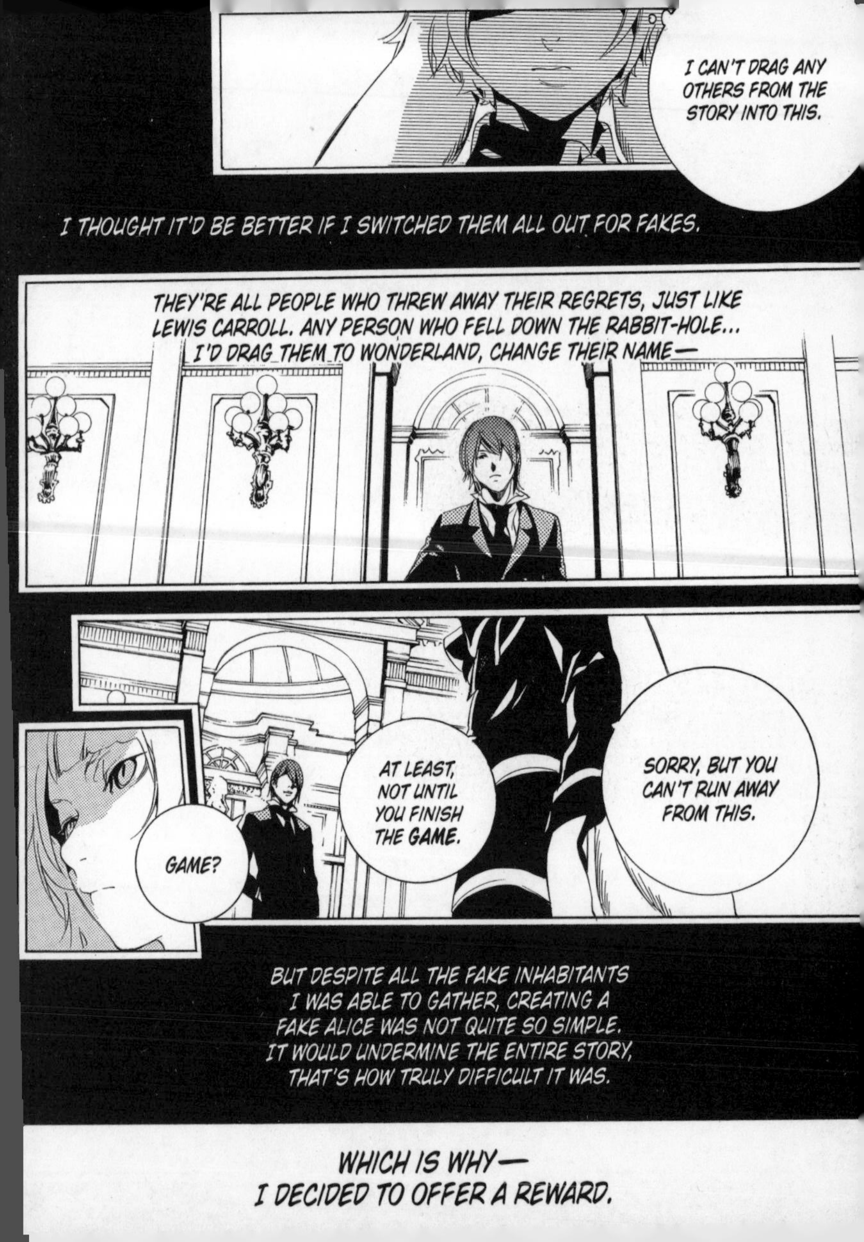
I CAN'T DRAG ANY OTHERS FROM THE STORY INTO THIS.
I THOUGHT IT'D BE BETTER IF I SWITCHED THEM ALL OUT FOR FAKES.
THEY'RE ALL PEOPLE WHO THREW AWAY THEIR REGRETS, JUST LIKE LEWIS CARROLL. ANY PERSON WHO FELL DOWN THE RABBIT-HOLE... I'D DRAG THEM TO WONDERLAND, CHANGE THEIR NAME—
SORRY, BUT YOU CAN'T RUN AWAY FROM THIS.
AT LEAST, NOT UNTIL YOU FINISH THE GAME.
GAME?
BUT DESPITE ALL THE FAKE INHABITANTS I WAS ABLE TO GATHER, CREATING A FAKE ALICE WAS NOT QUITE SO SIMPLE. IT WOULD UNDERMINE THE ENTIRE STORY, THAT'S HOW TRULY DIFFICULT IT WAS.
WHICH IS WHY—
I DECIDED TO OFFER A REWARD.

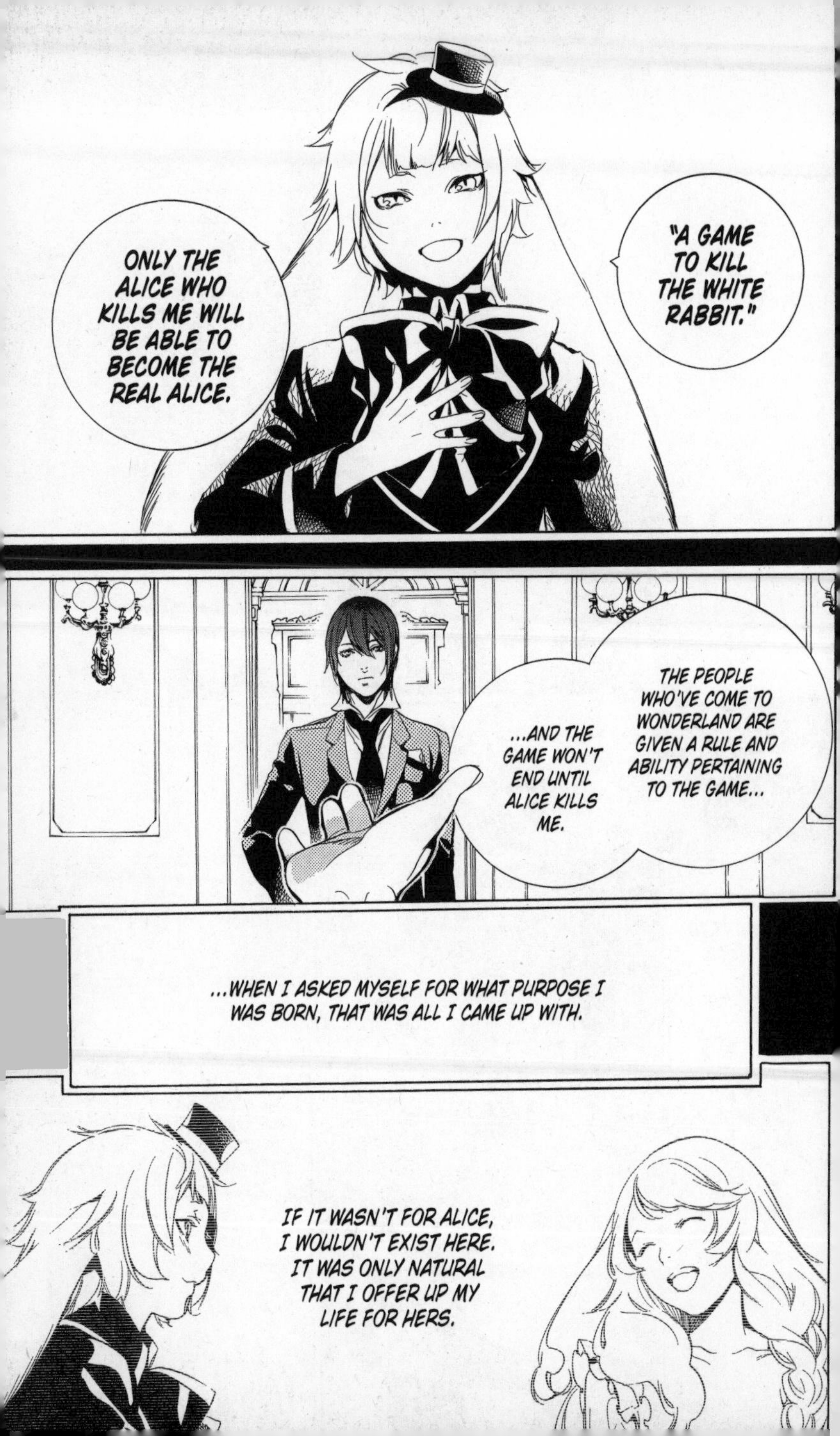
"A GAME TO KILL THE WHITE RABBIT."
ONLY THE ALICE WHO KILLS ME WILL BE ABLE TO BECOME THE REAL ALICE.
THE PEOPLE WHO'VE COME TO WONDERLAND ARE GIVEN A RULE AND ABILITY PERTAINING TO THE GAME...
...AND THE GAME WON'T END UNTIL ALICE KILLS ME.
...WHEN I ASKED MYSELF FOR WHAT PURPOSE I WAS BORN, THAT WAS ALL I CAME UP WITH.
IF IT WASN'T FOR ALICE, I WOULDN'T EXIST HERE. IT WAS ONLY NATURAL THAT I OFFER UP MY LIFE FOR HERS.

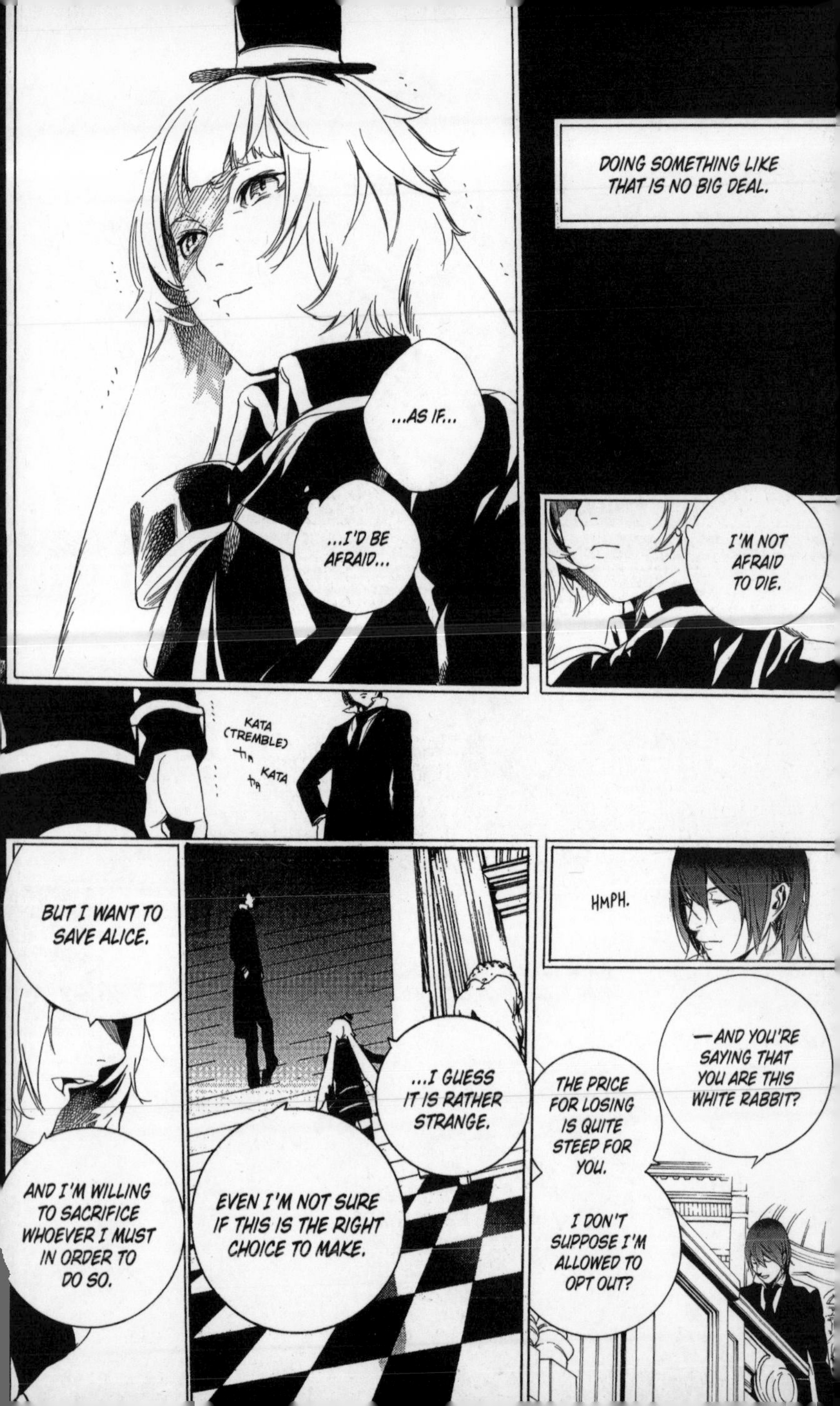
DOING SOMETHING LIKE THAT IS NO BIG DEAL.
I'M NOT AFRAID TO DIE.
...AS IF...
...I'D BE AFRAID...
KATA (TREMBLE) KATA
HMPH.
—AND YOU'RE SAYING THAT YOU ARE THIS WHITE RABBIT?
THE PRICE FOR LOSING IS QUITE STEEP FOR YOU.
I DON'T SUPPOSE I'M ALLOWED TO OPT OUT?
...I GUESS IT IS RATHER STRANGE.
EVEN I'M NOT SURE IF THIS IS THE RIGHT CHOICE TO MAKE.
BUT I WANT TO SAVE ALICE.
AND I'M WILLING TO SACRIFICE WHOEVER I MUST IN ORDER TO DO SO.

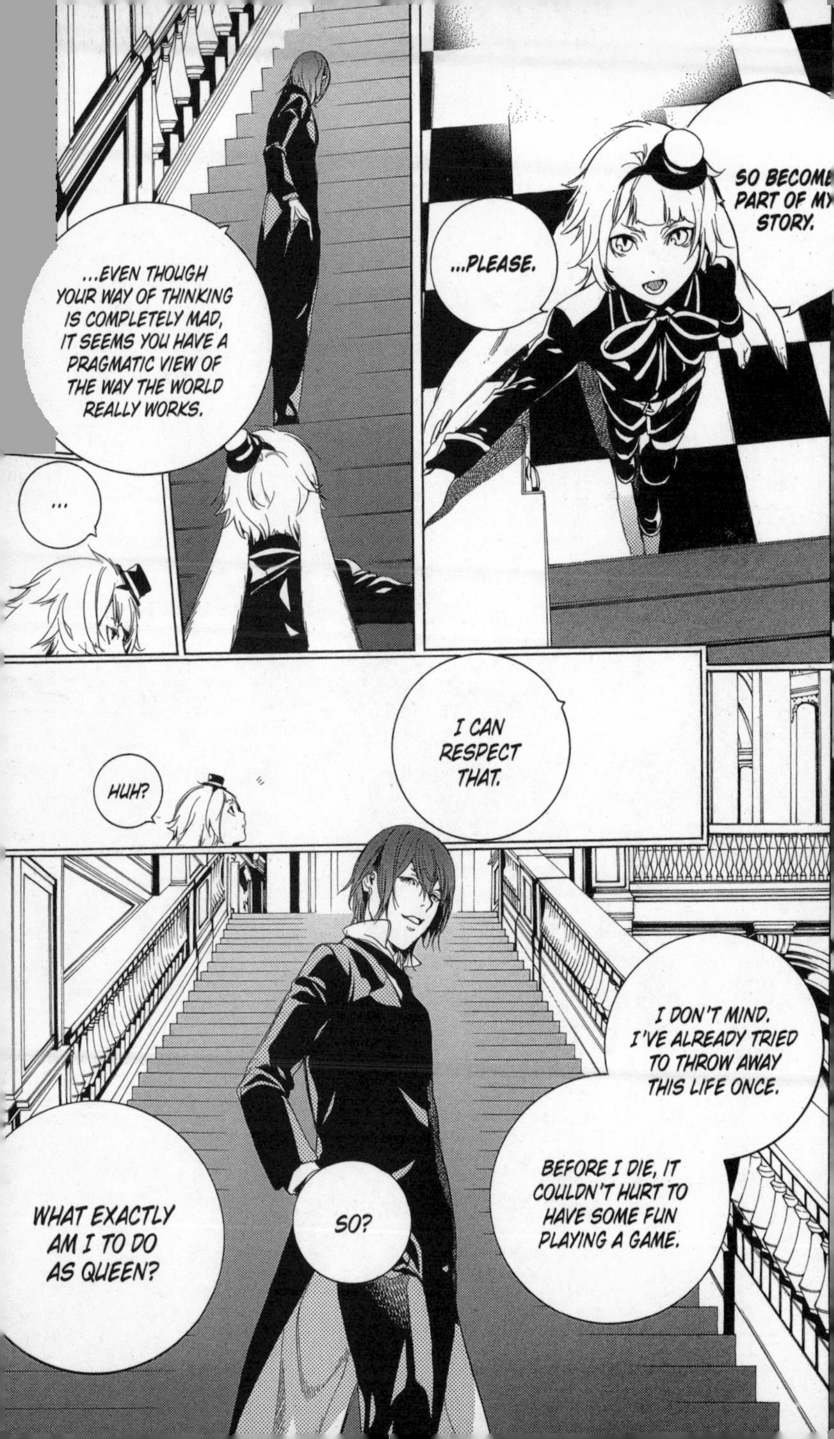
SO BECOME PART OF MY STORY.
...PLEASE.
...EVEN THOUGH YOUR WAY OF THINKING IS COMPLETELY MAD, IT SEEMS YOU HAVE A PRAGMATIC VIEW OF THE WAY THE WORLD REALLY WORKS.
...
I CAN RESPECT THAT.
HUH?
I DON'T MIND. I'VE ALREADY TRIED TO THROW AWAY THIS LIFE ONCE.
BEFORE I DIE, IT COULDN'T HURT TO HAVE SOME FUN PLAYING A GAME.
SO?
WHAT EXACTLY AM I TO DO AS QUEEN?

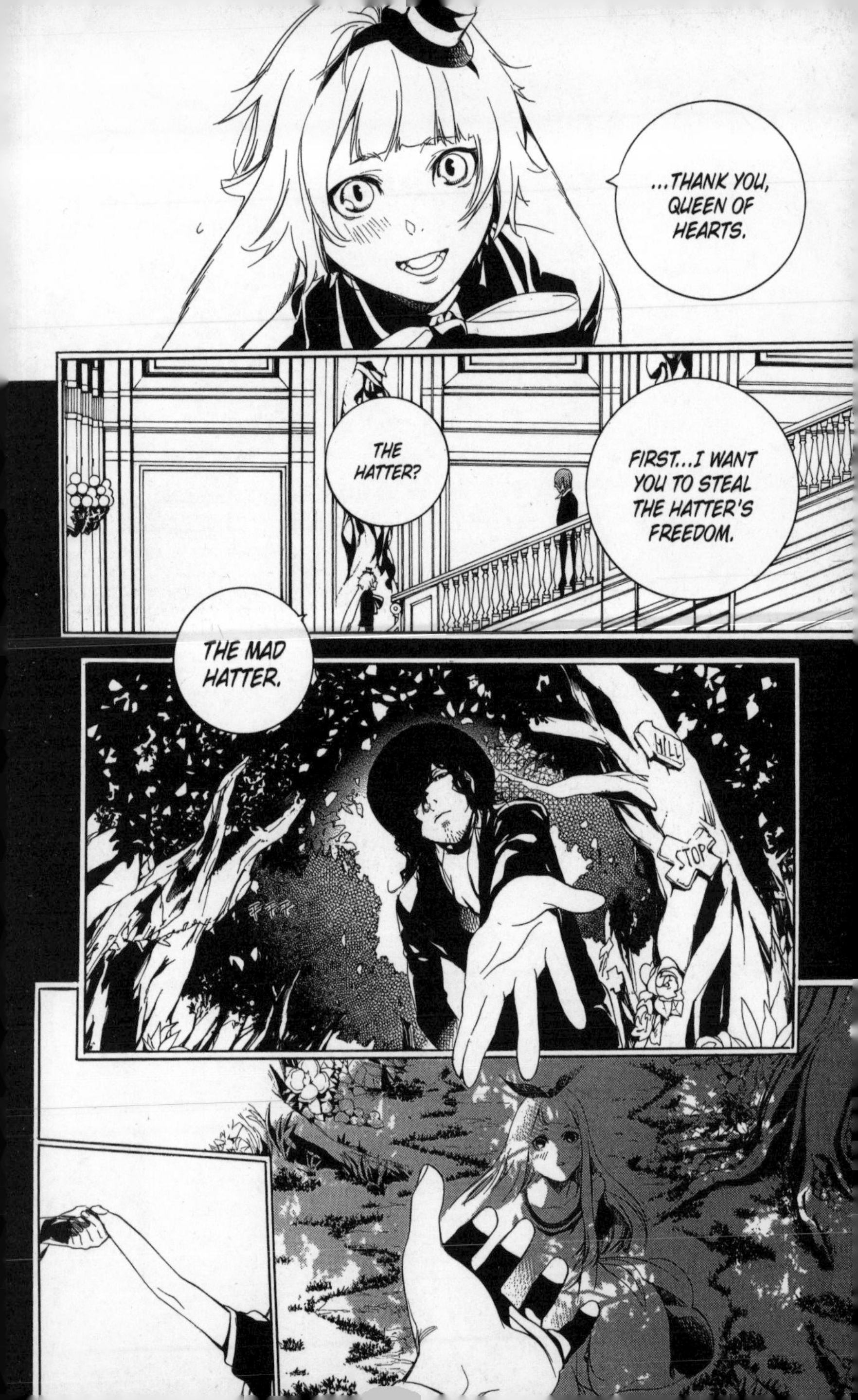
...THANK YOU, QUEEN OF HEARTS.
FIRST...I WANT YOU TO STEAL THE HATTER'S FREEDOM.
THE HATTER?
THE MAD HATTER.
STOP

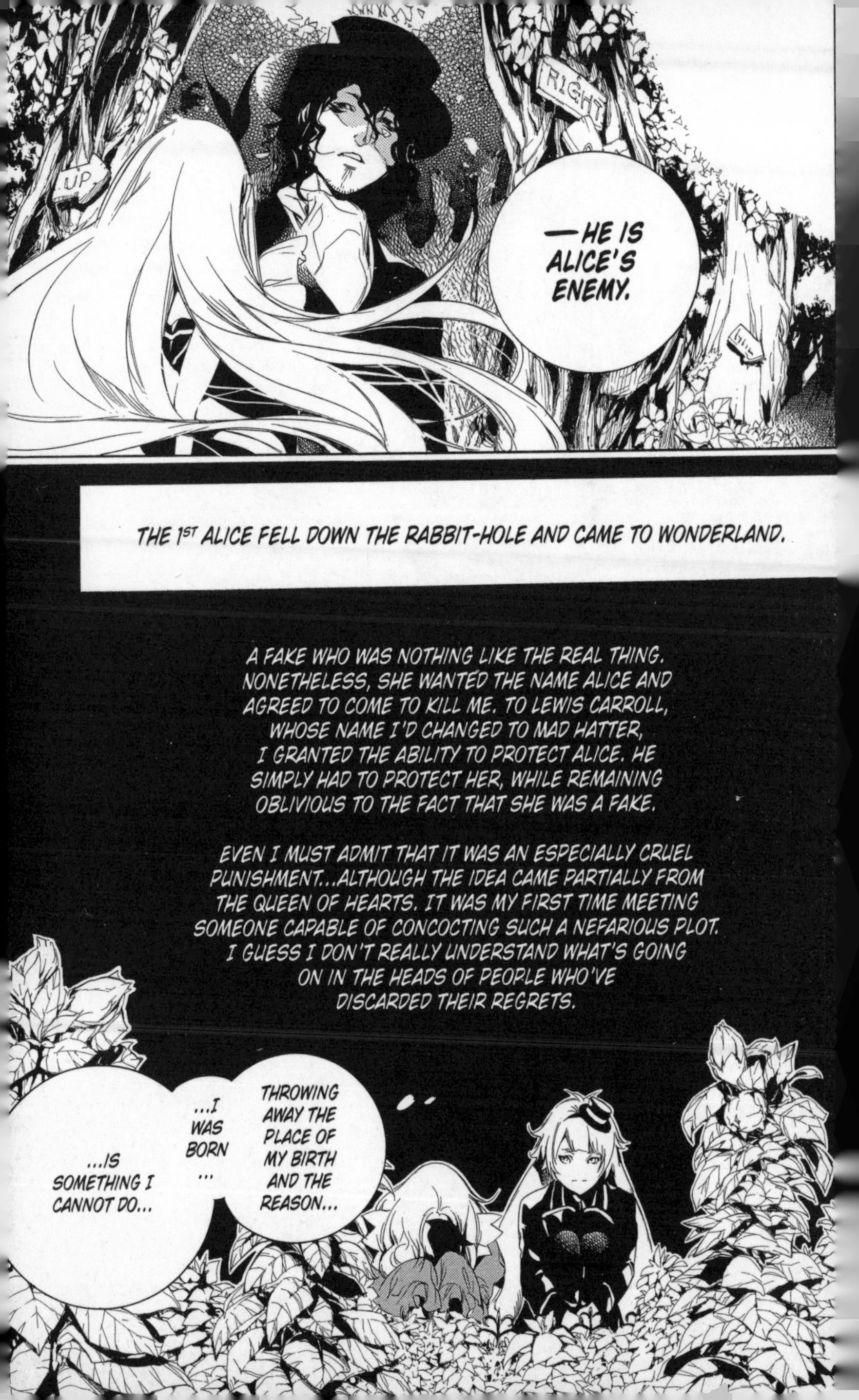
RIGHT
UP
—HE IS ALICE'S ENEMY.
THE 1ST ALICE FELL DOWN THE RABBIT-HOLE AND CAME TO WONDERLAND.
A FAKE WHO WAS NOTHING LIKE THE REAL THING. NONETHELESS, SHE WANTED THE NAME ALICE AND AGREED TO COME TO KILL ME. TO LEWIS CARROLL, WHOSE NAME I'D CHANGED TO MAD HATTER, I GRANTED THE ABILITY TO PROTECT ALICE. HE SIMPLY HAD TO PROTECT HER, WHILE REMAINING OBLIVIOUS TO THE FACT THAT SHE WAS A FAKE.
EVEN I MUST ADMIT THAT IT WAS AN ESPECIALLY CRUEL PUNISHMENT...ALTHOUGH THE IDEA CAME PARTIALLY FROM THE QUEEN OF HEARTS. IT WAS MY FIRST TIME MEETING SOMEONE CAPABLE OF CONCOCTING SUCH A NEFARIOUS PLOT. I GUESS I DON'T REALLY UNDERSTAND WHAT'S GOING ON IN THE HEADS OF PEOPLE WHO'VE DISCARDED THEIR REGRETS.
THROWING AWAY THE PLACE OF MY BIRTH AND THE REASON...
...I WAS BORN ...
...IS SOMETHING I CANNOT DO...

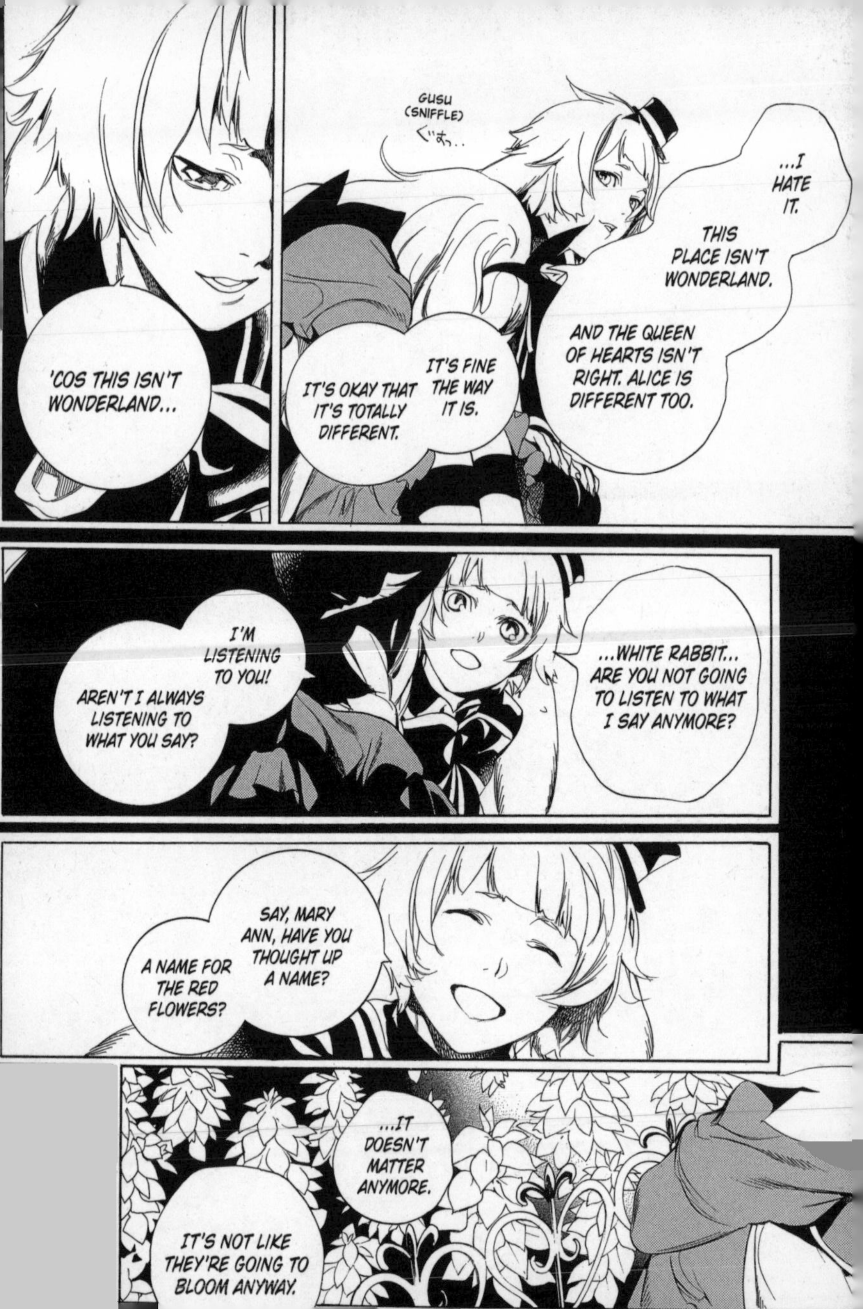
...I HATE IT.
THIS PLACE ISN'T WONDERLAND.
AND THE QUEEN OF HEARTS ISN'T RIGHT. ALICE IS DIFFERENT TOO.
GUSU (SNIFFLE) ぐすっ...
IT'S FINE THE WAY IT IS.
IT'S OKAY THAT IT'S TOTALLY DIFFERENT.
'COS THIS ISN'T WONDERLAND...
...WHITE RABBIT... ARE YOU NOT GOING TO LISTEN TO WHAT I SAY ANYMORE?
I'M LISTENING TO YOU!
AREN'T I ALWAYS LISTENING TO WHAT YOU SAY?
SAY, MARY ANN, HAVE YOU THOUGHT UP A NAME?
A NAME FOR THE RED FLOWERS?
...IT DOESN'T MATTER ANYMORE.
IT'S NOT LIKE THEY'RE GOING TO BLOOM ANYWAY.

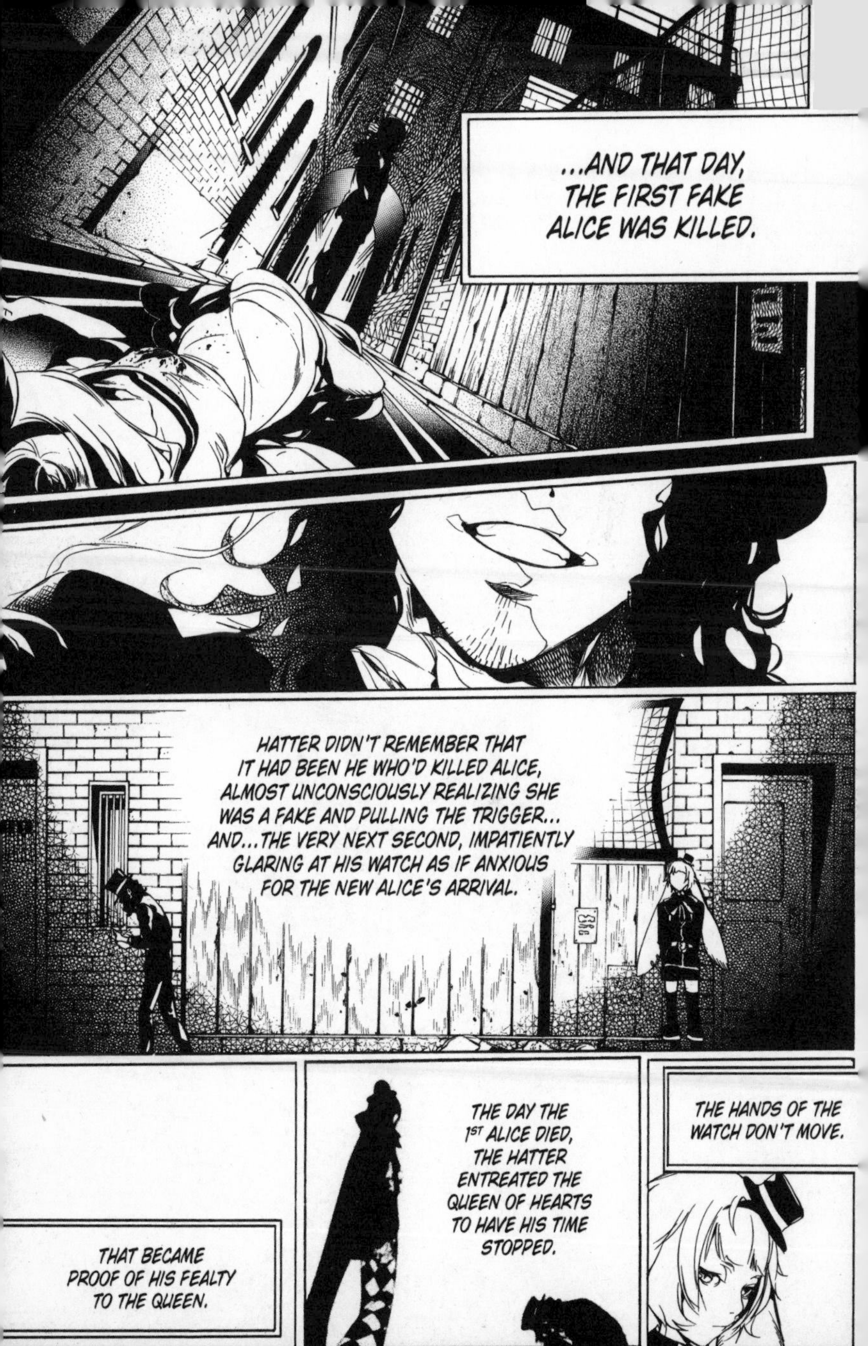
...AND THAT DAY, THE FIRST FAKE ALICE WAS KILLED.
HATTER DIDN'T REMEMBER THAT IT HAD BEEN HE WHO'D KILLED ALICE, ALMOST UNCONSCIOUSLY REALIZING SHE WAS A FAKE AND PULLING THE TRIGGER... AND...THE VERY NEXT SECOND, IMPATIENTLY GLARING AT HIS WATCH AS IF ANXIOUS FOR THE NEW ALICE'S ARRIVAL.
THE HANDS OF THE WATCH DON'T MOVE.
THE DAY THE 1ST ALICE DIED, THE HATTER ENTREATED THE QUEEN OF HEARTS TO HAVE HIS TIME STOPPED.
THAT BECAME PROOF OF HIS FEALTY TO THE QUEEN.

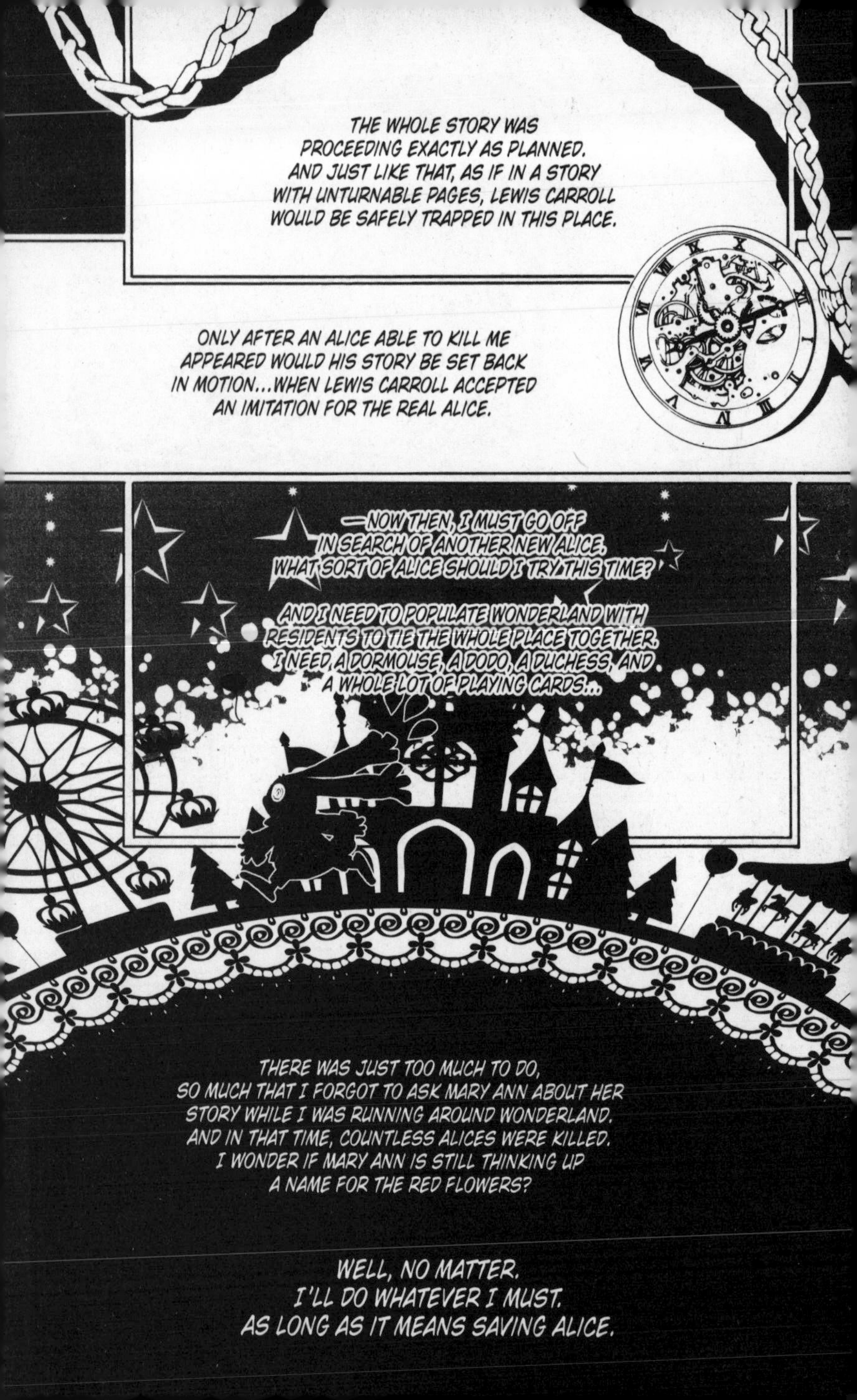
THE WHOLE STORY WAS PROCEEDING EXACTLY AS PLANNED. AND JUST LIKE THAT, AS IF IN A STORY WITH UNTURNABLE PAGES, LEWIS CARROLL WOULD BE SAFELY TRAPPED IN THIS PLACE.
ONLY AFTER AN ALICE ABLE TO KILL ME APPEARED WOULD HIS STORY BE SET BACK IN MOTION...WHEN LEWIS CARROLL ACCEPTED AN IMITATION FOR THE REAL ALICE.
—NOW THEN, I MUST GO OFF IN SEARCH OF ANOTHER NEW ALICE. WHAT SORT OF ALICE SHOULD I TRY THIS TIME?
AND I NEED TO POPULATE WONDERLAND WITH RESIDENTS TO TIE THE WHOLE PLACE TOGETHER. I NEED A DORMOUSE, A DODO, A DUCHESS, AND A WHOLE LOT OF PLAYING CARDS...
THERE WAS JUST TOO MUCH TO DO, SO MUCH THAT I FORGOT TO ASK MARY ANN ABOUT HER STORY WHILE I WAS RUNNING AROUND WONDERLAND. AND IN THAT TIME, COUNTLESS ALICES WERE KILLED. I WONDER IF MARY ANN IS STILL THINKING UP A NAME FOR THE RED FLOWERS?
WELL, NO MATTER. I'LL DO WHATEVER I MUST. AS LONG AS IT MEANS SAVING ALICE.

I WILL

SAVE

ALICE.

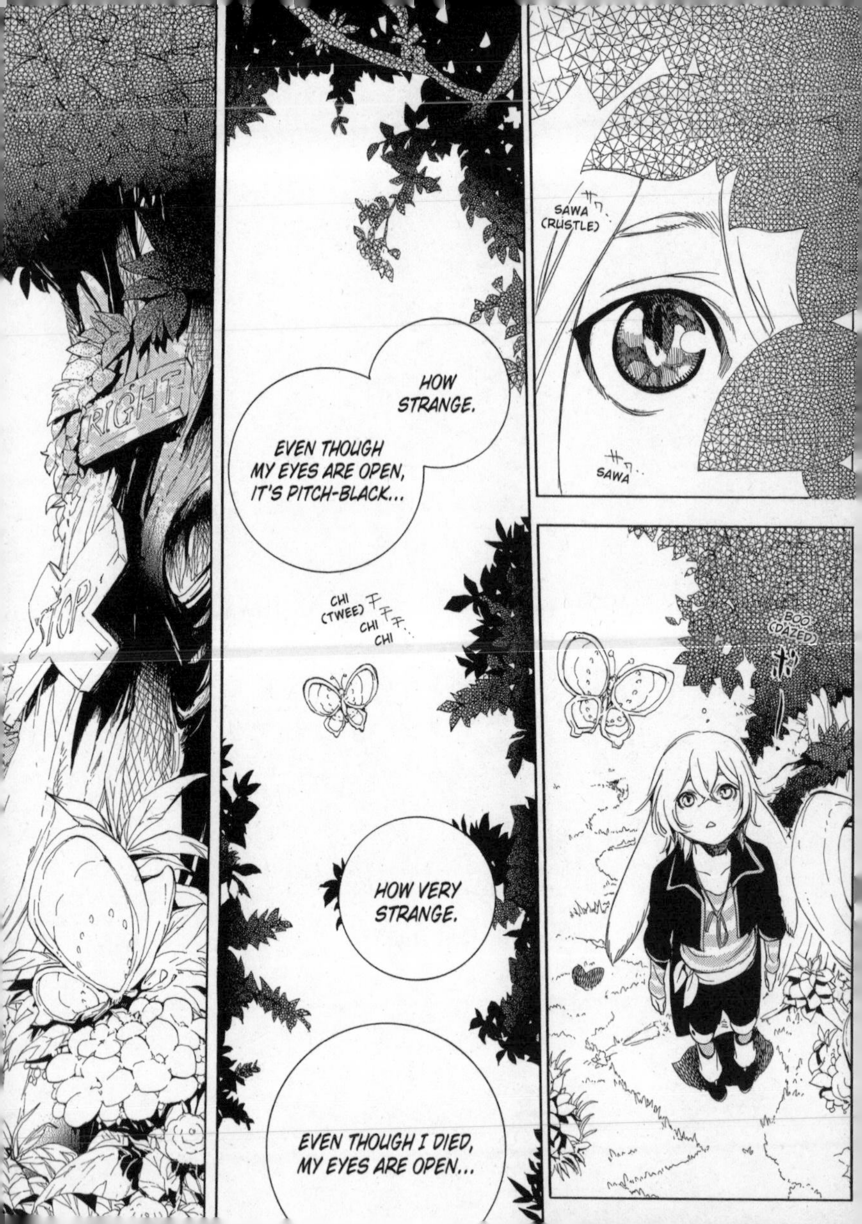
SAWA (RUSTLE)
SAWA
BOO (DAZED)
HOW STRANGE.
EVEN THOUGH MY EYES ARE OPEN, IT'S PITCH-BLACK...
CHI (TWEE) CHI CHI
HOW VERY STRANGE.
EVEN THOUGH I DIED, MY EYES ARE OPEN...
RIGHT
STOP

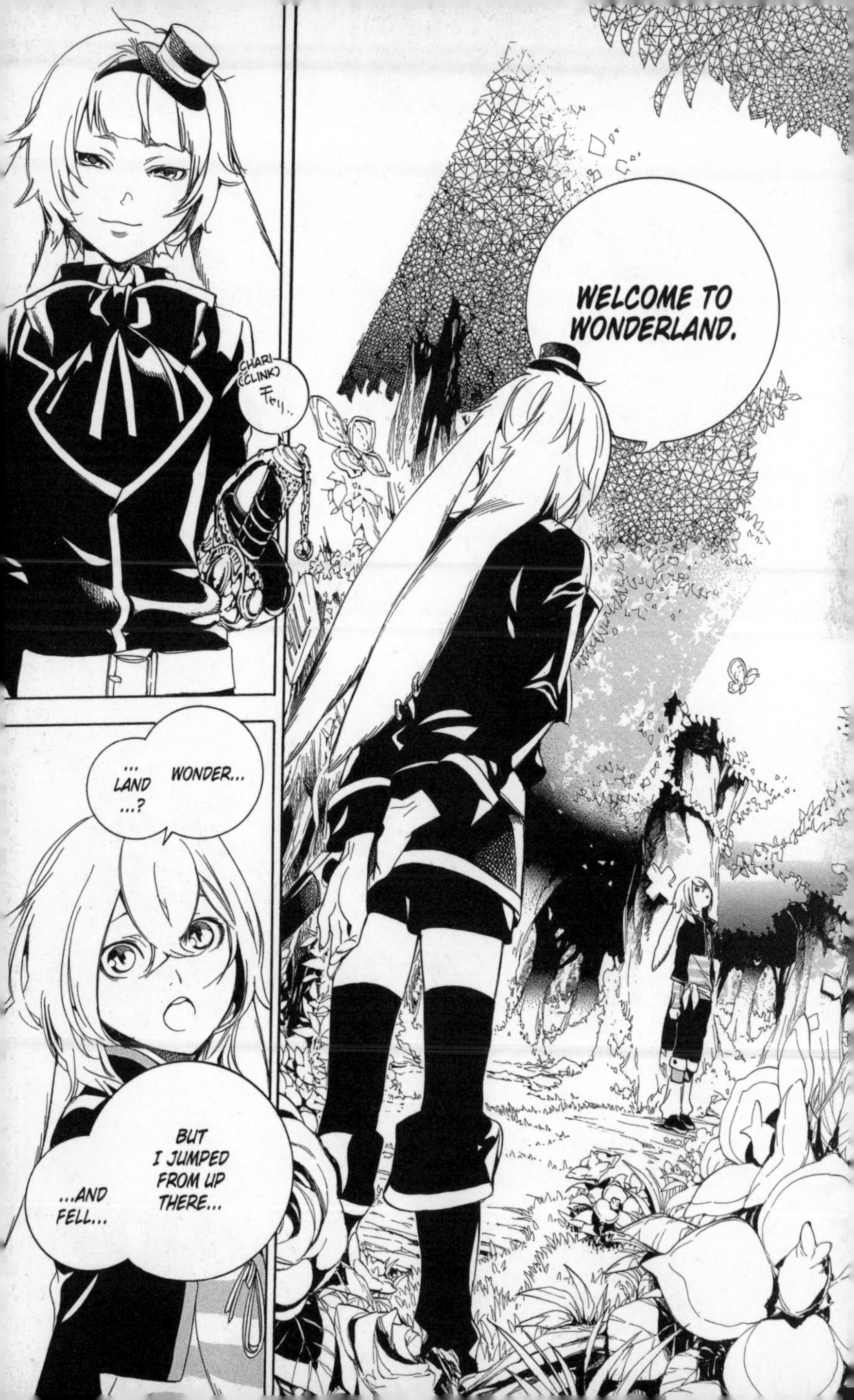
WELCOME TO WONDERLAND.
CHARI (CLINK)
チャリ..
WONDER...
... LAND ...?
BUT I JUMPED FROM UP THERE...
...AND FELL...

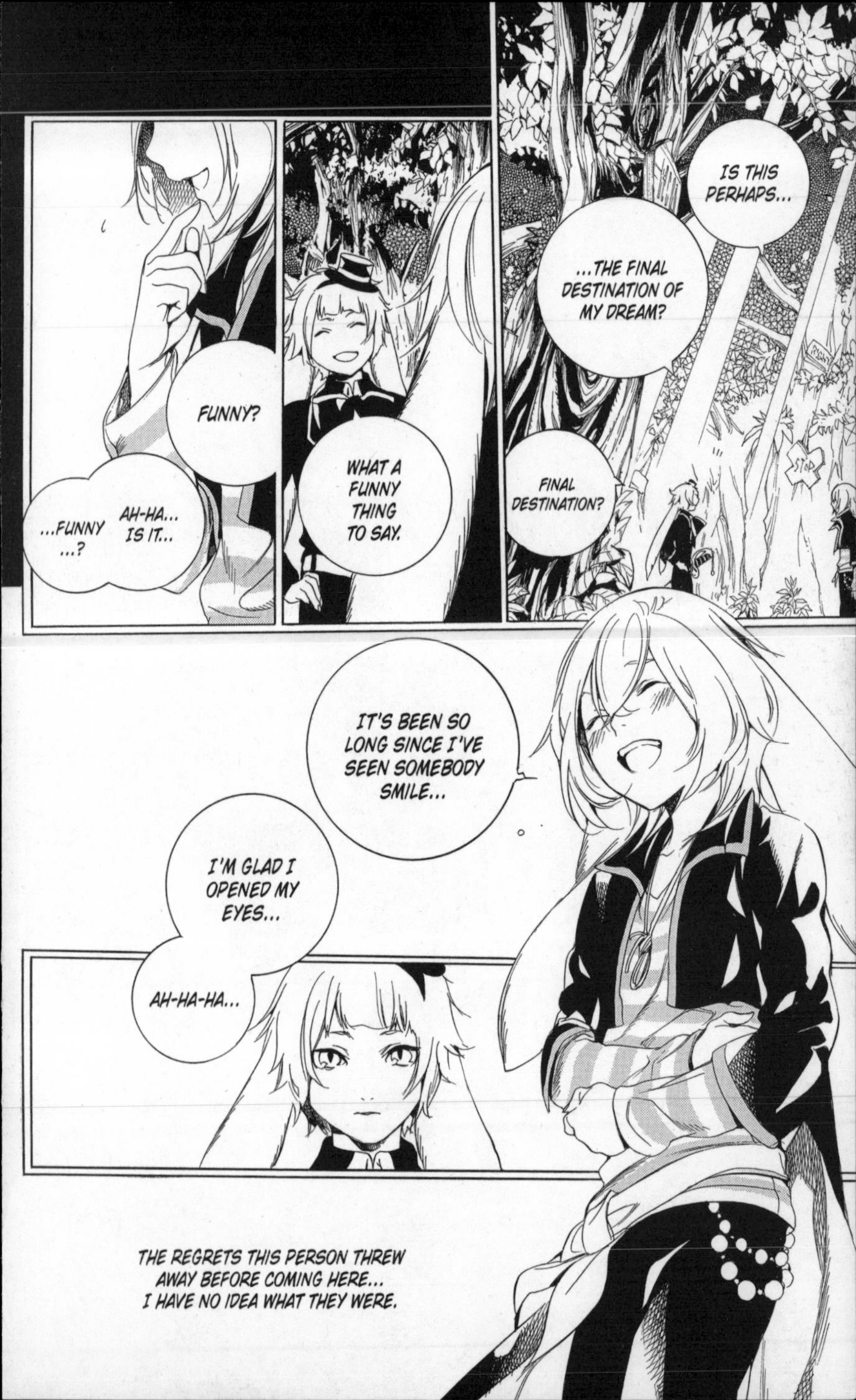
IS THIS PERHAPS...
...THE FINAL DESTINATION OF MY DREAM?
FINAL DESTINATION?
STOP
WHAT A FUNNY THING TO SAY.
FUNNY?
AH-HA... IS IT...
...FUNNY ...?
IT'S BEEN SO LONG SINCE I'VE SEEN SOMEBODY SMILE...
I'M GLAD I OPENED MY EYES...
AH-HA-HA...
THE REGRETS THIS PERSON THREW AWAY BEFORE COMING HERE... I HAVE NO IDEA WHAT THEY WERE.

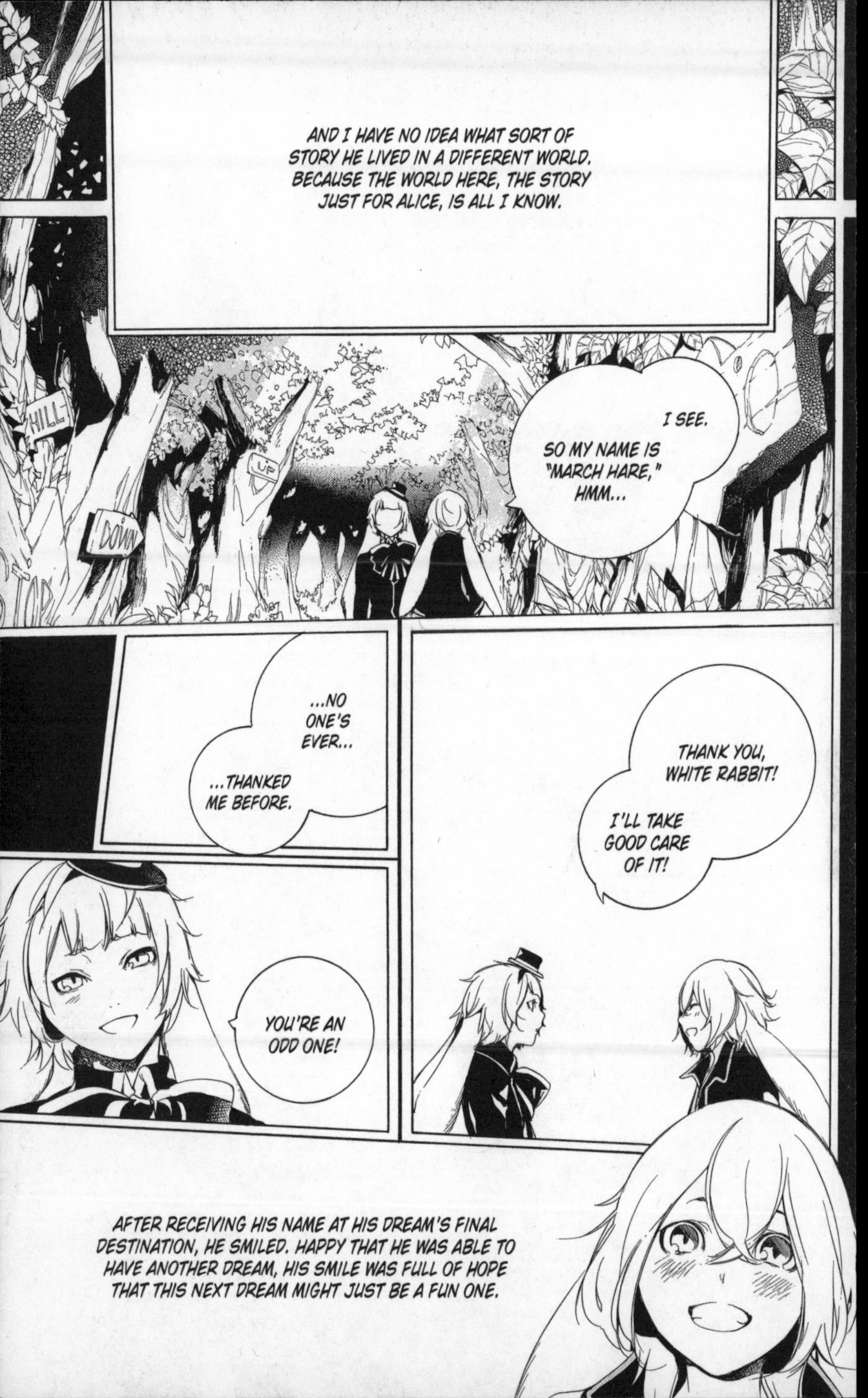
AND I HAVE NO IDEA WHAT SORT OF STORY HE LIVED IN A DIFFERENT WORLD. BECAUSE THE WORLD HERE, THE STORY JUST FOR ALICE, IS ALL I KNOW.
I SEE.
SO MY NAME IS "MARCH HARE," HMM...
HILL
UP
DOWN
THANK YOU, WHITE RABBIT!
I'LL TAKE GOOD CARE OF IT!
...NO ONE'S EVER...
...THANKED ME BEFORE.
YOU'RE AN ODD ONE!
AFTER RECEIVING HIS NAME AT HIS DREAM'S FINAL DESTINATION, HE SMILED. HAPPY THAT HE WAS ABLE TO HAVE ANOTHER DREAM, HIS SMILE WAS FULL OF HOPE THAT THIS NEXT DREAM MIGHT JUST BE A FUN ONE.

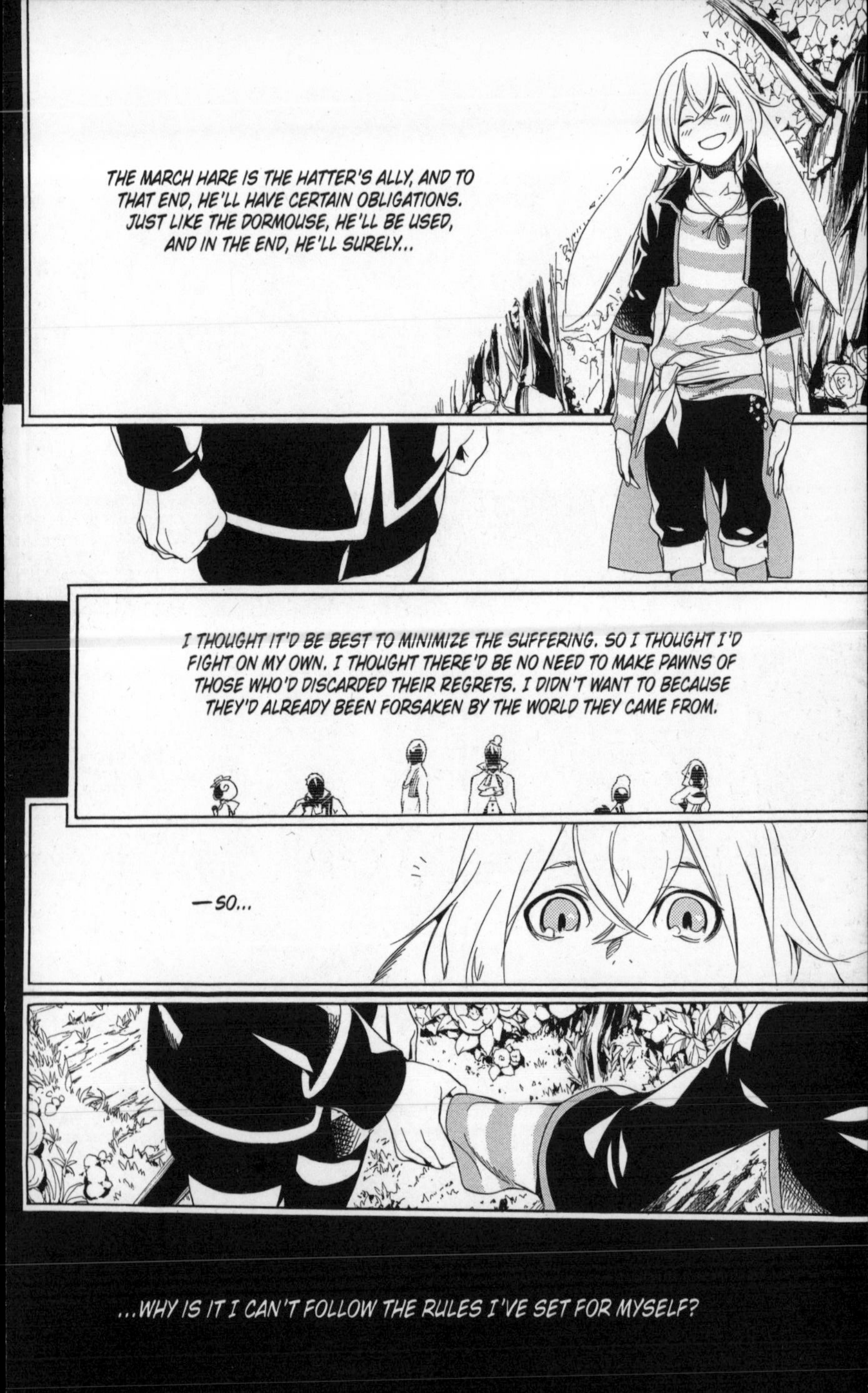
THE MARCH HARE IS THE HATTER'S ALLY, AND TO THAT END, HE'LL HAVE CERTAIN OBLIGATIONS. JUST LIKE THE DORMOUSE, HE'LL BE USED, AND IN THE END, HE'LL SURELY...
I THOUGHT IT'D BE BEST TO MINIMIZE THE SUFFERING. SO I THOUGHT I'D FIGHT ON MY OWN. I THOUGHT THERE'D BE NO NEED TO MAKE PAWNS OF THOSE WHO'D DISCARDED THEIR REGRETS. I DIDN'T WANT TO BECAUSE THEY'D ALREADY BEEN FORSAKEN BY THE WORLD THEY CAME FROM.
—SO...
...WHY IS IT I CAN'T FOLLOW THE RULES I'VE SET FOR MYSELF?

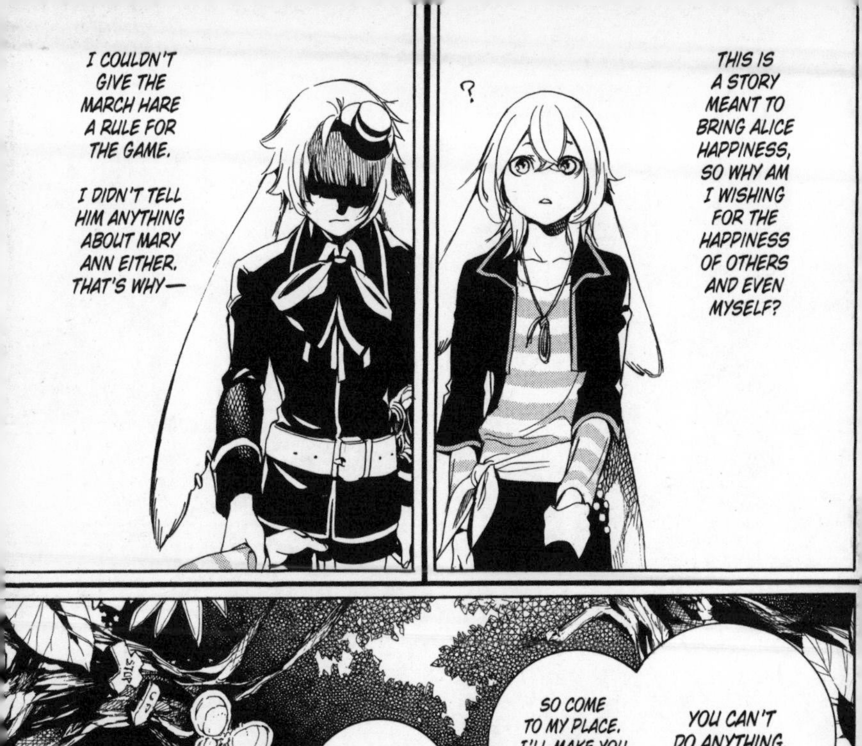
THIS IS A STORY MEANT TO BRING ALICE HAPPINESS, SO WHY AM I WISHING FOR THE HAPPINESS OF OTHERS AND EVEN MYSELF?
?
I COULDN'T GIVE THE MARCH HARE A RULE FOR THE GAME.
I DIDN'T TELL HIM ANYTHING ABOUT MARY ANN EITHER. THAT'S WHY—
YOU CAN'T DO ANYTHING, CAN YOU?
SO COME TO MY PLACE. I'LL MAKE YOU SOMETHING TO EAT.
IS THAT ANOTHER RULE?
...DUMMY.
DOESN'T THAT GO WITHOUT SAYING?

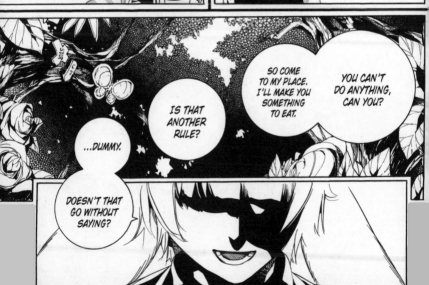

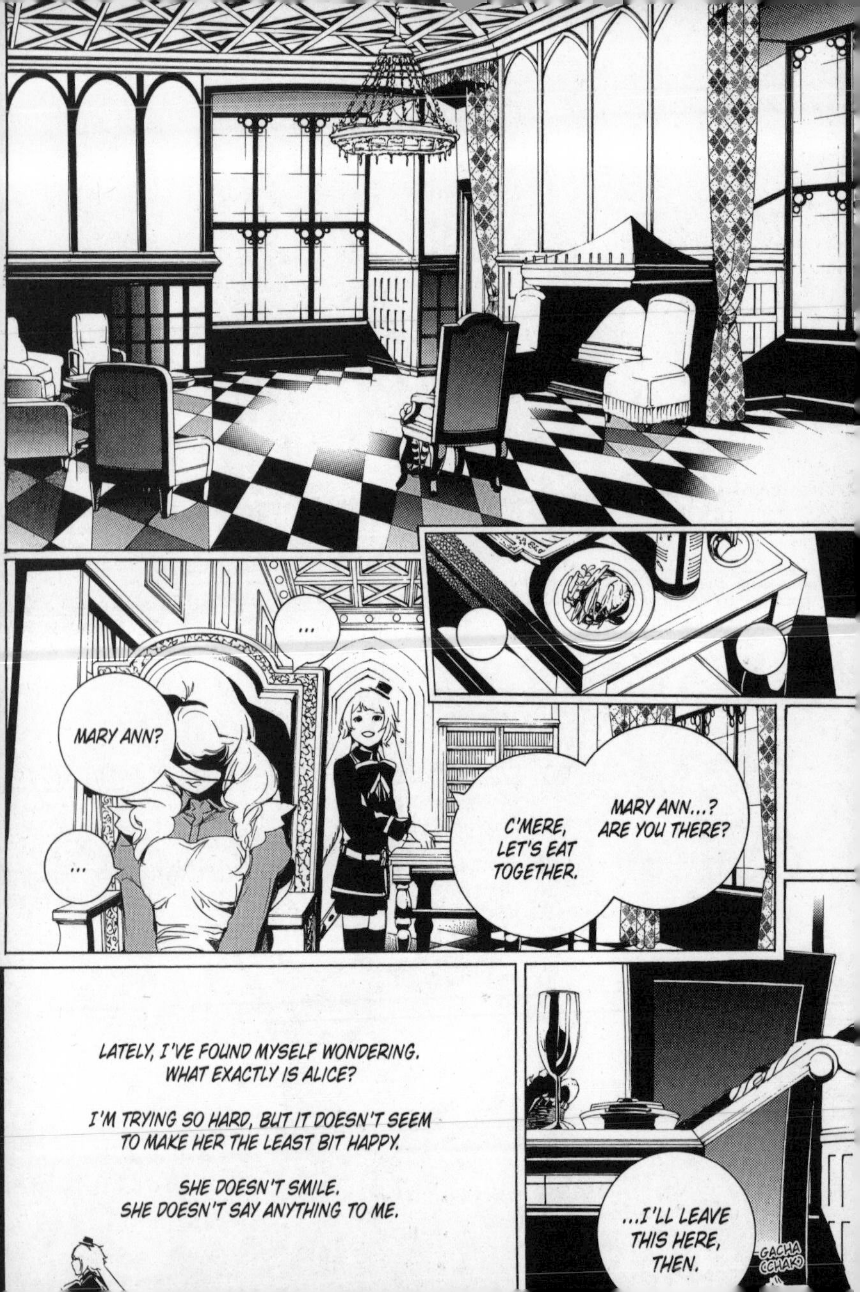
MARY ANN...? ARE YOU THERE?
C'MERE, LET'S EAT TOGETHER.
...
MARY ANN?
...
...I'LL LEAVE THIS HERE, THEN.
GACHA (CHAK)
LATELY, I'VE FOUND MYSELF WONDERING. WHAT EXACTLY IS ALICE?
I'M TRYING SO HARD, BUT IT DOESN'T SEEM TO MAKE HER THE LEAST BIT HAPPY.
SHE DOESN'T SMILE. SHE DOESN'T SAY ANYTHING TO ME.

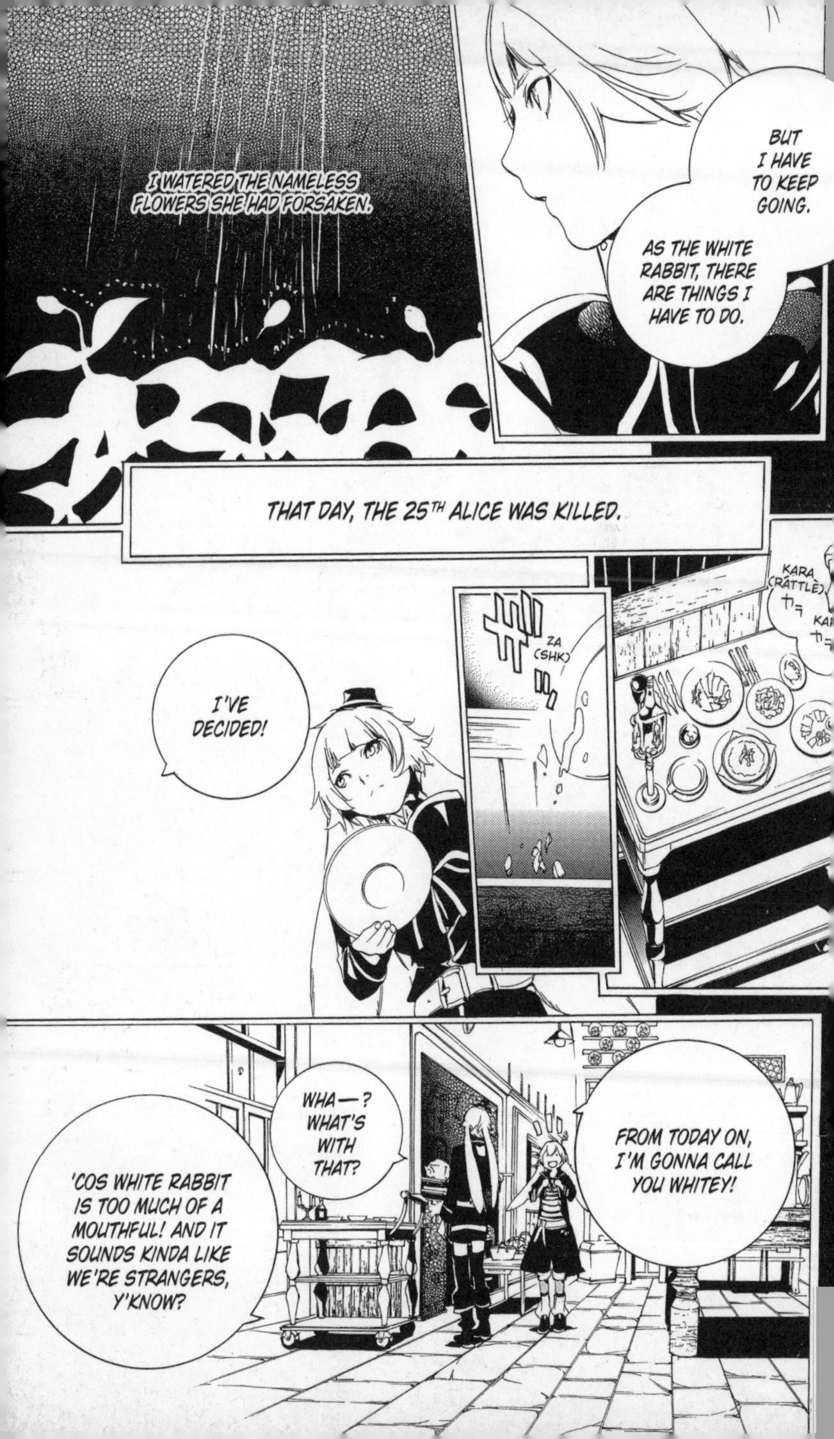
BUT I HAVE TO KEEP GOING.
AS THE WHITE RABBIT, THERE ARE THINGS I HAVE TO DO.
I WATERED THE NAMELESS FLOWERS SHE HAD FORSAKEN.
THAT DAY, THE 25TH ALICE WAS KILLED.
KARA (RATTLE)
ZA (SHK)
I'VE DECIDED!
FROM TODAY ON, I'M GONNA CALL YOU WHITEY!
WHA—? WHAT'S WITH THAT?
'COS WHITE RABBIT IS TOO MUCH OF A MOUTHFUL! AND IT SOUNDS KINDA LIKE WE'RE STRANGERS, Y'KNOW?

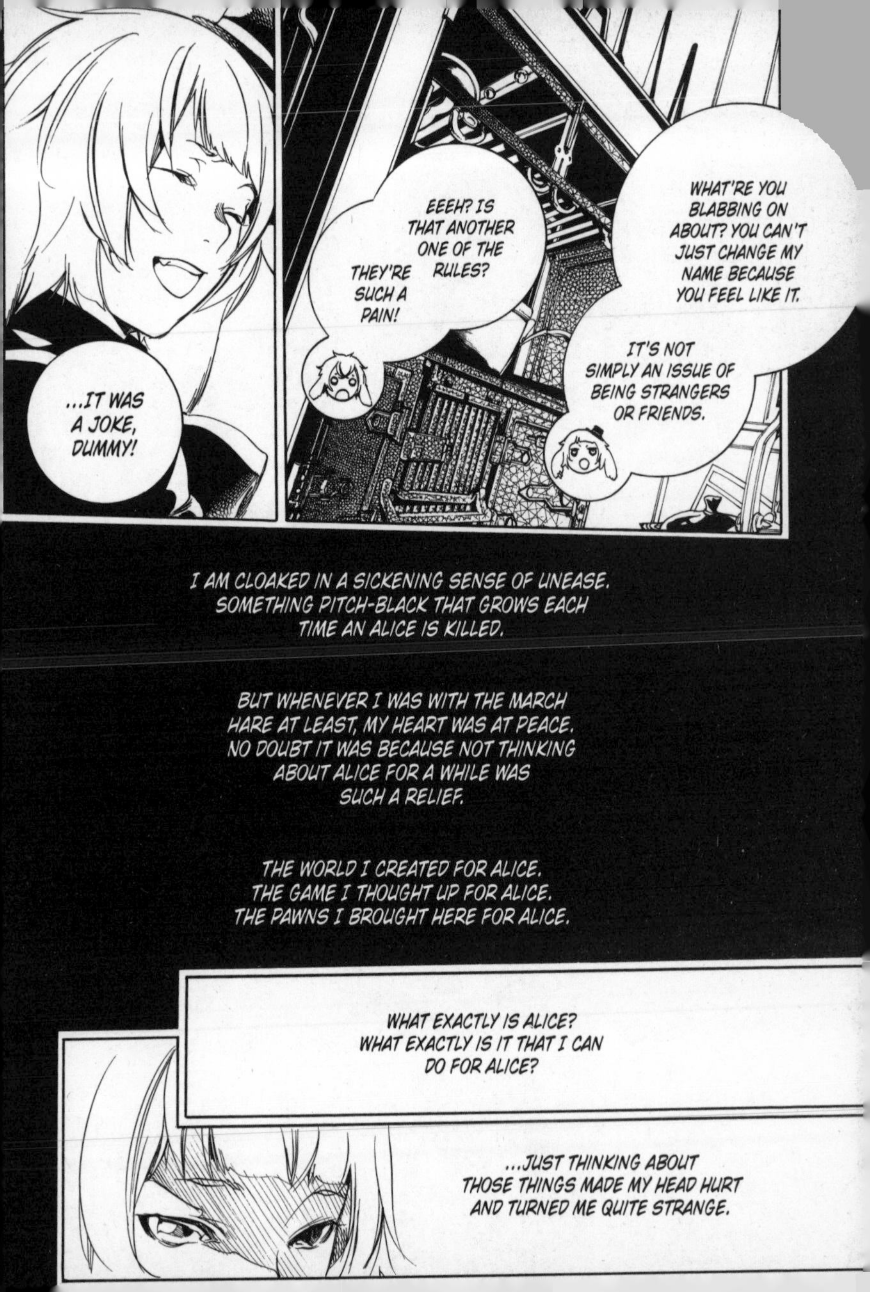
WHAT'RE YOU BLABBING ON ABOUT? YOU CAN'T JUST CHANGE MY NAME BECAUSE YOU FEEL LIKE IT.
EEEH? IS THAT ANOTHER ONE OF THE RULES?
THEY'RE SUCH A PAIN!
IT'S NOT SIMPLY AN ISSUE OF BEING STRANGERS OR FRIENDS.
...IT WAS A JOKE, DUMMY!
I AM CLOAKED IN A SICKENING SENSE OF UNEASE. SOMETHING PITCH-BLACK THAT GROWS EACH TIME AN ALICE IS KILLED.
BUT WHENEVER I WAS WITH THE MARCH HARE AT LEAST, MY HEART WAS AT PEACE. NO DOUBT IT WAS BECAUSE NOT THINKING ABOUT ALICE FOR A WHILE WAS SUCH A RELIEF.
THE WORLD I CREATED FOR ALICE. THE GAME I THOUGHT UP FOR ALICE. THE PAWNS I BROUGHT HERE FOR ALICE.
WHAT EXACTLY IS ALICE? WHAT EXACTLY IS IT THAT I CAN DO FOR ALICE?
...JUST THINKING ABOUT THOSE THINGS MADE MY HEAD HURT AND TURNED ME QUITE STRANGE.

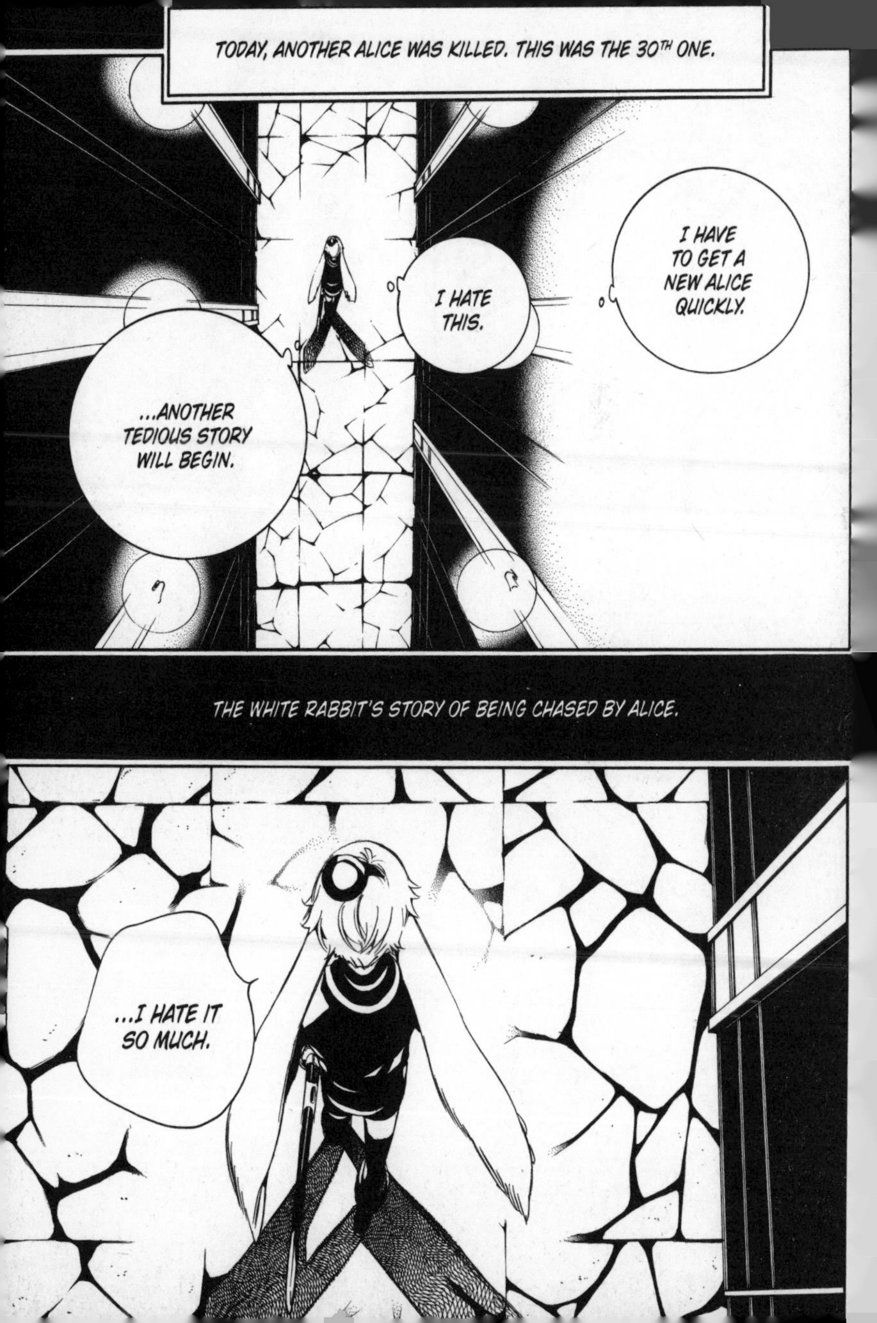
TODAY, ANOTHER ALICE WAS KILLED. THIS WAS THE 30TH ONE.
I HAVE TO GET A NEW ALICE QUICKLY.
I HATE THIS.
...ANOTHER TEDIOUS STORY WILL BEGIN.
THE WHITE RABBIT'S STORY OF BEING CHASED BY ALICE.
...I HATE IT SO MUCH.

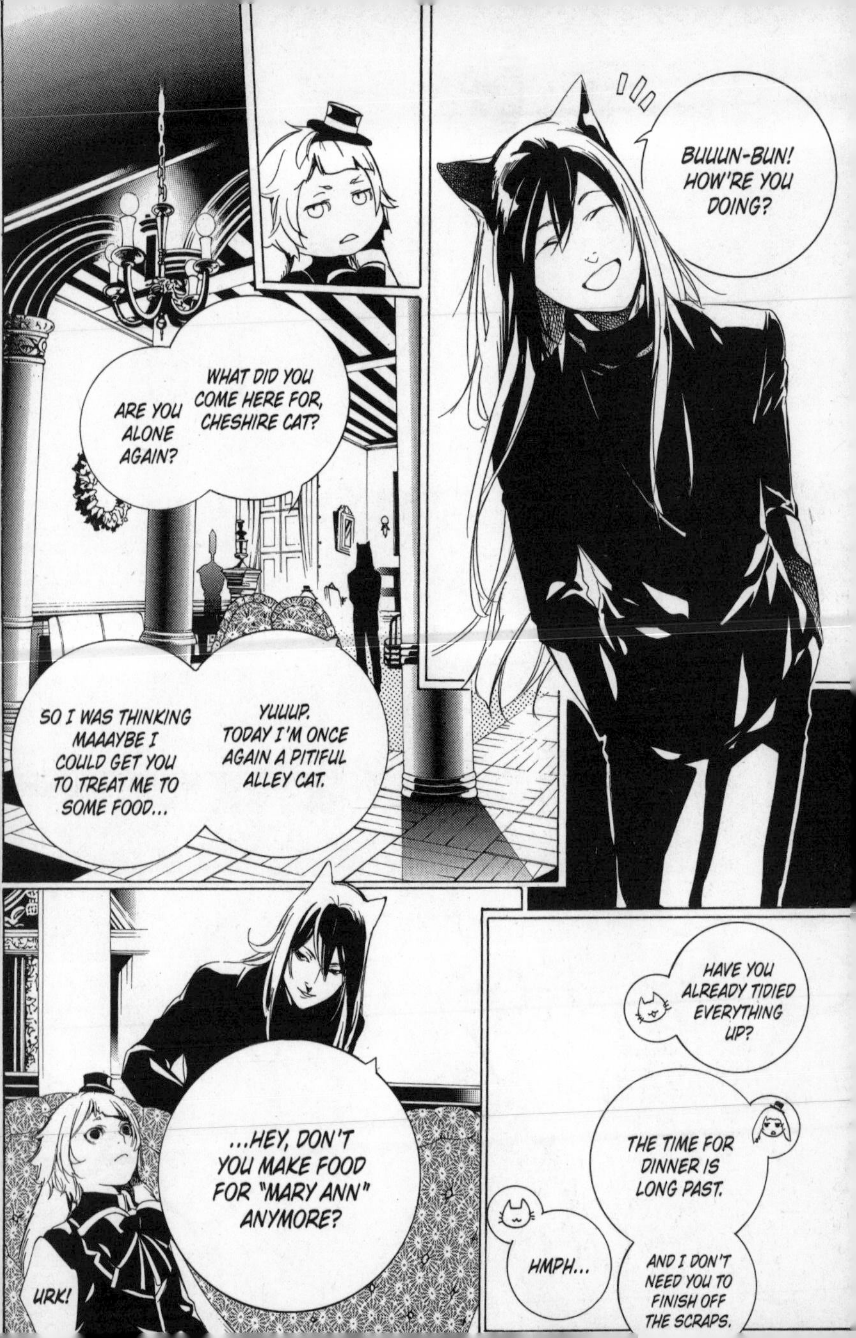
BUUUN-BUN! HOW'RE YOU DOING?
WHAT DID YOU COME HERE FOR, CHESHIRE CAT?
ARE YOU ALONE AGAIN?
YUUUP. TODAY I'M ONCE AGAIN A PITIFUL ALLEY CAT.
SO I WAS THINKING MAAAYBE I COULD GET YOU TO TREAT ME TO SOME FOOD...
HAVE YOU ALREADY TIDIED EVERYTHING UP?
THE TIME FOR DINNER IS LONG PAST.
AND I DON'T NEED YOU TO FINISH OFF THE SCRAPS.
HMPH...
...HEY, DON'T YOU MAKE FOOD FOR "MARY ANN" ANYMORE?
URK!

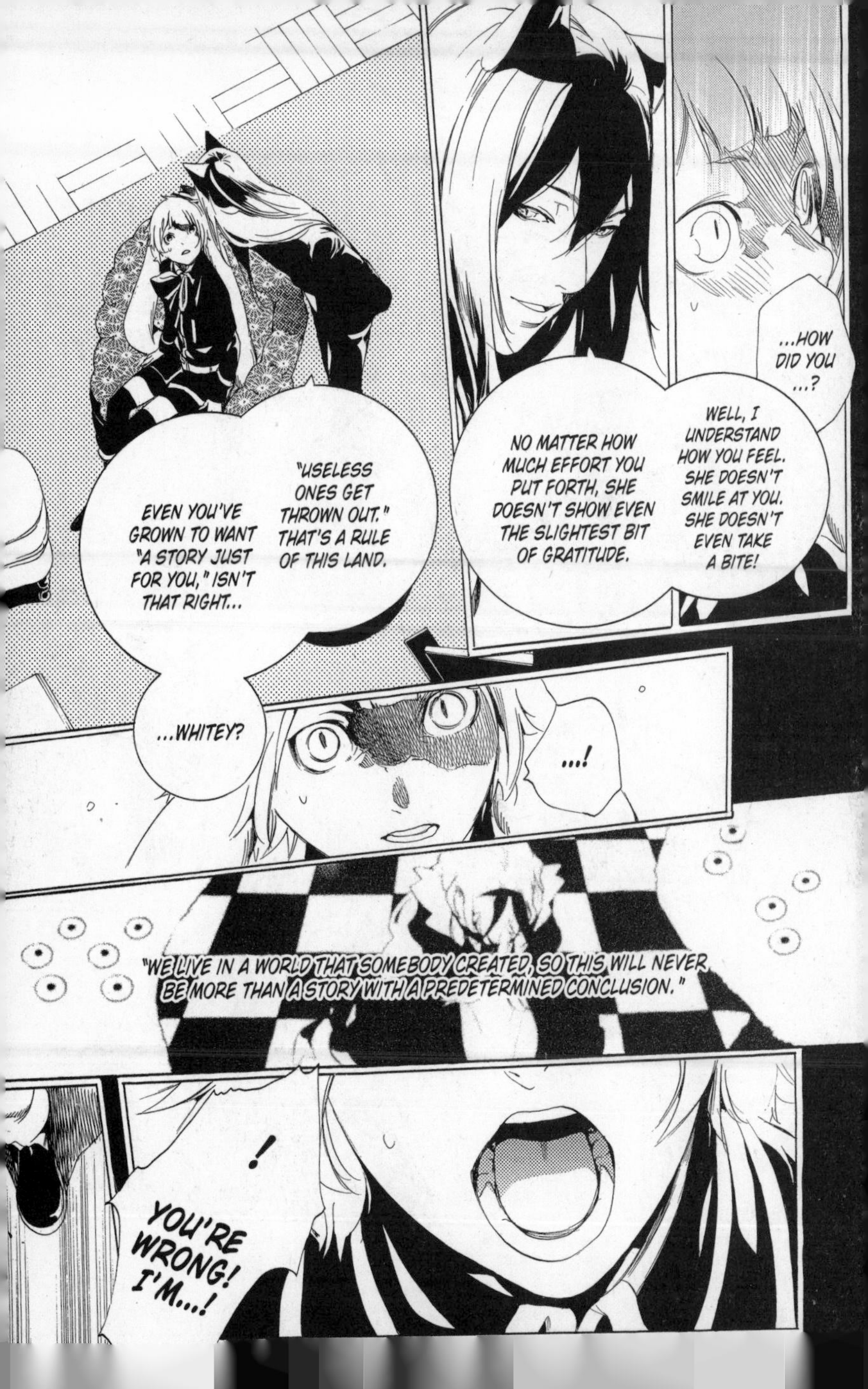
...HOW DID YOU ...?
WELL, I UNDERSTAND HOW YOU FEEL. SHE DOESN'T SMILE AT YOU. SHE DOESN'T EVEN TAKE A BITE!
NO MATTER HOW MUCH EFFORT YOU PUT FORTH, SHE DOESN'T SHOW EVEN THE SLIGHTEST BIT OF GRATITUDE.
"USELESS ONES GET THROWN OUT." THAT'S A RULE OF THIS LAND.
EVEN YOU'VE GROWN TO WANT "A STORY JUST FOR YOU," ISN'T THAT RIGHT...
...WHITEY?
...!
"WE LIVE IN A WORLD THAT SOMEBODY CREATED, SO THIS WILL NEVER BE MORE THAN A STORY WITH A PREDETERMINED CONCLUSION."
!
YOU'RE WRONG! I'M...!

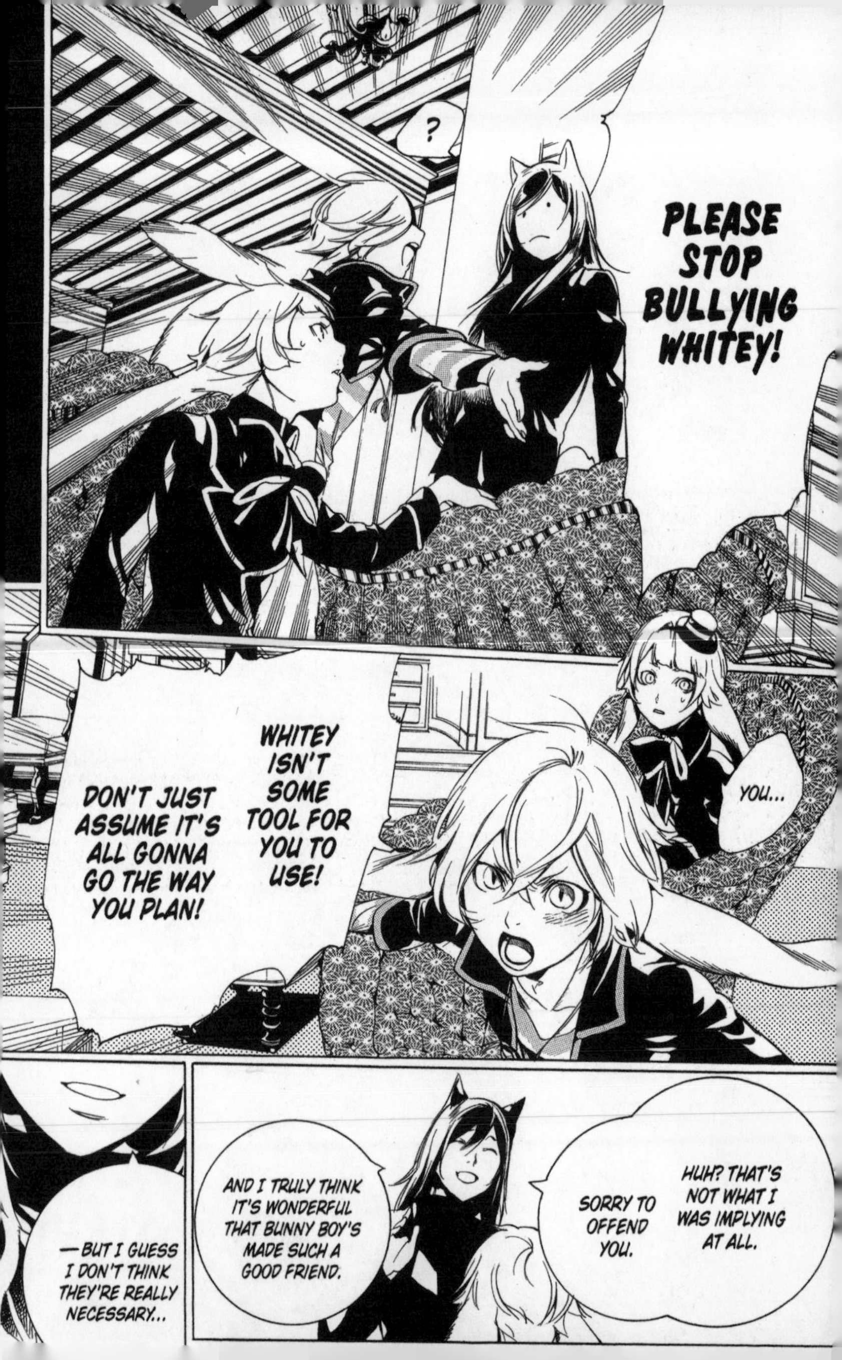
?
PLEASE STOP BULLYING WHITEY!
YOU...
WHITEY ISN'T SOME TOOL FOR YOU TO USE!
DON'T JUST ASSUME IT'S ALL GONNA GO THE WAY YOU PLAN!
HUH? THAT'S NOT WHAT I WAS IMPLYING AT ALL.
SORRY TO OFFEND YOU.
AND I TRULY THINK IT'S WONDERFUL THAT BUNNY BOY'S MADE SUCH A GOOD FRIEND.
—BUT I GUESS I DON'T THINK THEY'RE REALLY NECESSARY...

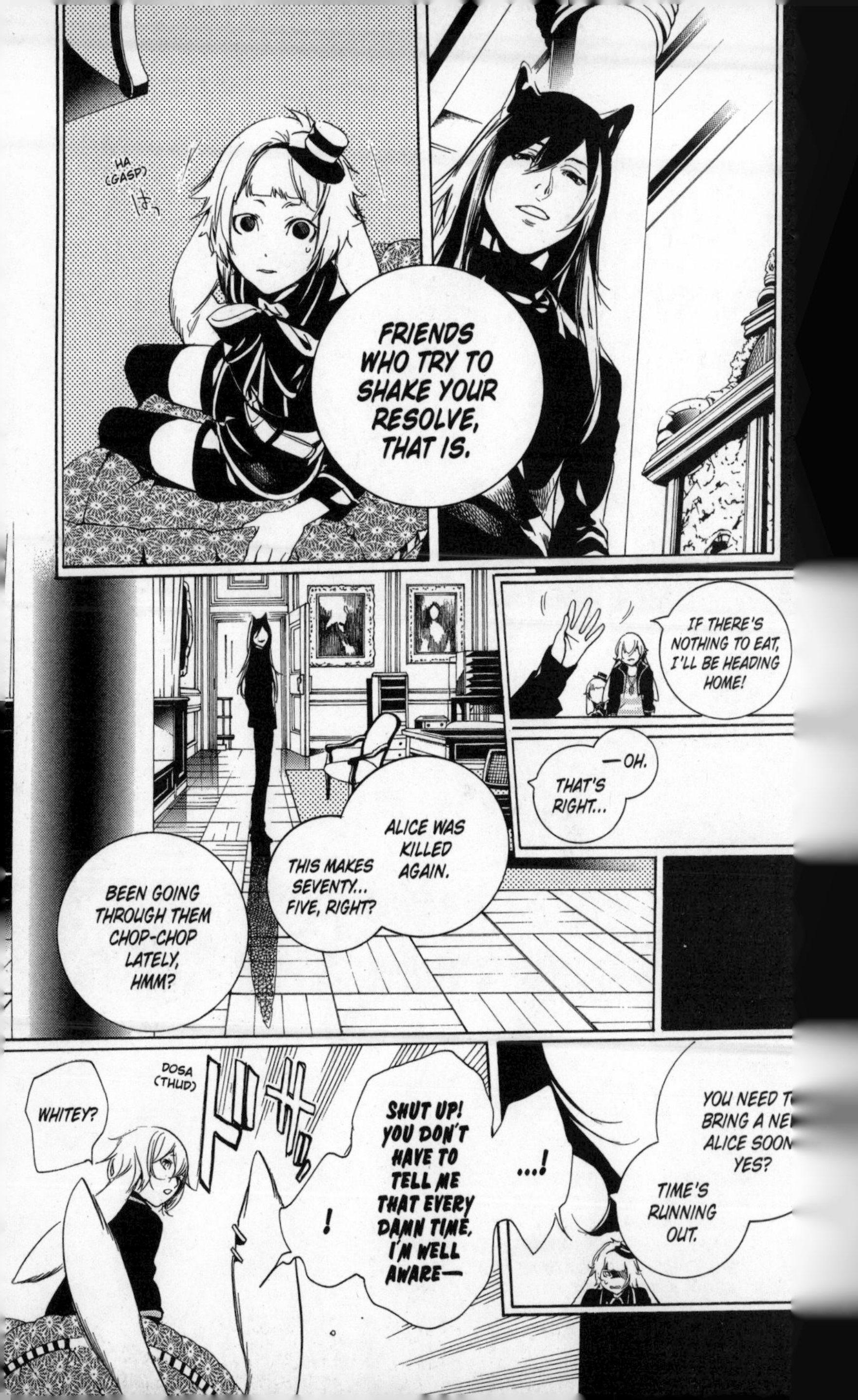
FRIENDS WHO TRY TO SHAKE YOUR RESOLVE, THAT IS.
HA (GASP)
はっ
IF THERE'S NOTHING TO EAT, I'LL BE HEADING HOME!
—OH.
THAT'S RIGHT...
ALICE WAS KILLED AGAIN.
THIS MAKES SEVENTY... FIVE, RIGHT?
BEEN GOING THROUGH THEM CHOP-CHOP LATELY, HMM?
YOU NEED T BRING A NE ALICE SOON YES?
TIME'S RUNNING OUT.
...!
SHUT UP! YOU DON'T HAVE TO TELL ME THAT EVERY DAMN TIME, I'M WELL AWARE—
!
DOSA (THUD)
WHITEY?

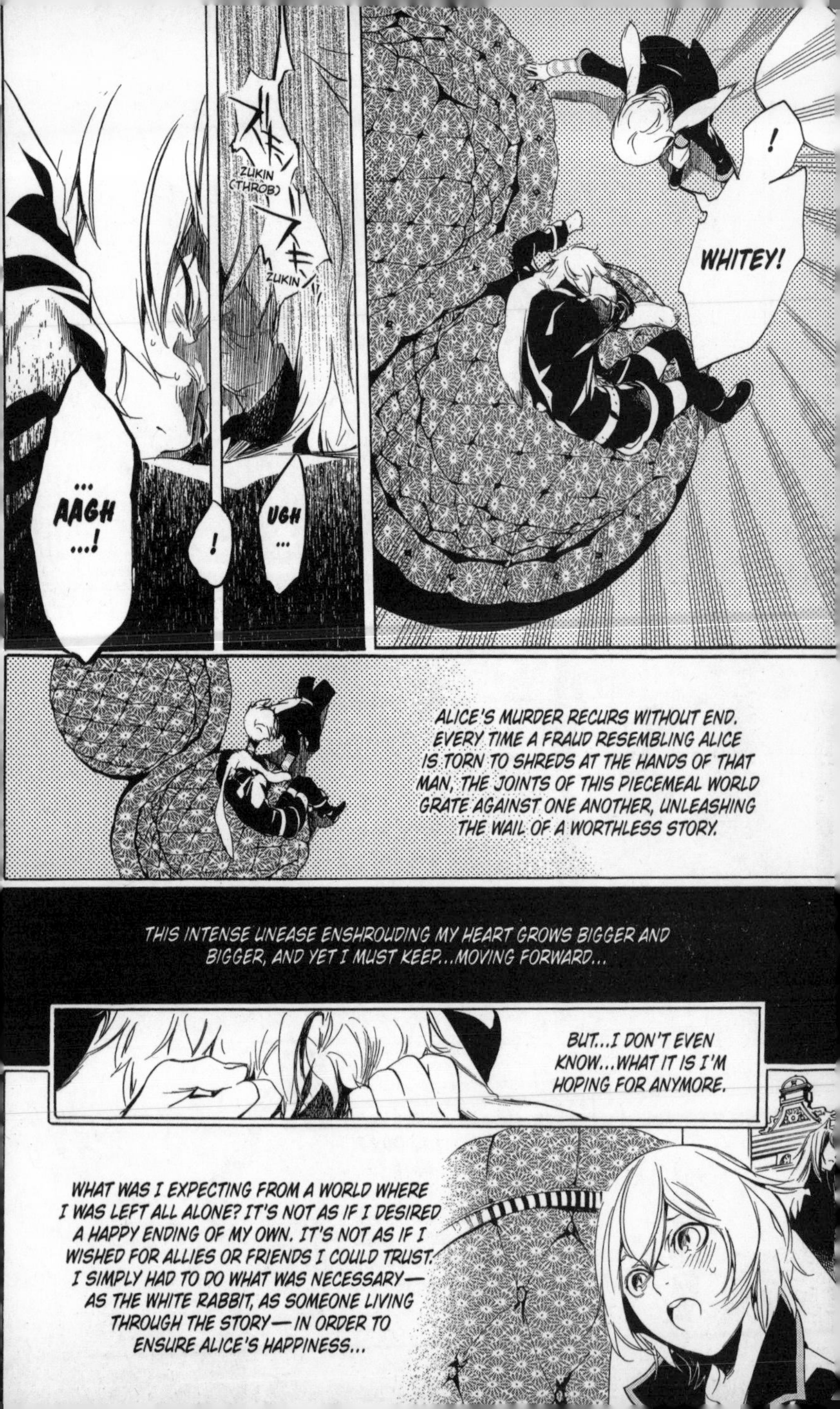
!
WHITEY!
ZUKIN (THROB)
ZUKIN
UGH...
!
...AAGH...!
ALICE'S MURDER RECURS WITHOUT END. EVERY TIME A FRAUD RESEMBLING ALICE IS TORN TO SHREDS AT THE HANDS OF THAT MAN, THE JOINTS OF THIS PIECEMEAL WORLD GRATE AGAINST ONE ANOTHER, UNLEASHING THE WAIL OF A WORTHLESS STORY.
THIS INTENSE UNEASE ENSHROUDING MY HEART GROWS BIGGER AND BIGGER, AND YET I MUST KEEP...MOVING FORWARD...
BUT...I DON'T EVEN KNOW...WHAT IT IS I'M HOPING FOR ANYMORE.
WHAT WAS I EXPECTING FROM A WORLD WHERE I WAS LEFT ALL ALONE? IT'S NOT AS IF I DESIRED A HAPPY ENDING OF MY OWN. IT'S NOT AS IF I WISHED FOR ALLIES OR FRIENDS I COULD TRUST. I SIMPLY HAD TO DO WHAT WAS NECESSARY—AS THE WHITE RABBIT, AS SOMEONE LIVING THROUGH THE STORY—IN ORDER TO ENSURE ALICE'S HAPPINESS...

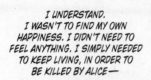

I UNDERSTAND.
I WASN'T TO FIND MY OWN
HAPPINESS. I DIDN'T NEED TO
FEEL ANYTHING. I SIMPLY NEEDED
TO KEEP LIVING, IN ORDER TO
BE KILLED BY ALICE—

WHITEY,
ARE
YOU ALL
RIGHT!?

WHITEY!

I DON'T HAVE MUCH RECOLLECTION OF WHAT'S
HAPPENED SINCE THEN. A LOT OF ALICES HAVE
BEEN KILLED. I'VE BROUGHT A LOT OF ALICES HERE.
THE TIME LEFT TO FINISH PIECING WONDERLAND
BACK TOGETHER HAS RUN OUT. I NO LONGER EVEN
COMPREHEND MY OWN NAME. STILL...I BELIEVE THAT
ALICE WILL COME KILL THE WHITE RABBIT AND THAT
IT'S JUST A BIT LONGER UNTIL SHE REACHES HER
HAPPY ENDING. JUST FOR A BIT LONGER, JUST A
LITTLE BIT LONGER, I HAVE TO KEEP MY EYES OPEN
AND KEEP ON BREATHING, AND I'LL BE—
I'LL BE...

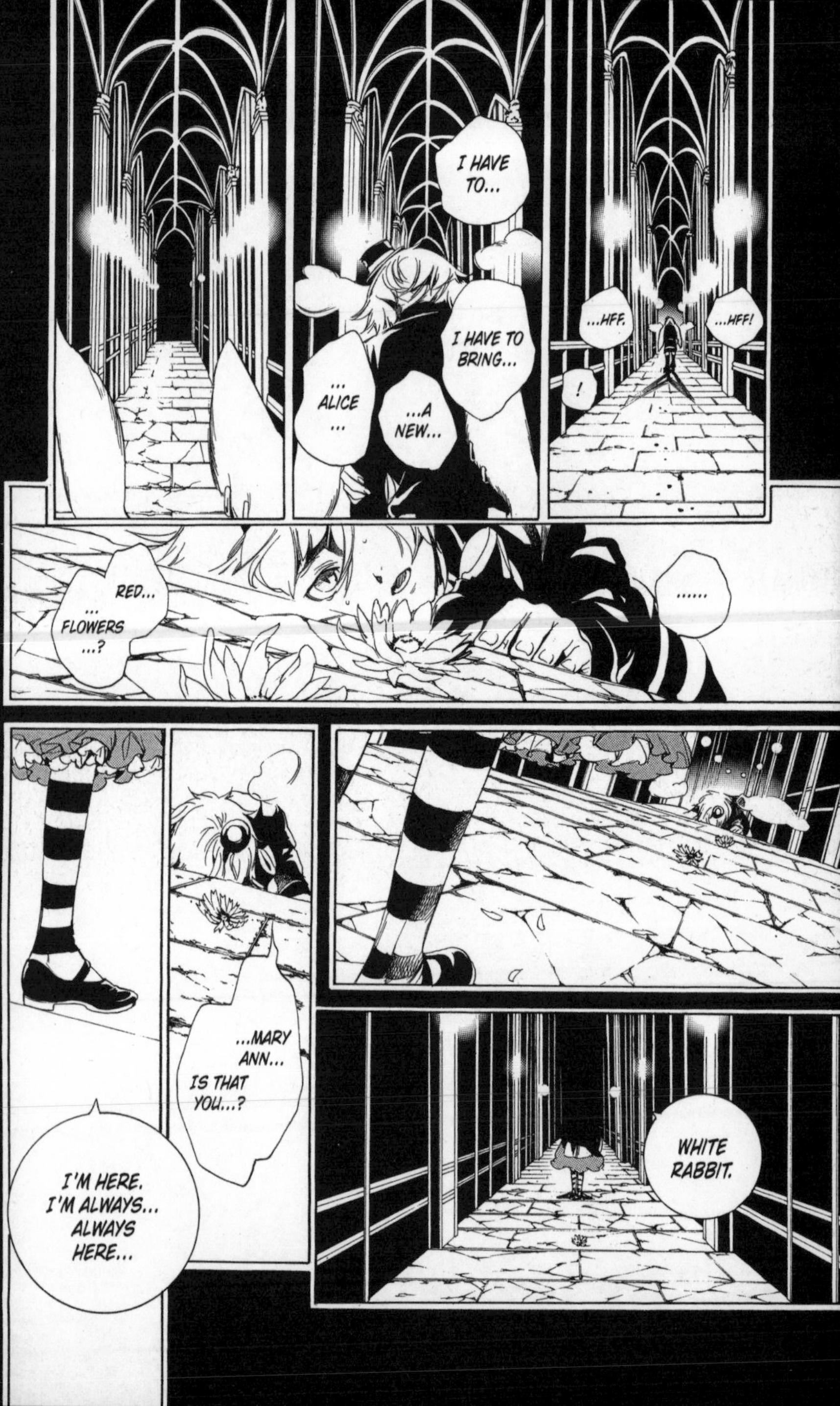
...HFF!
...HFF.
!
I HAVE TO...
I HAVE TO BRING...
...A NEW...
...ALICE...
......
RED... ...FLOWERS ...?
WHITE RABBIT.
...MARY ANN... IS THAT YOU...?
I'M HERE. I'M ALWAYS... ALWAYS HERE...

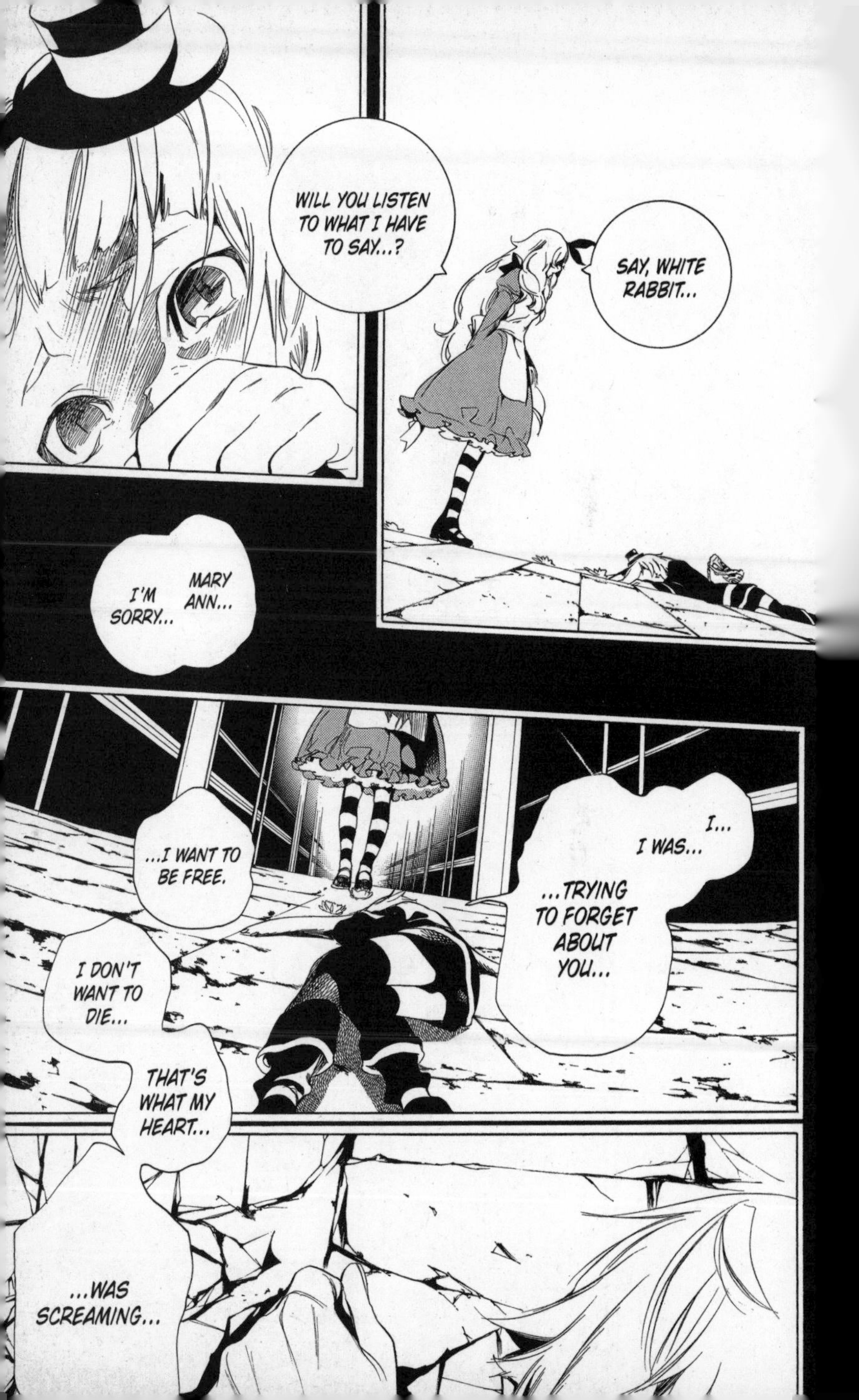
SAY, WHITE RABBIT...
WILL YOU LISTEN TO WHAT I HAVE TO SAY...?
MARY ANN... I'M SORRY...
I... I WAS...
...TRYING TO FORGET ABOUT YOU...
...I WANT TO BE FREE.
I DON'T WANT TO DIE...
THAT'S WHAT MY HEART...
...WAS SCREAMING...

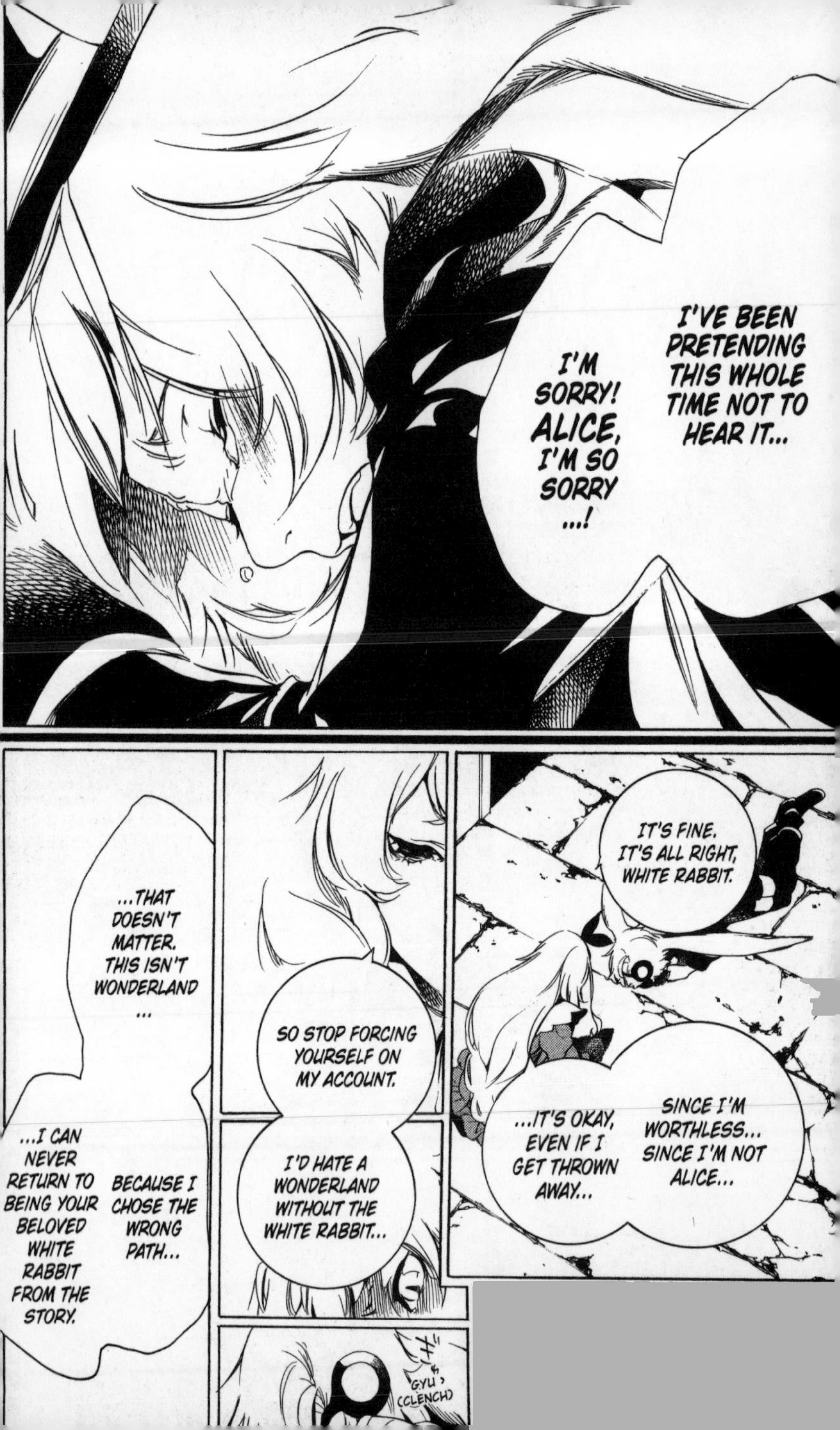
I'VE BEEN PRETENDING THIS WHOLE TIME NOT TO HEAR IT...
I'M SORRY! ALICE, I'M SO SORRY ...!
IT'S FINE. IT'S ALL RIGHT, WHITE RABBIT.
SINCE I'M WORTHLESS... SINCE I'M NOT ALICE...
...IT'S OKAY, EVEN IF I GET THROWN AWAY...
SO STOP FORCING YOURSELF ON MY ACCOUNT.
I'D HATE A WONDERLAND WITHOUT THE WHITE RABBIT...
GYU (CLENCH)
...THAT DOESN'T MATTER. THIS ISN'T WONDERLAND...
BECAUSE I CHOSE THE WRONG PATH...
...I CAN NEVER RETURN TO BEING YOUR BELOVED WHITE RABBIT FROM THE STORY.

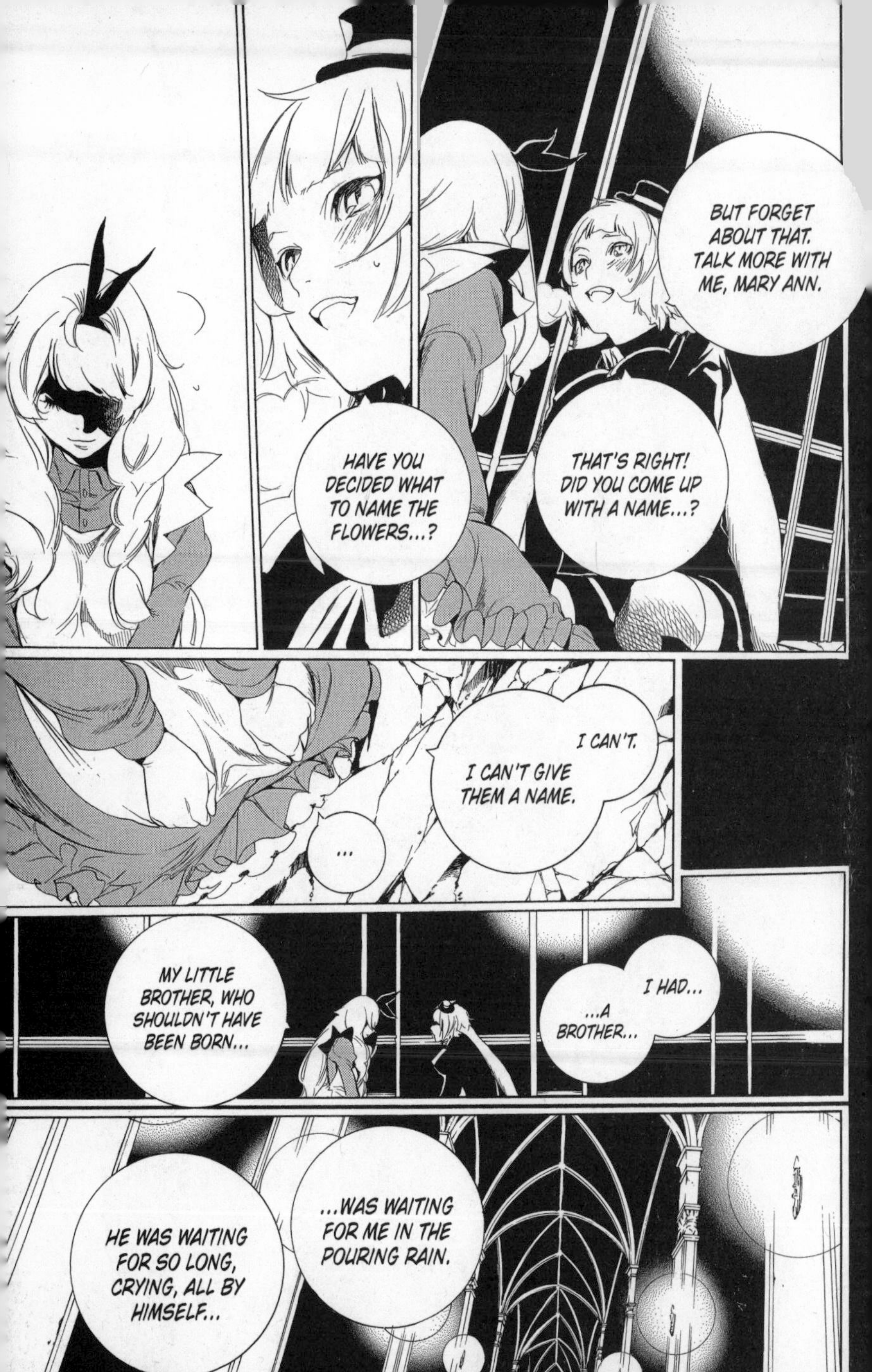
BUT FORGET ABOUT THAT. TALK MORE WITH ME, MARY ANN.
THAT'S RIGHT! DID YOU COME UP WITH A NAME...?
HAVE YOU DECIDED WHAT TO NAME THE FLOWERS...?
I CAN'T.
I CAN'T GIVE THEM A NAME.
...
I HAD...
...A BROTHER...
MY LITTLE BROTHER, WHO SHOULDN'T HAVE BEEN BORN...
...WAS WAITING FOR ME IN THE POURING RAIN.
HE WAS WAITING FOR SO LONG, CRYING, ALL BY HIMSELF...

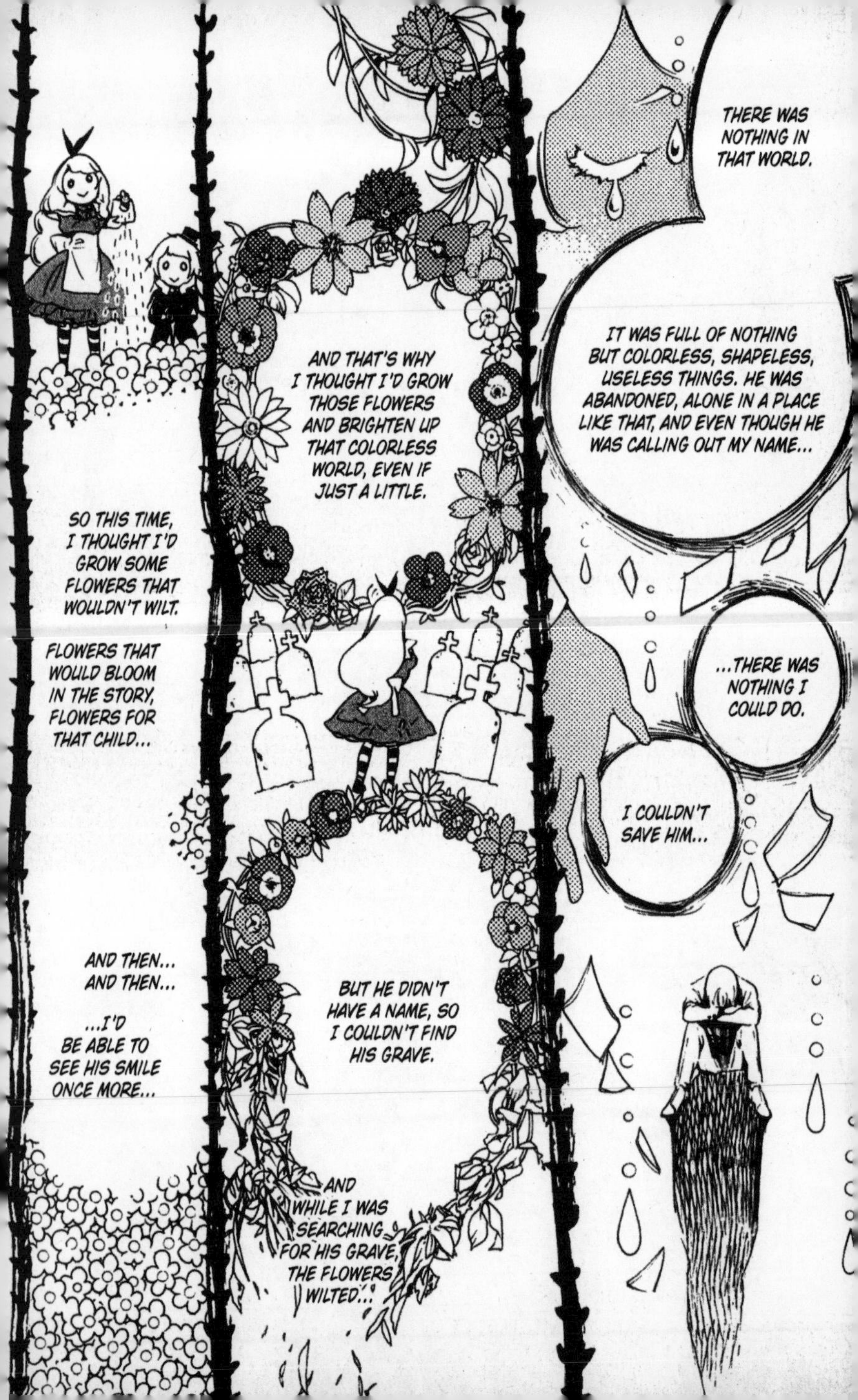
THERE WAS NOTHING IN THAT WORLD.
IT WAS FULL OF NOTHING BUT COLORLESS, SHAPELESS, USELESS THINGS. HE WAS ABANDONED, ALONE IN A PLACE LIKE THAT, AND EVEN THOUGH HE WAS CALLING OUT MY NAME...
...THERE WAS NOTHING I COULD DO.
I COULDN'T SAVE HIM...
AND THAT'S WHY I THOUGHT I'D GROW THOSE FLOWERS AND BRIGHTEN UP THAT COLORLESS WORLD, EVEN IF JUST A LITTLE.
BUT HE DIDN'T HAVE A NAME, SO I COULDN'T FIND HIS GRAVE.
AND WHILE I WAS SEARCHING FOR HIS GRAVE, THE FLOWERS WILTED...
SO THIS TIME, I THOUGHT I'D GROW SOME FLOWERS THAT WOULDN'T WILT.
FLOWERS THAT WOULD BLOOM IN THE STORY, FLOWERS FOR THAT CHILD...
AND THEN... AND THEN...
...I'D BE ABLE TO SEE HIS SMILE ONCE MORE...

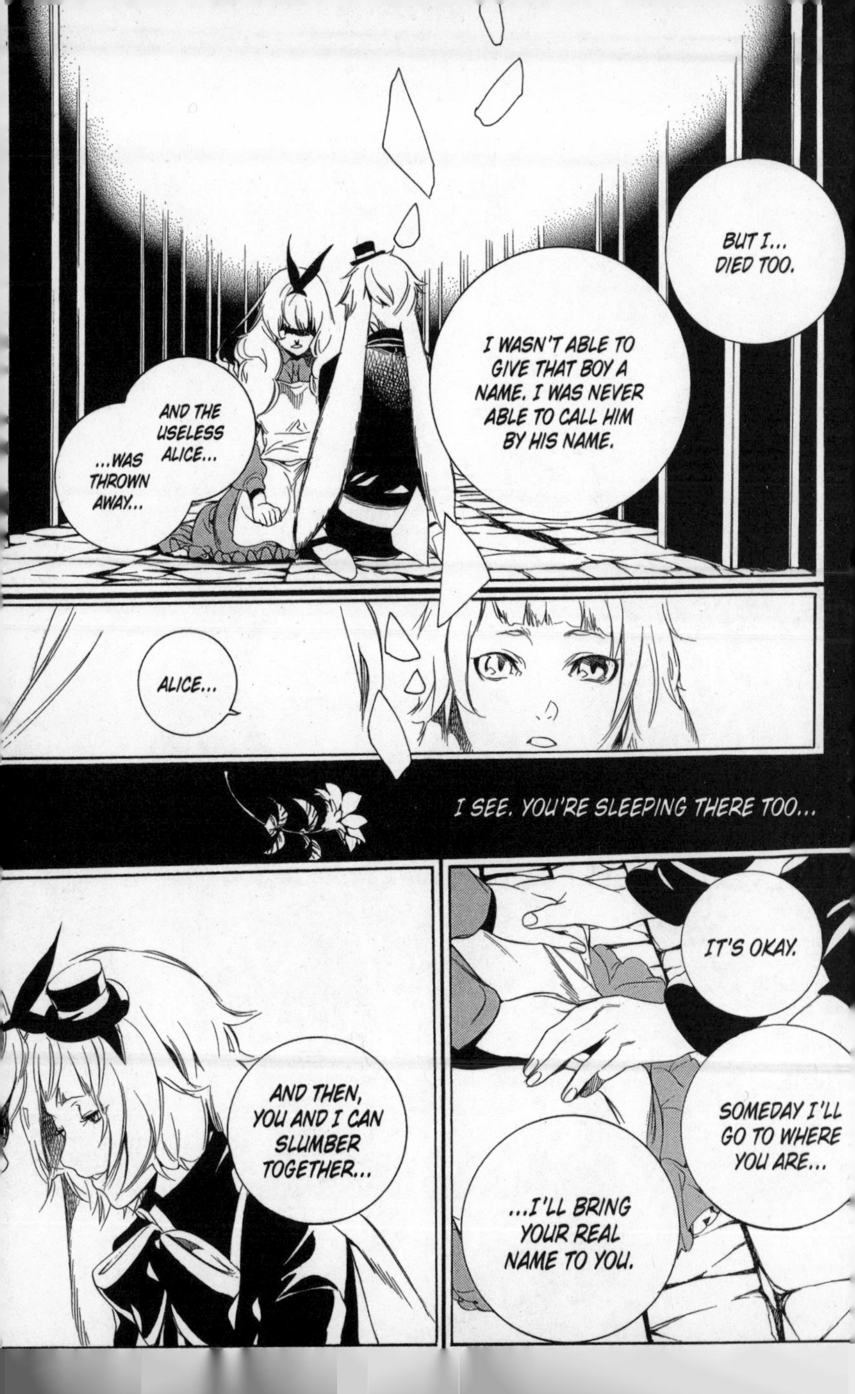
BUT I... DIED TOO.
I WASN'T ABLE TO GIVE THAT BOY A NAME. I WAS NEVER ABLE TO CALL HIM BY HIS NAME.
AND THE USELESS ALICE...
...WAS THROWN AWAY...
ALICE...
I SEE. YOU'RE SLEEPING THERE TOO...
IT'S OKAY.
SOMEDAY I'LL GO TO WHERE YOU ARE...
...I'LL BRING YOUR REAL NAME TO YOU.
AND THEN, YOU AND I CAN SLUMBER TOGETHER...

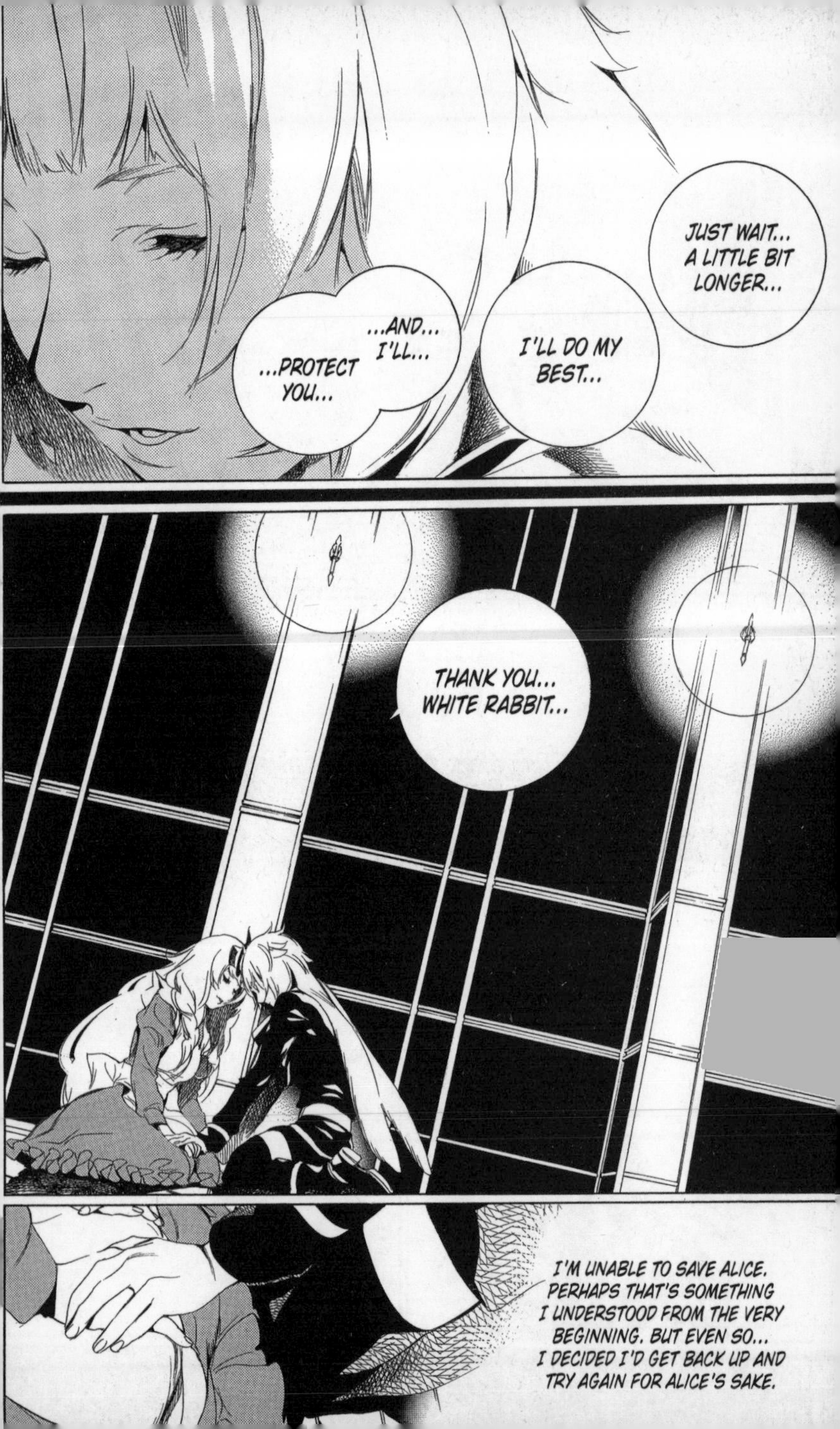
JUST WAIT... A LITTLE BIT LONGER...
I'LL DO MY BEST...
...AND... I'LL...
...PROTECT YOU...
THANK YOU... WHITE RABBIT...
I'M UNABLE TO SAVE ALICE. PERHAPS THAT'S SOMETHING I UNDERSTOOD FROM THE VERY BEGINNING. BUT EVEN SO... I DECIDED I'D GET BACK UP AND TRY AGAIN FOR ALICE'S SAKE.

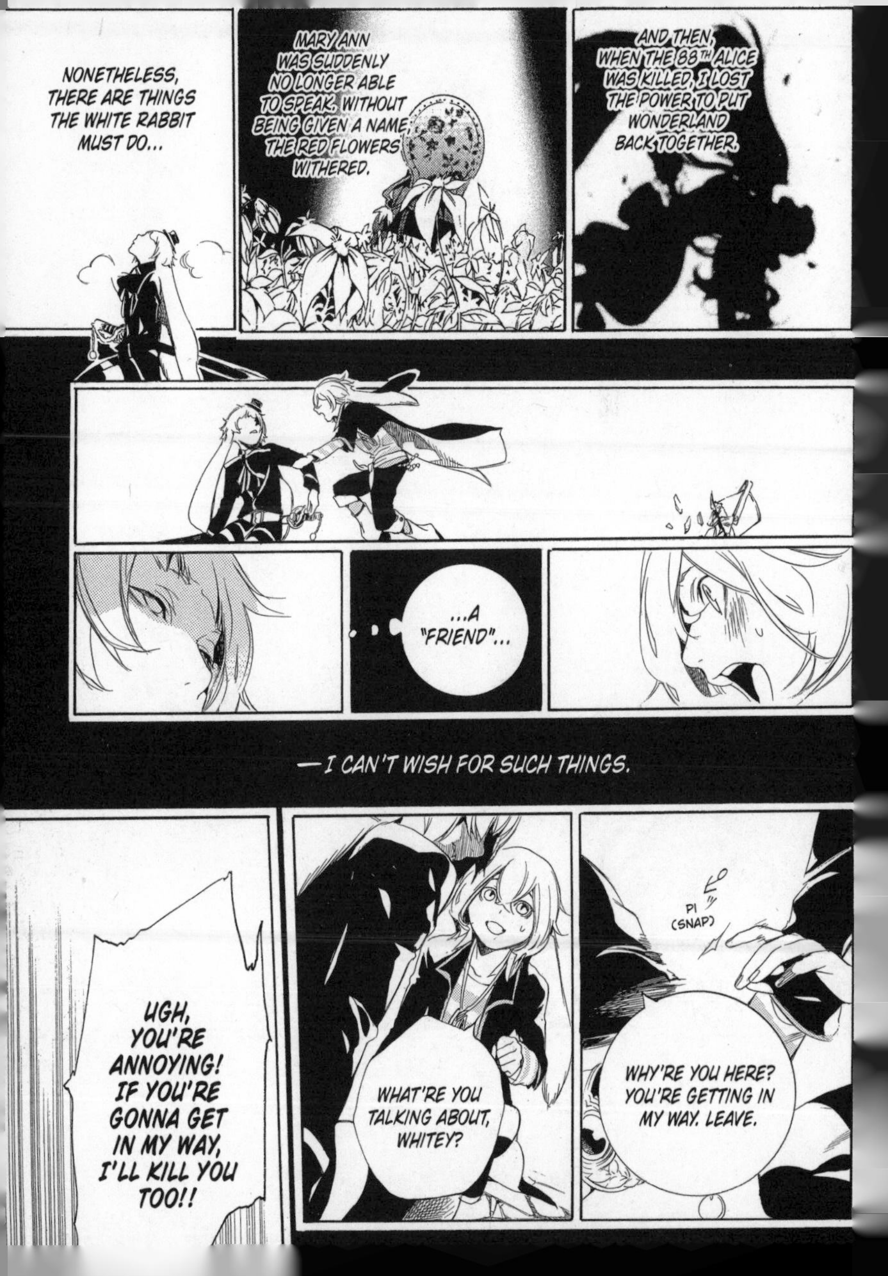
AND THEN, WHEN THE 88TH ALICE WAS KILLED, I LOST THE POWER TO PUT WONDERLAND BACK TOGETHER.
MARY ANN WAS SUDDENLY NO LONGER ABLE TO SPEAK. WITHOUT BEING GIVEN A NAME, THE RED FLOWERS WITHERED.
NONETHELESS, THERE ARE THINGS THE WHITE RABBIT MUST DO...
...A "FRIEND"...
—I CAN'T WISH FOR SUCH THINGS.
PI (SNAP)
WHY'RE YOU HERE? YOU'RE GETTING IN MY WAY. LEAVE.
WHAT'RE YOU TALKING ABOUT, WHITEY?
UGH, YOU'RE ANNOYING! IF YOU'RE GONNA GET IN MY WAY, I'LL KILL YOU TOO!!

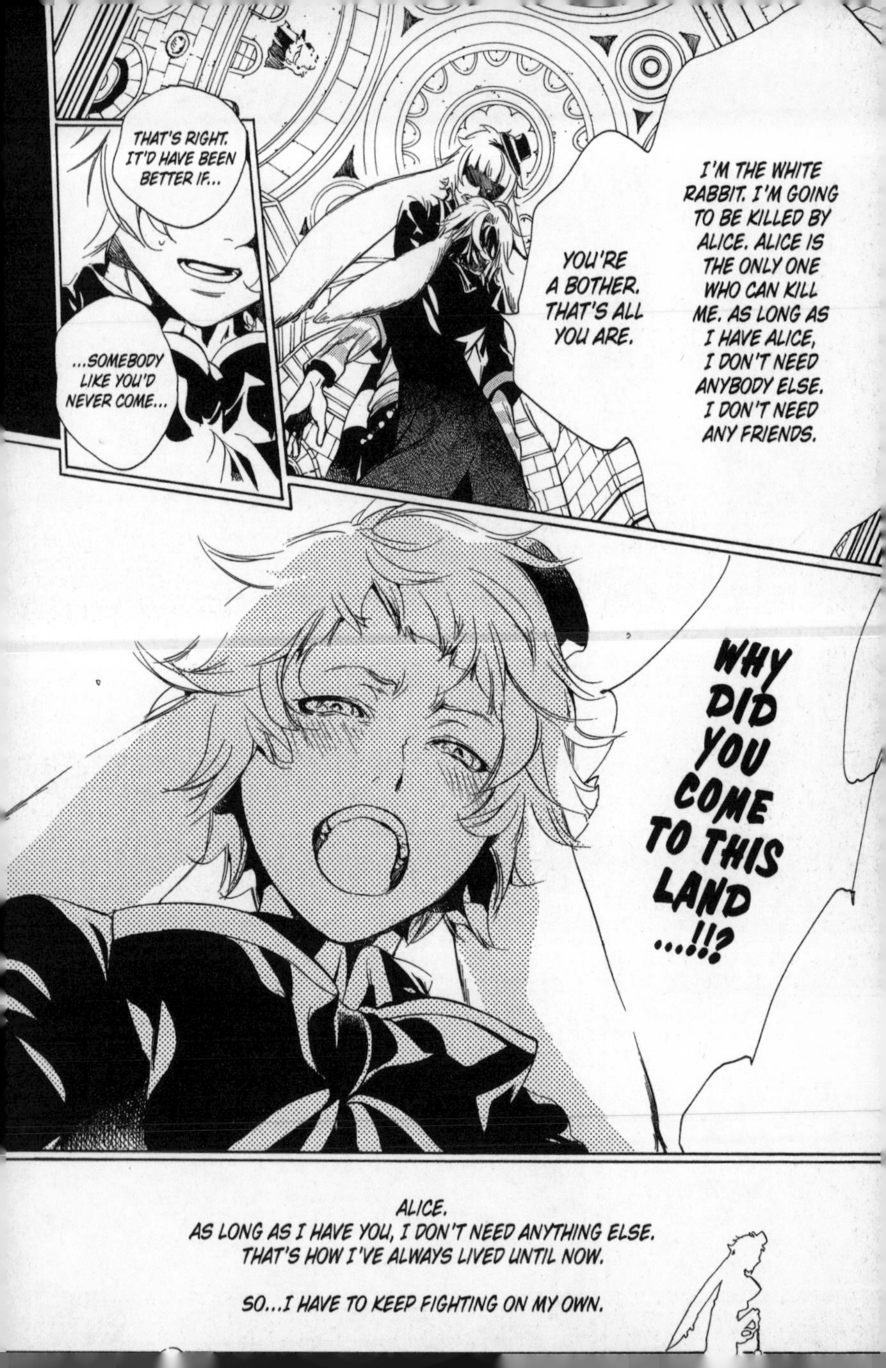
I'M THE WHITE RABBIT. I'M GOING TO BE KILLED BY ALICE. ALICE IS THE ONLY ONE WHO CAN KILL ME. AS LONG AS I HAVE ALICE, I DON'T NEED ANYBODY ELSE. I DON'T NEED ANY FRIENDS.
YOU'RE A BOTHER. THAT'S ALL YOU ARE.
THAT'S RIGHT. IT'D HAVE BEEN BETTER IF...
...SOMEBODY LIKE YOU'D NEVER COME...
WHY DID YOU COME TO THIS LAND ...!!?
ALICE.
AS LONG AS I HAVE YOU, I DON'T NEED ANYTHING ELSE.
THAT'S HOW I'VE ALWAYS LIVED UNTIL NOW.
SO...I HAVE TO KEEP FIGHTING ON MY OWN.

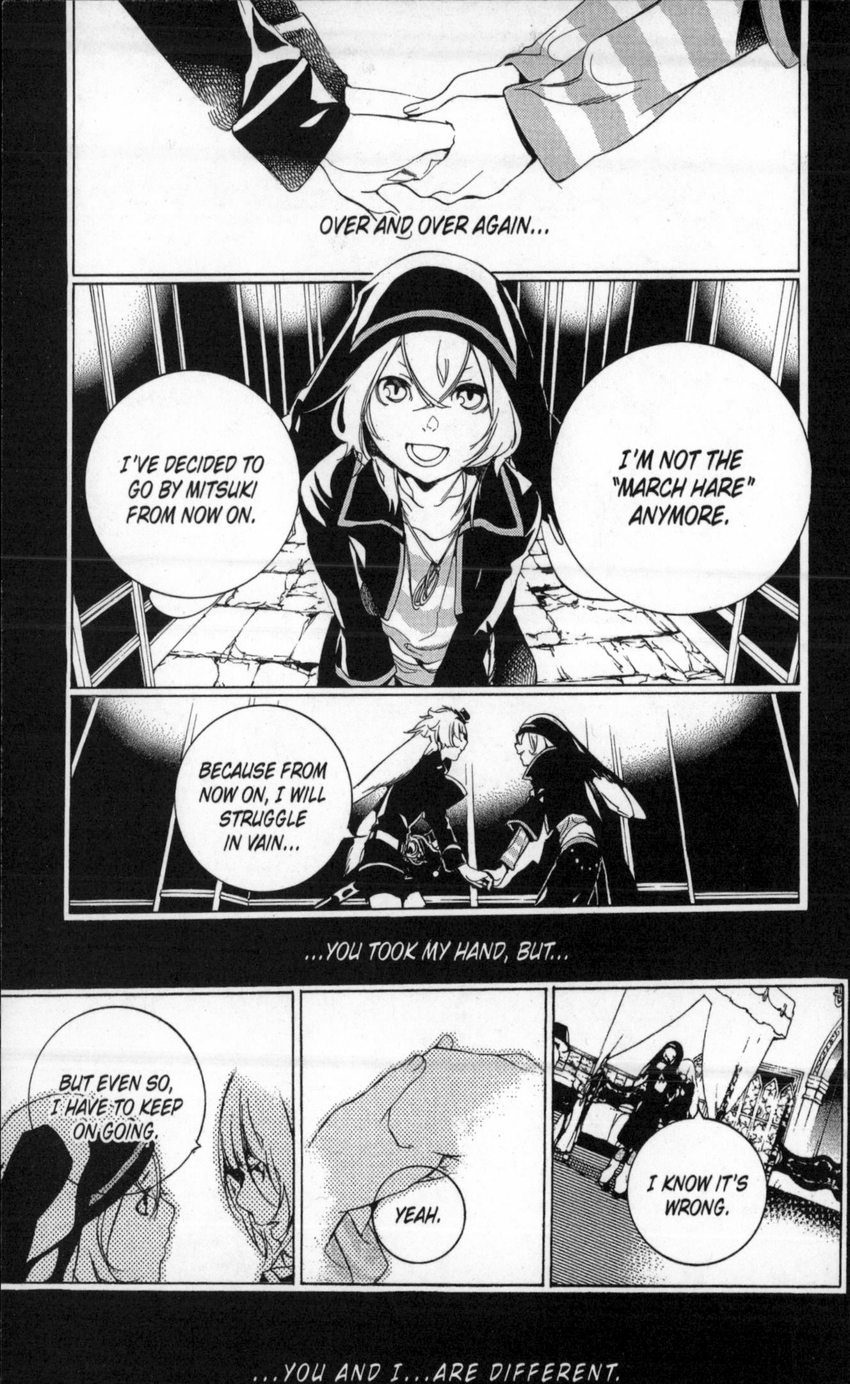
OVER AND OVER AGAIN...
I'M NOT THE "MARCH HARE" ANYMORE.
I'VE DECIDED TO GO BY MITSUKI FROM NOW ON.
BECAUSE FROM NOW ON, I WILL STRUGGLE IN VAIN...
...YOU TOOK MY HAND, BUT...
I KNOW IT'S WRONG.
YEAH.
BUT EVEN SO, I HAVE TO KEEP ON GOING.
...YOU AND I...ARE DIFFERENT

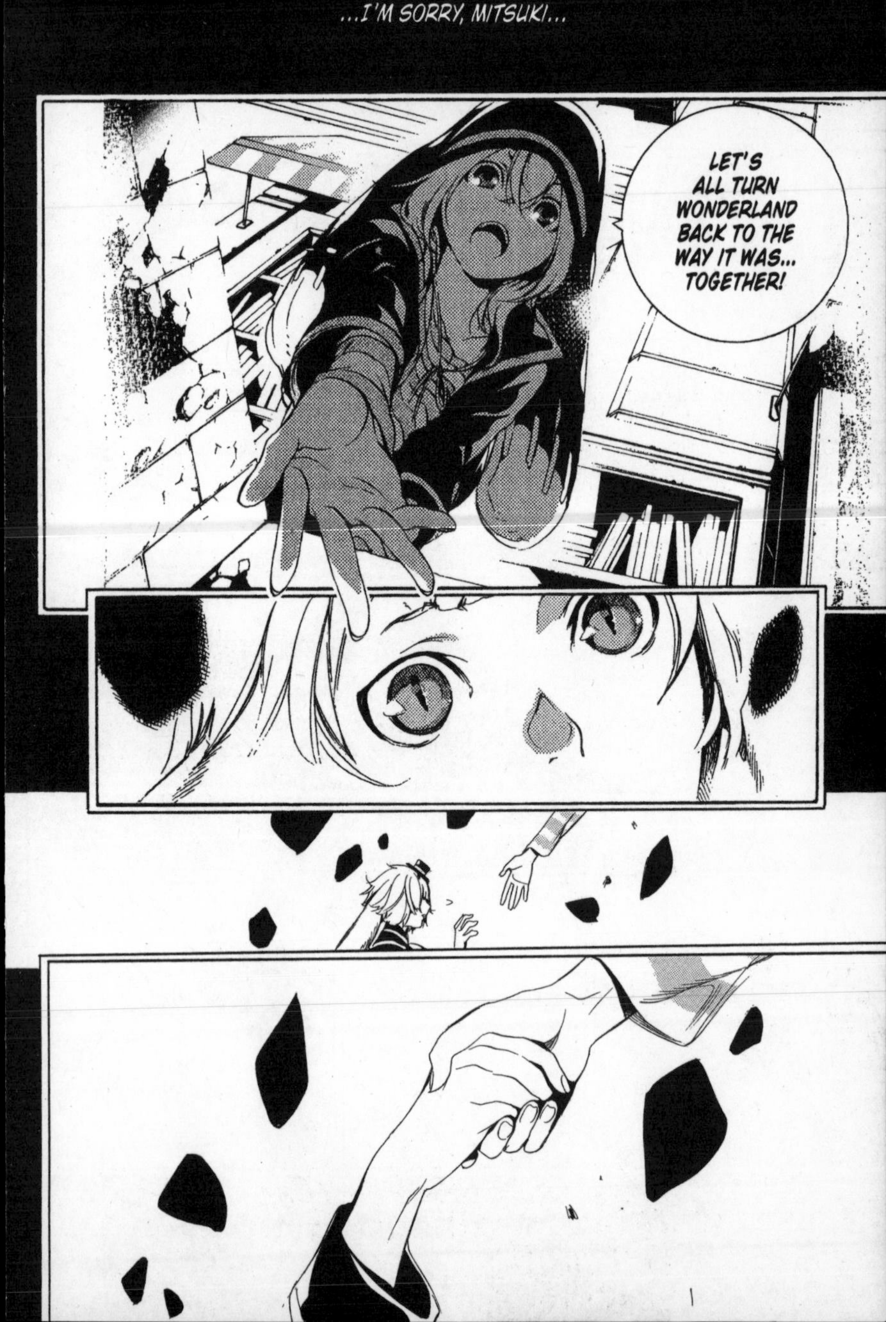
...I'M SORRY, MITSUKI...
LET'S ALL TURN WONDERLAND BACK TO THE WAY IT WAS... TOGETHER!

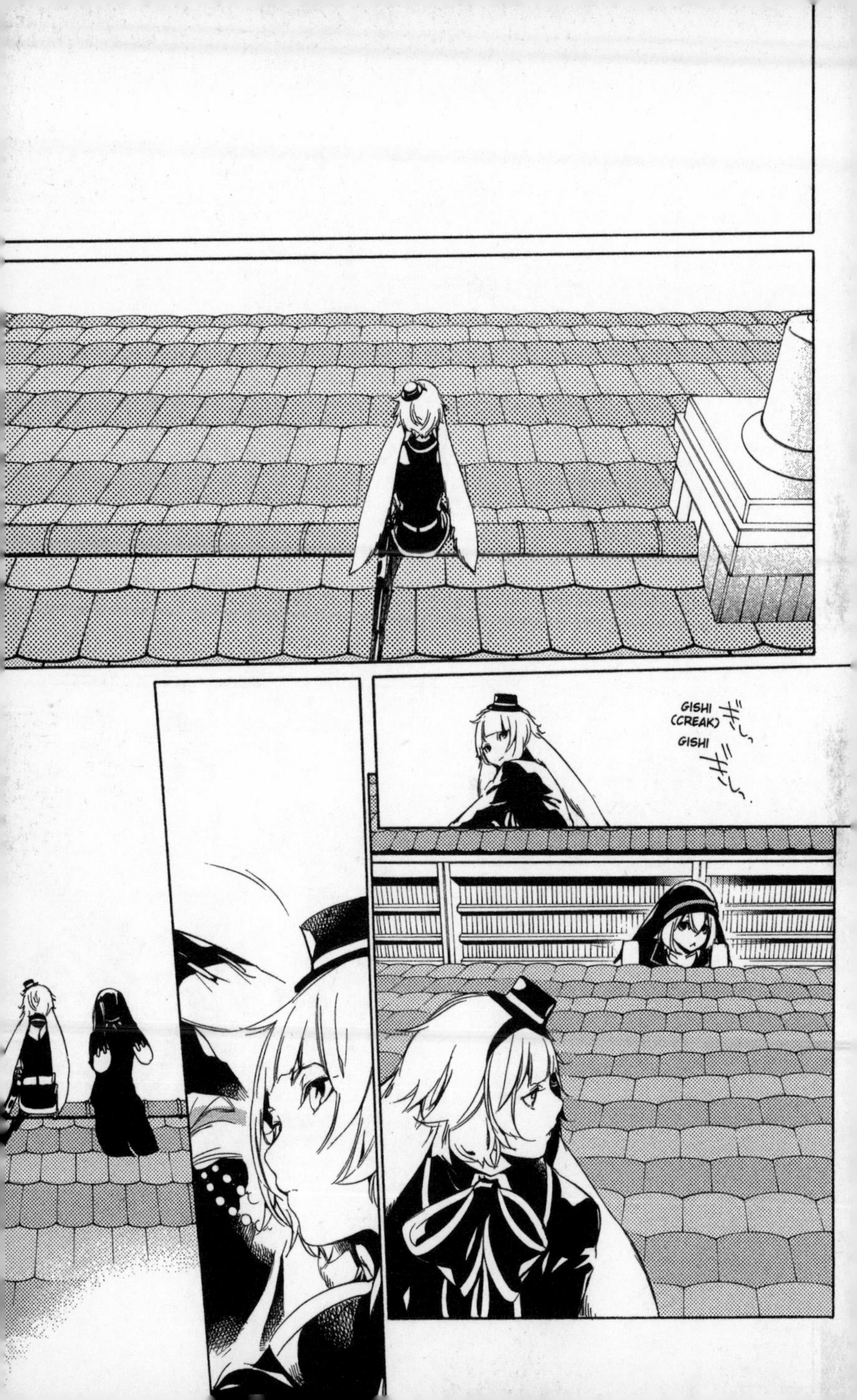
GISHI (CREAK)
ぎし
GISHI
ぎし

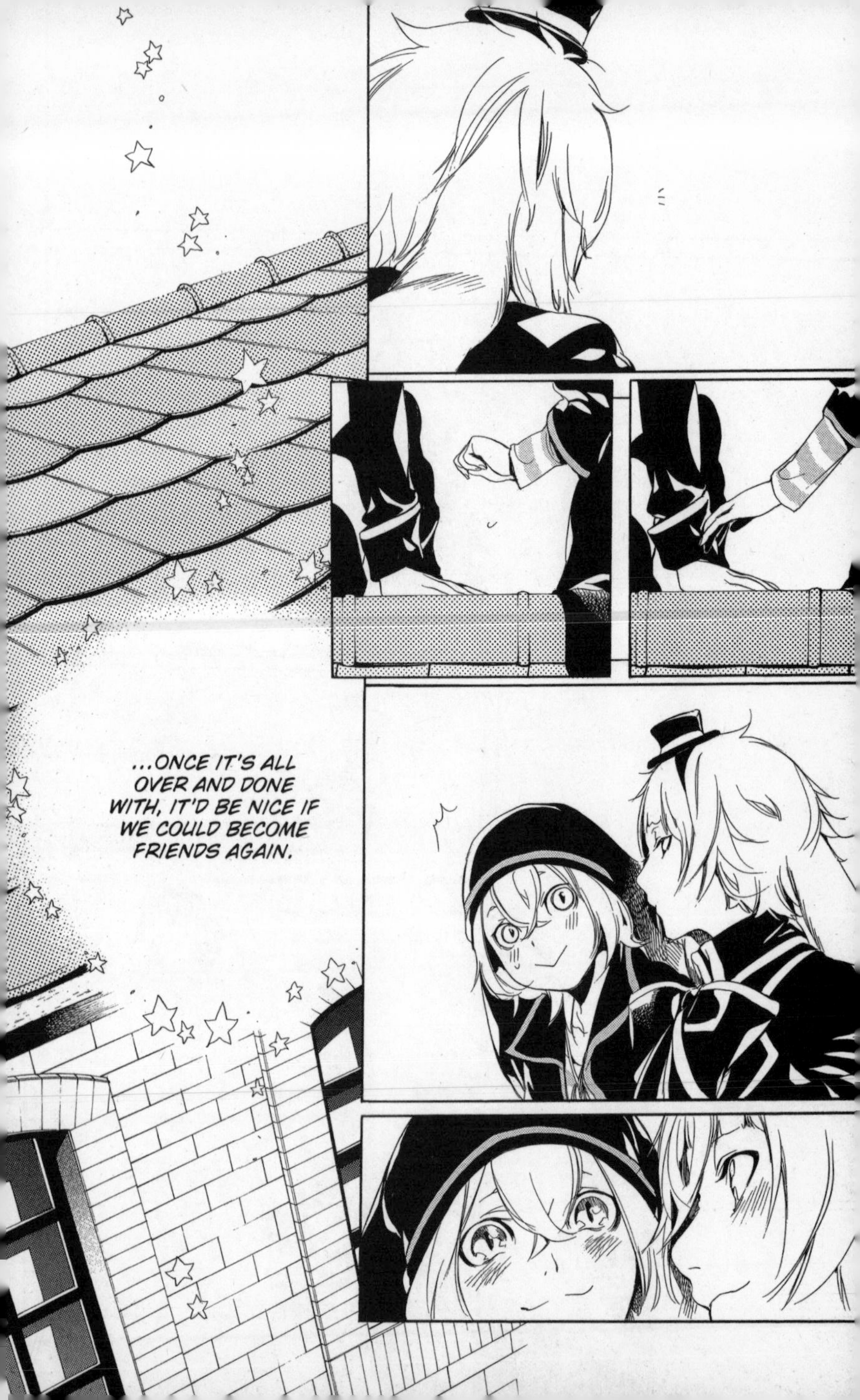
...ONCE IT'S ALL OVER AND DONE WITH, IT'D BE NICE IF WE COULD BECOME FRIENDS AGAIN.

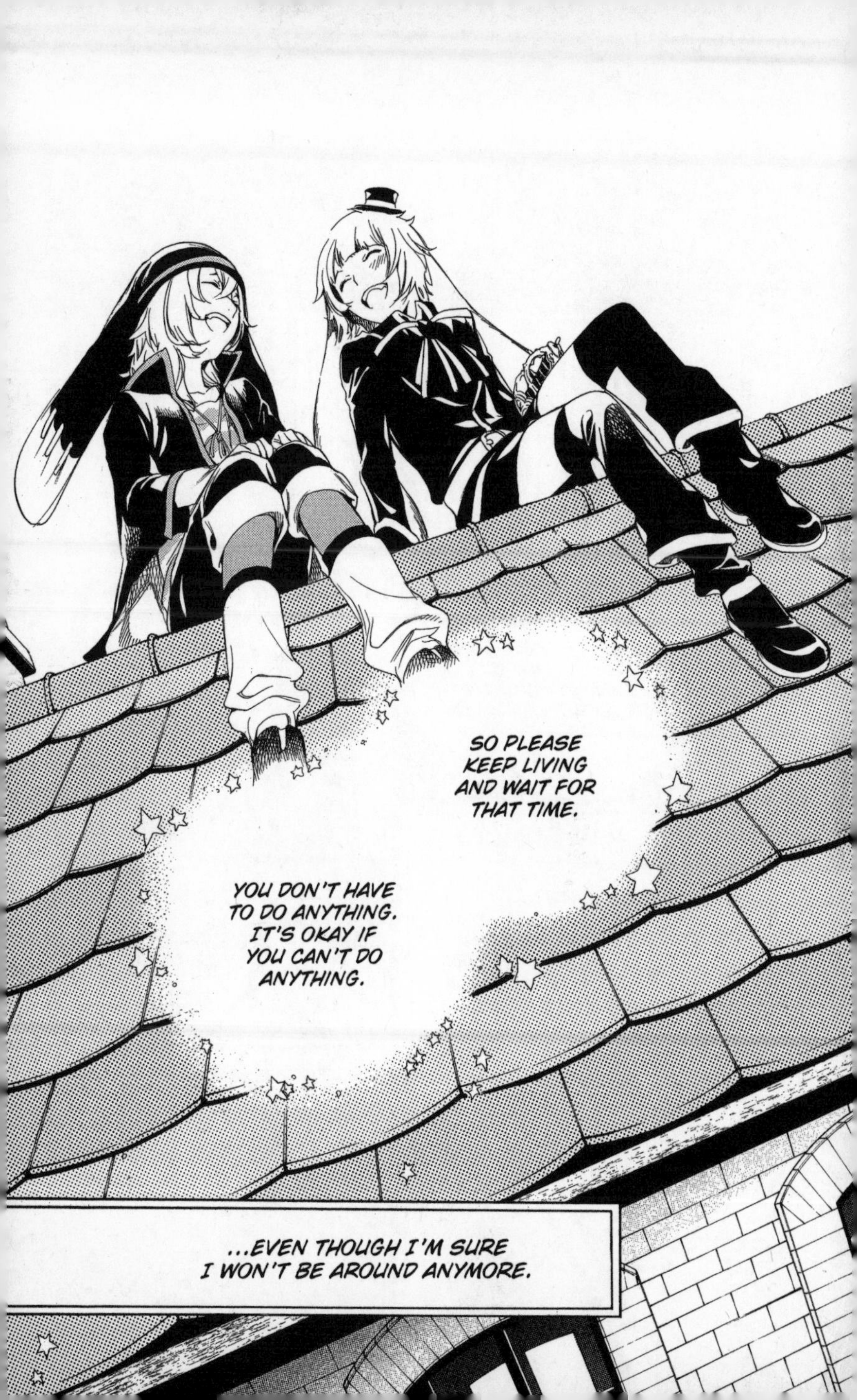
SO PLEASE KEEP LIVING AND WAIT FOR THAT TIME.
YOU DON'T HAVE TO DO ANYTHING. IT'S OKAY IF YOU CAN'T DO ANYTHING.
...EVEN THOUGH I'M SURE I WON'T BE AROUND ANYMORE.

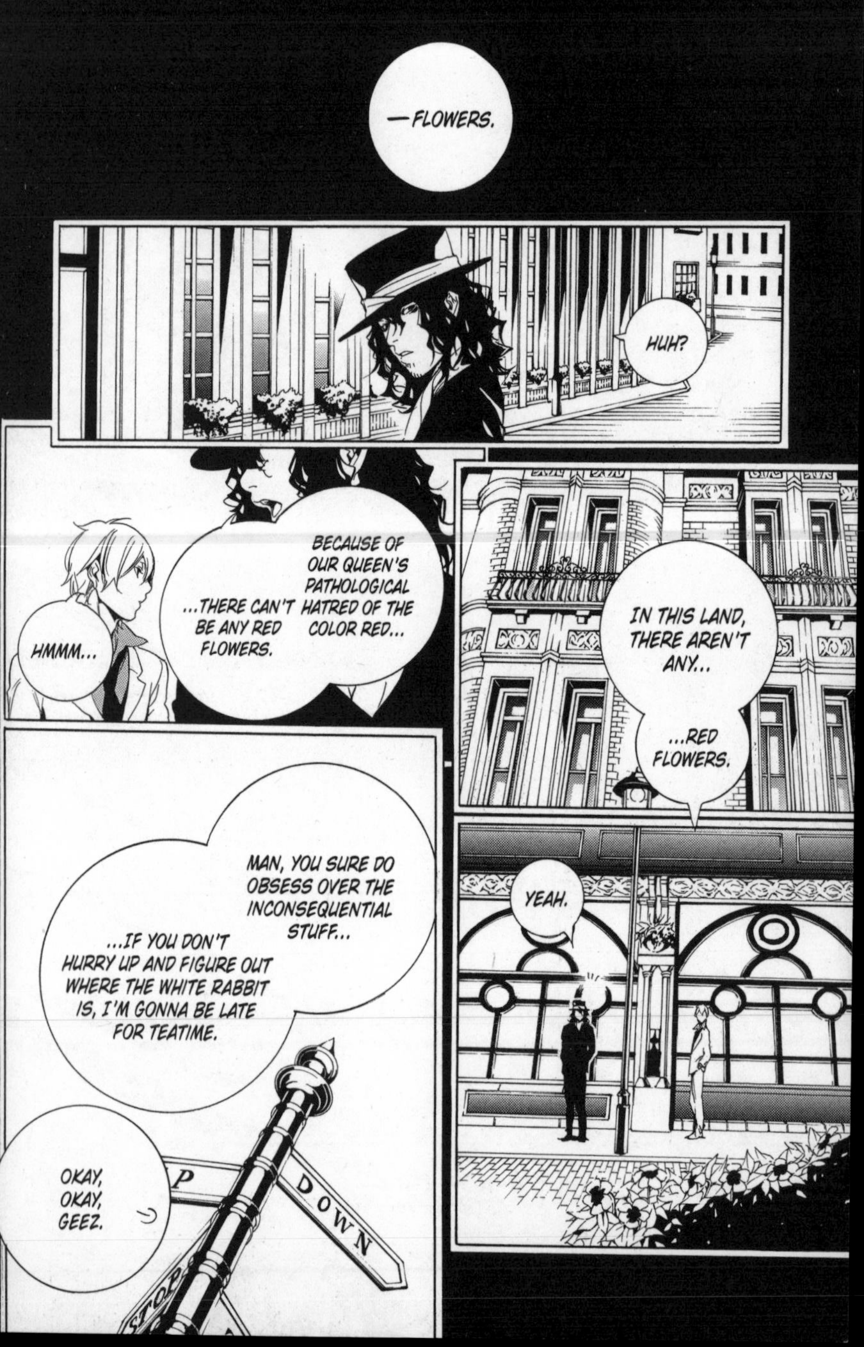
—FLOWERS.
HUH?
IN THIS LAND, THERE AREN'T ANY...
...RED FLOWERS.
BECAUSE OF OUR QUEEN'S PATHOLOGICAL HATRED OF THE COLOR RED...
...THERE CAN'T BE ANY RED FLOWERS.
HMMM...
YEAH.
MAN, YOU SURE DO OBSESS OVER THE INCONSEQUENTIAL STUFF...
...IF YOU DON'T HURRY UP AND FIGURE OUT WHERE THE WHITE RABBIT IS, I'M GONNA BE LATE FOR TEATIME.
OKAY, OKAY, GEEZ.
DOWN
STOP

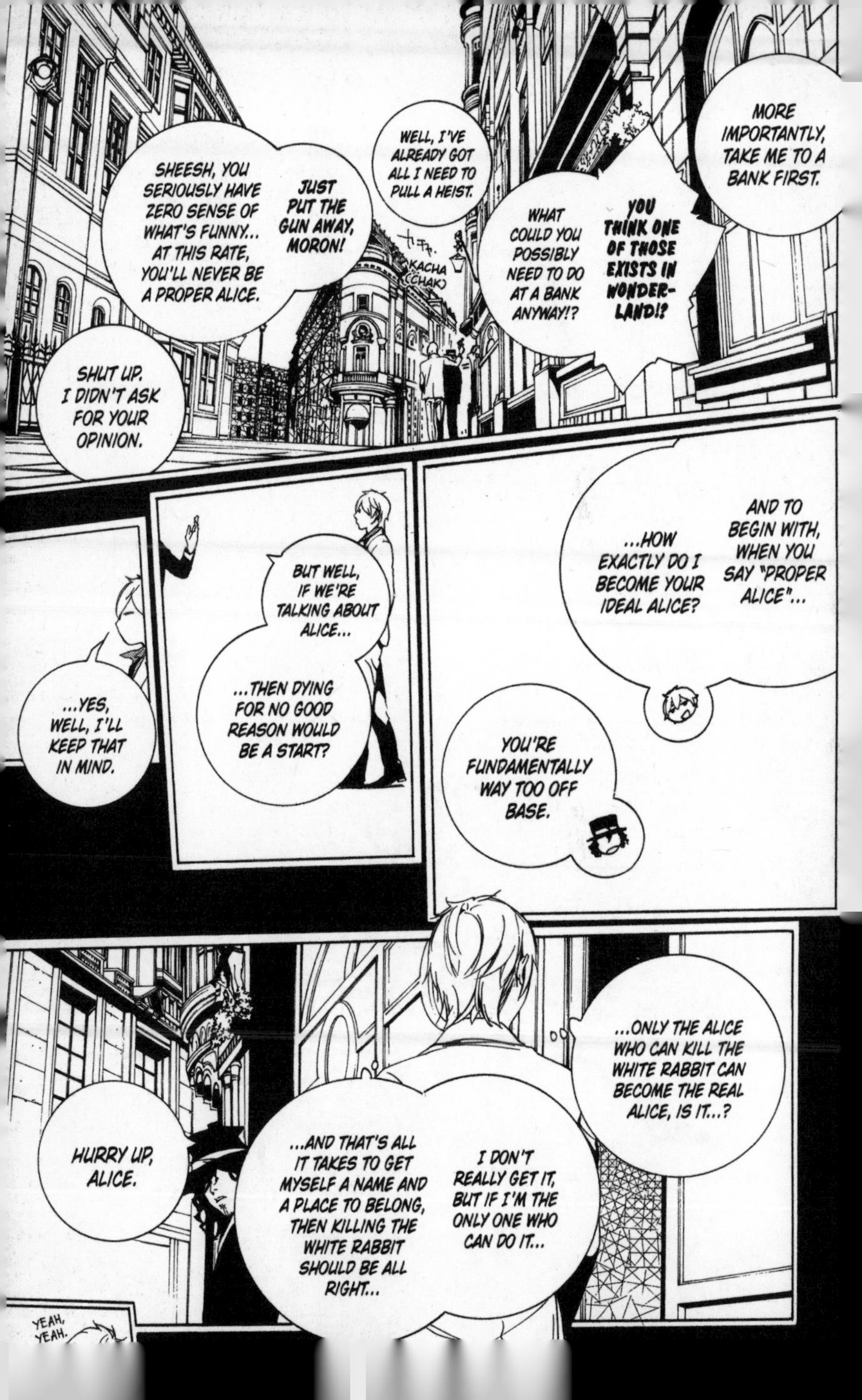
MORE IMPORTANTLY, TAKE ME TO A BANK FIRST.
YOU THINK ONE OF THOSE EXISTS IN WONDERLAND!?
WHAT COULD YOU POSSIBLY NEED TO DO AT A BANK ANYWAY!?
WELL, I'VE ALREADY GOT ALL I NEED TO PULL A HEIST.
KACHA (CHAK)
JUST PUT THE GUN AWAY, MORON!
SHEESH, YOU SERIOUSLY HAVE ZERO SENSE OF WHAT'S FUNNY... AT THIS RATE, YOU'LL NEVER BE A PROPER ALICE.
SHUT UP. I DIDN'T ASK FOR YOUR OPINION.
AND TO BEGIN WITH, WHEN YOU SAY "PROPER ALICE"...
...HOW EXACTLY DO I BECOME YOUR IDEAL ALICE?
YOU'RE FUNDAMENTALLY WAY TOO OFF BASE.
BUT WELL, IF WE'RE TALKING ABOUT ALICE...
...THEN DYING FOR NO GOOD REASON WOULD BE A START?
...YES, WELL, I'LL KEEP THAT IN MIND.
...ONLY THE ALICE WHO CAN KILL THE WHITE RABBIT CAN BECOME THE REAL ALICE, IS IT...?
I DON'T REALLY GET IT, BUT IF I'M THE ONLY ONE WHO CAN DO IT...
...AND THAT'S ALL IT TAKES TO GET MYSELF A NAME AND A PLACE TO BELONG, THEN KILLING THE WHITE RABBIT SHOULD BE ALL RIGHT...
HURRY UP, ALICE.
YEAH, YEAH.

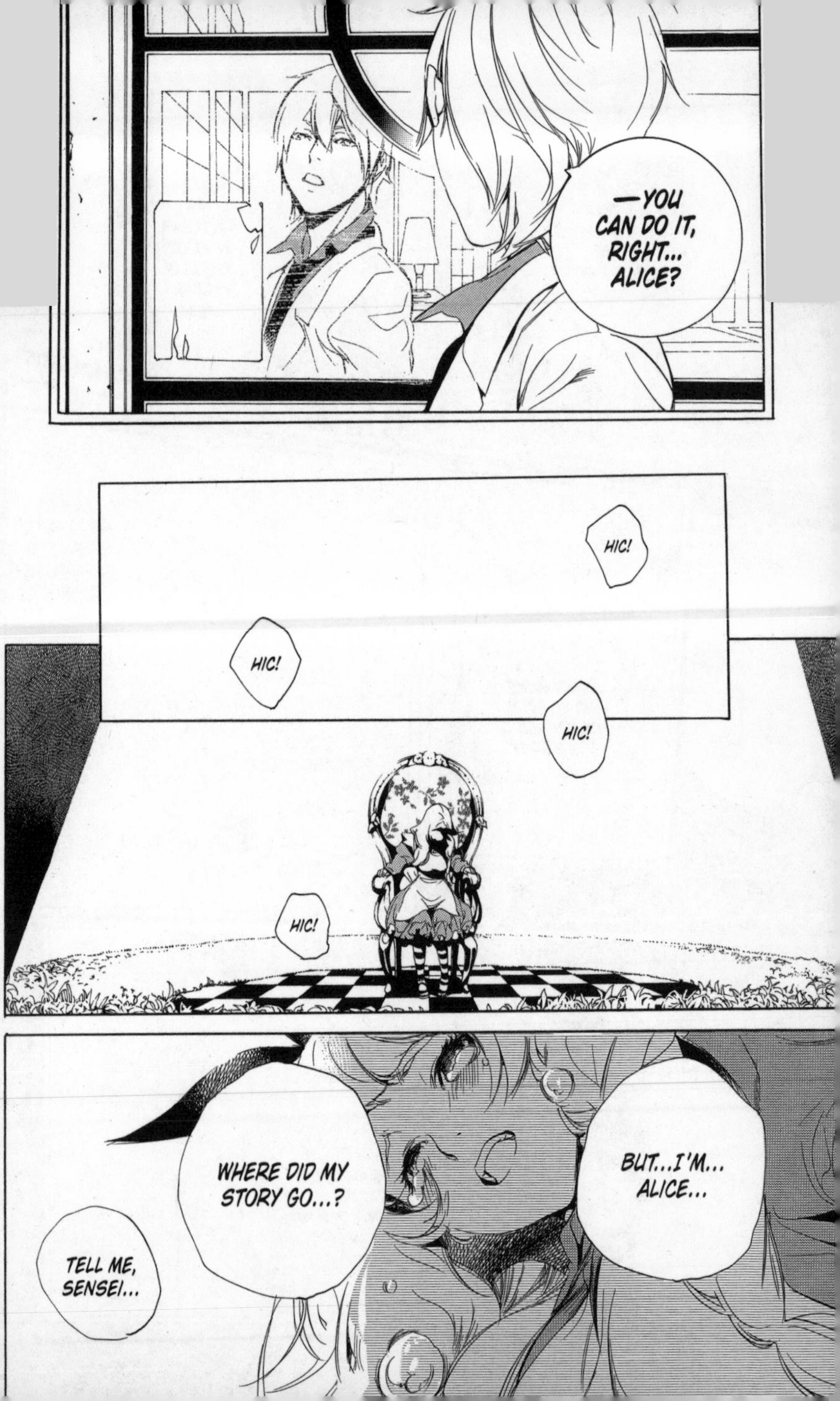
—YOU CAN DO IT, RIGHT... ALICE?
HIC!
HIC!
HIC!
HIC!
BUT...I'M... ALICE...
WHERE DID MY STORY GO...?
TELL ME, SENSEI...

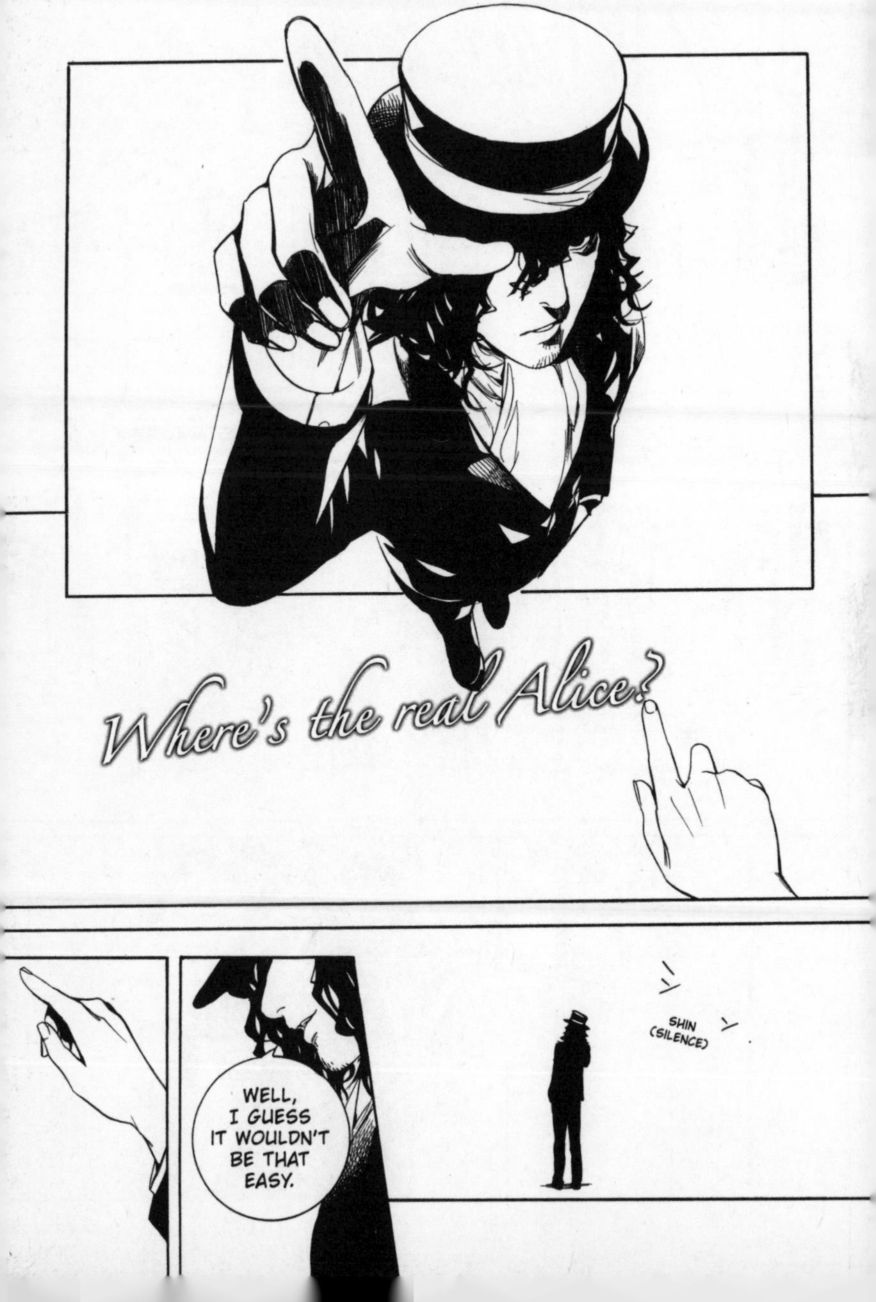
Where's the real Alice?
SHIN
(SILENCE)
WELL, I GUESS IT WOULDN'T BE THAT EASY.

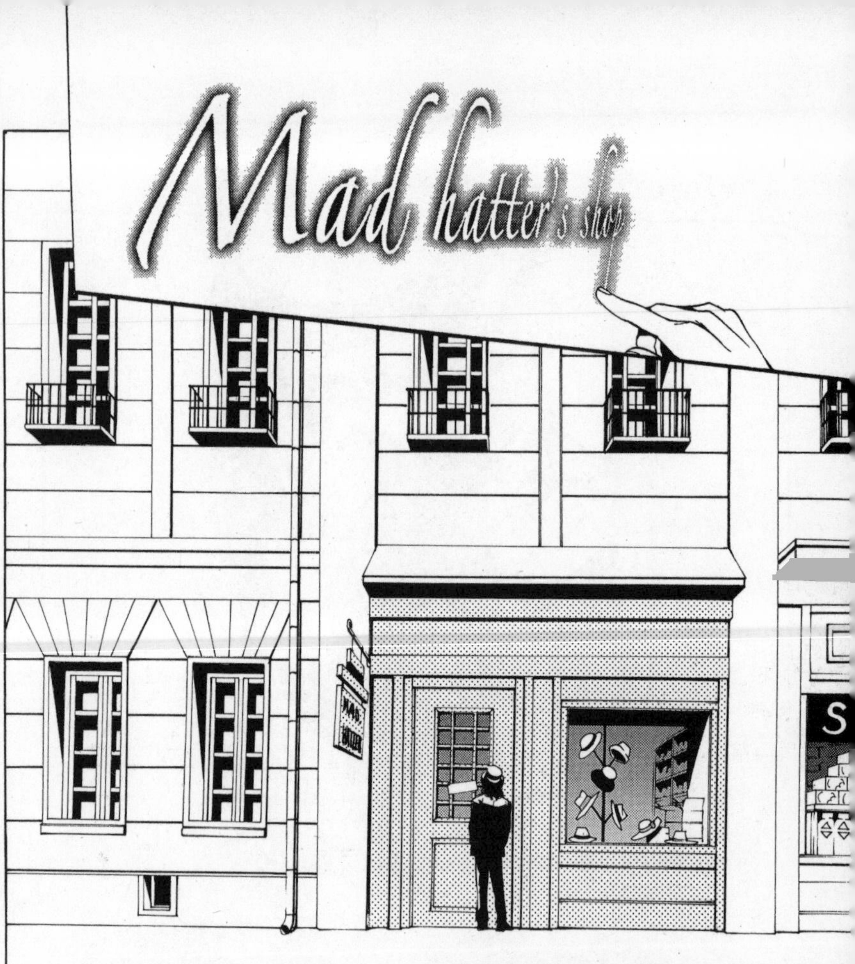
Mad hatter's shop

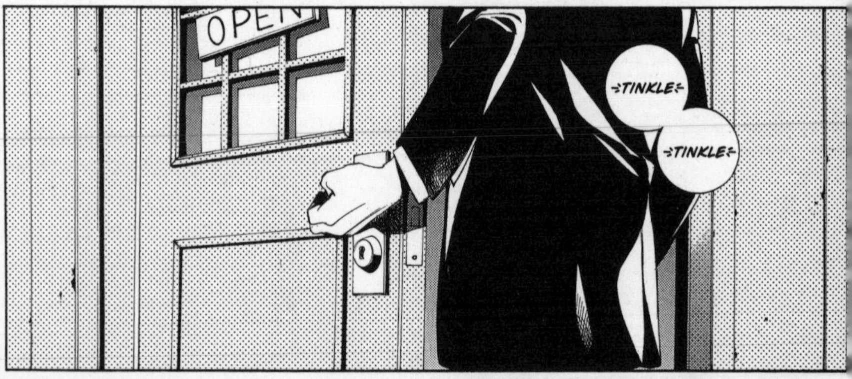
OPEN
TINKLE
TINKLE

Chapter 64

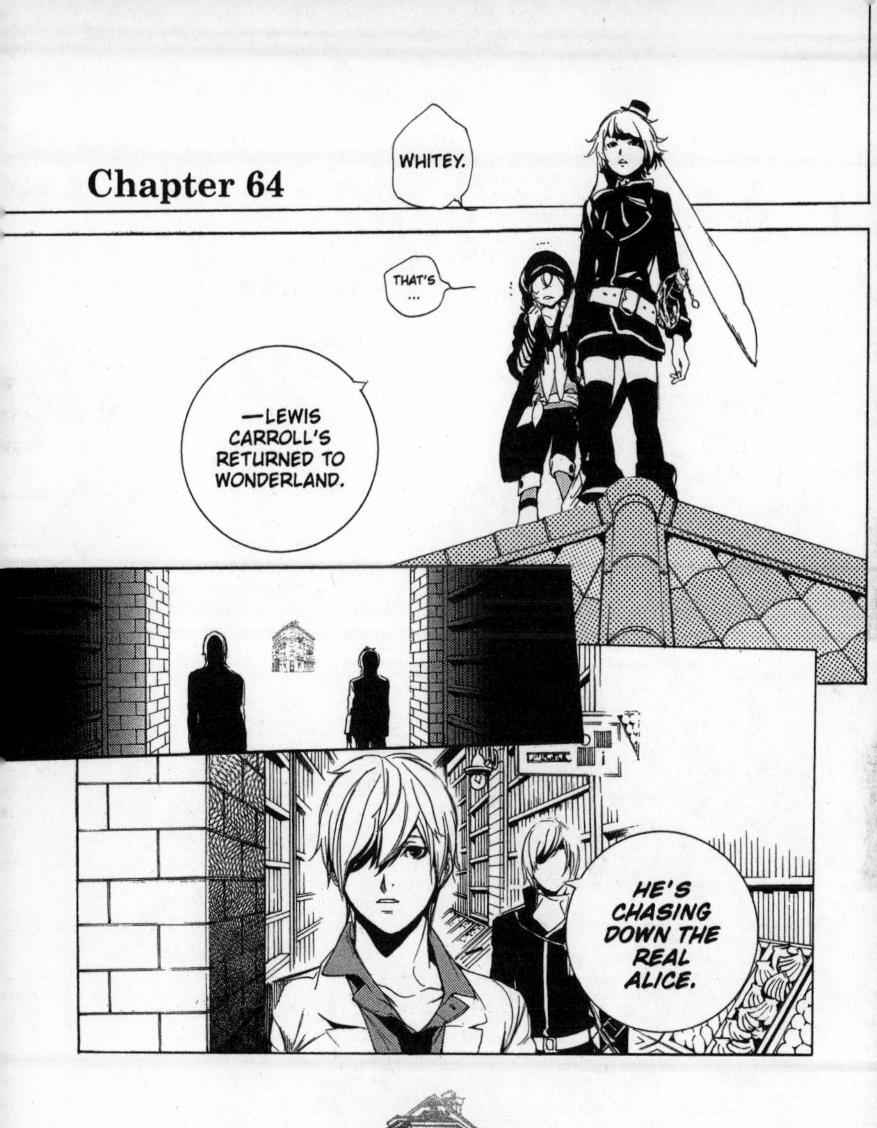
WHITEY.
THAT'S ...
—LEWIS CARROLL'S RETURNED TO WONDERLAND.
HE'S CHASING DOWN THE REAL ALICE.

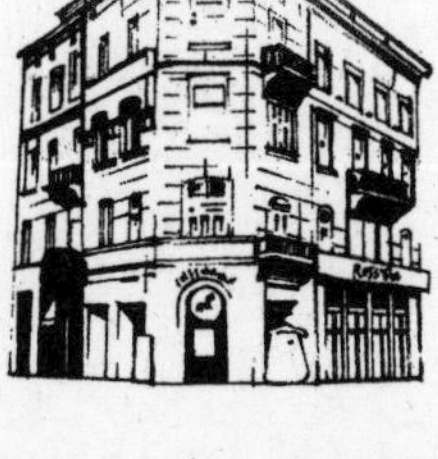

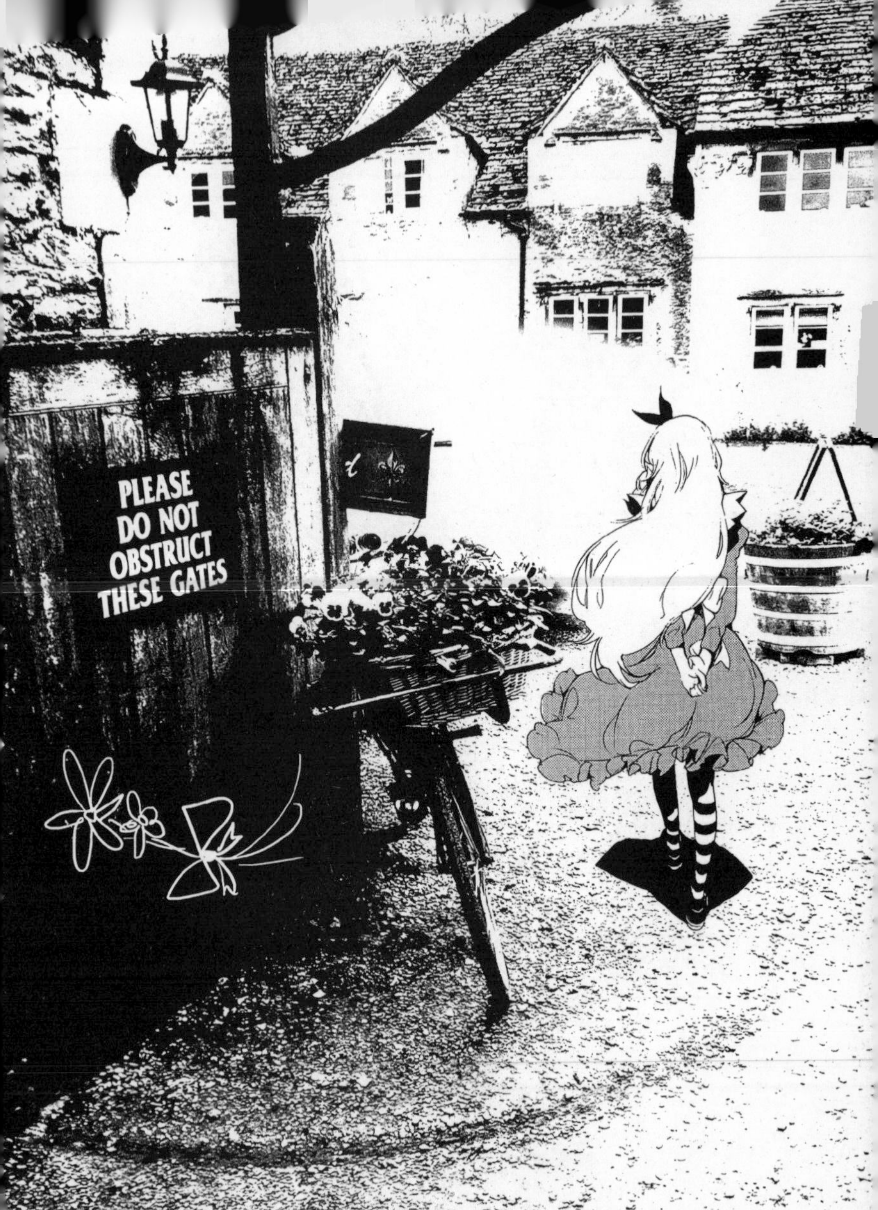
PLEASE
DO NOT
OBSTRUCT
THESE GATES

Chapter 64 Ordinaries of Life.

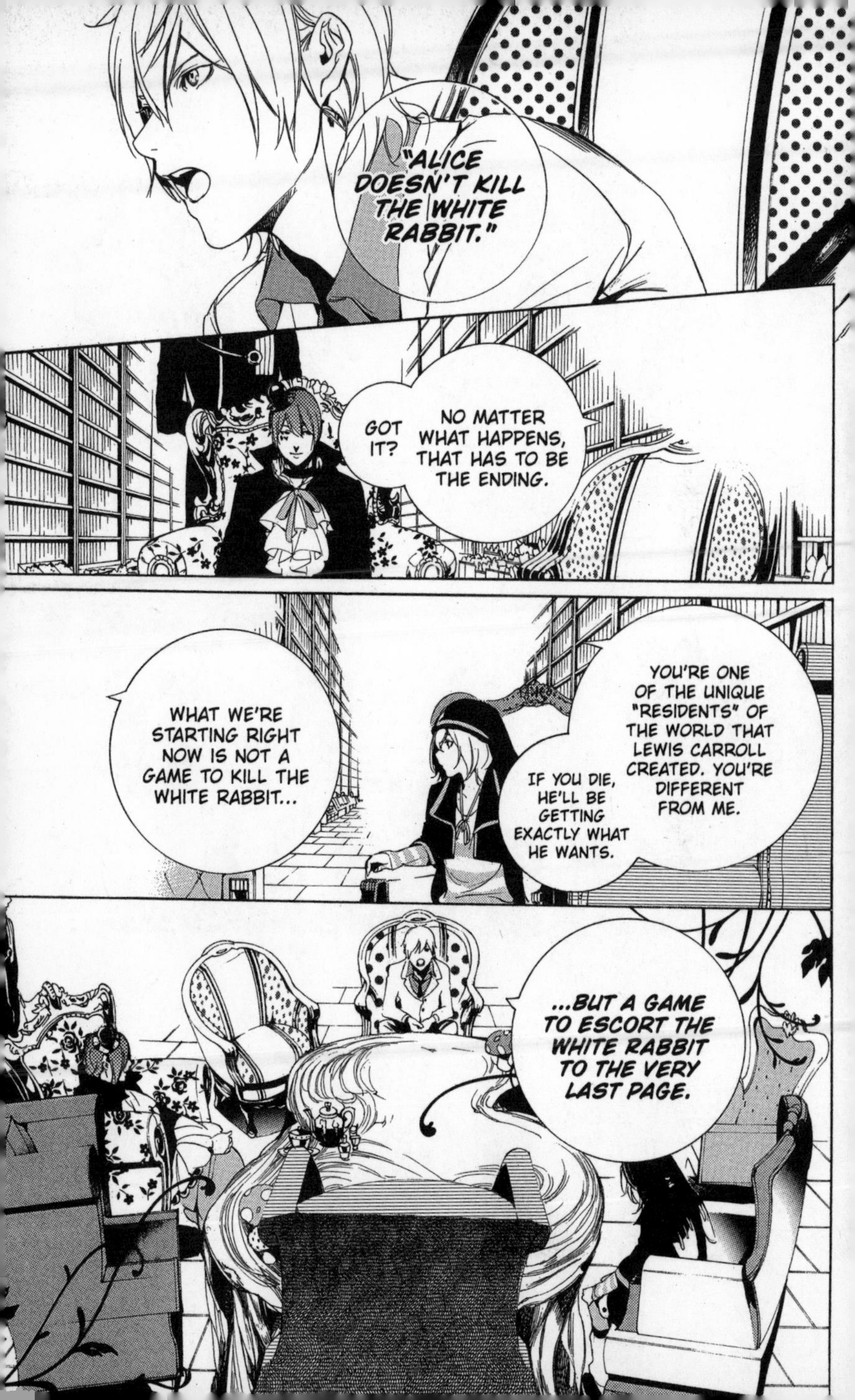
"ALICE DOESN'T KILL THE WHITE RABBIT."
NO MATTER WHAT HAPPENS, THAT HAS TO BE THE ENDING.
GOT IT?
YOU'RE ONE OF THE UNIQUE "RESIDENTS" OF THE WORLD THAT LEWIS CARROLL CREATED. YOU'RE DIFFERENT FROM ME.
IF YOU DIE, HE'LL BE GETTING EXACTLY WHAT HE WANTS.
WHAT WE'RE STARTING RIGHT NOW IS NOT A GAME TO KILL THE WHITE RABBIT...
...BUT A GAME TO ESCORT THE WHITE RABBIT TO THE VERY LAST PAGE.

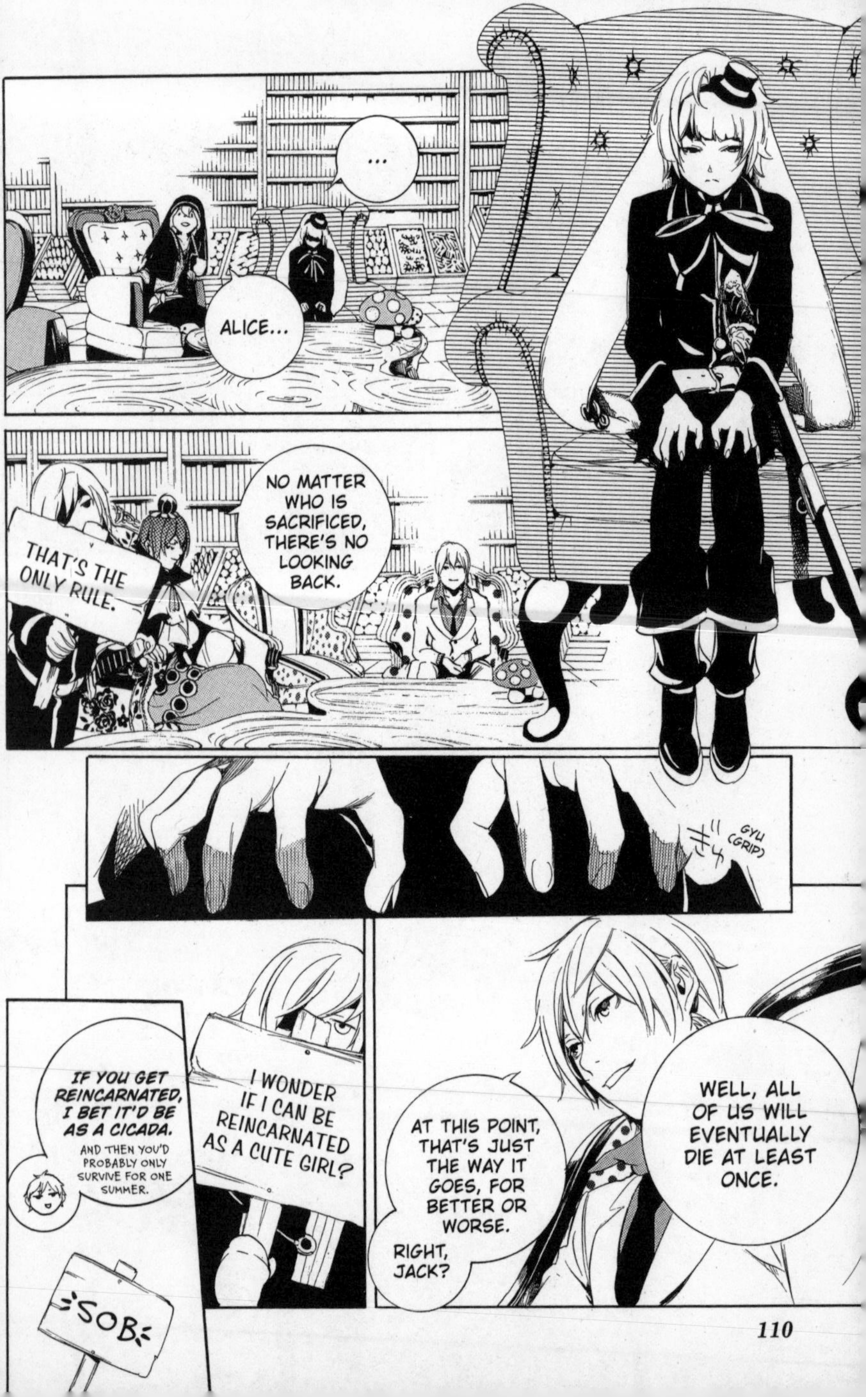
...
ALICE...
NO MATTER WHO IS SACRIFICED, THERE'S NO LOOKING BACK.
THAT'S THE ONLY RULE.
GYU (GRIP)
WELL, ALL OF US WILL EVENTUALLY DIE AT LEAST ONCE.
AT THIS POINT, THAT'S JUST THE WAY IT GOES, FOR BETTER OR WORSE.
RIGHT, JACK?
I WONDER IF I CAN BE REINCARNATED AS A CUTE GIRL?
IF YOU GET REINCARNATED, I BET IT'D BE AS A CICADA.
AND THEN YOU'D PROBABLY ONLY SURVIVE FOR ONE SUMMER.
SOB

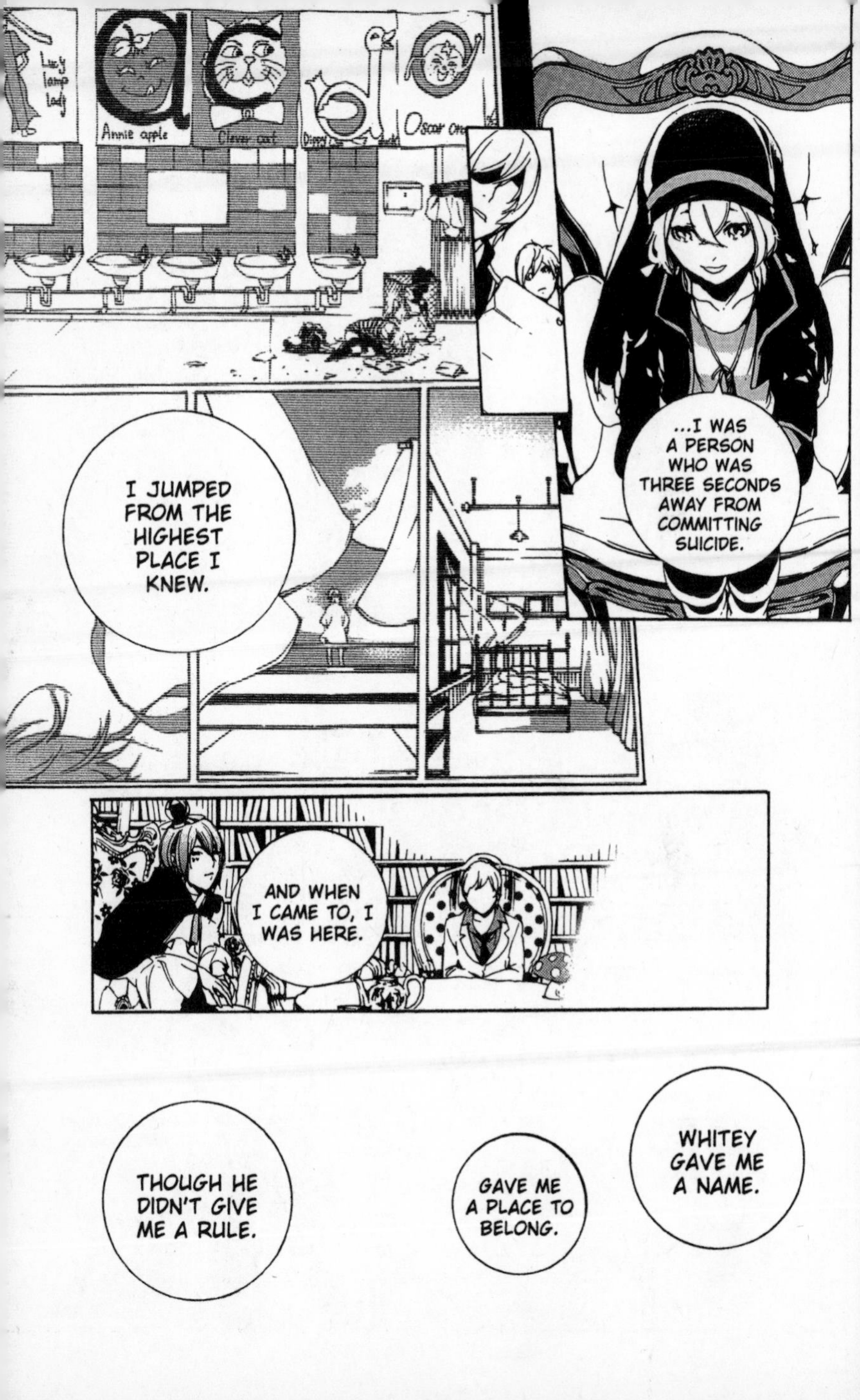
...I WAS A PERSON WHO WAS THREE SECONDS AWAY FROM COMMITTING SUICIDE.
Lucy lamp lady
Annie apple
Clever cat
I JUMPED FROM THE HIGHEST PLACE I KNEW.
AND WHEN I CAME TO, I WAS HERE.
WHITEY GAVE ME A NAME.
GAVE ME A PLACE TO BELONG.
THOUGH HE DIDN'T GIVE ME A RULE.

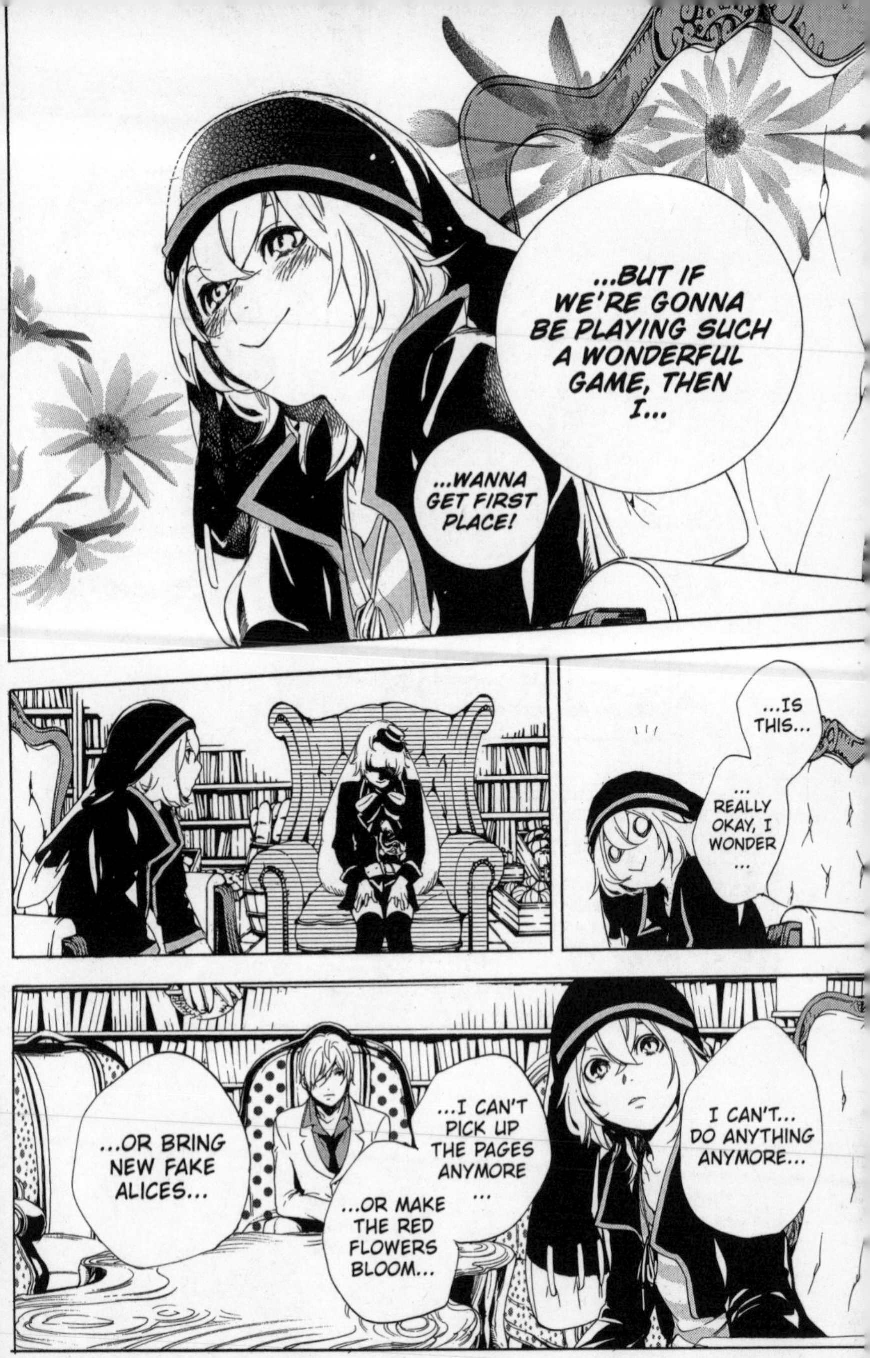
...BUT IF WE'RE GONNA BE PLAYING SUCH A WONDERFUL GAME, THEN I...
...WANNA GET FIRST PLACE!
...IS THIS...
...REALLY OKAY, I WONDER...
I CAN'T... DO ANYTHING ANYMORE...
...I CAN'T PICK UP THE PAGES ANYMORE...
...OR MAKE THE RED FLOWERS BLOOM...
...OR BRING NEW FAKE ALICES...

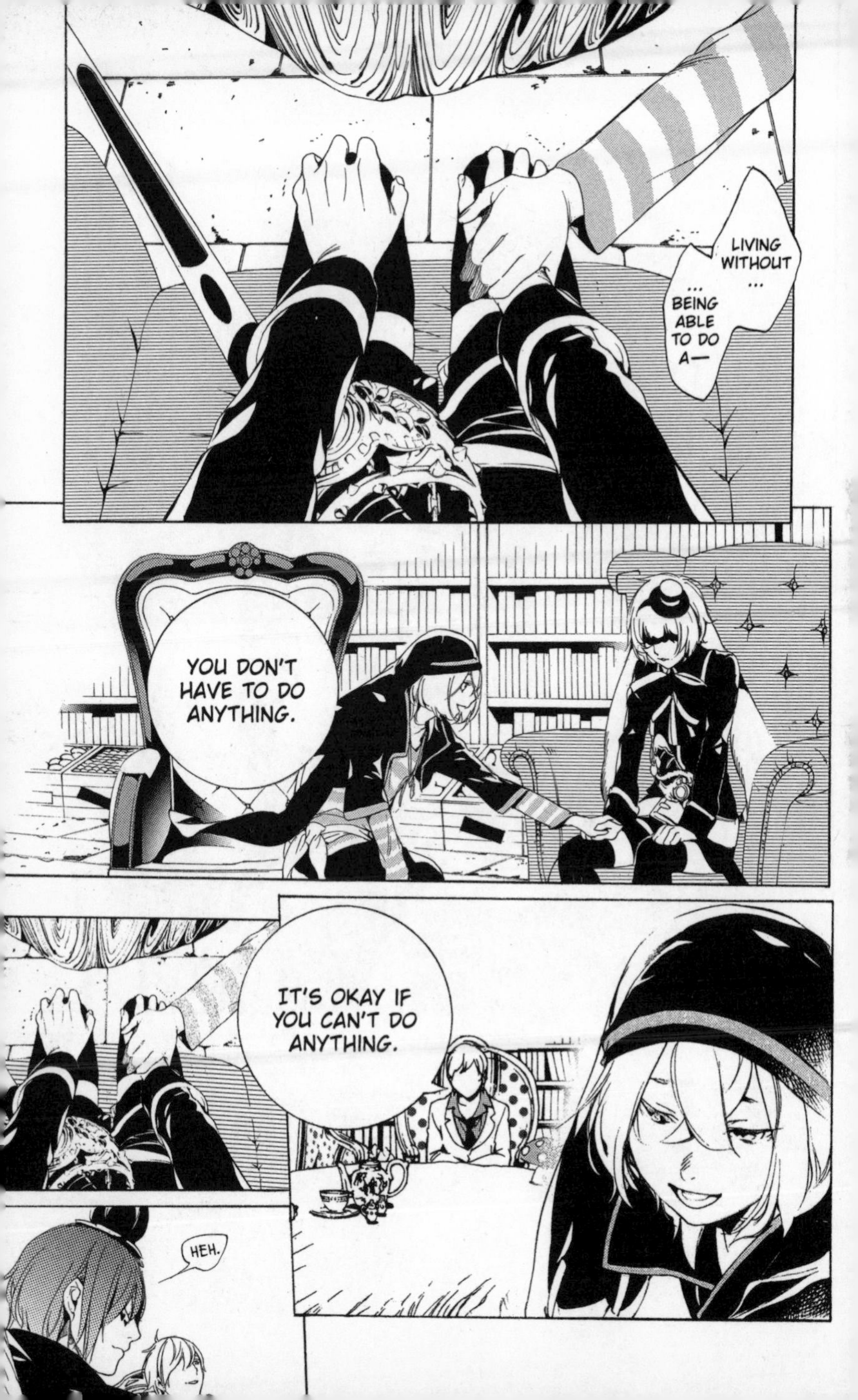
LIVING WITHOUT ... ... BEING ABLE TO DO A—
YOU DON'T HAVE TO DO ANYTHING.
IT'S OKAY IF YOU CAN'T DO ANYTHING.
HEH.

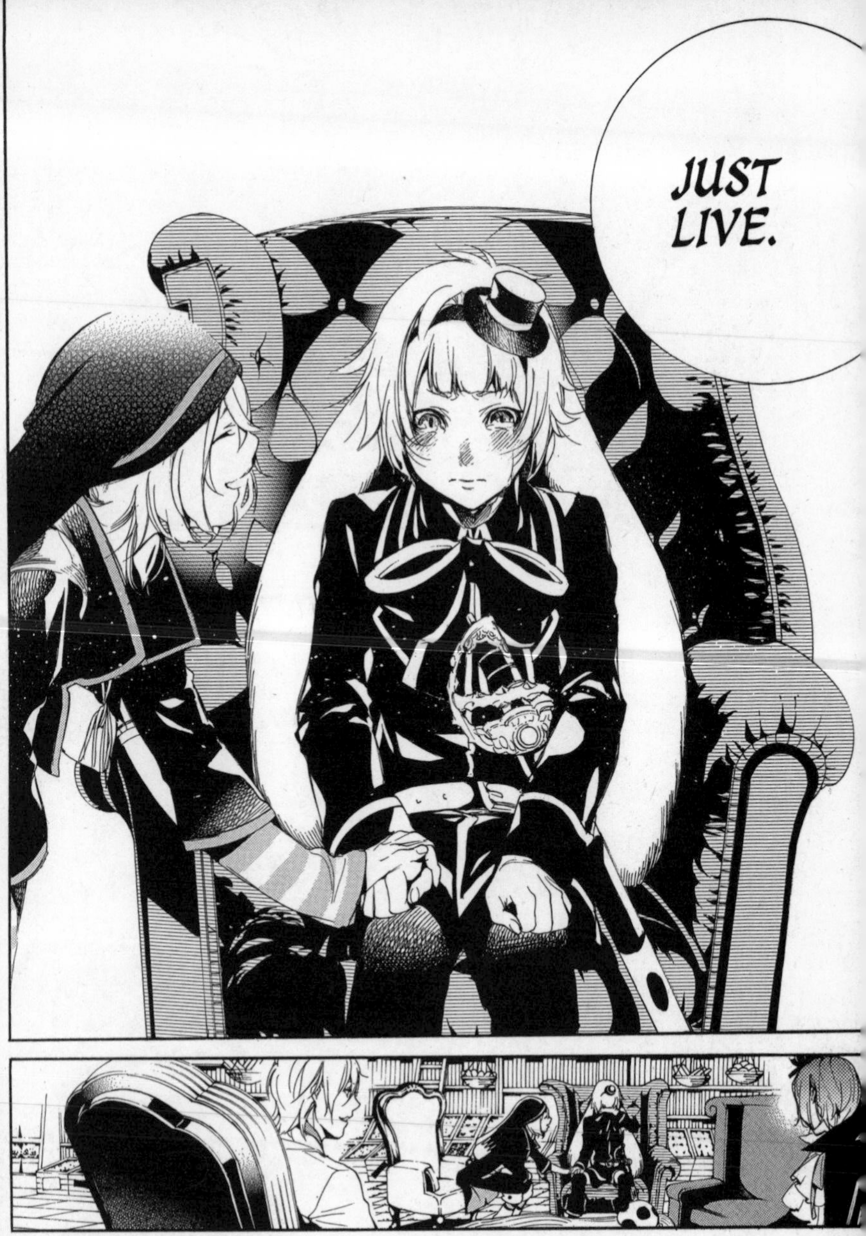
JUST LIVE.

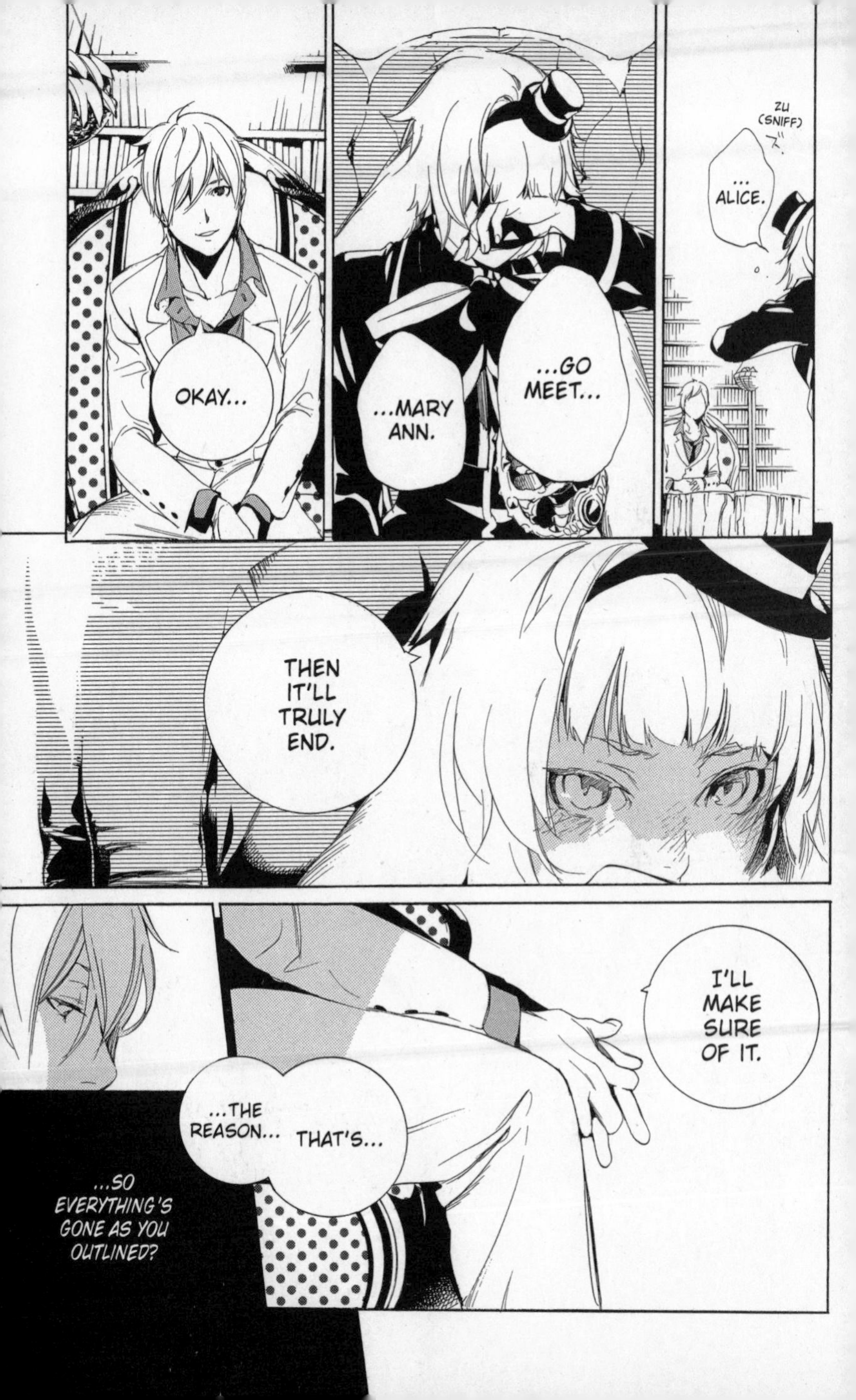

ZU (SNIFF)
...ALICE.
...GO MEET...
...MARY ANN.
OKAY...
THEN IT'LL TRULY END.
I'LL MAKE SURE OF IT.
THAT'S...
...THE REASON...
...SO EVERYTHING'S GONE AS YOU OUTLINED?

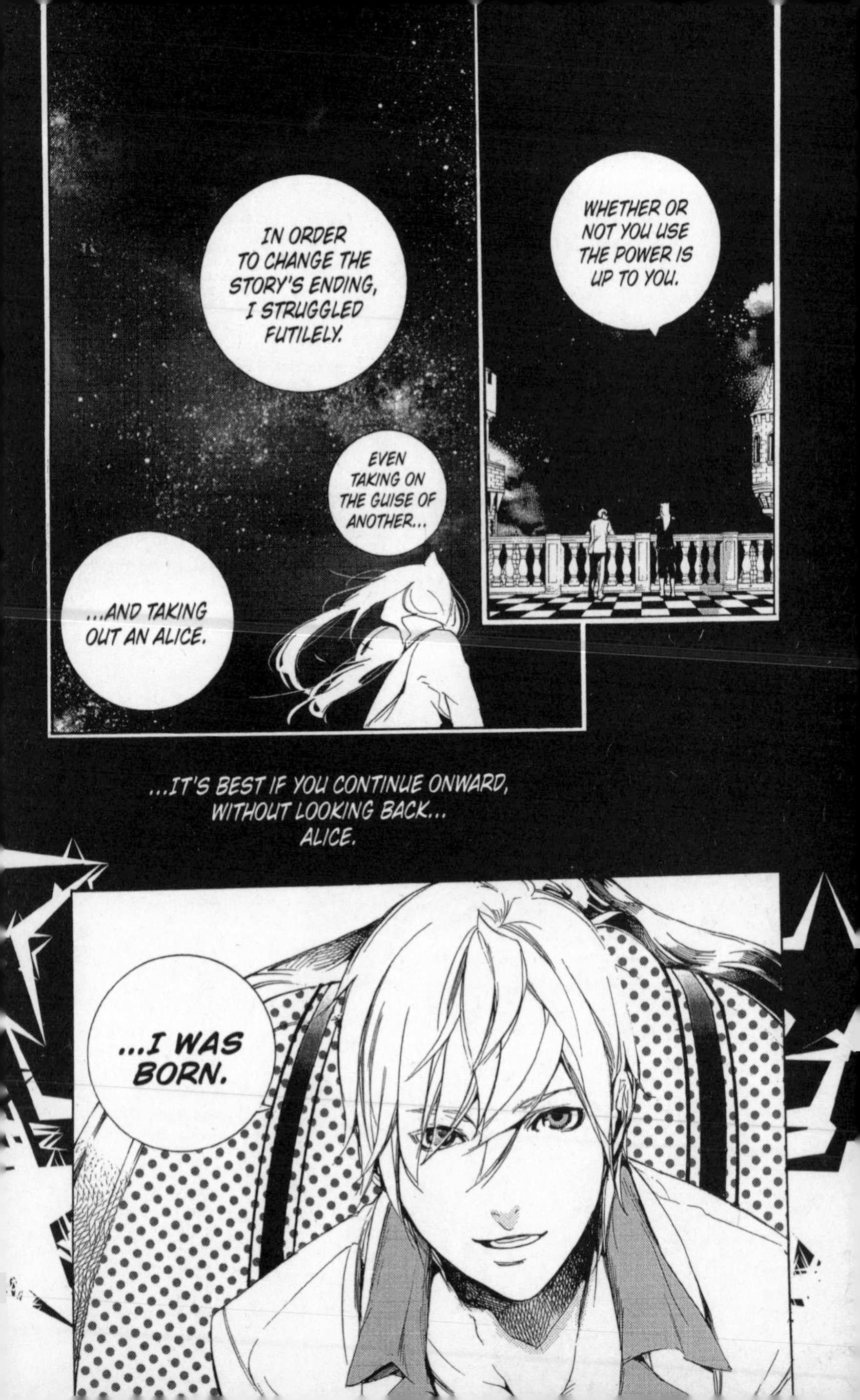
WHETHER OR NOT YOU USE THE POWER IS UP TO YOU.
IN ORDER TO CHANGE THE STORY'S ENDING, I STRUGGLED FUTILELY.
EVEN TAKING ON THE GUISE OF ANOTHER...
...AND TAKING OUT AN ALICE.
...IT'S BEST IF YOU CONTINUE ONWARD, WITHOUT LOOKING BACK... ALICE.
...I WAS BORN.

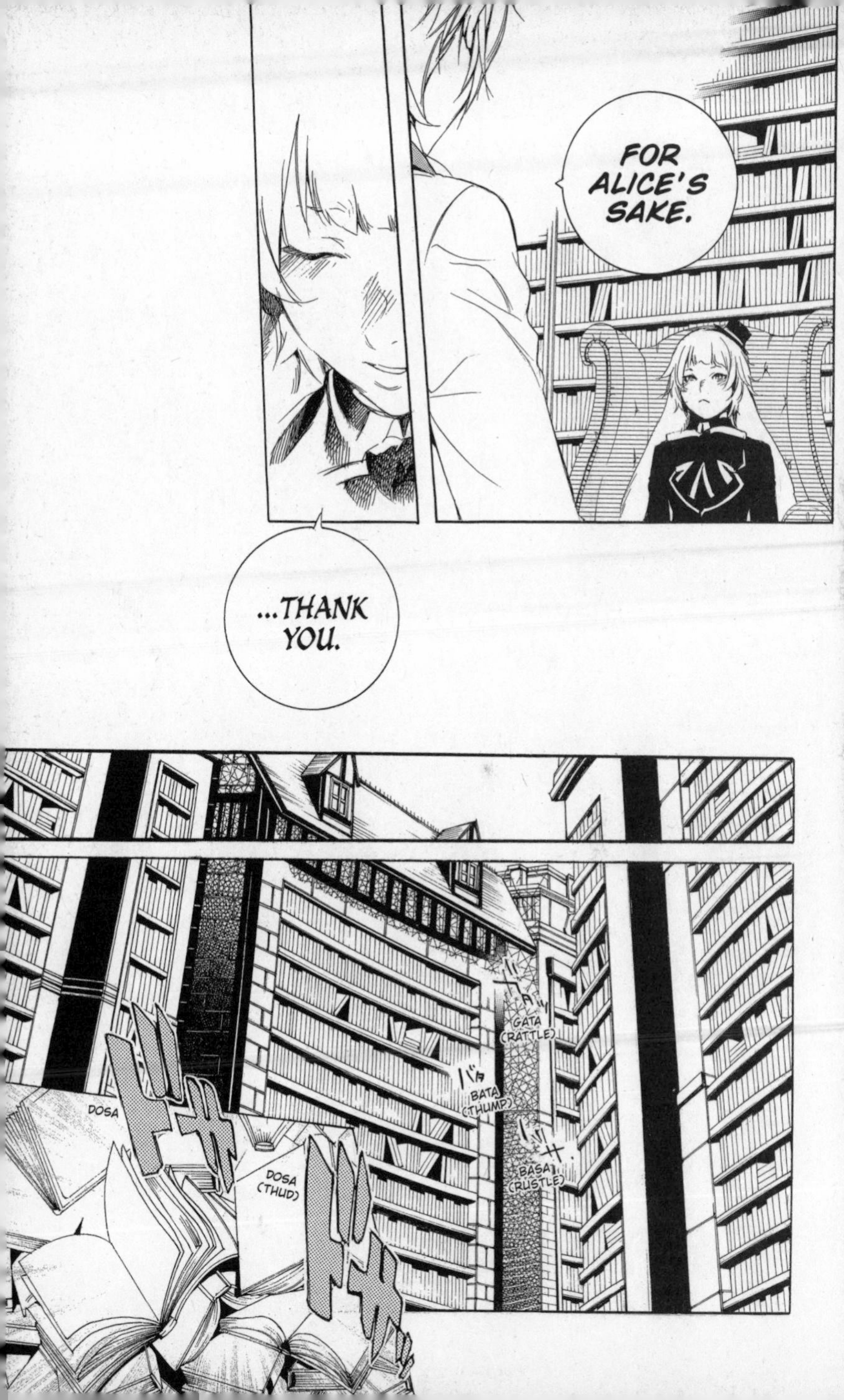

FOR ALICE'S SAKE.
...THANK YOU.
GATA (RATTLE)
BATA (THUMP)
BASA (RUSTLE)
DOSA (THUD)
DOSA

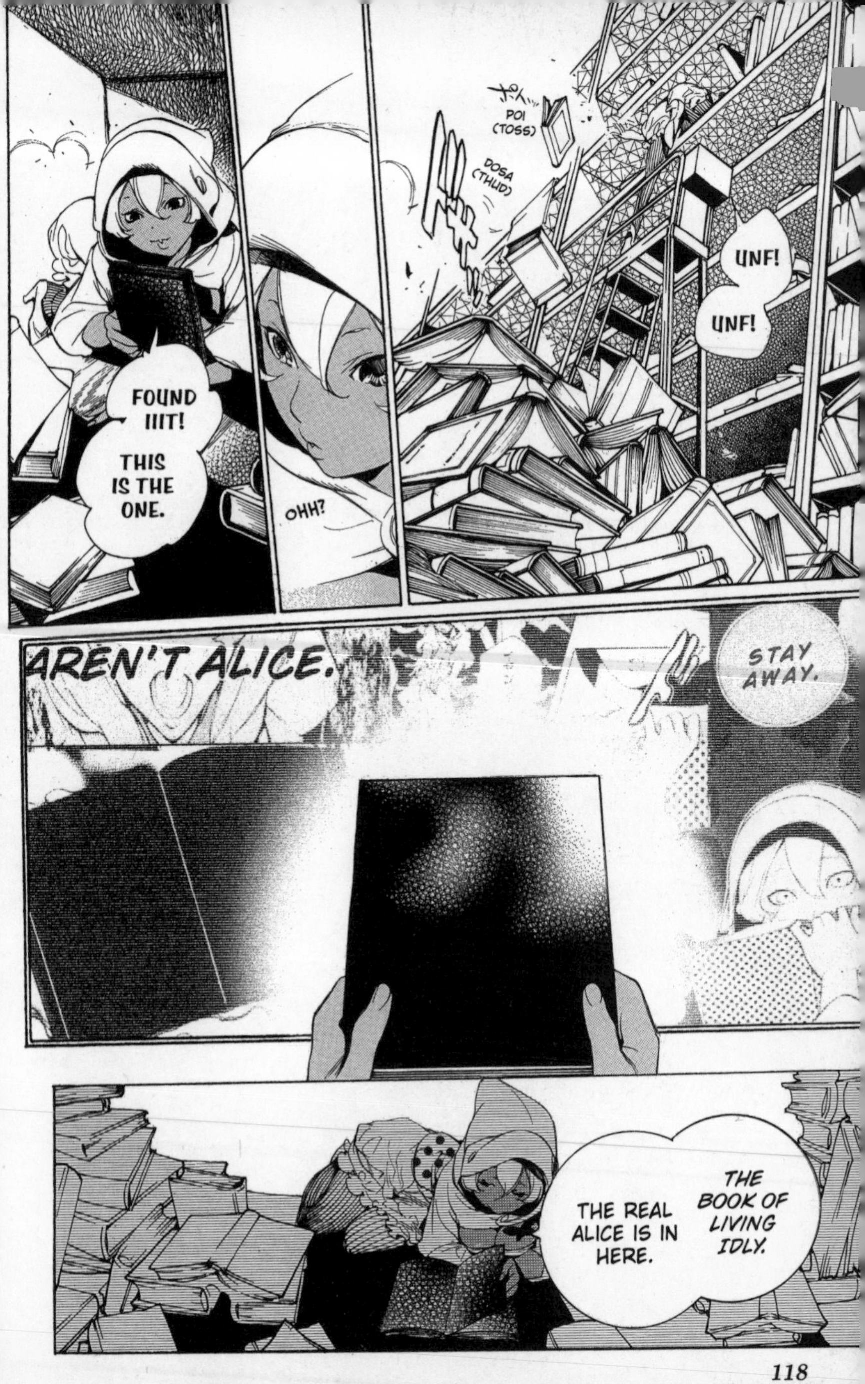
POI (TOSS)
DOSA (THUD)
UNF!
UNF!
OHH?
FOUND IIIT!
THIS IS THE ONE.
STAY AWAY.
AREN'T ALICE.
THE BOOK OF LIVING IDLY.
THE REAL ALICE IS IN HERE.

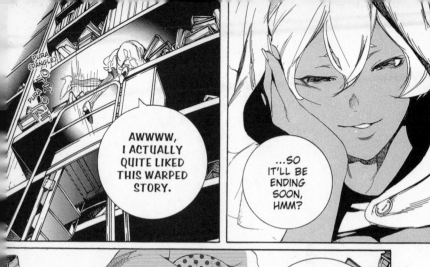

...SO IT'LL BE ENDING SOON, HMM?
PURA (DANGLE)
PURA
AWWWW, I ACTUALLY QUITE LIKED THIS WARPED STORY.
—IN THAT CASE, SHALL I TELL YOU HOW TO KEEP IT FROM ENDING?
EH?
DAN (BLAM)

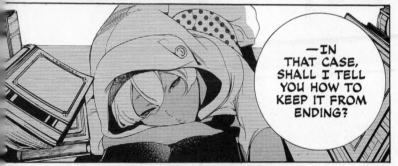

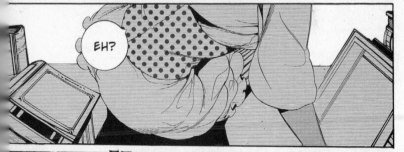

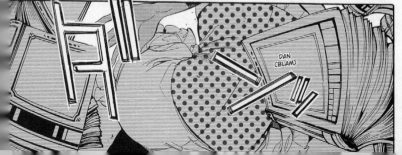

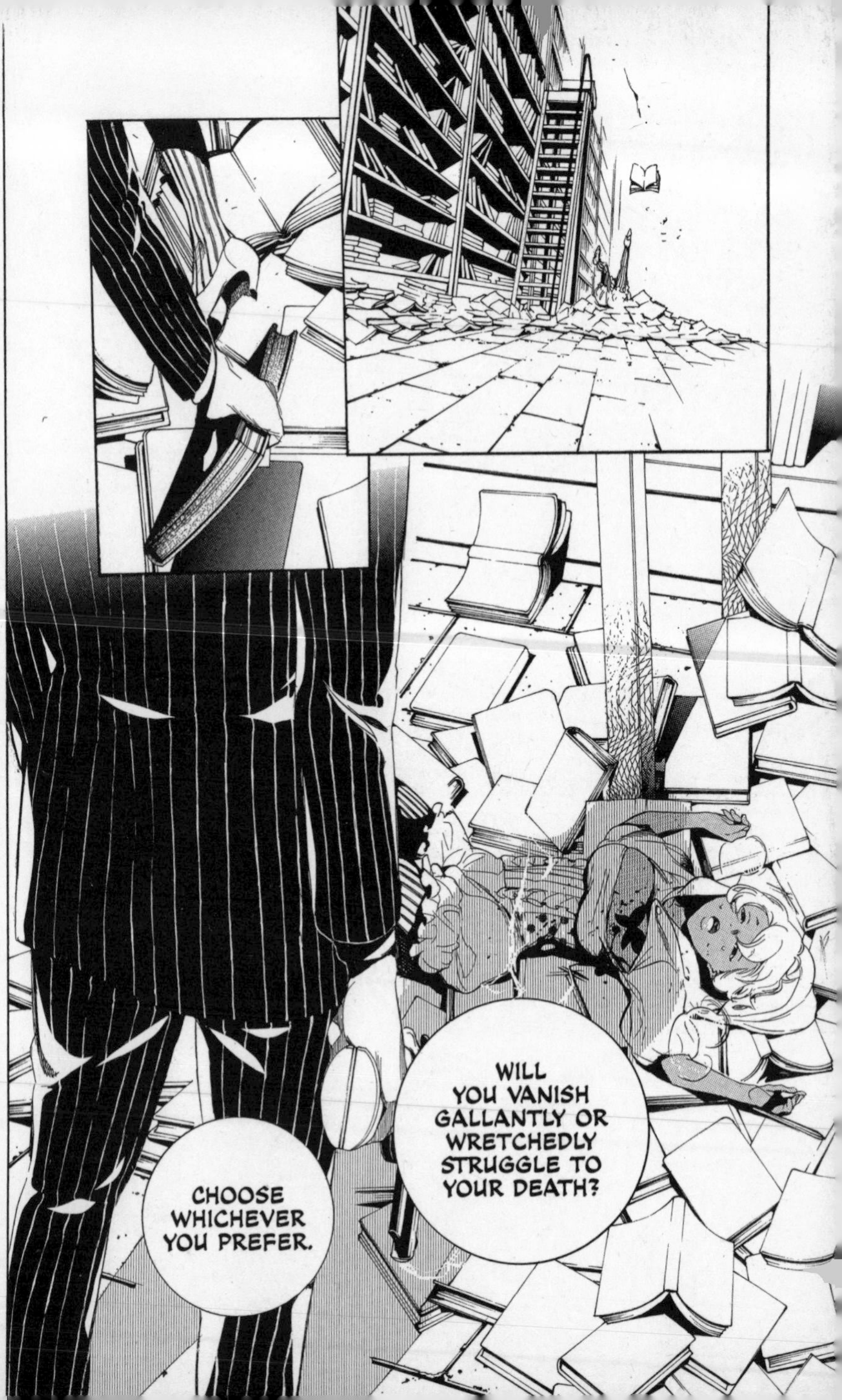
WILL YOU VANISH GALLANTLY OR WRETCHEDLY STRUGGLE TO YOUR DEATH?
CHOOSE WHICHEVER YOU PREFER.

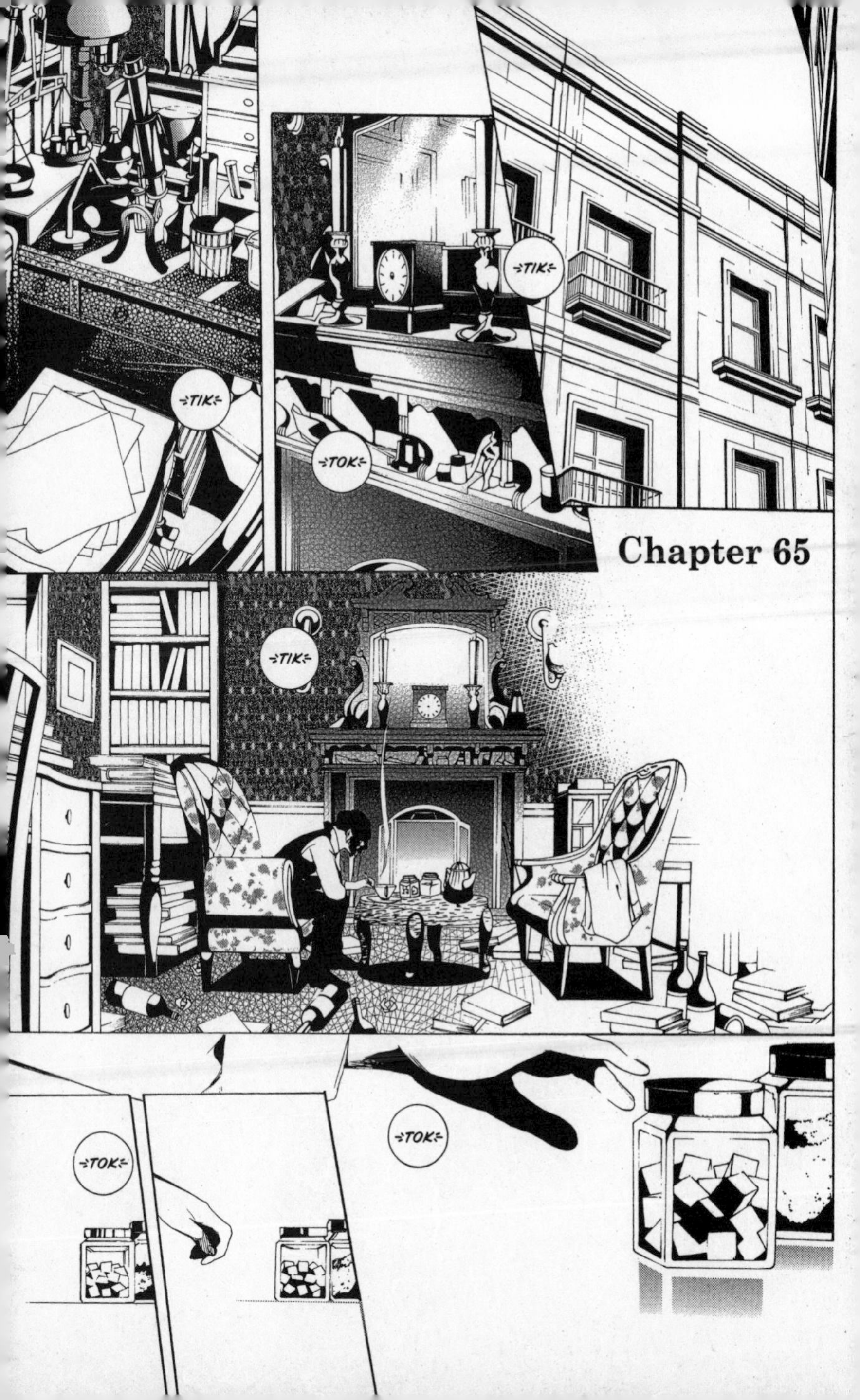
Chapter 65
TIK
TOK
TIK
TIK
TOK
TOK

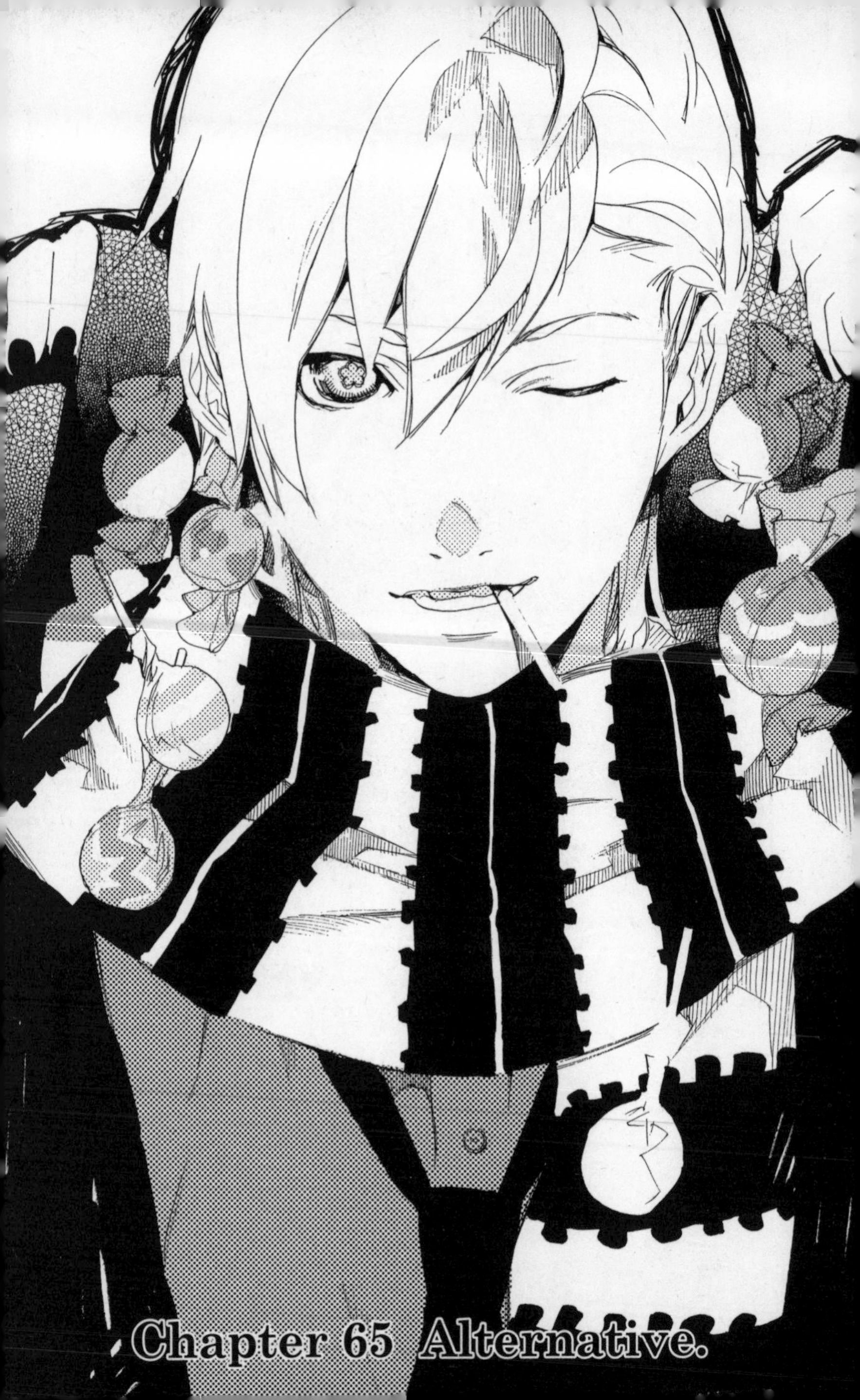

Chapter 65 Alternative.

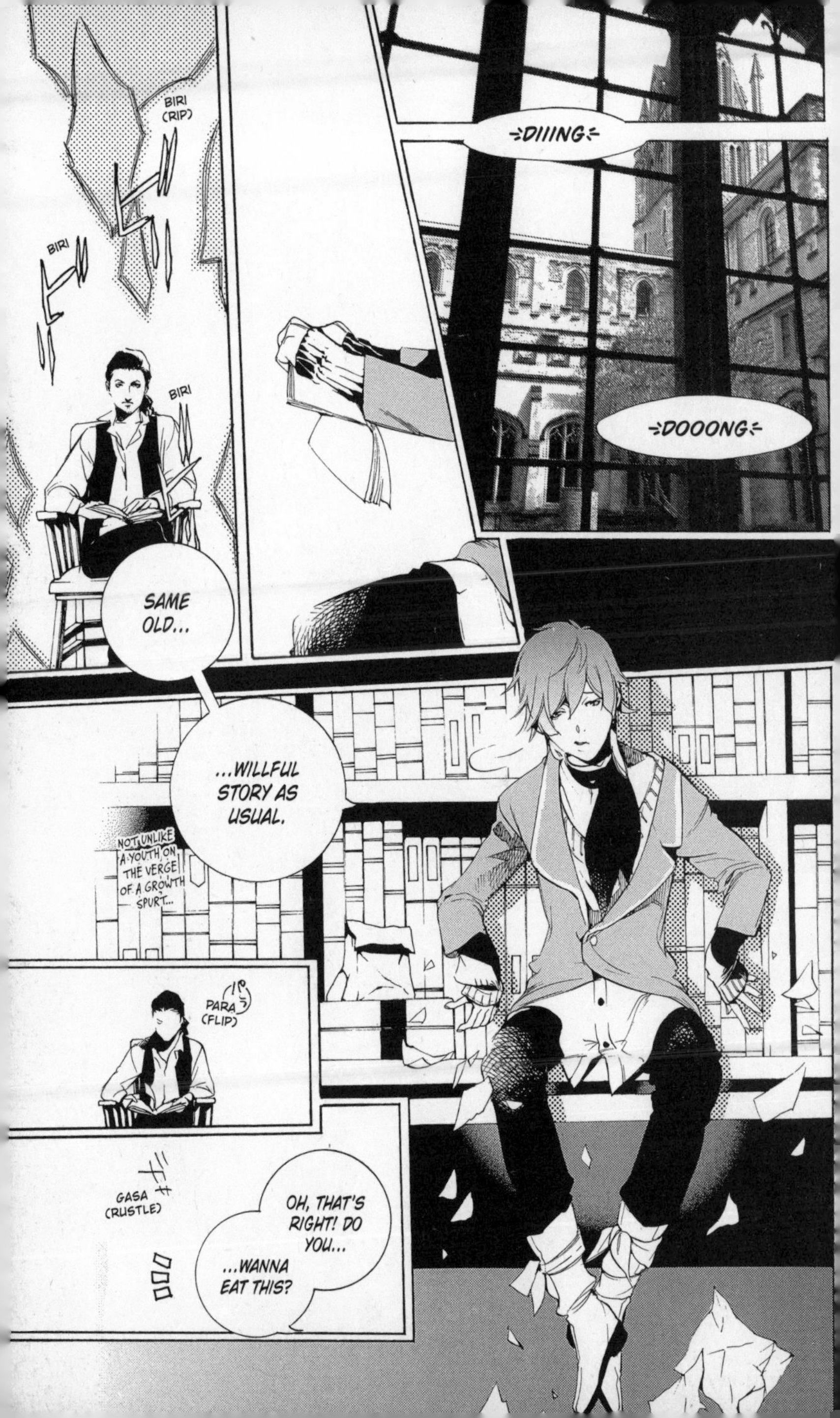

-DIIING-
-DOOONG-
BIRI (RIP)
BIRI
BIRI
SAME OLD...
...WILLFUL STORY AS USUAL.
NOT UNLIKE A YOUTH ON THE VERGE OF A GROWTH SPURT...
PARA (FLIP)
GASA (RUSTLE)
OH, THAT'S RIGHT! DO YOU...
...WANNA EAT THIS?

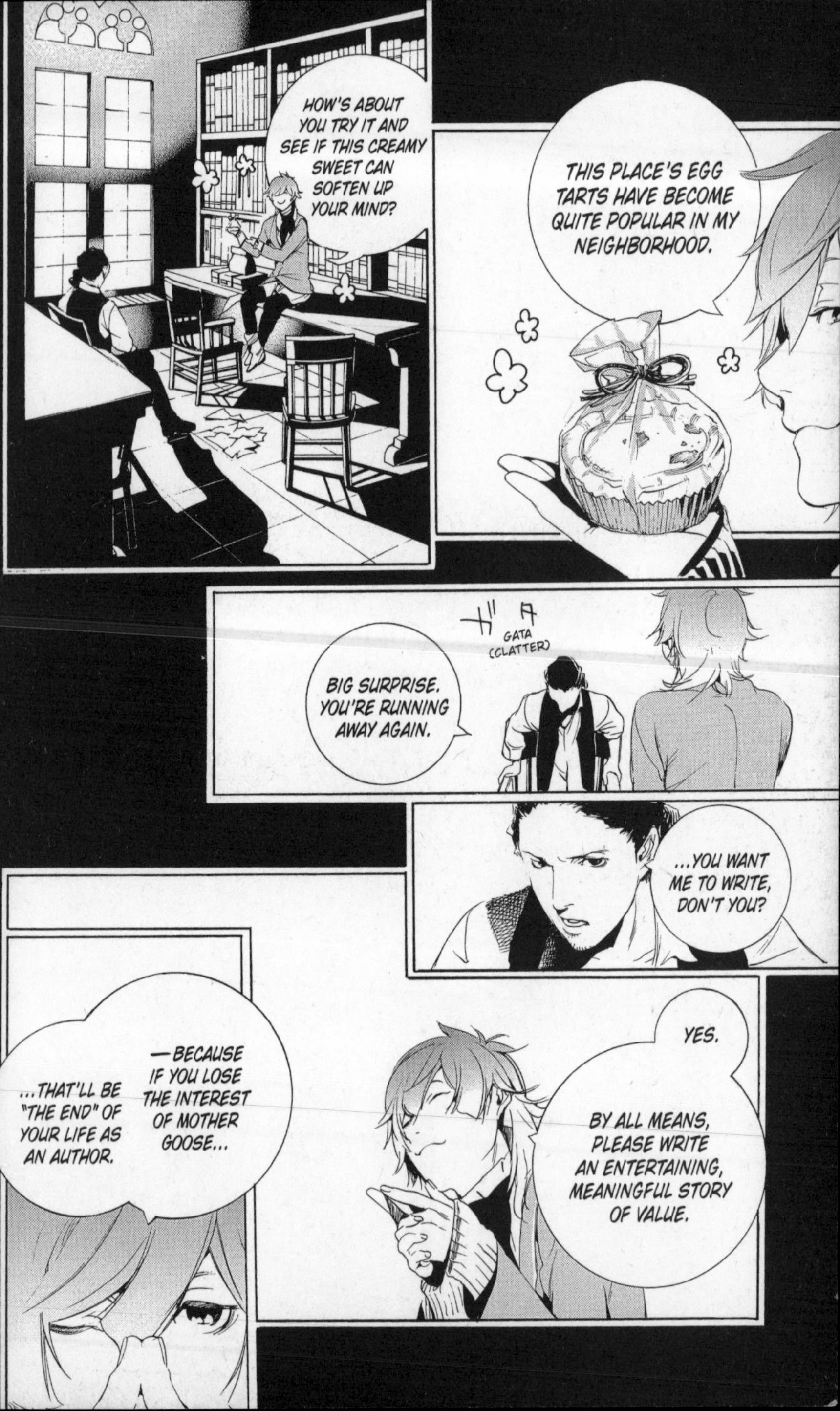
THIS PLACE'S EGG TARTS HAVE BECOME QUITE POPULAR IN MY NEIGHBORHOOD.
HOW'S ABOUT YOU TRY IT AND SEE IF THIS CREAMY SWEET CAN SOFTEN UP YOUR MIND?
ガタ
GATA (CLATTER)
BIG SURPRISE. YOU'RE RUNNING AWAY AGAIN.
...YOU WANT ME TO WRITE, DON'T YOU?
YES.
BY ALL MEANS, PLEASE WRITE AN ENTERTAINING, MEANINGFUL STORY OF VALUE.
—BECAUSE IF YOU LOSE THE INTEREST OF MOTHER GOOSE...
...THAT'LL BE "THE END" OF YOUR LIFE AS AN AUTHOR.

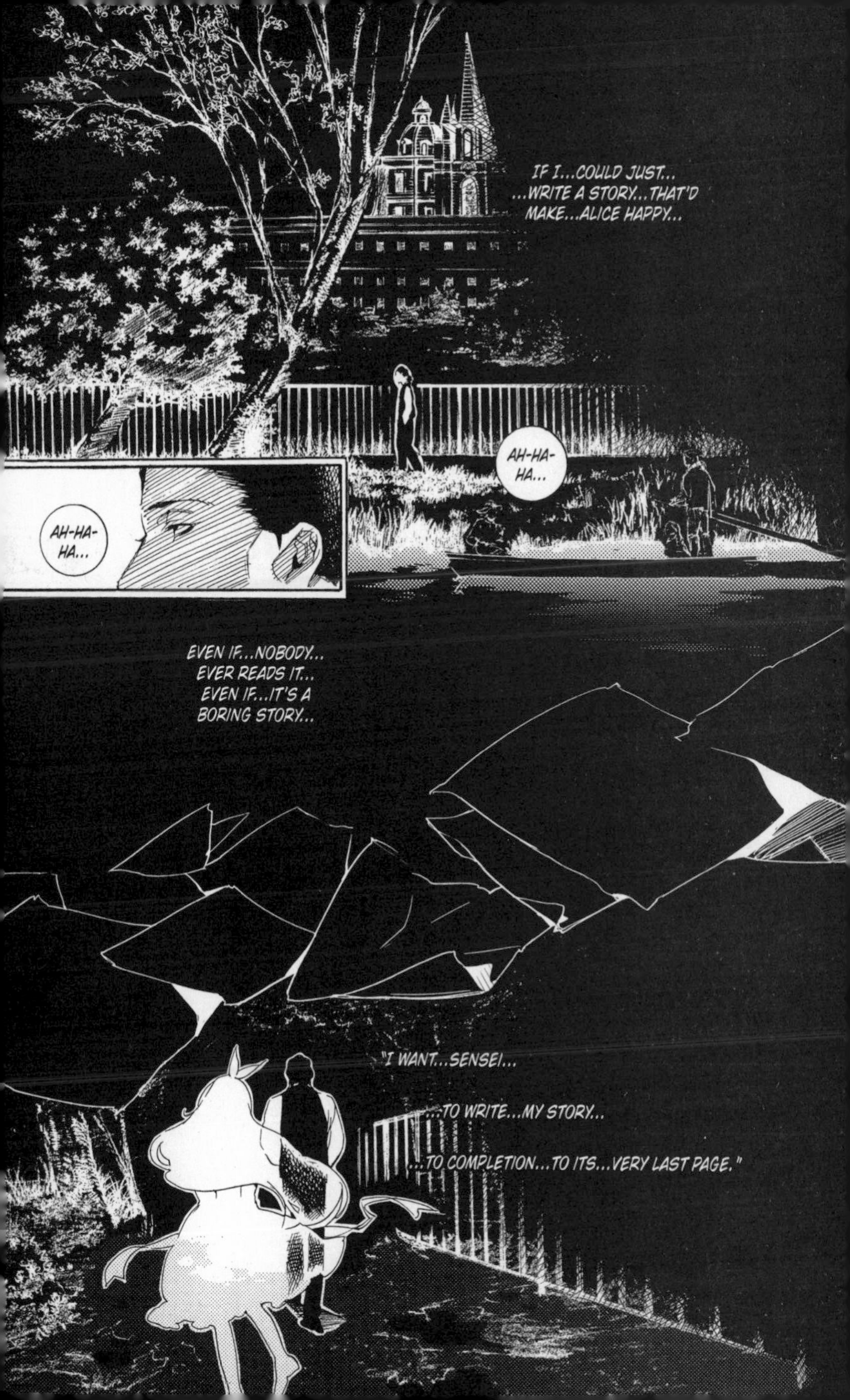
IF I...COULD JUST...
...WRITE A STORY...THAT'D
MAKE...ALICE HAPPY...
AH-HA-HA...
AH-HA-HA...
EVEN IF...NOBODY...
EVER READS IT...
EVEN IF...IT'S A
BORING STORY...
"I WANT...SENSEI...
...TO WRITE...MY STORY...
...TO COMPLETION...TO ITS...VERY LAST PAGE."

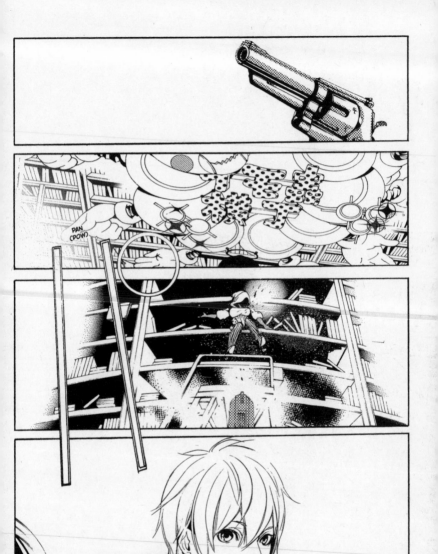

PAN
(POW)

126

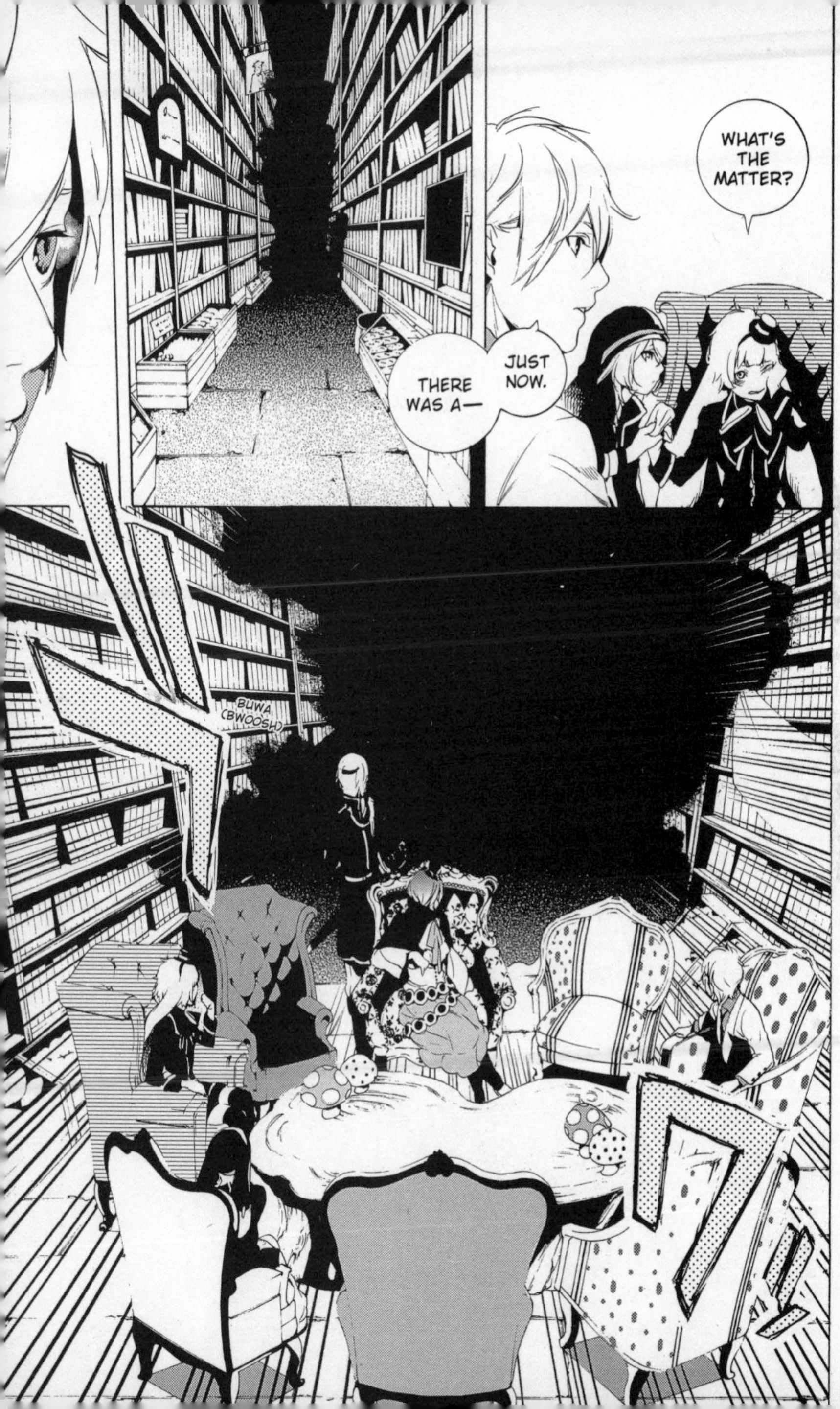
WHAT'S THE MATTER?
JUST NOW.
THERE WAS A—
BUWA (BWOOSH)

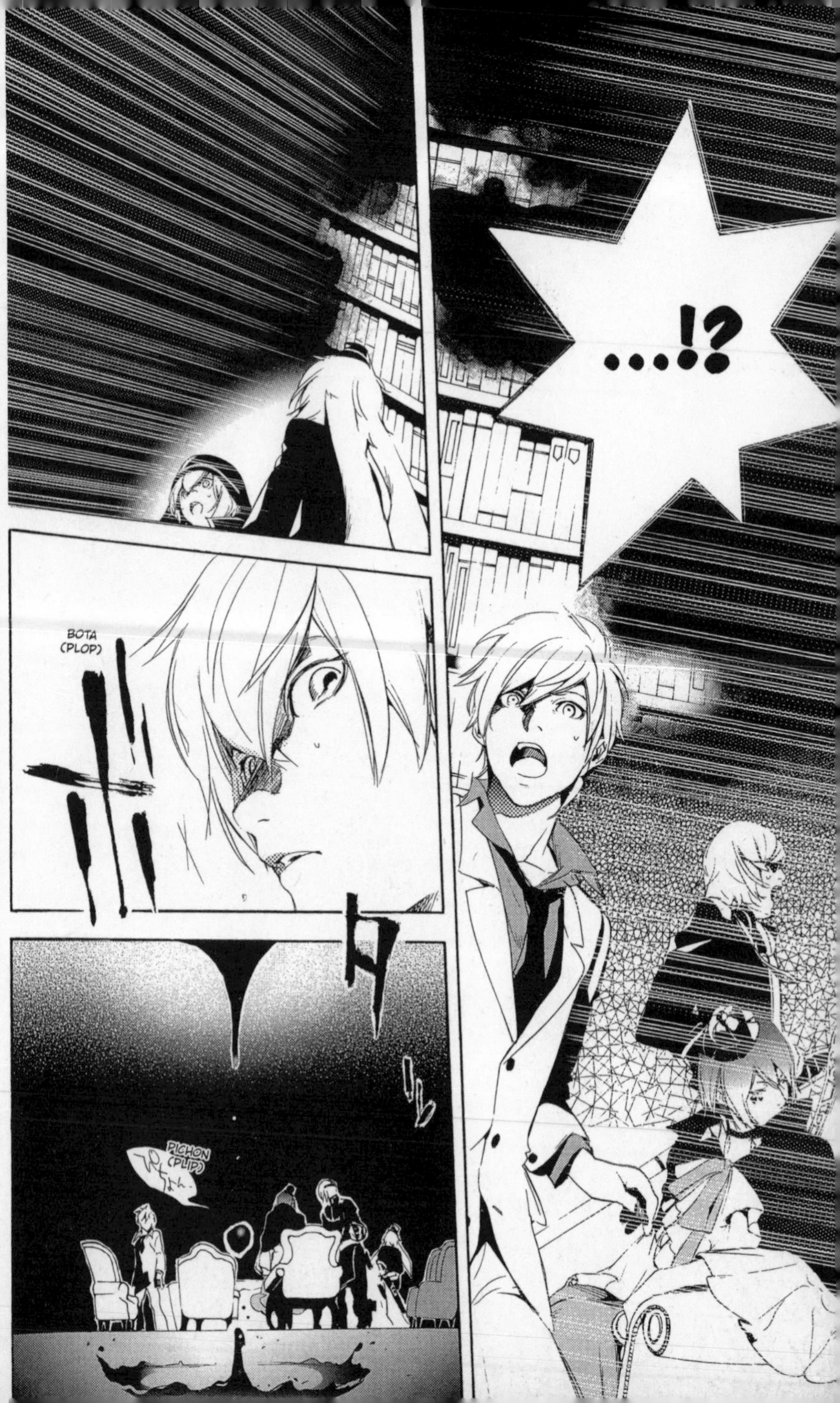
...!?
BOTA (PLOP)
PICHON (PLIP)

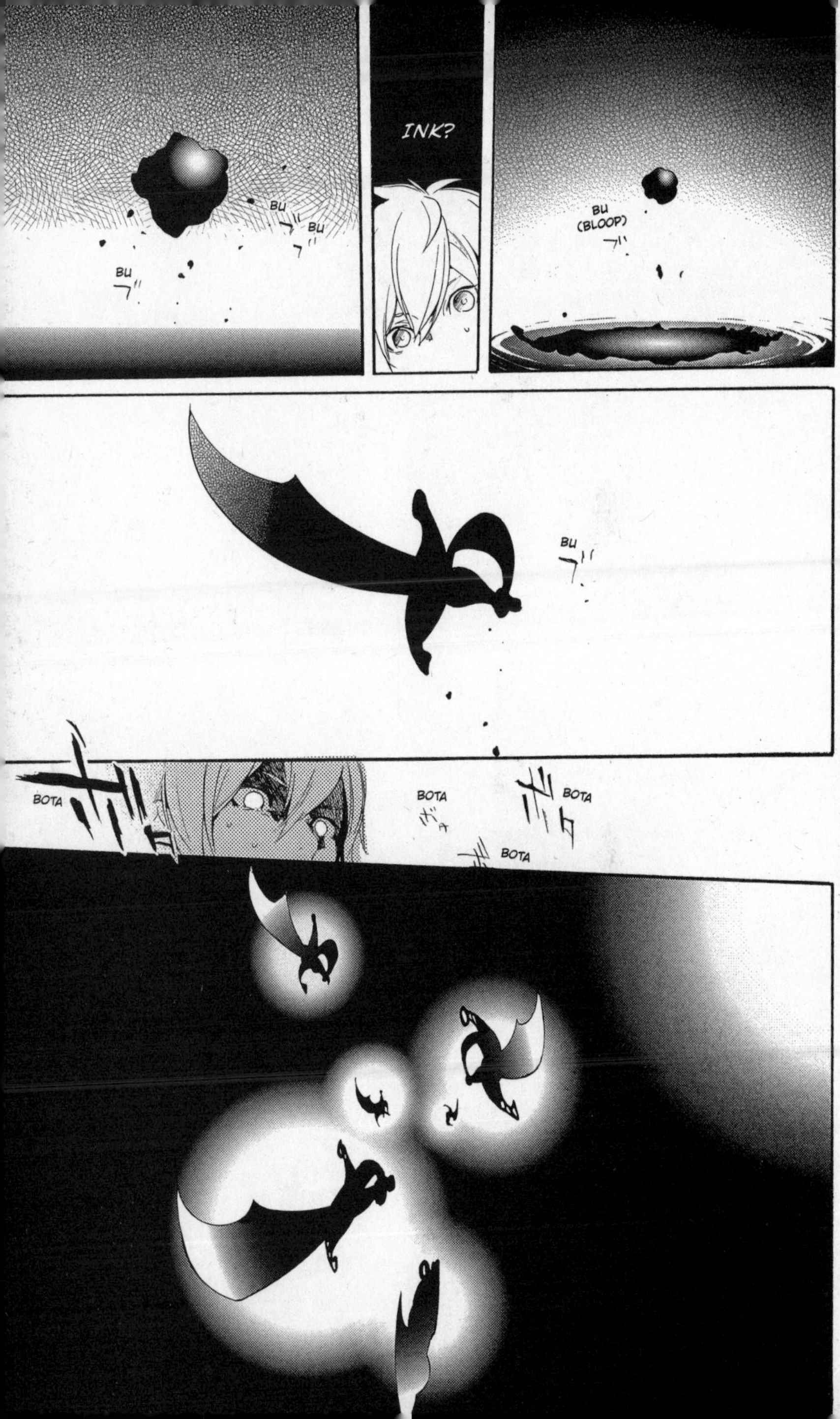
BU
(BLOOP)
INK?
BU
BU
BU
BU
BOTA
BOTA
BOTA
BOTA

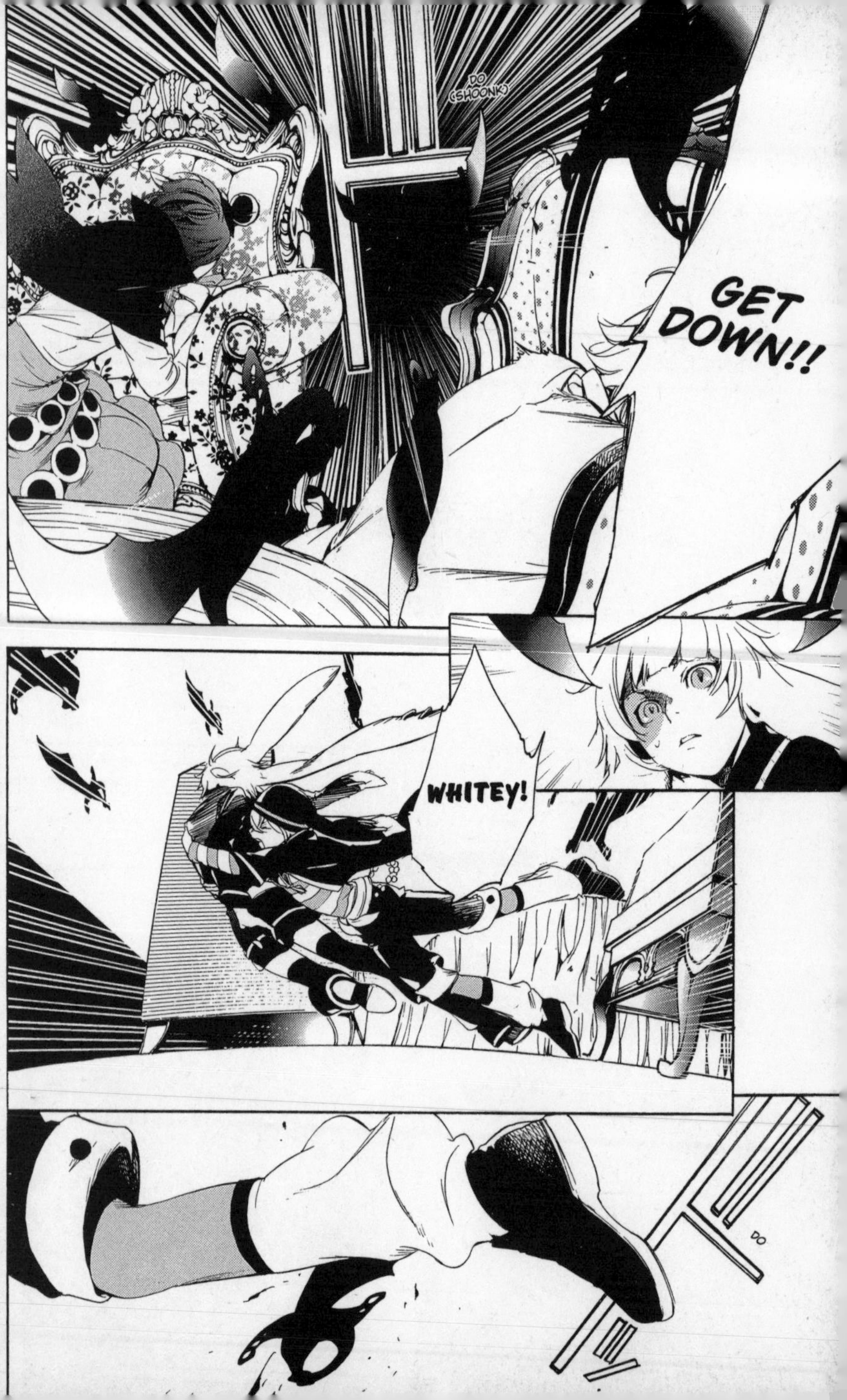
GET DOWN!!
DO (SHOONK)
WHITEY!
DO

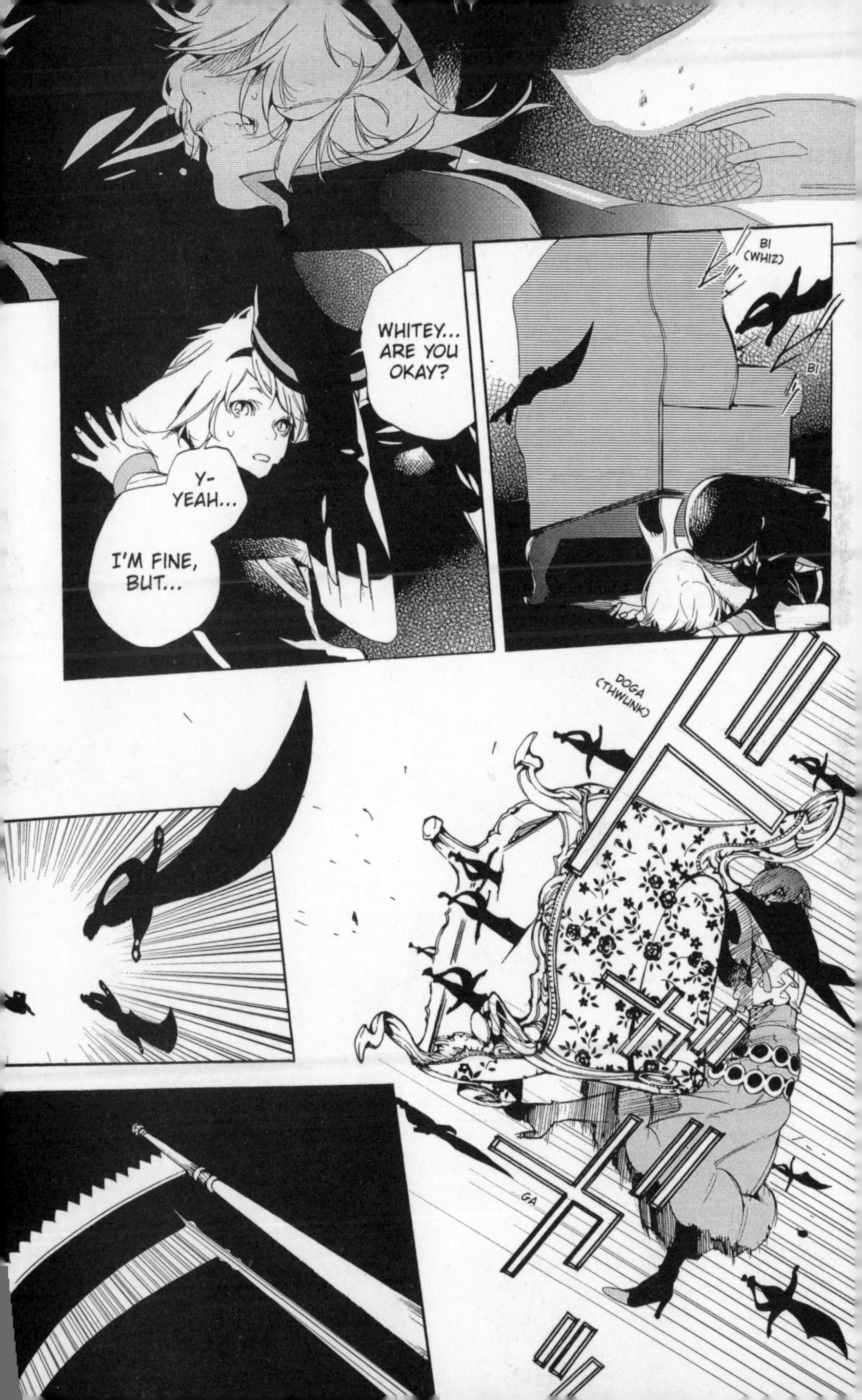
BI
(WHIZ)
BI
WHITEY... ARE YOU OKAY?
Y-YEAH...
I'M FINE, BUT...
DOGA
(THWUNK)
GA

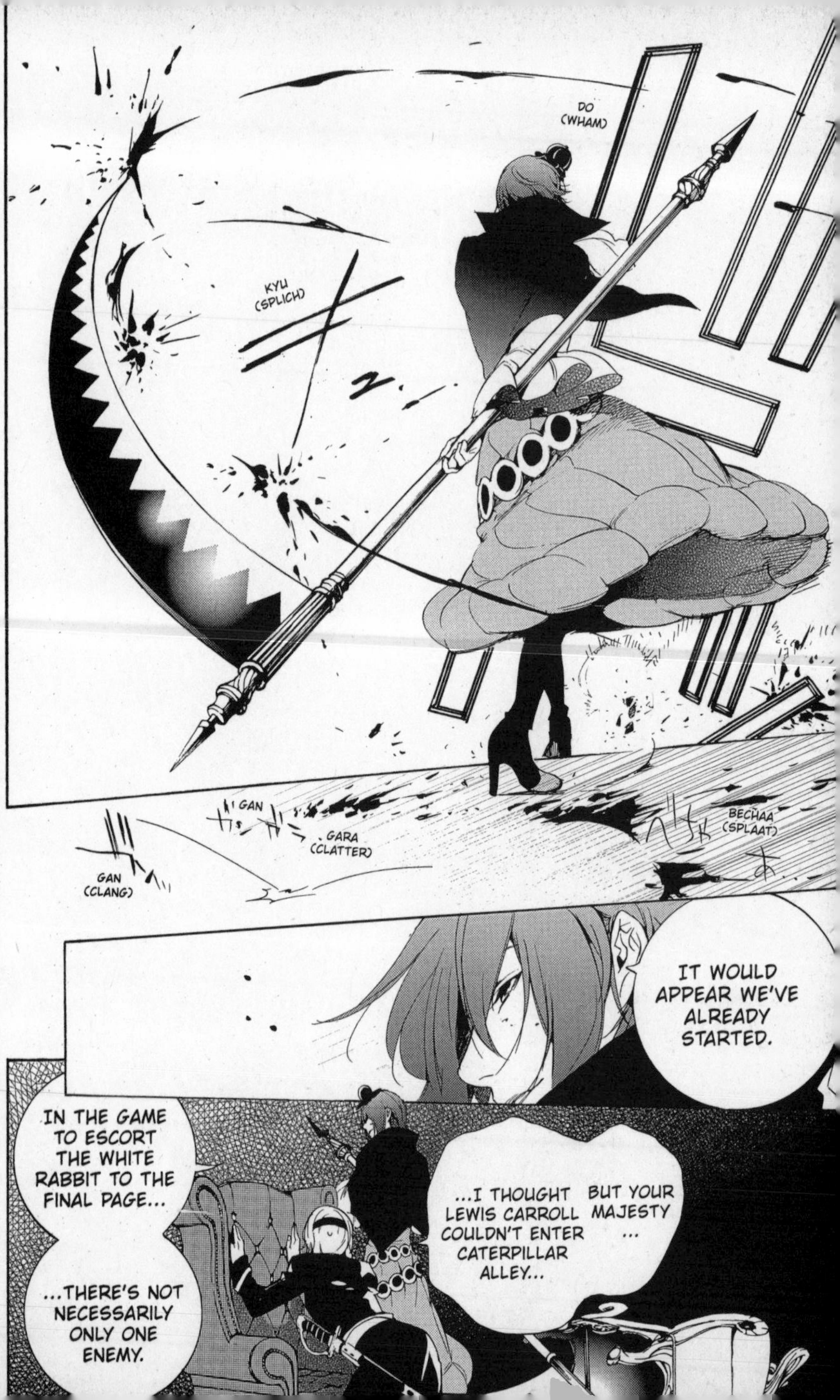
DO (WHAM)
KYU (SPLICH)
BECHAA (SPLAAT)
GAN
GARA (CLATTER)
GAN (CLANG)
IT WOULD APPEAR WE'VE ALREADY STARTED.
BUT YOUR MAJESTY...
...I THOUGHT LEWIS CARROLL COULDN'T ENTER CATERPILLAR ALLEY...
IN THE GAME TO ESCORT THE WHITE RABBIT TO THE FINAL PAGE...
...THERE'S NOT NECESSARILY ONLY ONE ENEMY.

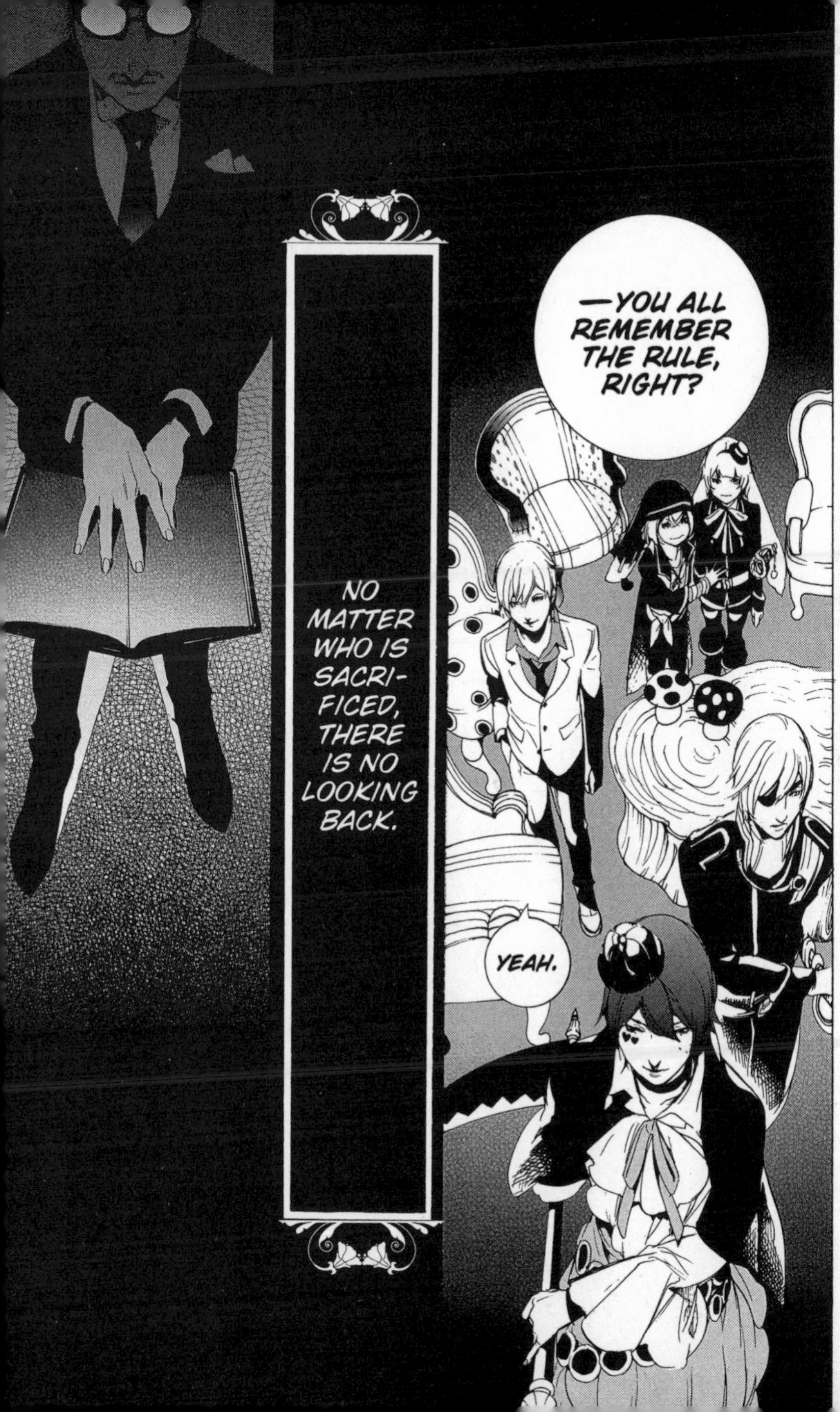
—YOU ALL REMEMBER THE RULE, RIGHT?
YEAH.
NO MATTER WHO IS SACRI-FICED, THERE IS NO LOOKING BACK.

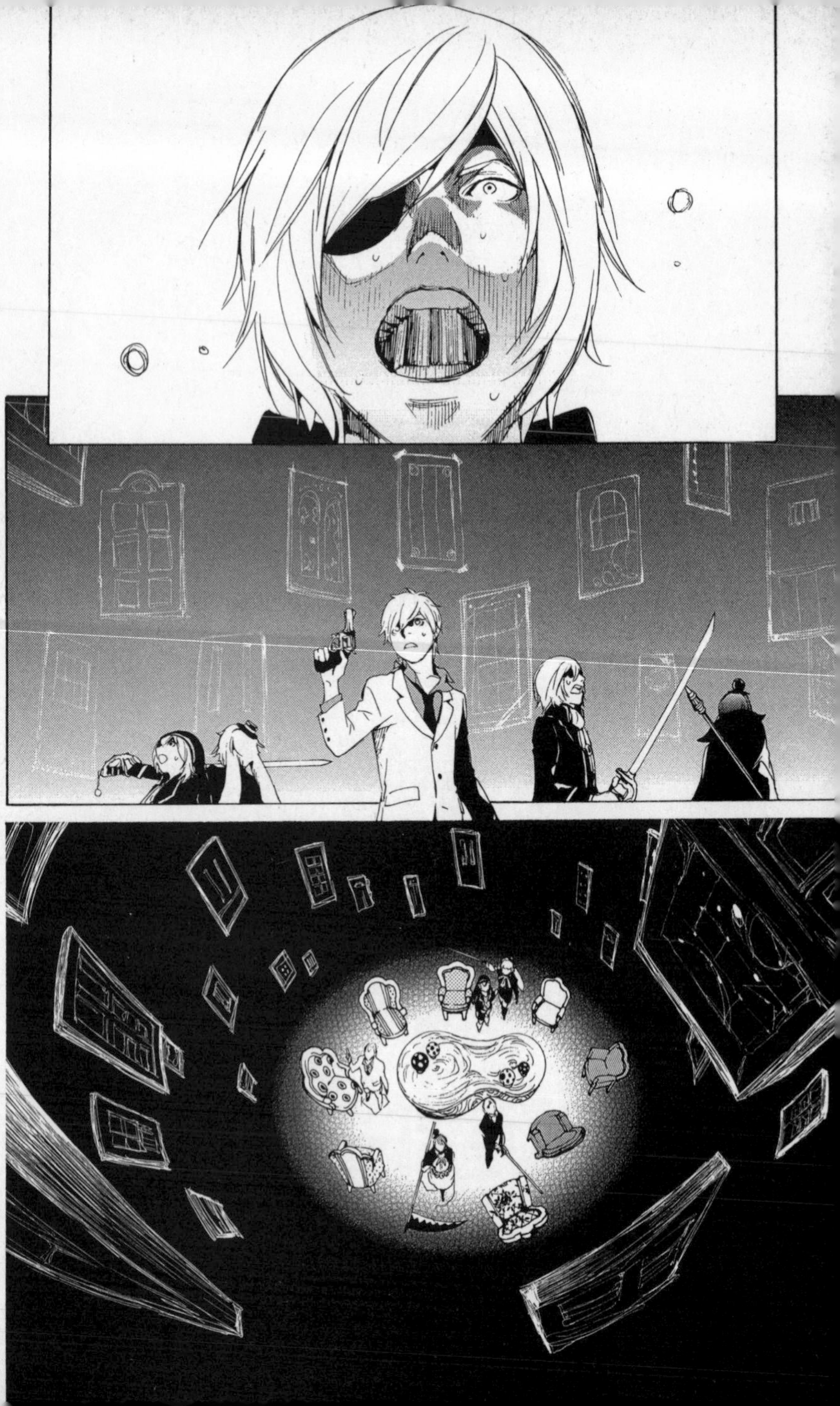

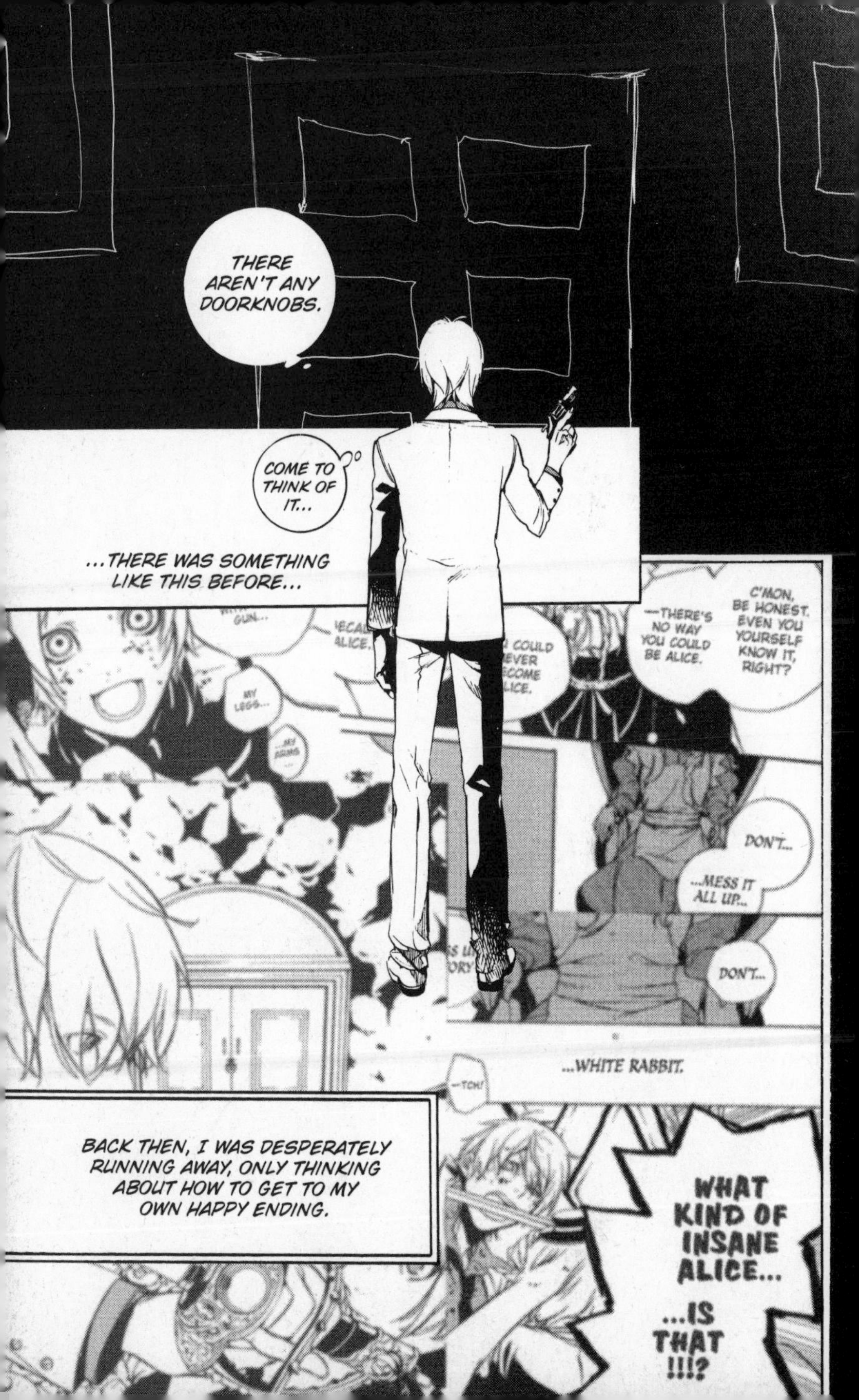
THERE AREN'T ANY DOORKNOBS.
COME TO THINK OF IT...
...THERE WAS SOMETHING LIKE THIS BEFORE...
C'MON, BE HONEST. EVEN YOU YOURSELF KNOW IT, RIGHT?
—THERE'S NO WAY YOU COULD BE ALICE.
MY LEGS...
...MY ARMS...
DON'T...
...MESS IT ALL UP...
DON'T...
...WHITE RABBIT.
—TCH!
WHAT KIND OF INSANE ALICE...
...IS THAT !!!?
BACK THEN, I WAS DESPERATELY RUNNING AWAY, ONLY THINKING ABOUT HOW TO GET TO MY OWN HAPPY ENDING.

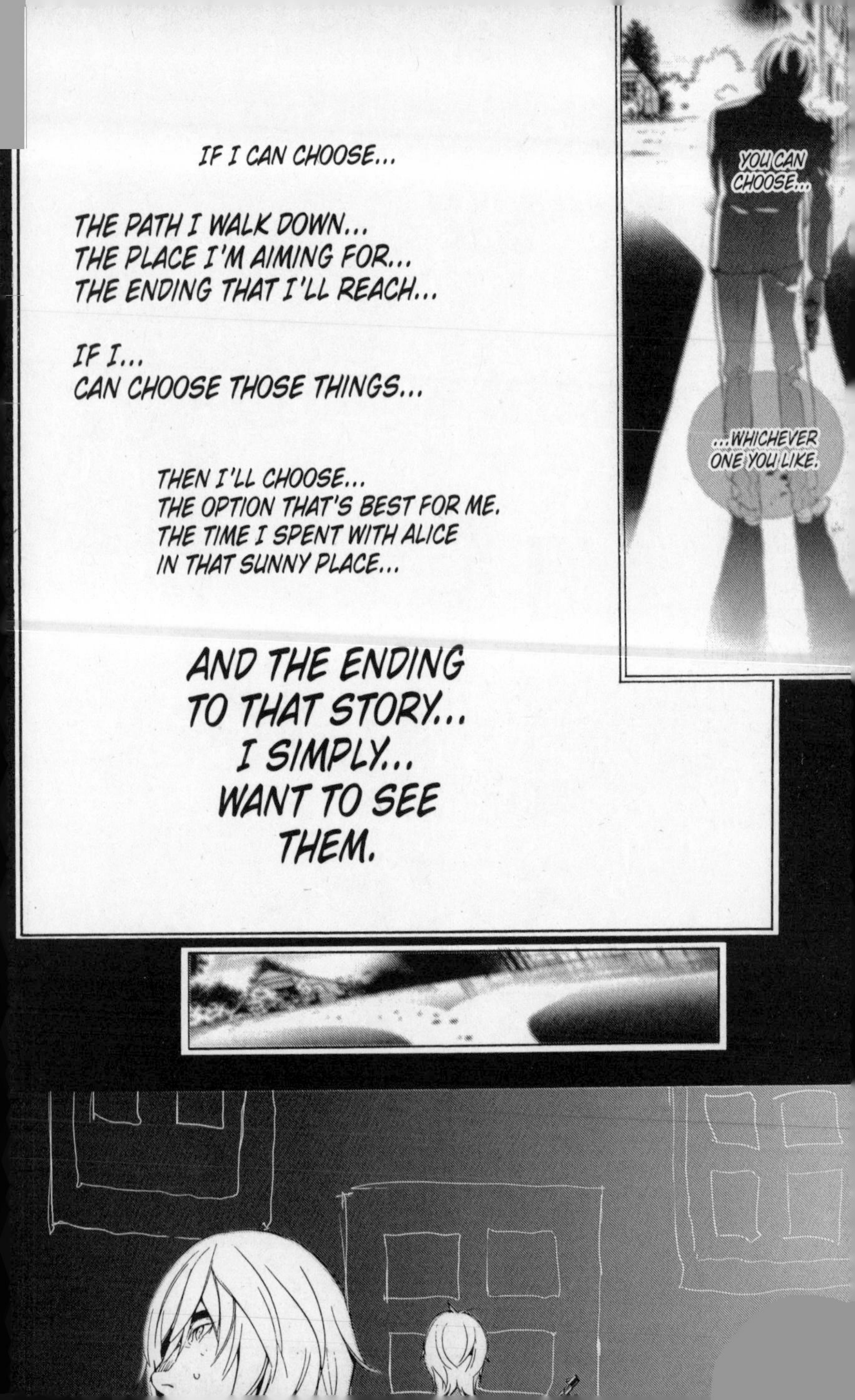
YOU CAN CHOOSE...
...WHICHEVER ONE YOU LIKE.
IF I CAN CHOOSE...
THE PATH I WALK DOWN... THE PLACE I'M AIMING FOR... THE ENDING THAT I'LL REACH...
IF I... CAN CHOOSE THOSE THINGS...
THEN I'LL CHOOSE... THE OPTION THAT'S BEST FOR ME. THE TIME I SPENT WITH ALICE IN THAT SUNNY PLACE...
AND THE ENDING TO THAT STORY... I SIMPLY... WANT TO SEE THEM.

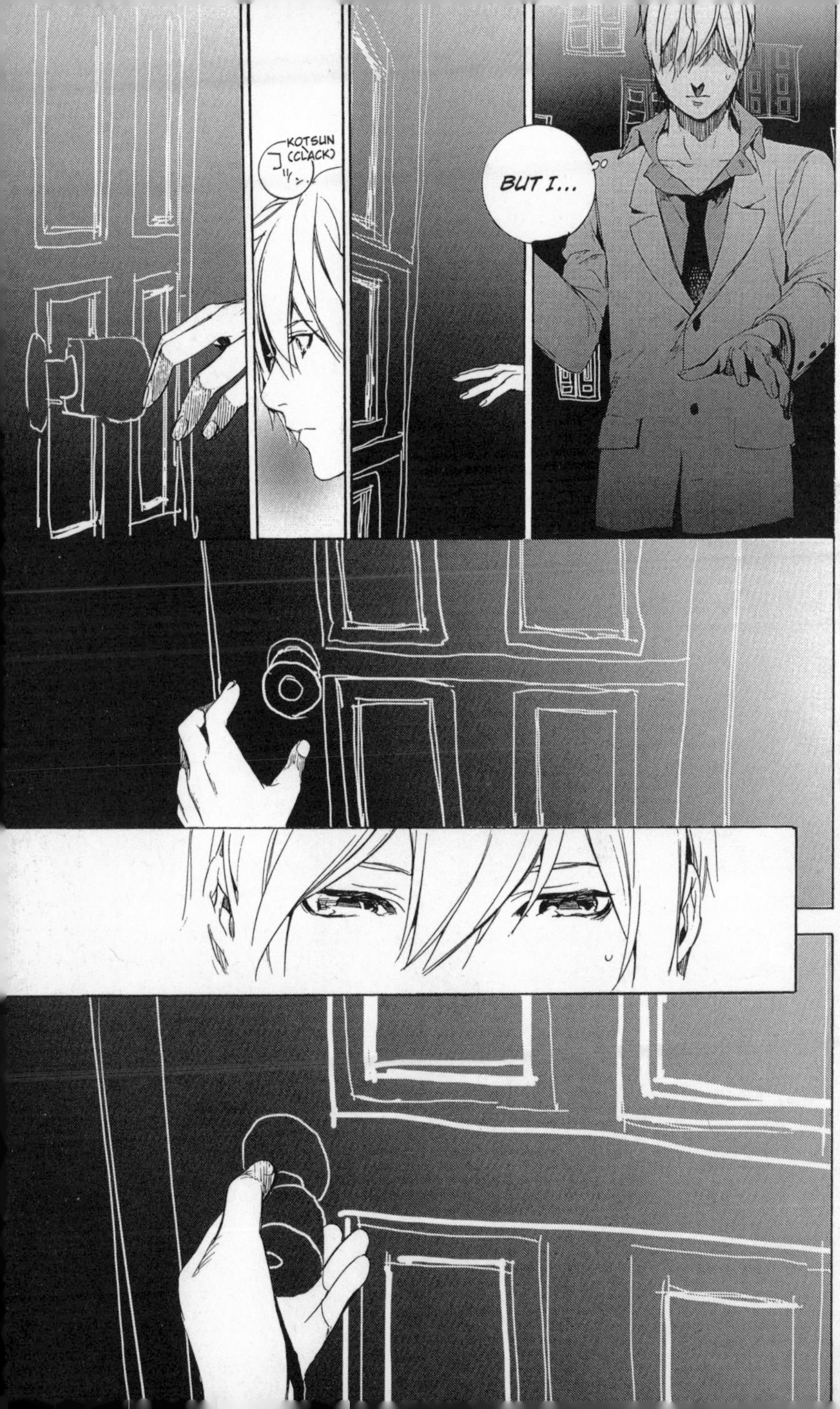
BUT I...
KOTSUN (CLACK)

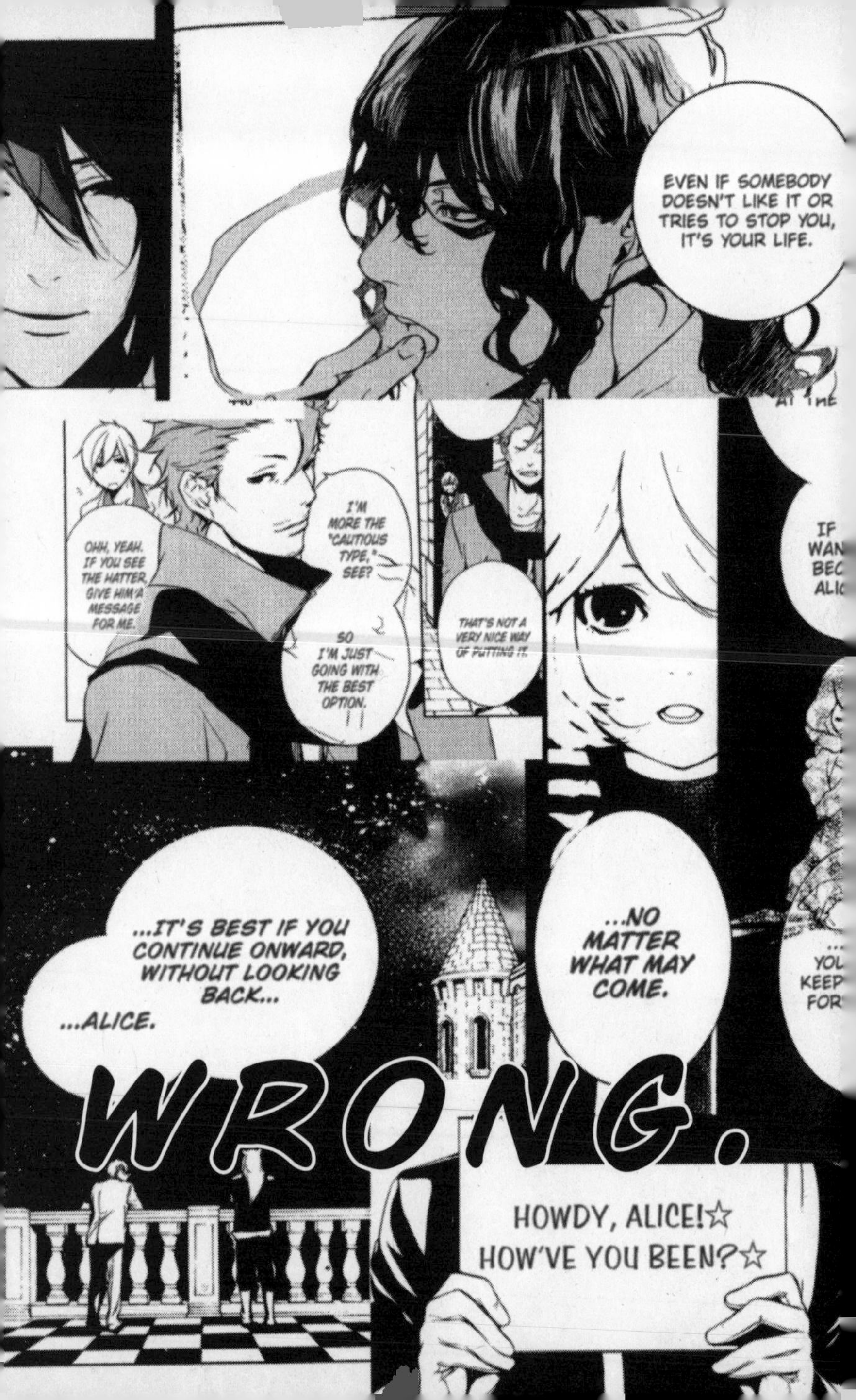

EVEN IF SOMEBODY DOESN'T LIKE IT OR TRIES TO STOP YOU, IT'S YOUR LIFE.
THAT'S NOT A VERY NICE WAY OF PUTTING IT.
I'M MORE THE "CAUTIOUS TYPE," SEE?
OHH, YEAH. IF YOU SEE THE HATTER, GIVE HIM A MESSAGE FOR ME.
SO I'M JUST GOING WITH THE BEST OPTION.
...NO MATTER WHAT MAY COME.
...IT'S BEST IF YOU CONTINUE ONWARD, WITHOUT LOOKING BACK...
...ALICE.
WRONG.
HOWDY, ALICE!☆ HOW'VE YOU BEEN?☆

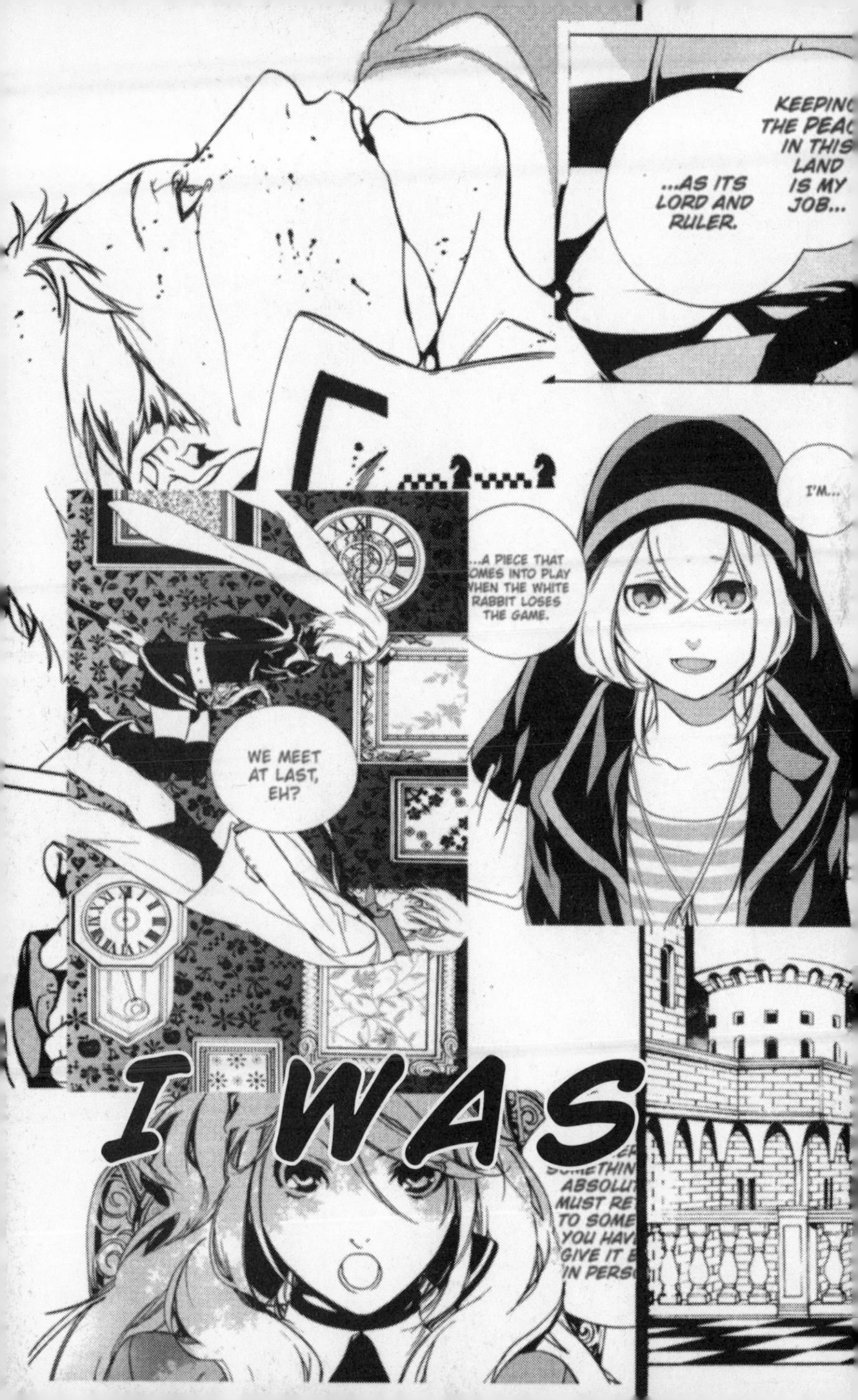
KEEPING THE PEAC IN THIS LAND IS MY JOB...
...AS ITS LORD AND RULER.
I'M...
...A PIECE THAT OMES INTO PLAY WHEN THE WHITE RABBIT LOSES THE GAME.
WE MEET AT LAST, EH?
I WAS
SOMETHIN ABSOLUT MUST RE TO SOME YOU HAVE GIVE IT IN PERSO

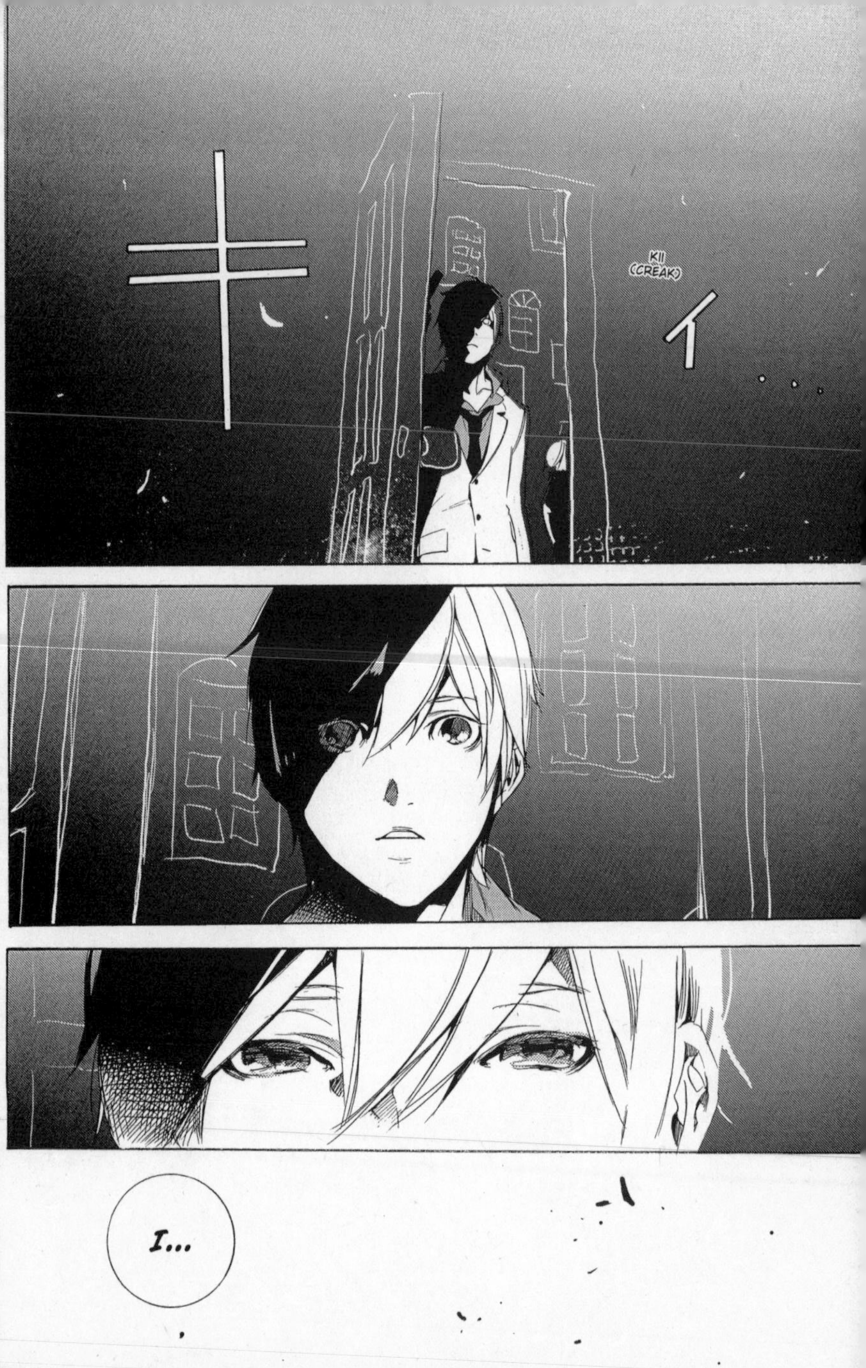
KII (CREAK)
I...

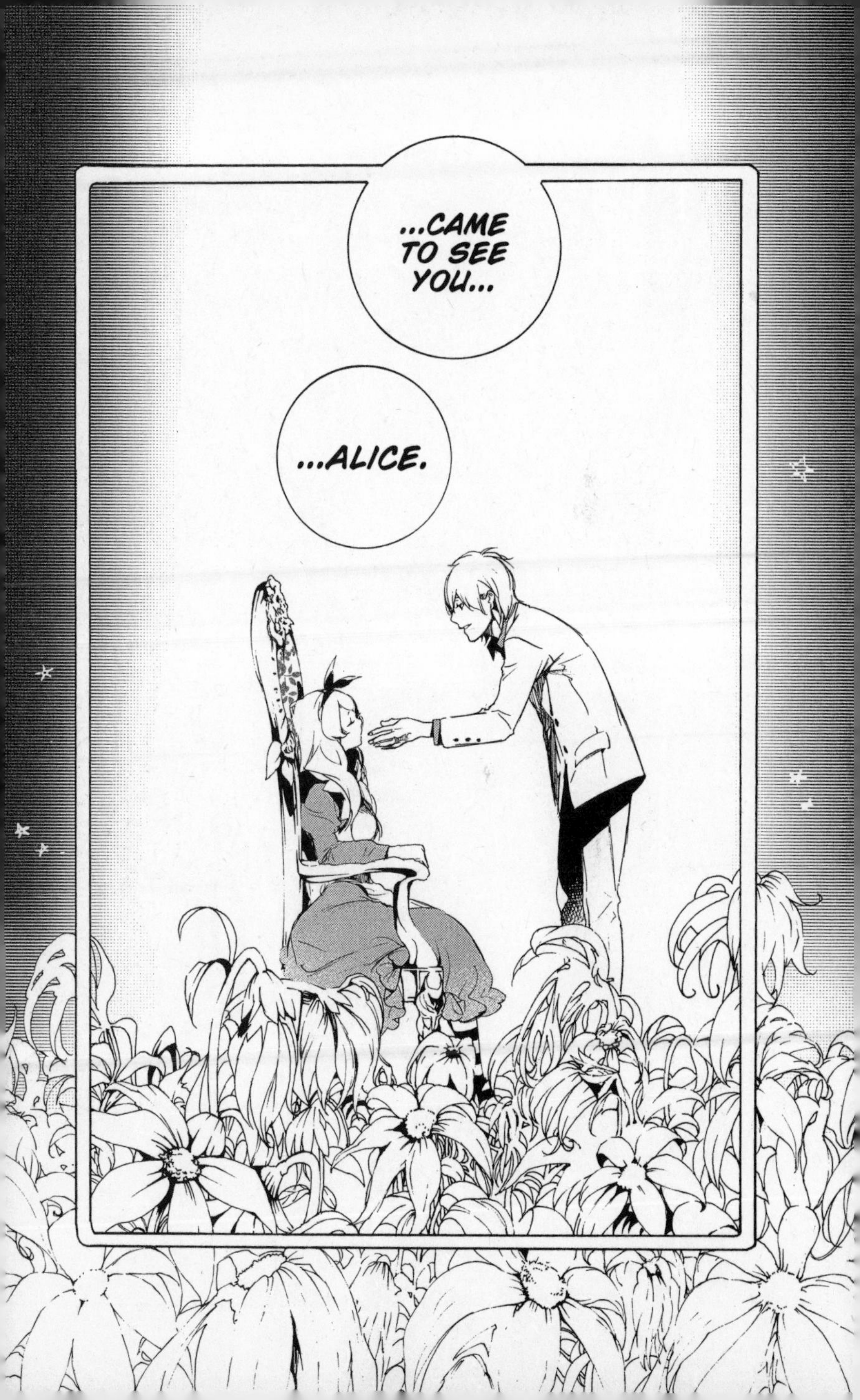
...CAME TO SEE YOU...
...ALICE.

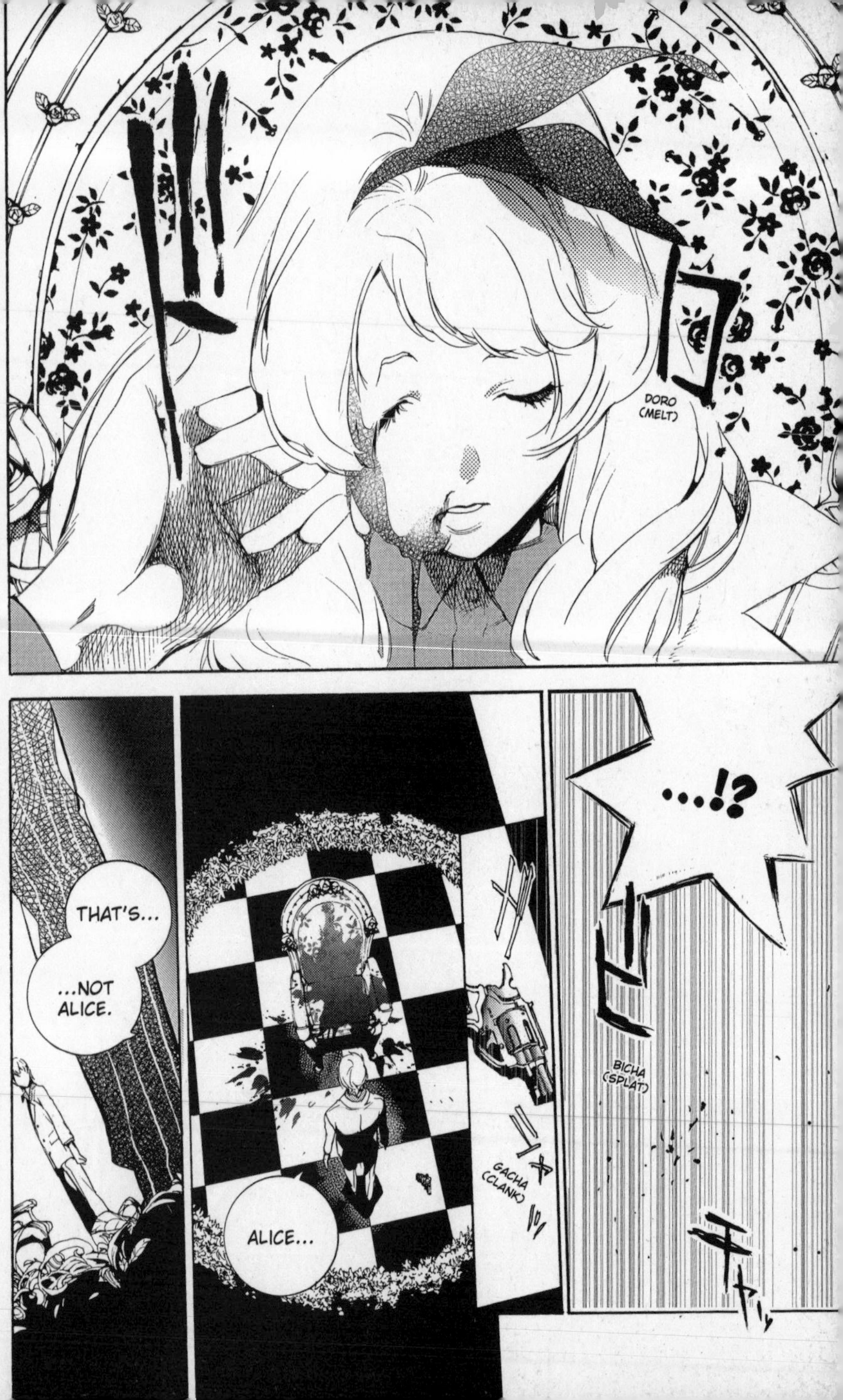
DORO
(MELT)
...!?
BICHA
(SPLAT)
GACHA
(CLANK)
ALICE...
THAT'S...
...NOT ALICE.

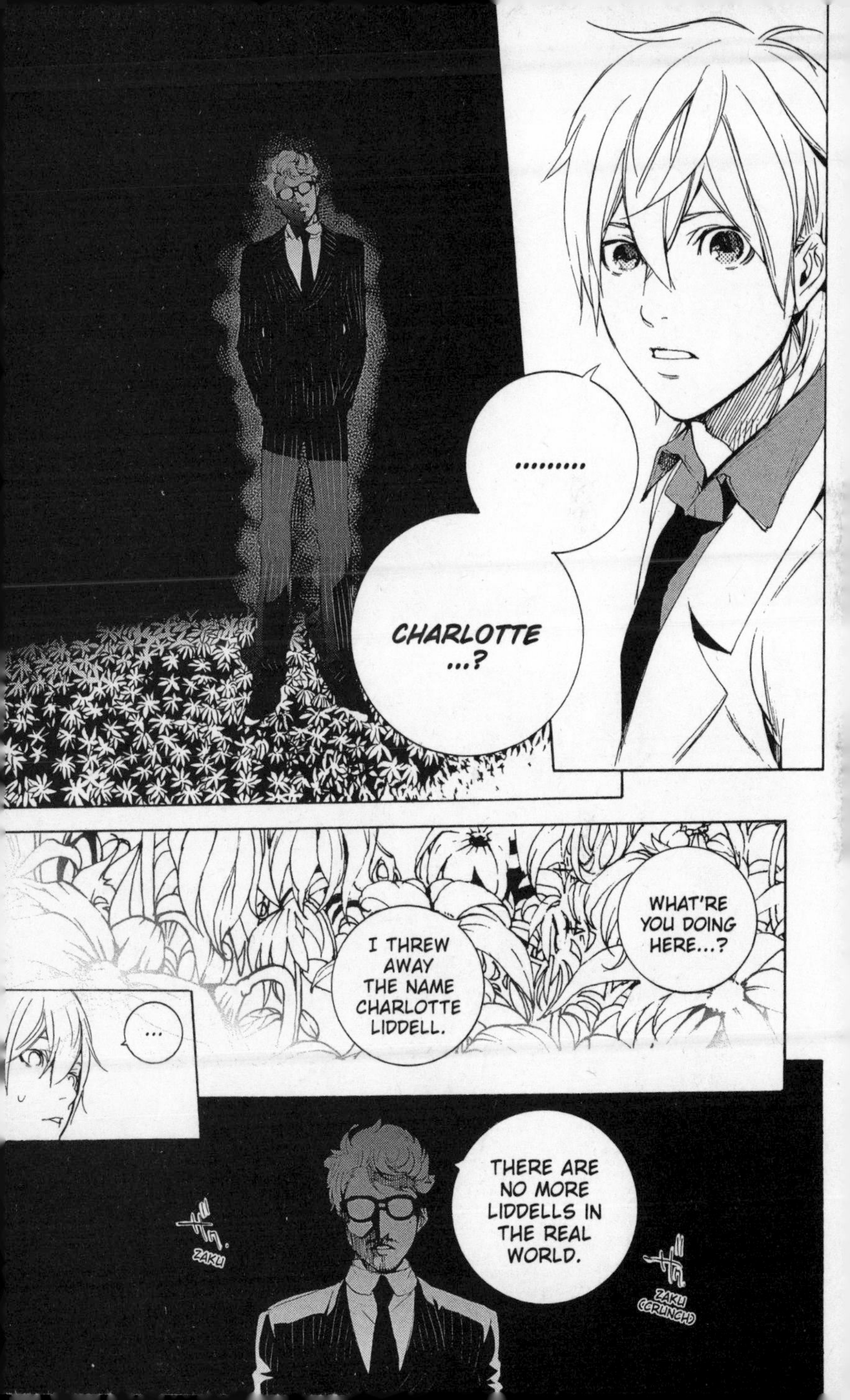
....
CHARLOTTE ...?
WHAT'RE YOU DOING HERE...?
I THREW AWAY THE NAME CHARLOTTE LIDDELL.
...
THERE ARE NO MORE LIDDELLS IN THE REAL WORLD.
ZAKU (CRUNCH)
ZAKU

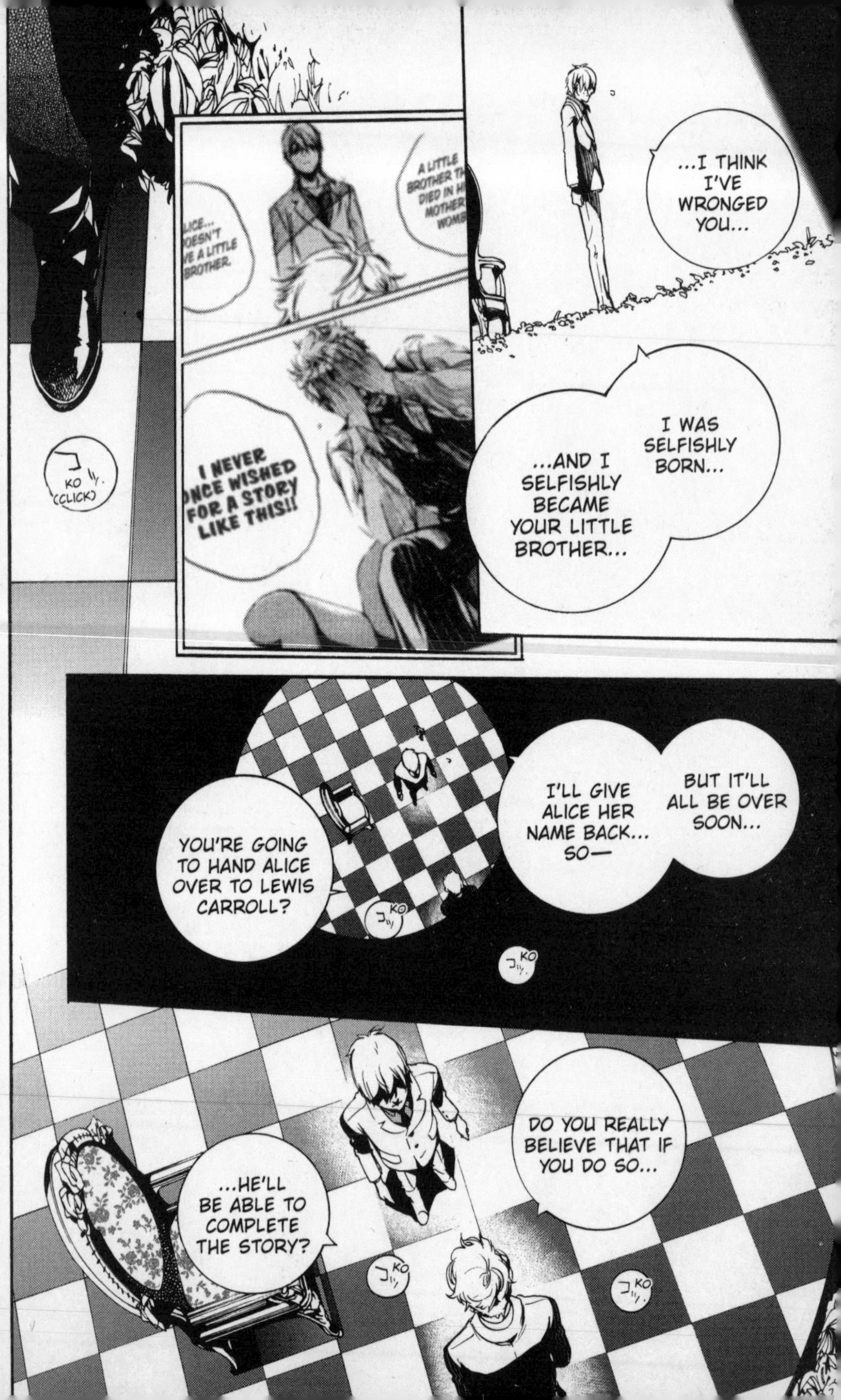
...I THINK I'VE WRONGED YOU...
I WAS SELFISHLY BORN...
...AND I SELFISHLY BECAME YOUR LITTLE BROTHER...
A LITTLE BROTHER TH DIED IN HI MOTHER WOMB
ALICE... OESN'T VE A LITTLE BROTHER.
I NEVER NCE WISHED FOR A STORY LIKE THIS!!
コッ KO (CLICK)
BUT IT'LL ALL BE OVER SOON...
I'LL GIVE ALICE HER NAME BACK... SO—
YOU'RE GOING TO HAND ALICE OVER TO LEWIS CARROLL?
コッ KO
コッ KO
DO YOU REALLY BELIEVE THAT IF YOU DO SO...
...HE'LL BE ABLE TO COMPLETE THE STORY?
コッ KO
コッ KO

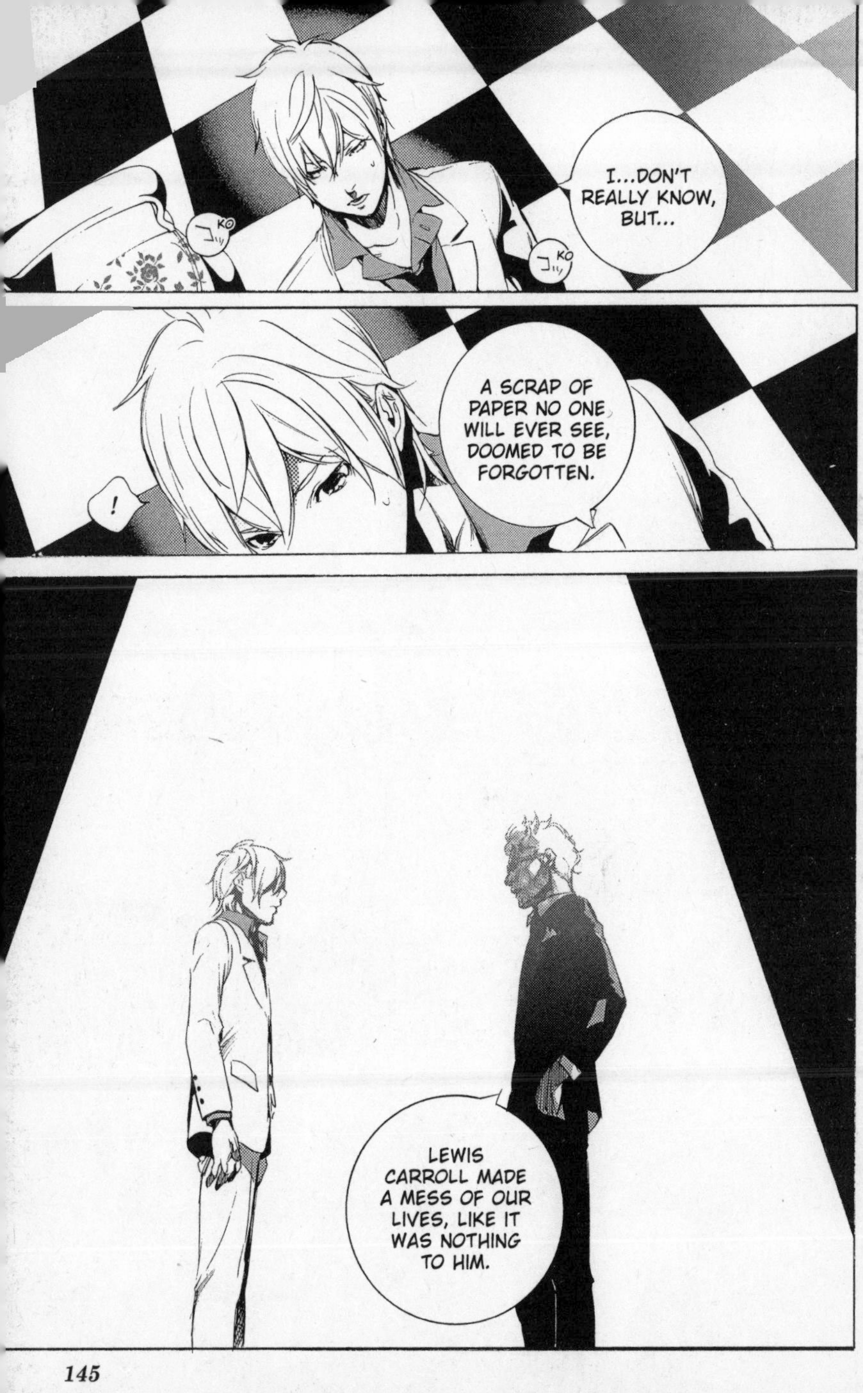
I...DON'T REALLY KNOW, BUT...
KO
KO
A SCRAP OF PAPER NO ONE WILL EVER SEE, DOOMED TO BE FORGOTTEN.
!
LEWIS CARROLL MADE A MESS OF OUR LIVES, LIKE IT WAS NOTHING TO HIM.

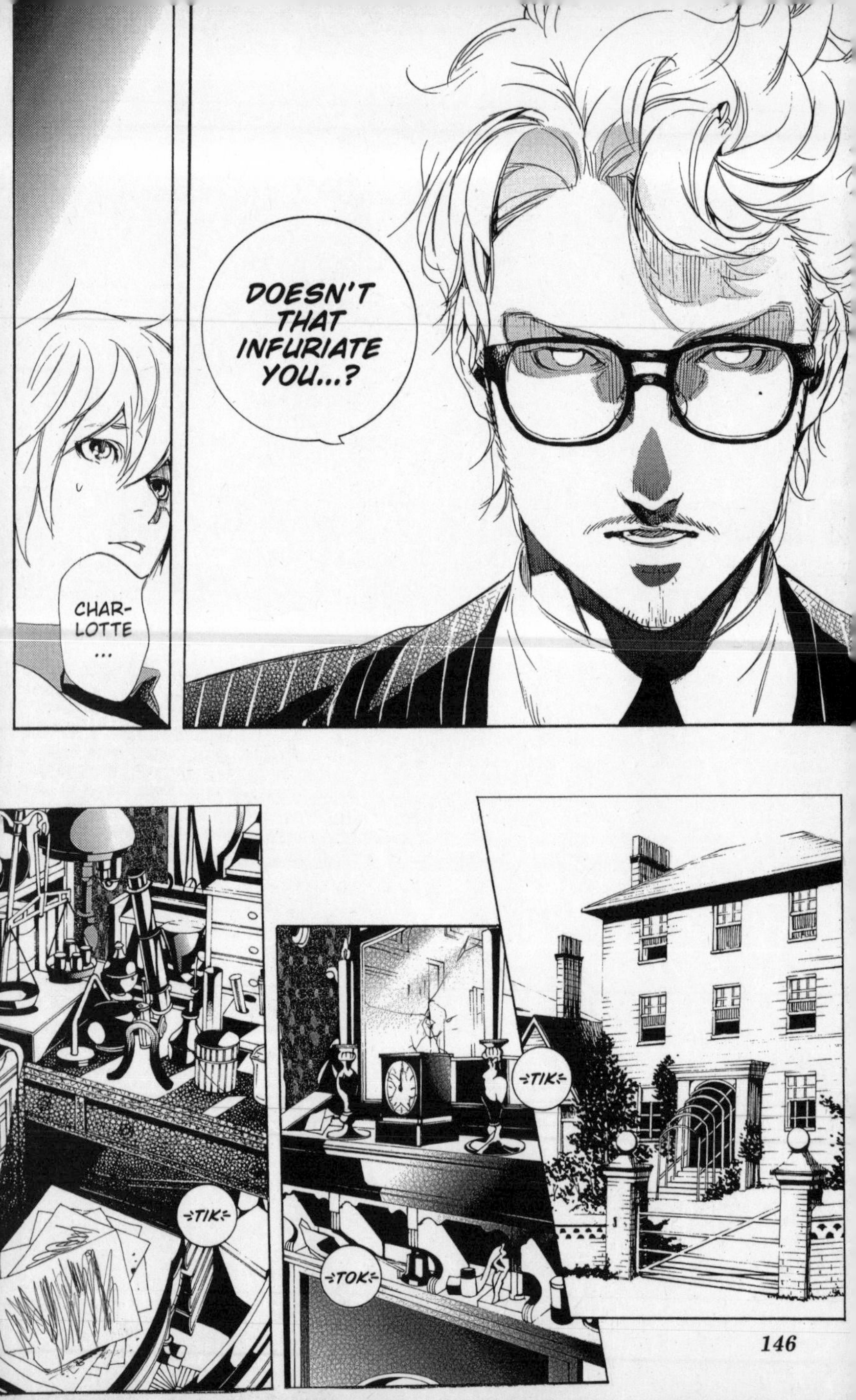
DOESN'T THAT INFURIATE YOU...?
CHAR-LOTTE ...
TIK
TOK
TIK

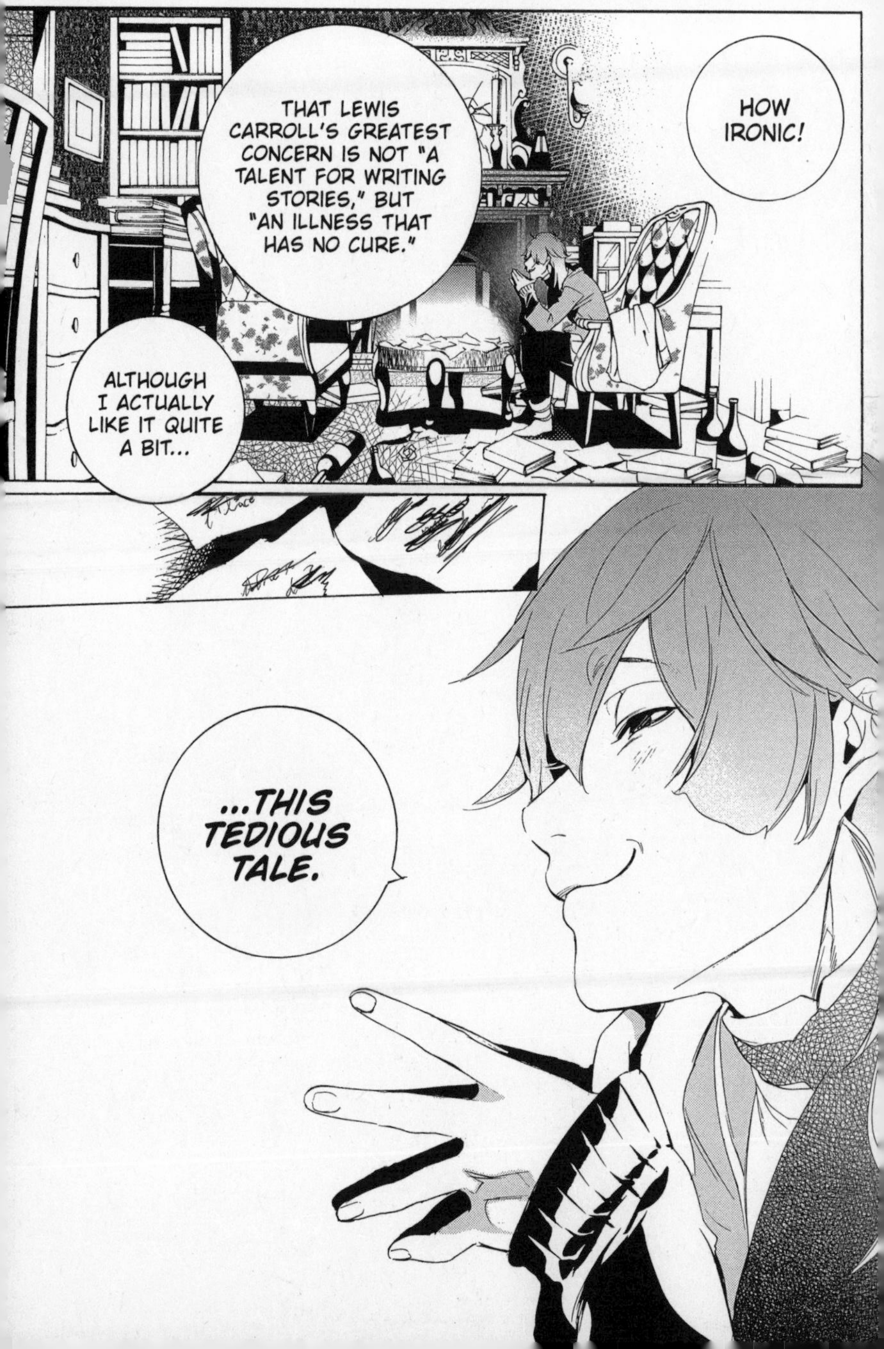
HOW IRONIC!
THAT LEWIS CARROLL'S GREATEST CONCERN IS NOT "A TALENT FOR WRITING STORIES," BUT "AN ILLNESS THAT HAS NO CURE."
ALTHOUGH I ACTUALLY LIKE IT QUITE A BIT...
...THIS TEDIOUS TALE.

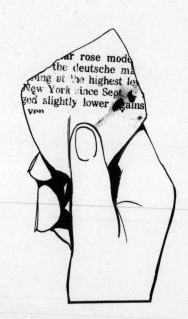

ar rose mode
the deutsche ma
ing at the highest le
New York since Sep
ged slightly lower gains
ven

Chapter 66 Little Bill.

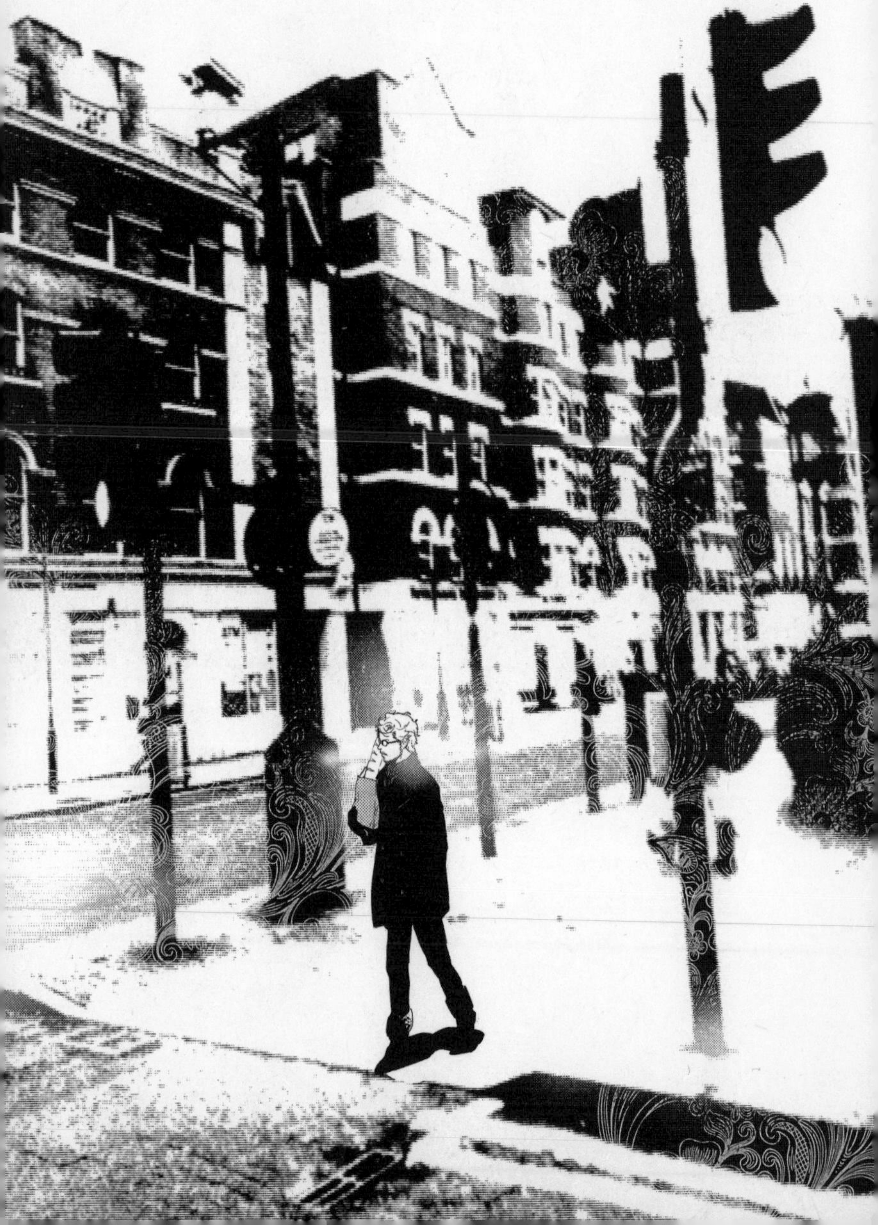

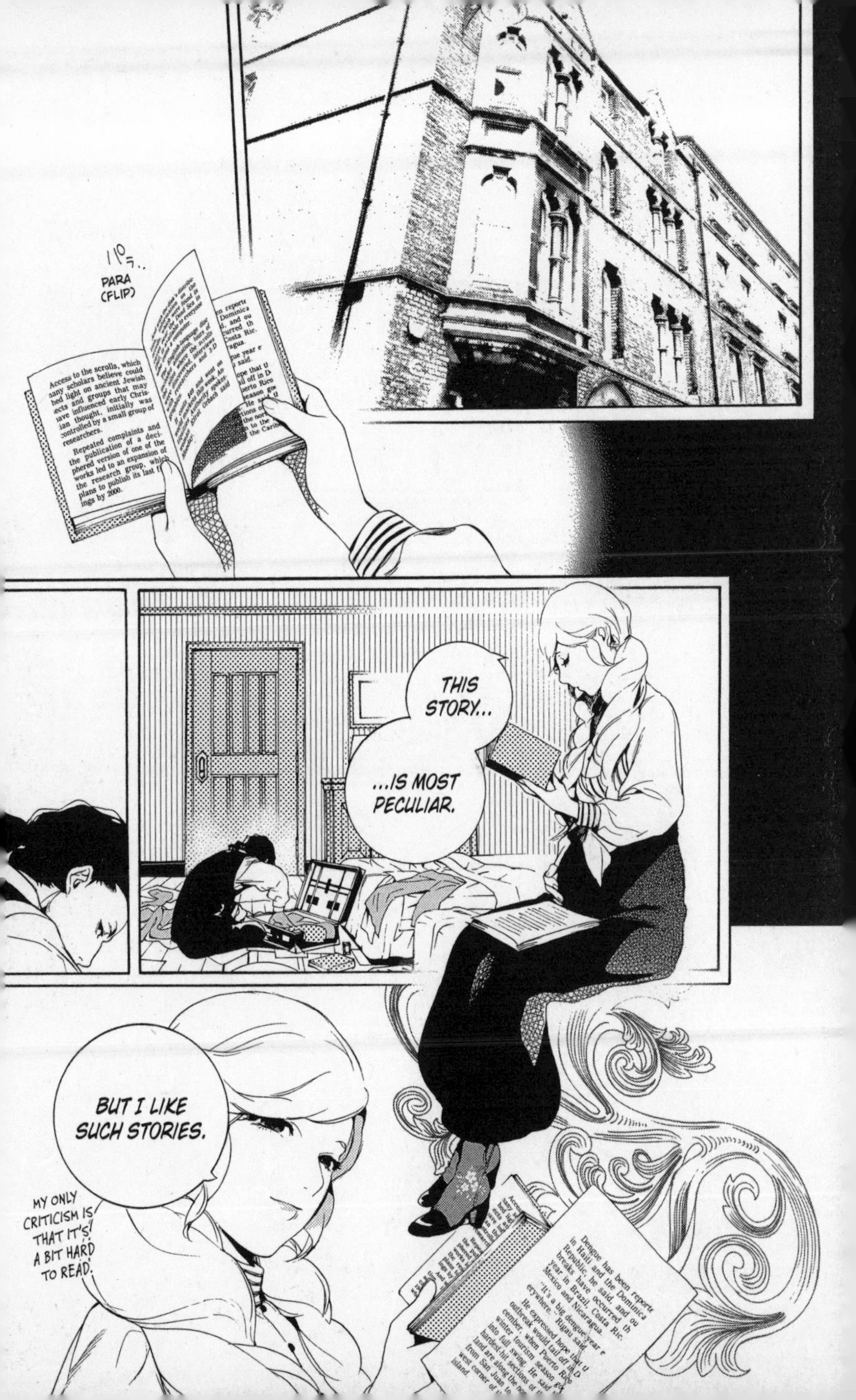

パラ..
PARA (FLIP)
Access to the scrolls, which nany scholars believe could hed light on ancient Jewish ects and groups that may ave influenced early Chrisian thought, initially was controlled by a small group of researchers.
Repeated complaints and the publication of a deciphered version of one of the works led to an expansion of the research group, which plans to publish its last fi ings by 2000.
THIS STORY...
...IS MOST PECULIAR.
BUT I LIKE SUCH STORIES.
MY ONLY CRITICISM IS THAT IT'S A BIT HARD TO READ.

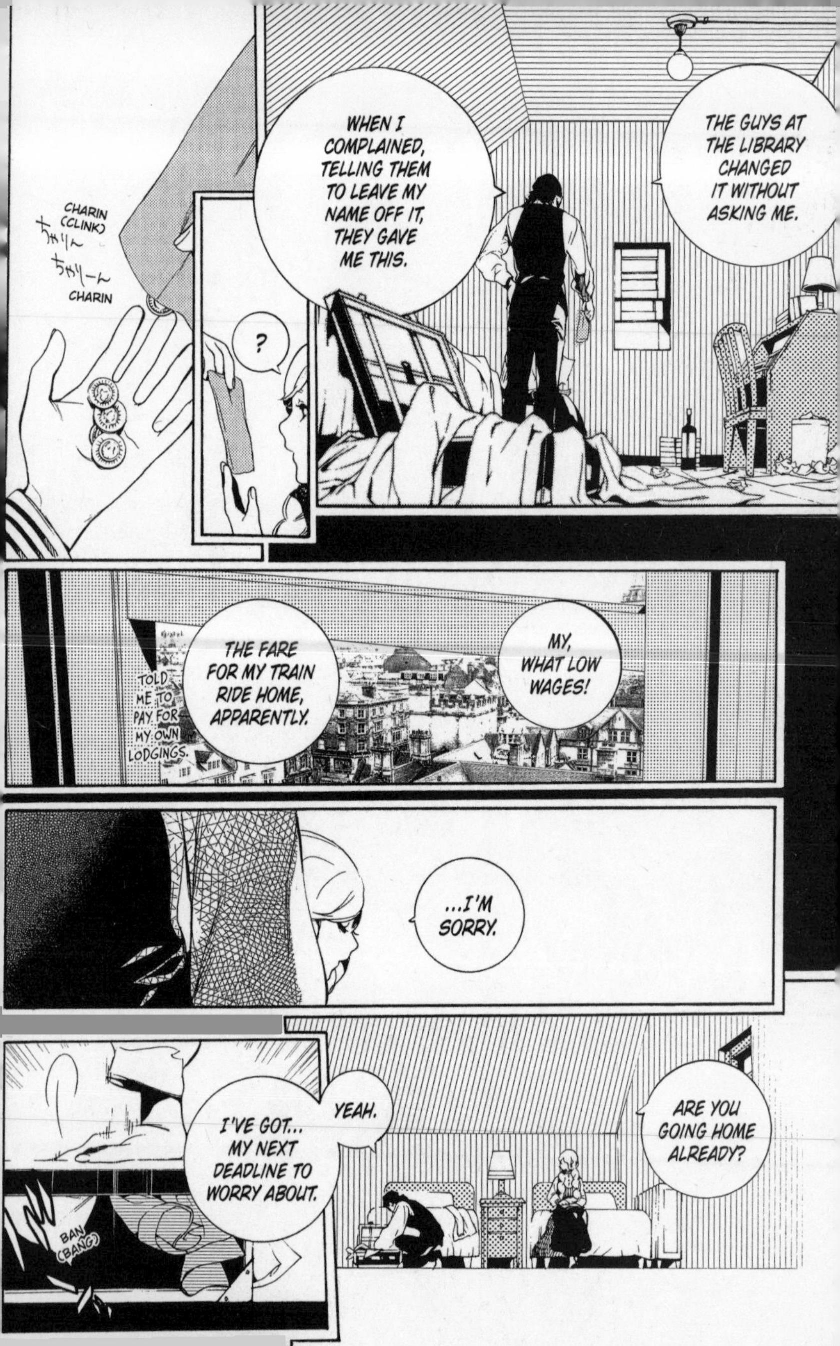
THE GUYS AT THE LIBRARY CHANGED IT WITHOUT ASKING ME.
WHEN I COMPLAINED, TELLING THEM TO LEAVE MY NAME OFF IT, THEY GAVE ME THIS.
?
CHARIN (CLINK)
ちゃりん
ちゃりーん
CHARIN
MY, WHAT LOW WAGES!
THE FARE FOR MY TRAIN RIDE HOME, APPARENTLY.
TOLD ME TO PAY FOR MY OWN LODGINGS.
...I'M SORRY.
ARE YOU GOING HOME ALREADY?
YEAH.
I'VE GOT... MY NEXT DEADLINE TO WORRY ABOUT.
BAN (BANG)

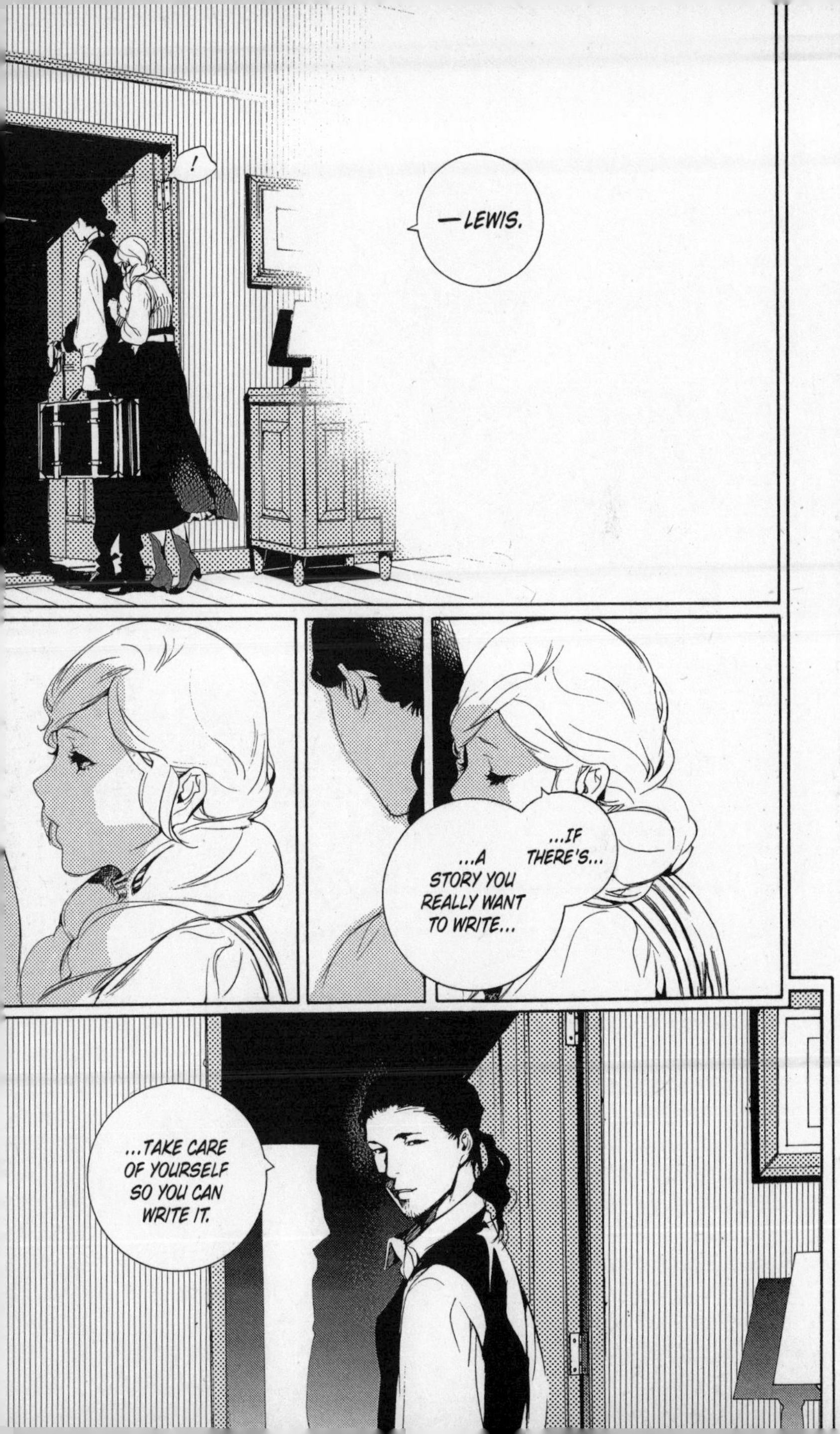
—LEWIS.
!
...IF THERE'S... ...A STORY YOU REALLY WANT TO WRITE...
...TAKE CARE OF YOURSELF SO YOU CAN WRITE IT.

GI
(CREAK)

BATAN
(SHUT)

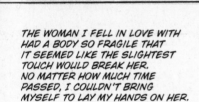

THE WOMAN I FELL IN LOVE WITH
HAD A BODY SO FRAGILE THAT
IT SEEMED LIKE THE SLIGHTEST
TOUCH WOULD BREAK HER.
NO MATTER HOW MUCH TIME
PASSED, I COULDN'T BRING
MYSELF TO LAY MY HANDS ON HER.

SO SHE WAS STOLEN FROM ME.

IT'S A TALE AS OLD AS TIME.

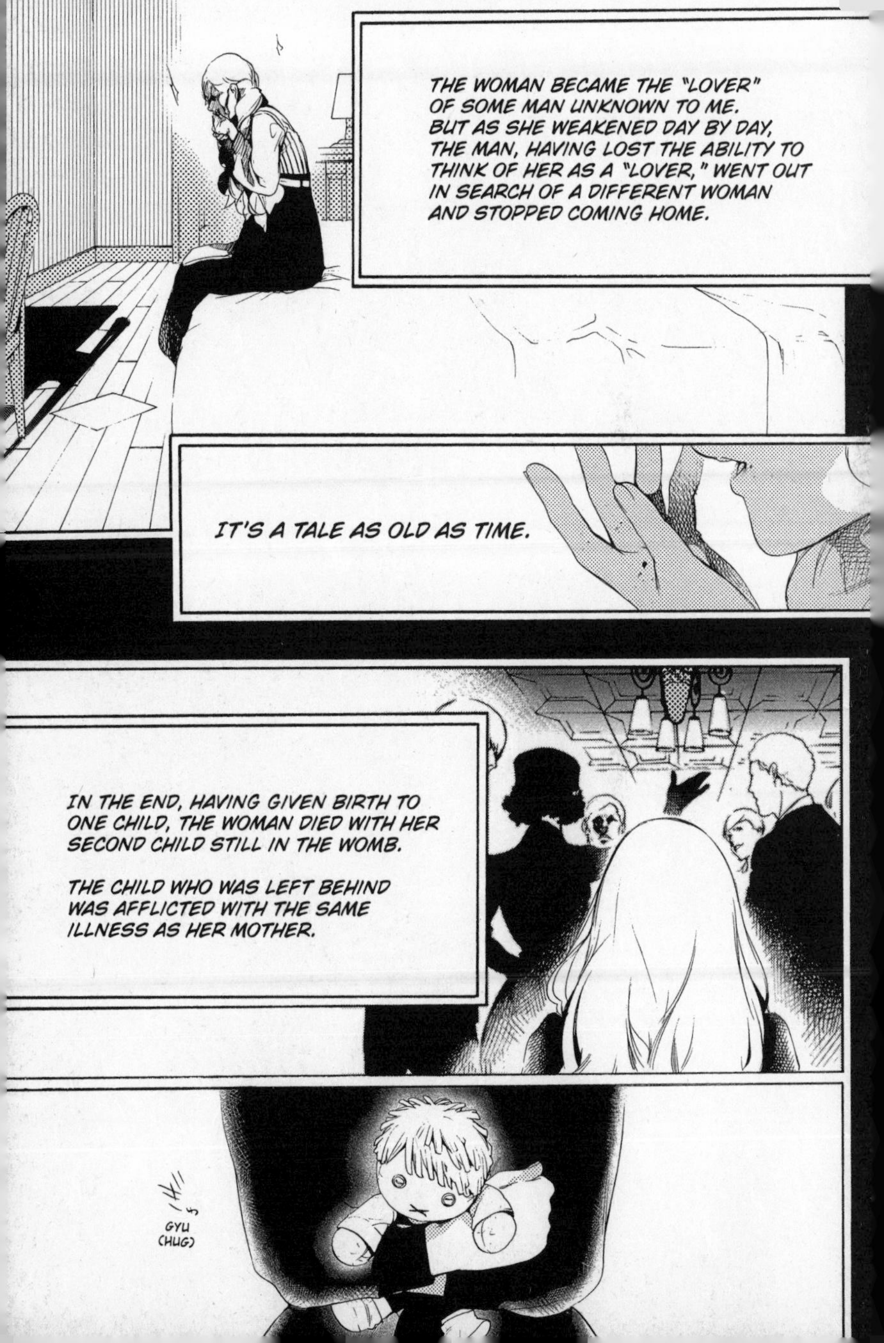
THE WOMAN BECAME THE "LOVER" OF SOME MAN UNKNOWN TO ME. BUT AS SHE WEAKENED DAY BY DAY, THE MAN, HAVING LOST THE ABILITY TO THINK OF HER AS A "LOVER," WENT OUT IN SEARCH OF A DIFFERENT WOMAN AND STOPPED COMING HOME.
IT'S A TALE AS OLD AS TIME.
IN THE END, HAVING GIVEN BIRTH TO ONE CHILD, THE WOMAN DIED WITH HER SECOND CHILD STILL IN THE WOMB.
THE CHILD WHO WAS LEFT BEHIND WAS AFFLICTED WITH THE SAME ILLNESS AS HER MOTHER.
GYU (HUG)

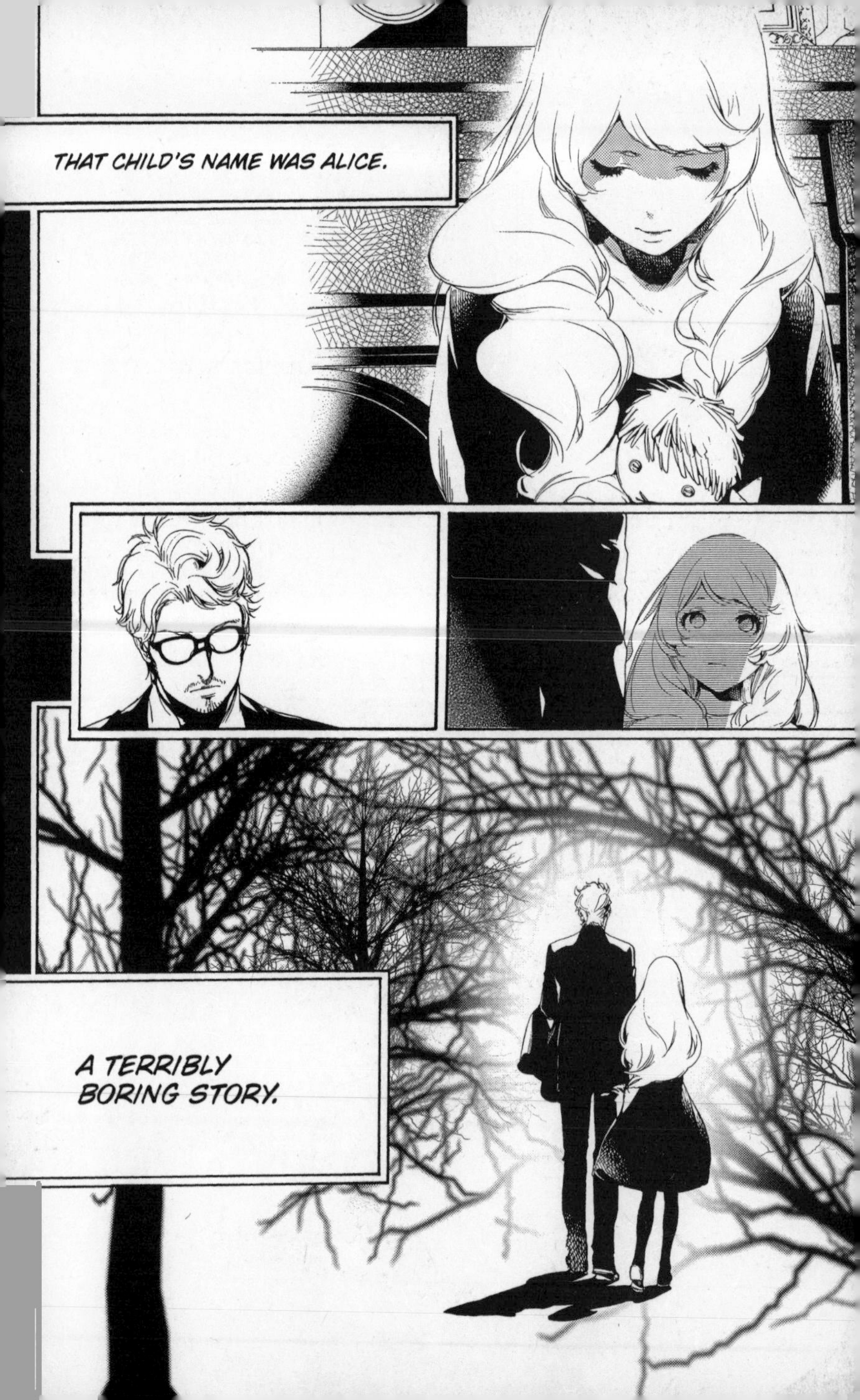
THAT CHILD'S NAME WAS ALICE.
A TERRIBLY BORING STORY.

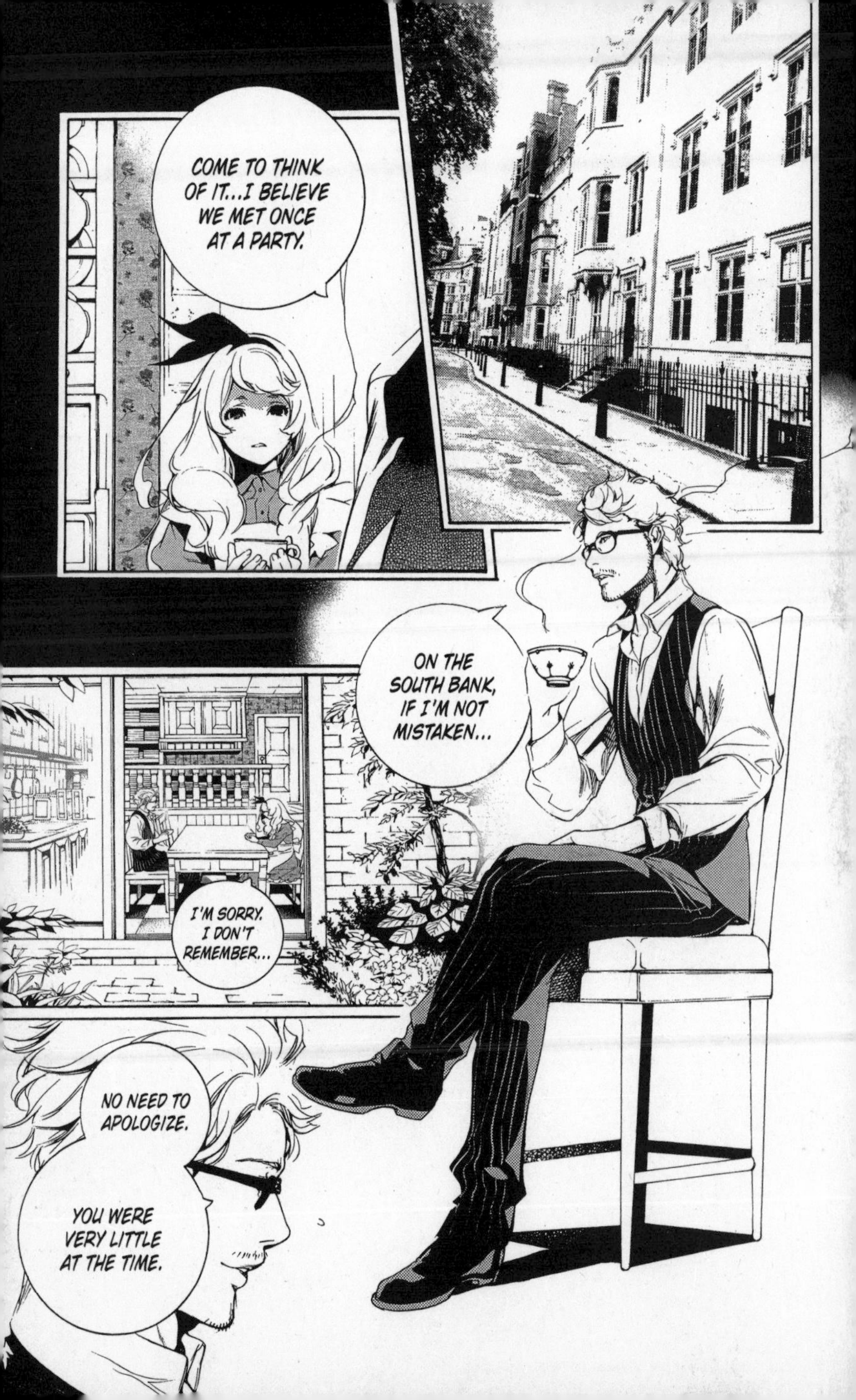
COME TO THINK OF IT...I BELIEVE WE MET ONCE AT A PARTY.
ON THE SOUTH BANK, IF I'M NOT MISTAKEN...
I'M SORRY. I DON'T REMEMBER...
NO NEED TO APOLOGIZE.
YOU WERE VERY LITTLE AT THE TIME.

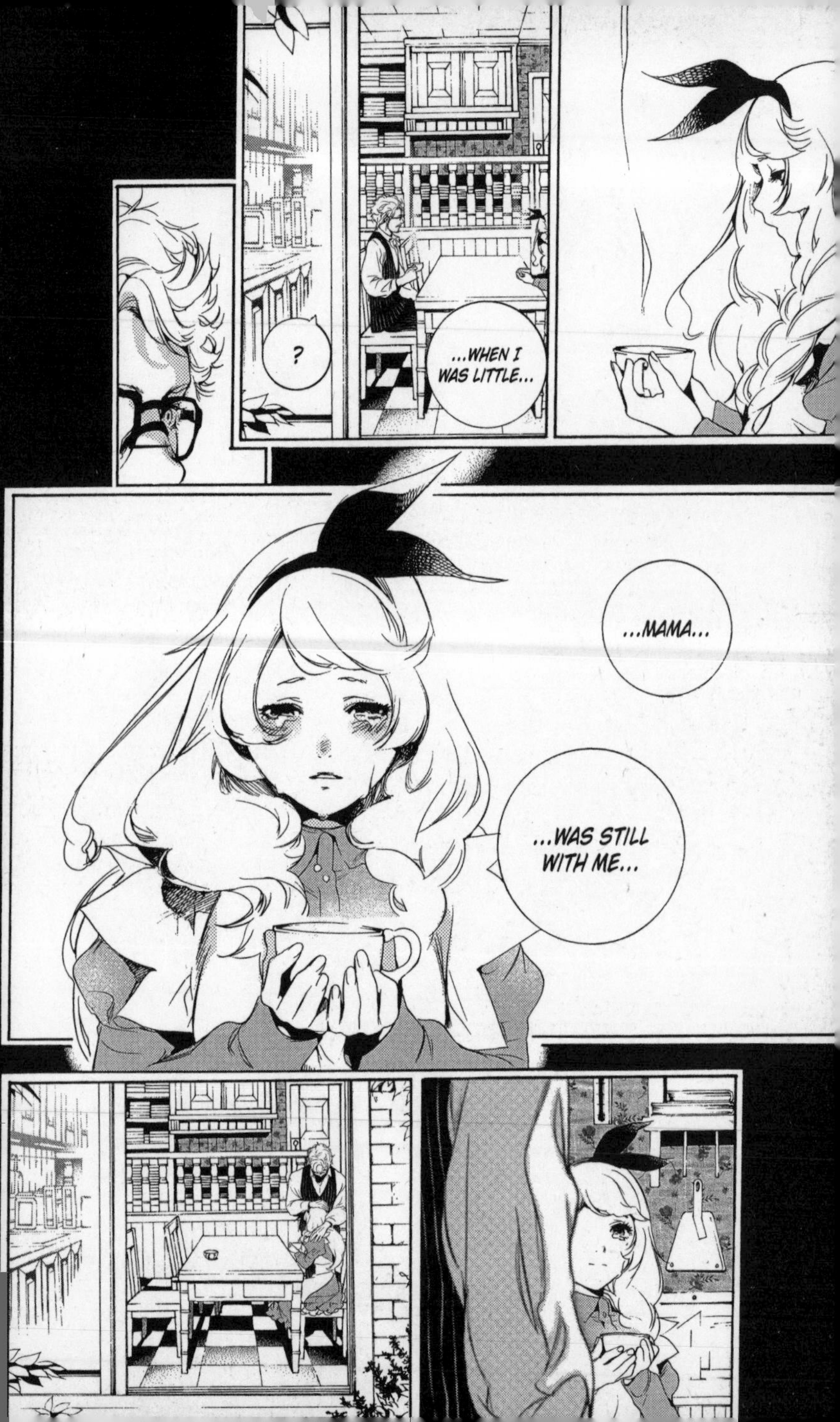
...WHEN I WAS LITTLE...
?
...MAMA...
...WAS STILL WITH ME...

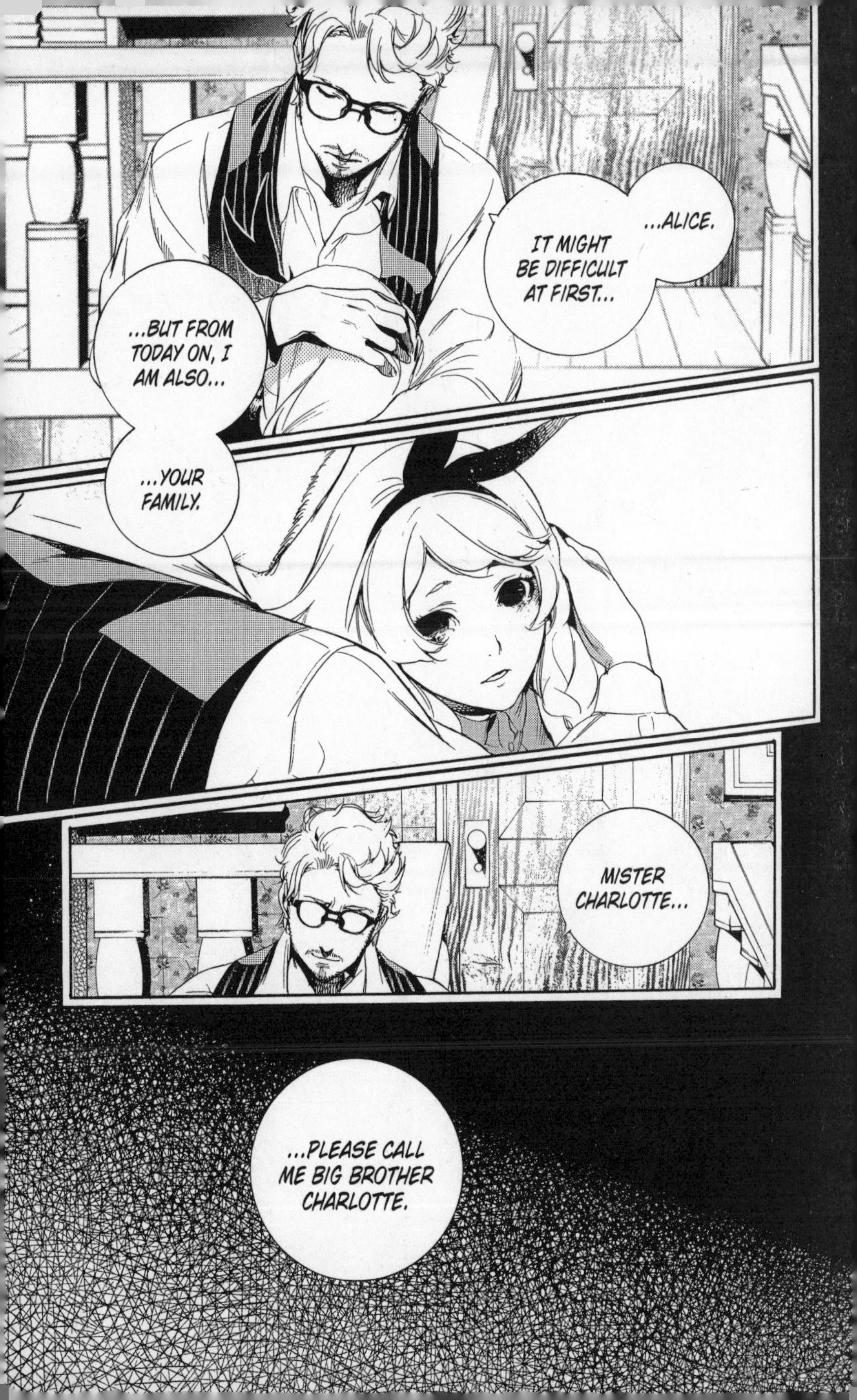
...ALICE.
IT MIGHT BE DIFFICULT AT FIRST...
...BUT FROM TODAY ON, I AM ALSO...
...YOUR FAMILY.
MISTER CHARLOTTE...
...PLEASE CALL ME BIG BROTHER CHARLOTTE.

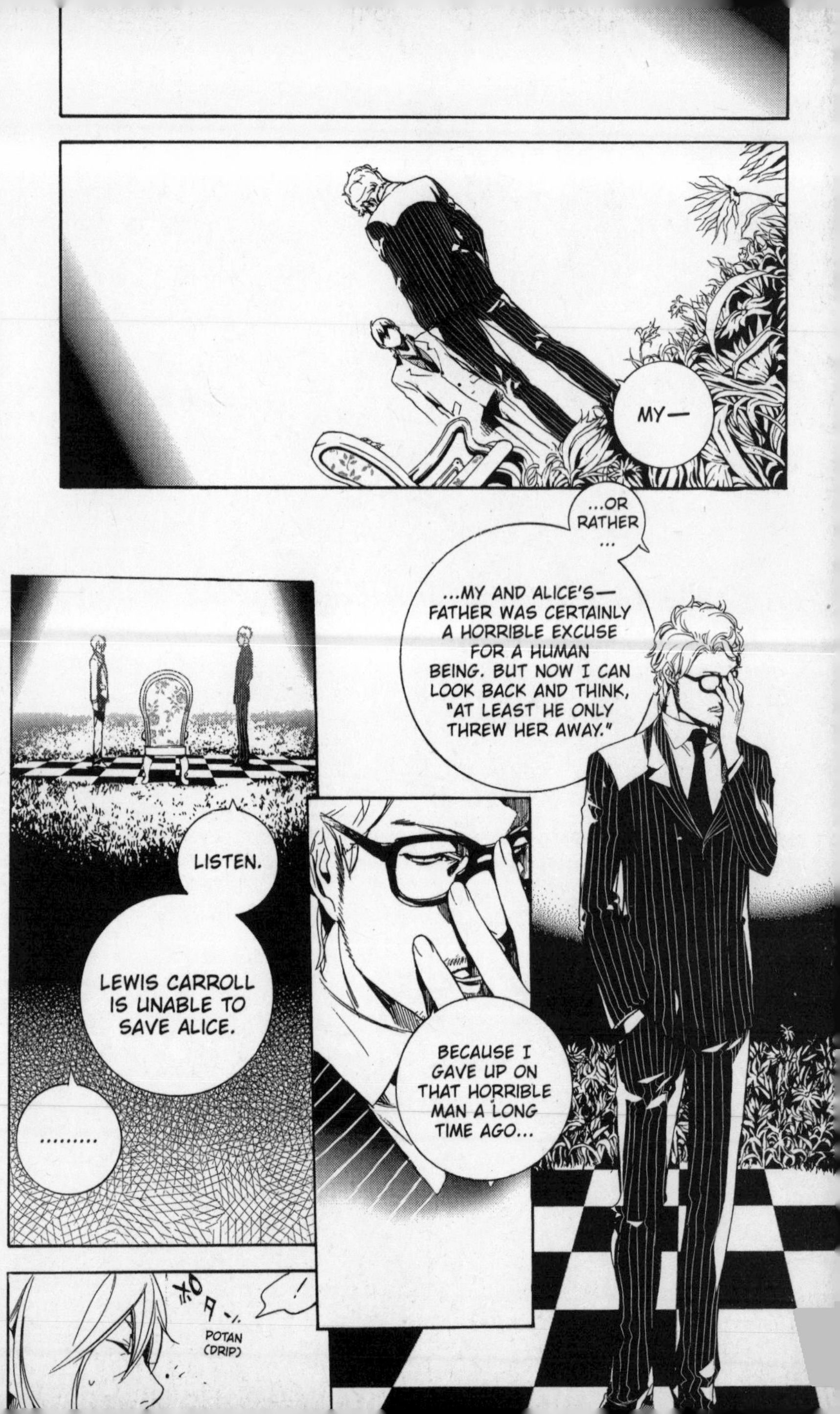
MY—
...OR RATHER ...
...MY AND ALICE'S— FATHER WAS CERTAINLY A HORRIBLE EXCUSE FOR A HUMAN BEING. BUT NOW I CAN LOOK BACK AND THINK, "AT LEAST HE ONLY THREW HER AWAY."
BECAUSE I GAVE UP ON THAT HORRIBLE MAN A LONG TIME AGO...
LISTEN.
LEWIS CARROLL IS UNABLE TO SAVE ALICE.
....
!
POTAN (DRIP)

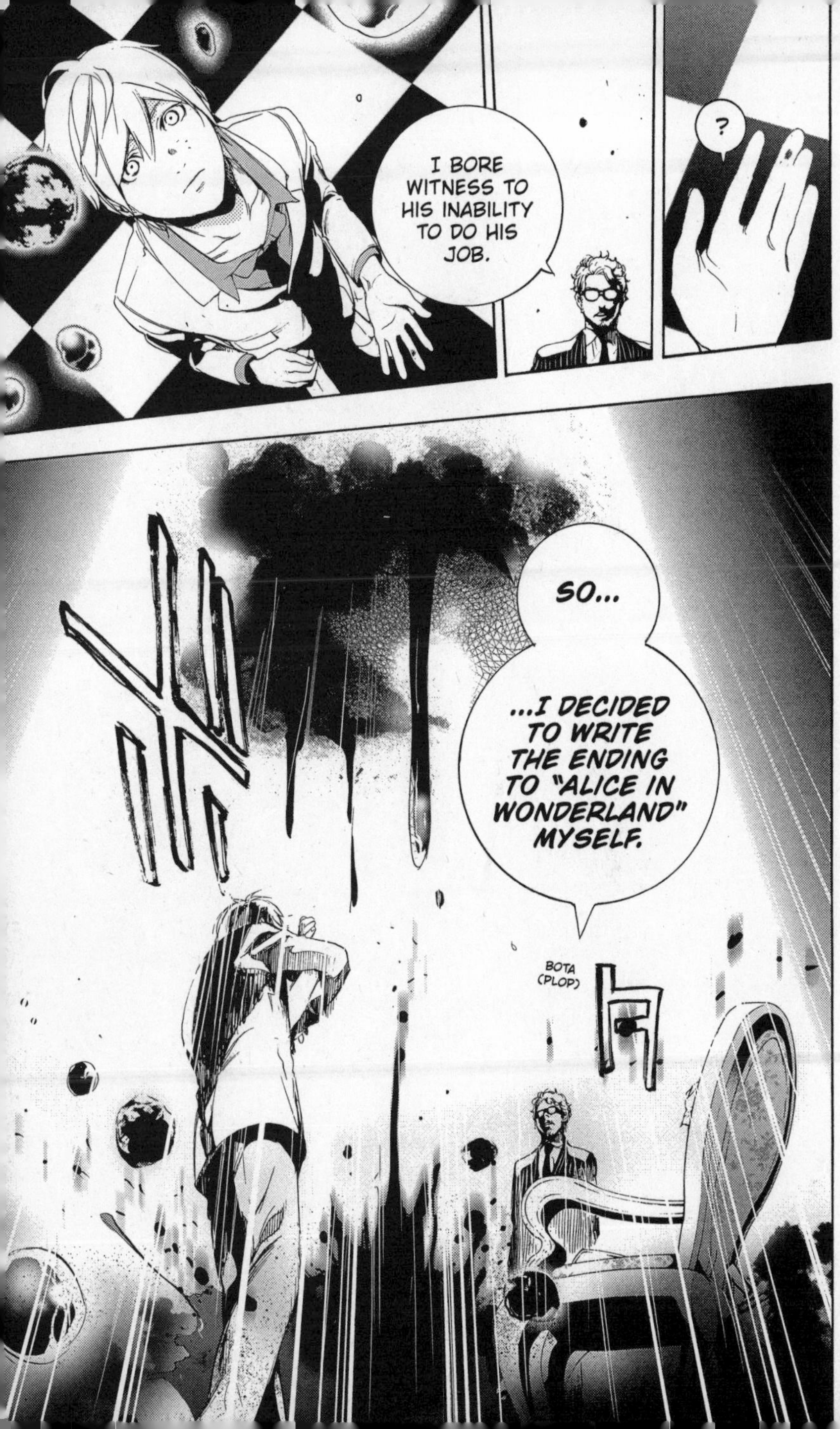
?
I BORE WITNESS TO HIS INABILITY TO DO HIS JOB.
SO...
...I DECIDED TO WRITE THE ENDING TO "ALICE IN WONDERLAND" MYSELF.
BOTA (PLOP)

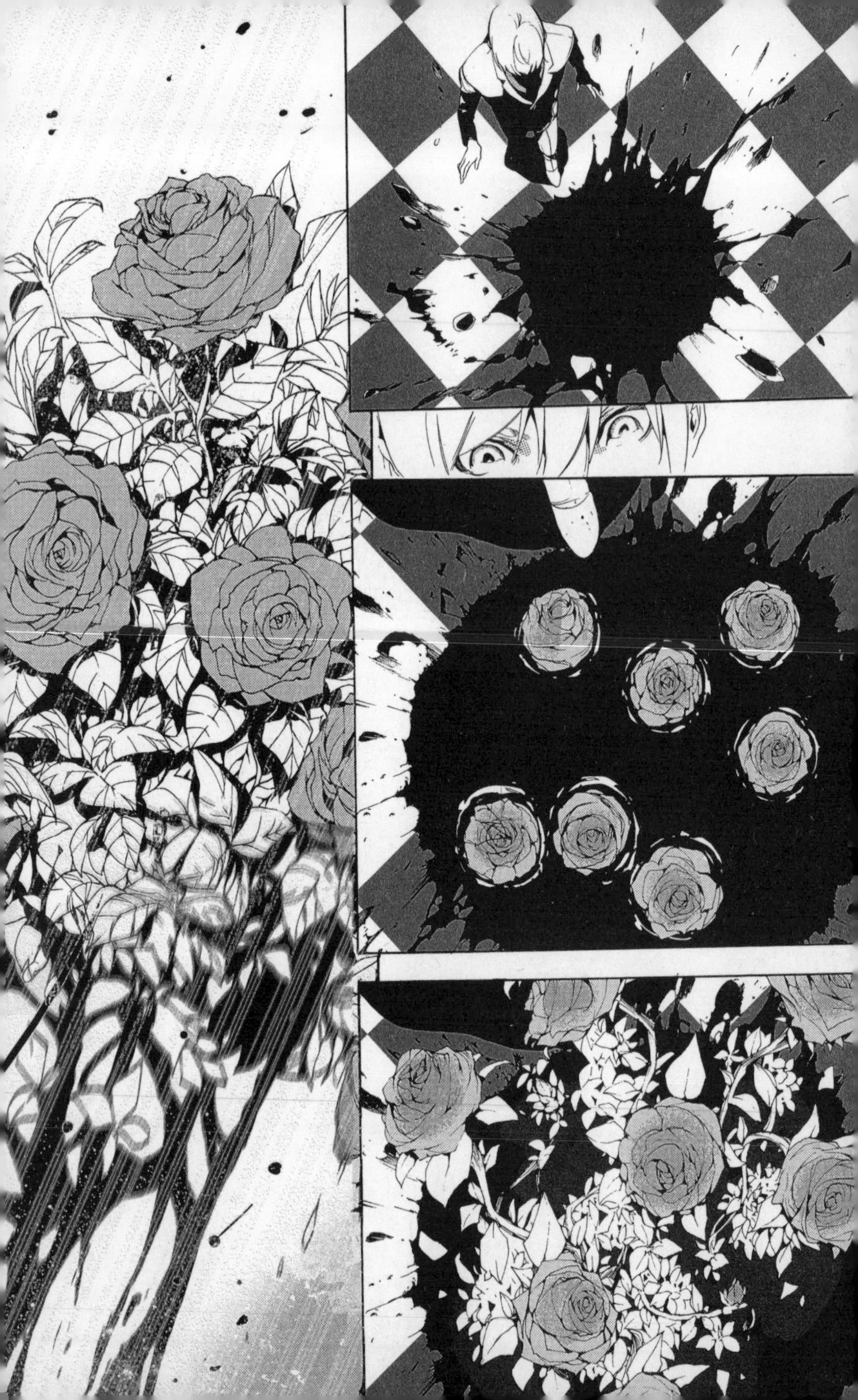

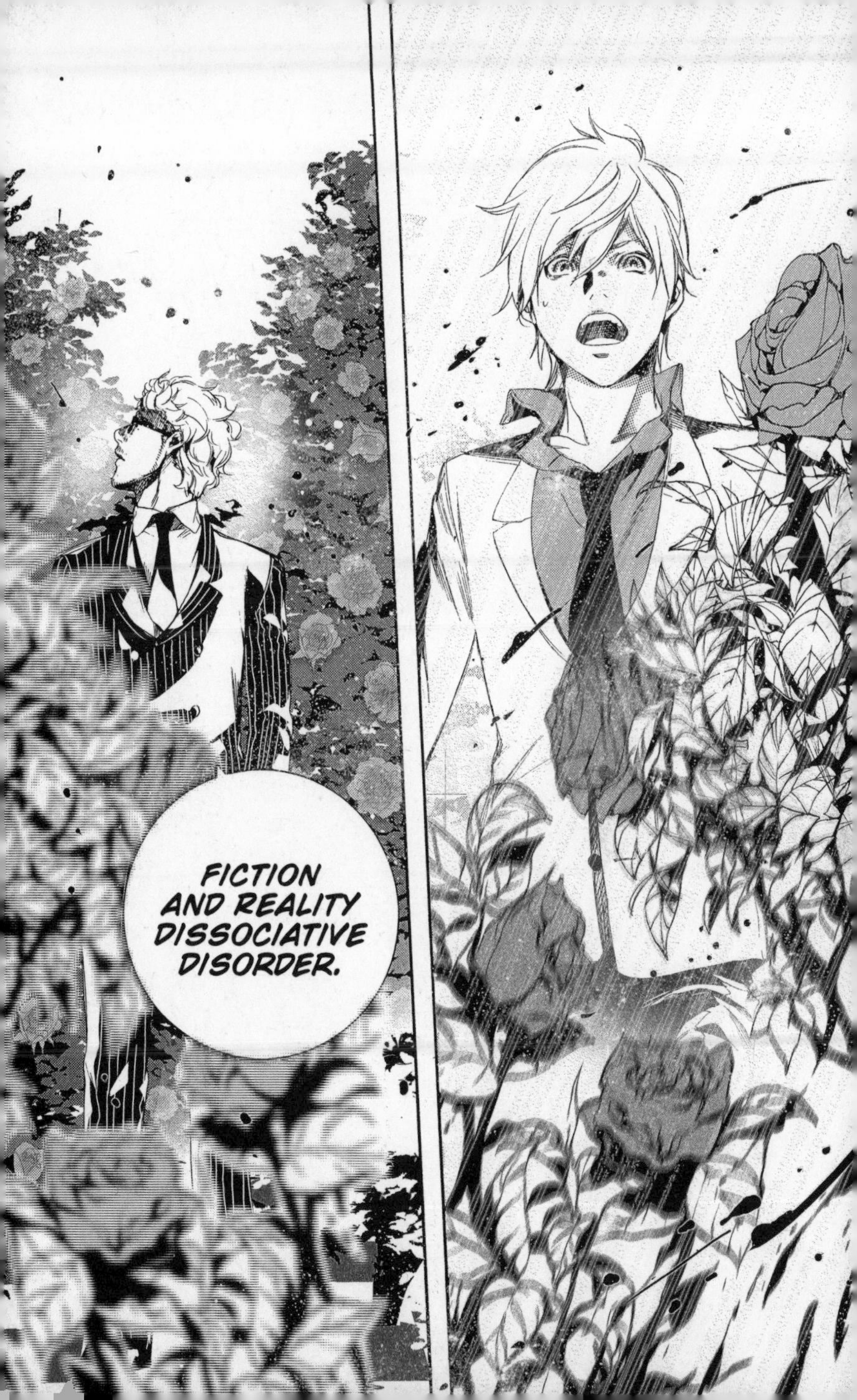
FICTION AND REALITY DISSOCIATIVE DISORDER.

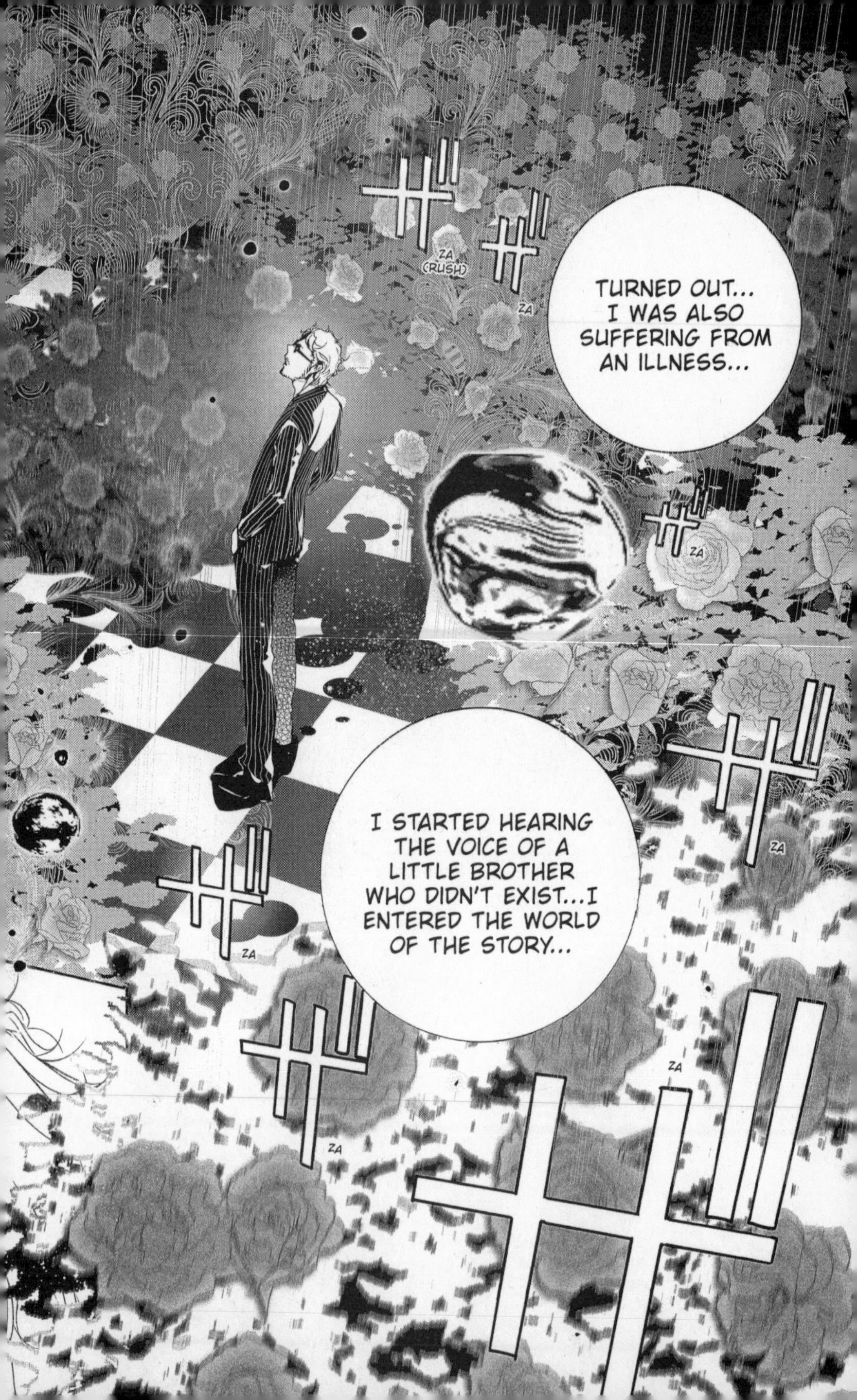
ZA
(RUSH)
ZA
TURNED OUT... I WAS ALSO SUFFERING FROM AN ILLNESS...
ZA
ZA
I STARTED HEARING THE VOICE OF A LITTLE BROTHER WHO DIDN'T EXIST...I ENTERED THE WORLD OF THE STORY...
ZA
ZA
ZA

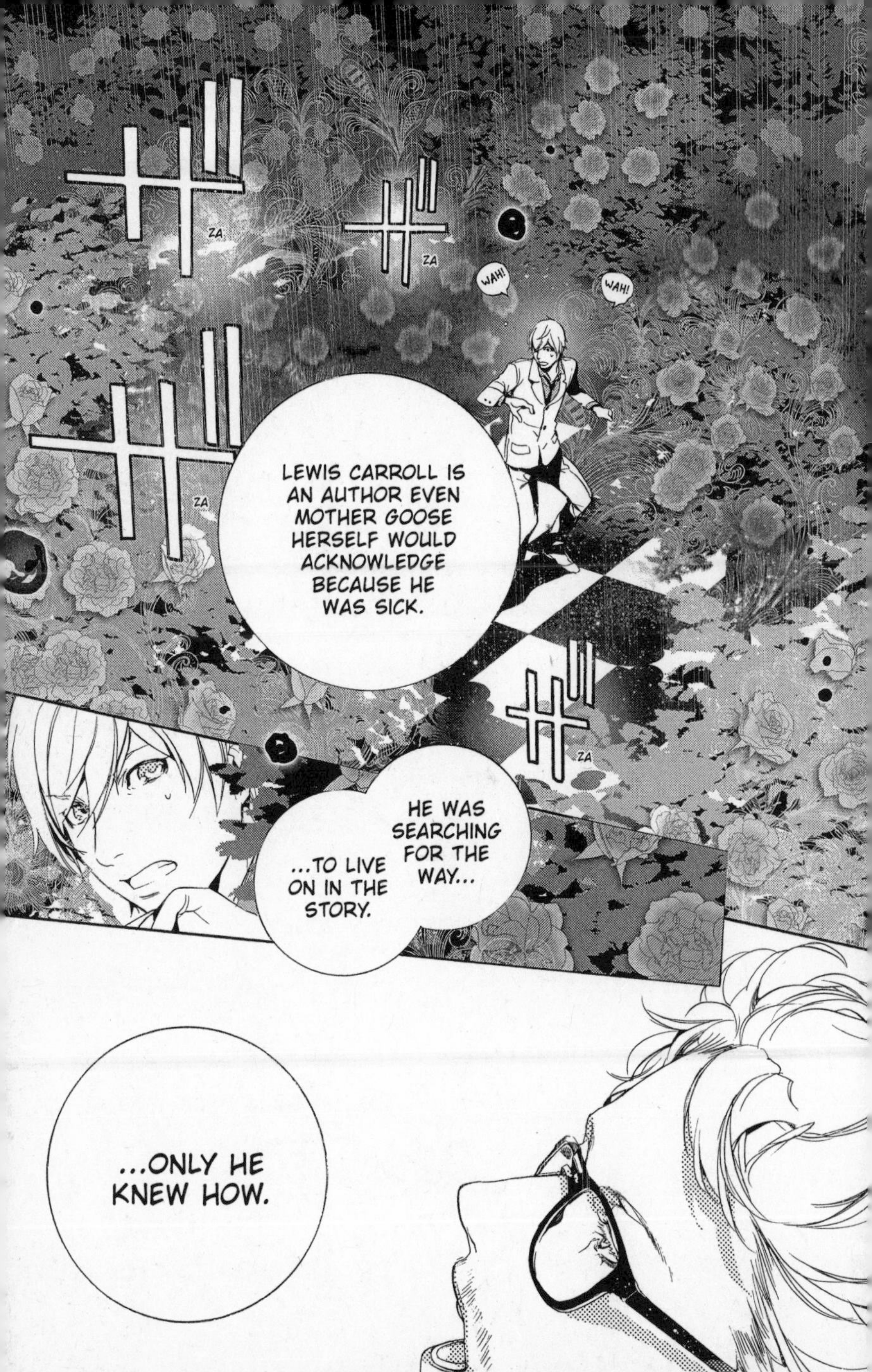
WAH!
WAH!
ZA
ZA
ZA
ZA
LEWIS CARROLL IS AN AUTHOR EVEN MOTHER GOOSE HERSELF WOULD ACKNOWLEDGE BECAUSE HE WAS SICK.
HE WAS SEARCHING FOR THE WAY...
...TO LIVE ON IN THE STORY.
...ONLY HE KNEW HOW.

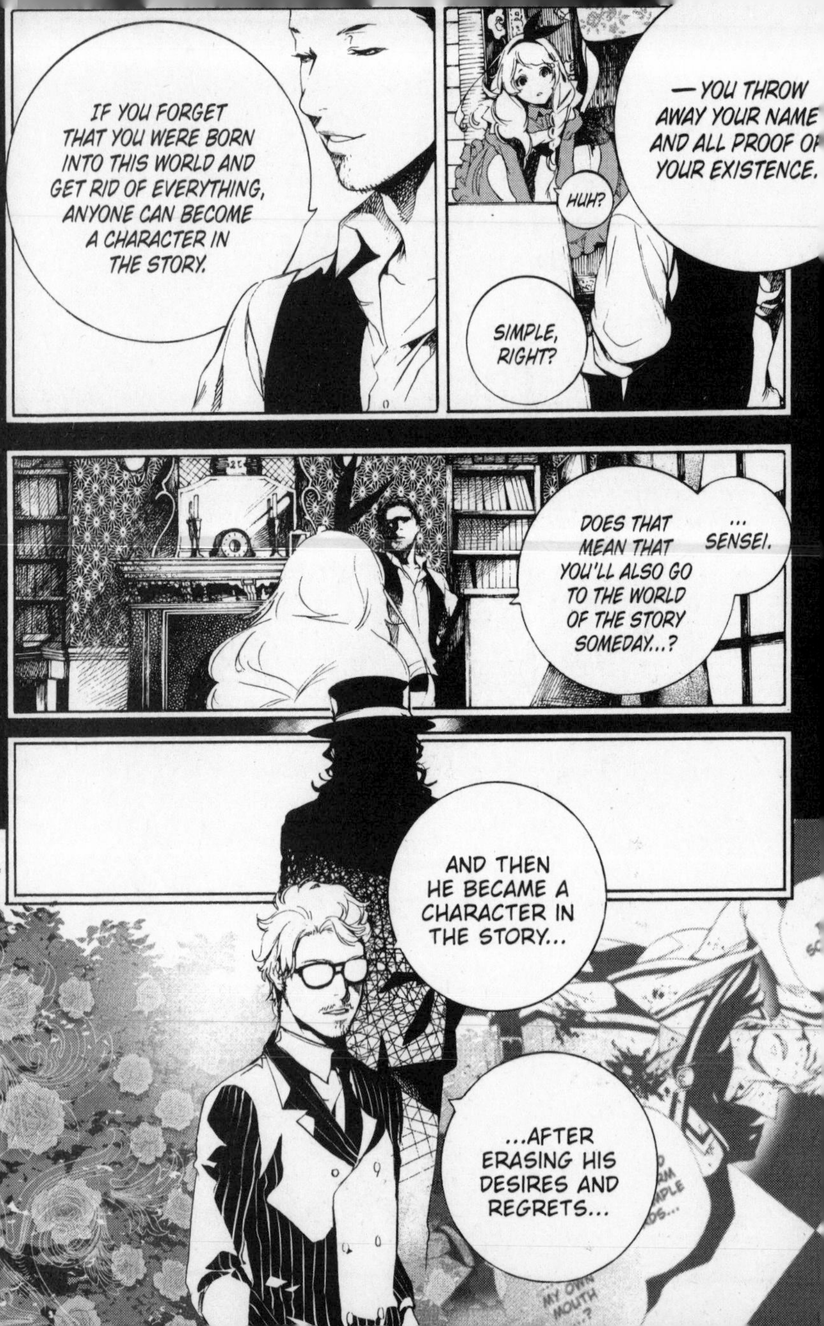
—YOU THROW AWAY YOUR NAME AND ALL PROOF OF YOUR EXISTENCE.
HUH?
SIMPLE, RIGHT?
IF YOU FORGET THAT YOU WERE BORN INTO THIS WORLD AND GET RID OF EVERYTHING, ANYONE CAN BECOME A CHARACTER IN THE STORY.
... SENSEI.
DOES THAT MEAN THAT YOU'LL ALSO GO TO THE WORLD OF THE STORY SOMEDAY...?
AND THEN HE BECAME A CHARACTER IN THE STORY...
...AFTER ERASING HIS DESIRES AND REGRETS...
...MY OWN MOUTH

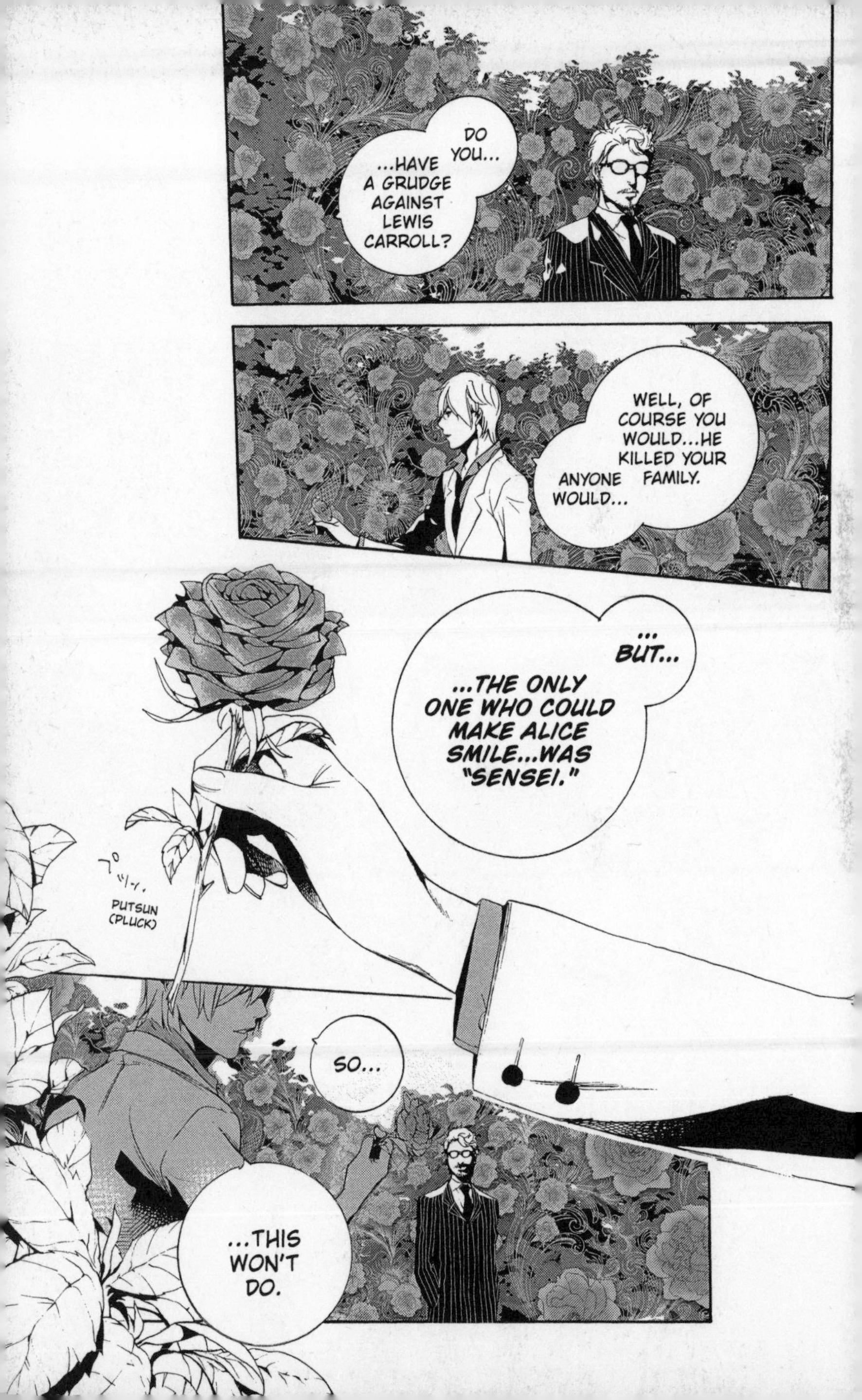
DO YOU... ...HAVE A GRUDGE AGAINST LEWIS CARROLL?
WELL, OF COURSE YOU WOULD...HE KILLED YOUR FAMILY.
ANYONE WOULD...
... BUT...
...THE ONLY ONE WHO COULD MAKE ALICE SMILE...WAS "SENSEI."
プツン
PUTSUN (PLUCK)
SO...
...THIS WON'T DO.

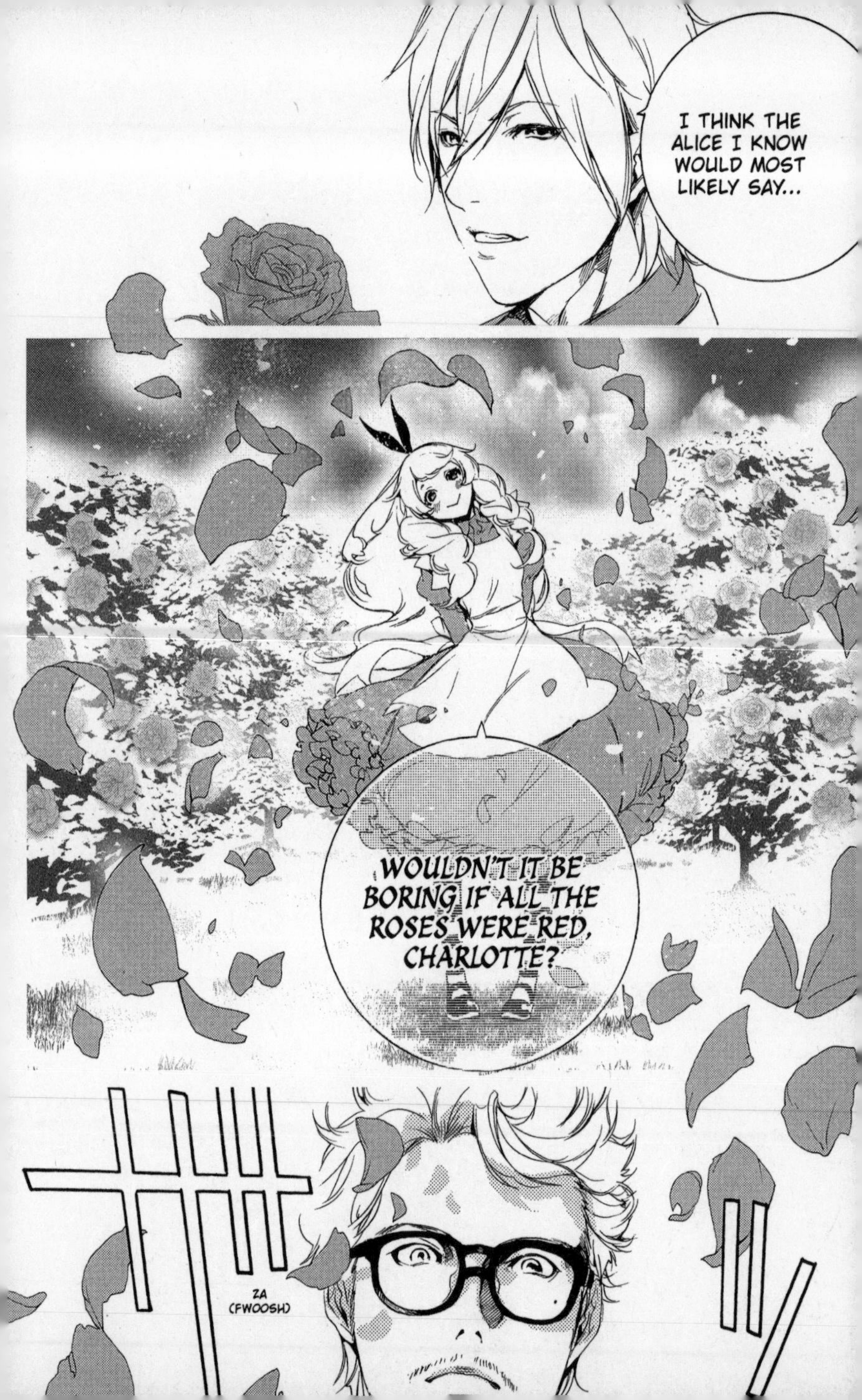
I THINK THE ALICE I KNOW WOULD MOST LIKELY SAY...
WOULDN'T IT BE BORING IF ALL THE ROSES WERE RED, CHARLOTTE?
ZA (FWOOSH)

"WHY ARE YOU PAINTING THOSE ROSES?"

FIVE AND SEVEN SAID NOTHING, BUT LOOKED AT TWO. TWO BEGAN IN A LOW VOICE...

"WHY THE FACT IS, YOU SEE, MISS, THIS HERE OUGHT TO HAVE BEEN A RED ROSE TREE, AND WE PUT A WHITE ONE IN BY MISTAKE; AND IF THE QUEEN WAS TO FIND IT OUT, WE SHOULD ALL HAVE OUR HEADS CUT OFF, YOU KNOW. SO YOU SEE, MISS, WE'RE DOING OUR BEST, AFORE SHE COMES, TO—"

AT THIS MOMENT, FIVE, WHO HAD BEEN ANXIOUSLY LOOKING ACROSS THE GARDEN, CALLED OUT...

"THE QUEEN! THE QUEEN!"

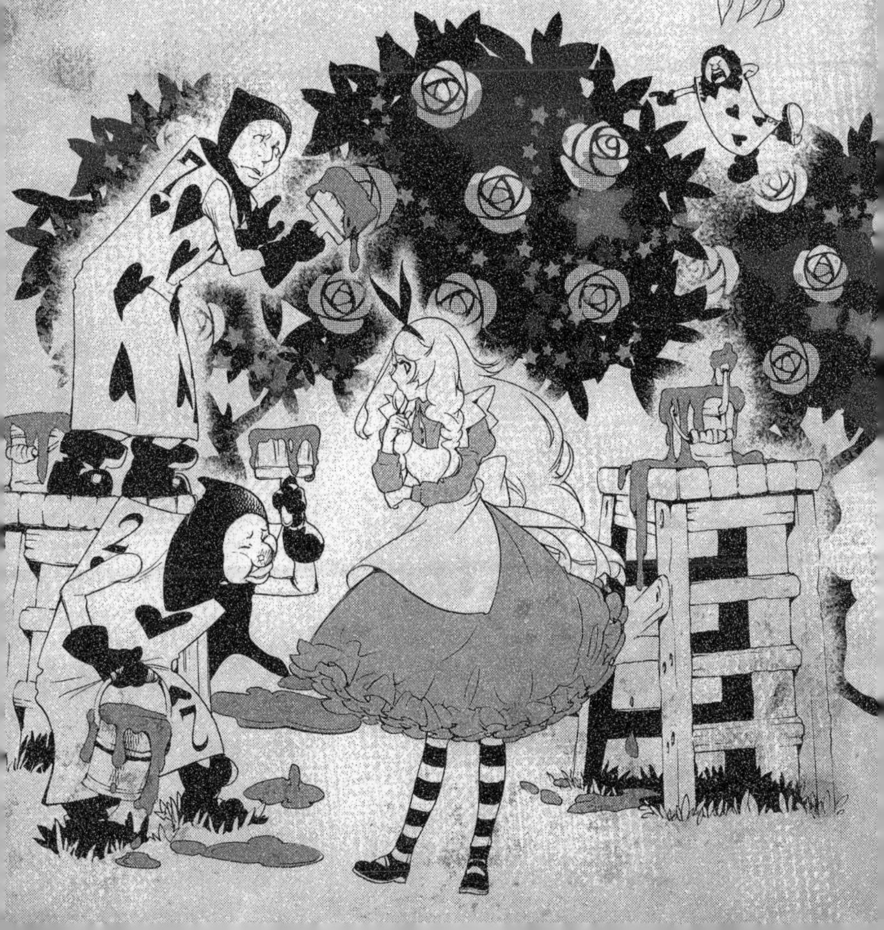

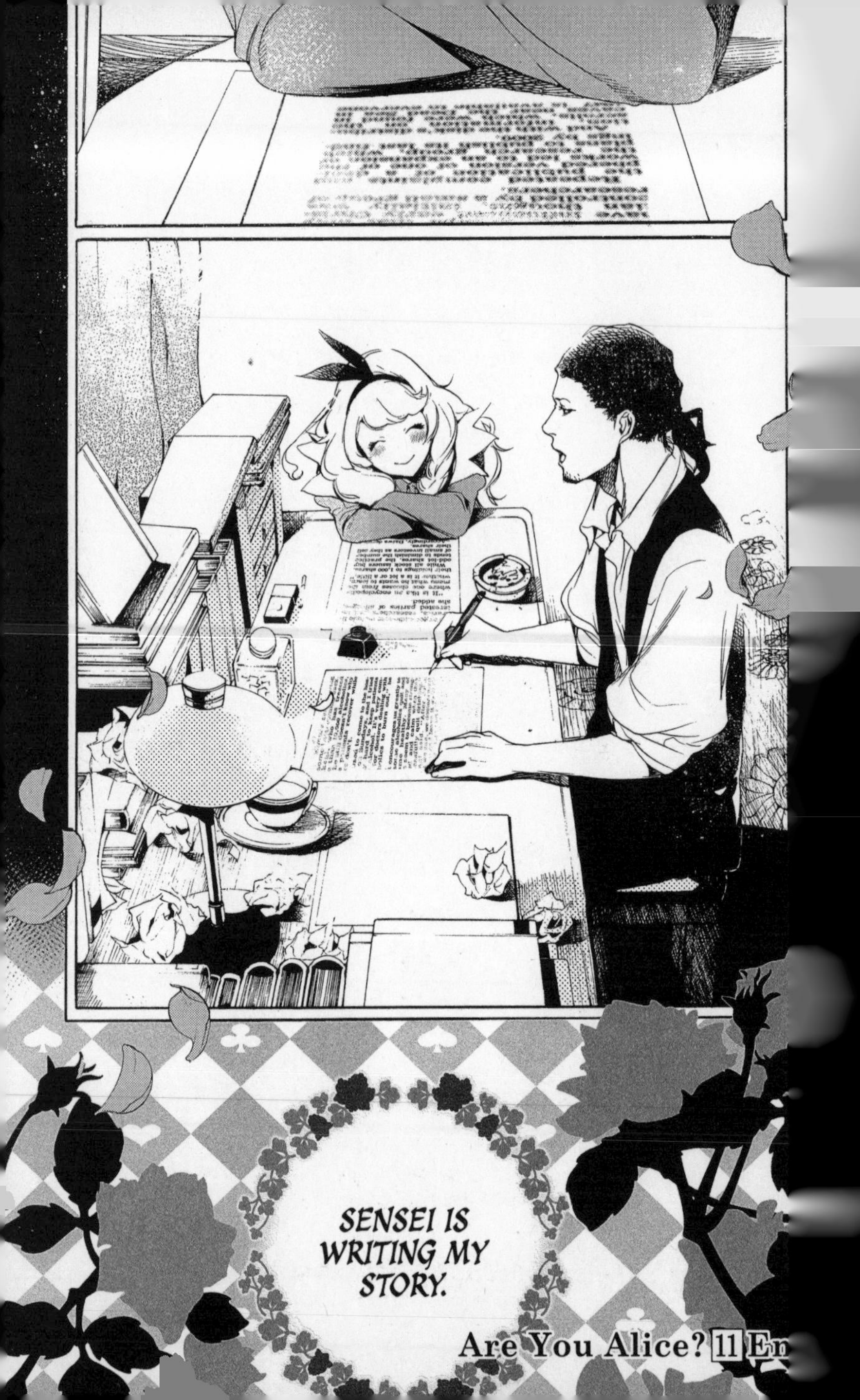
SENSEI IS WRITING MY STORY.
Are You Alice? 11 En

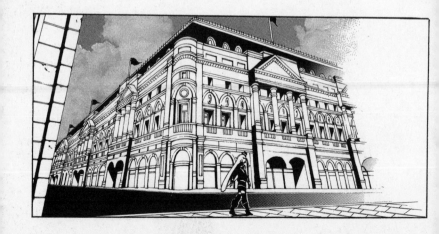

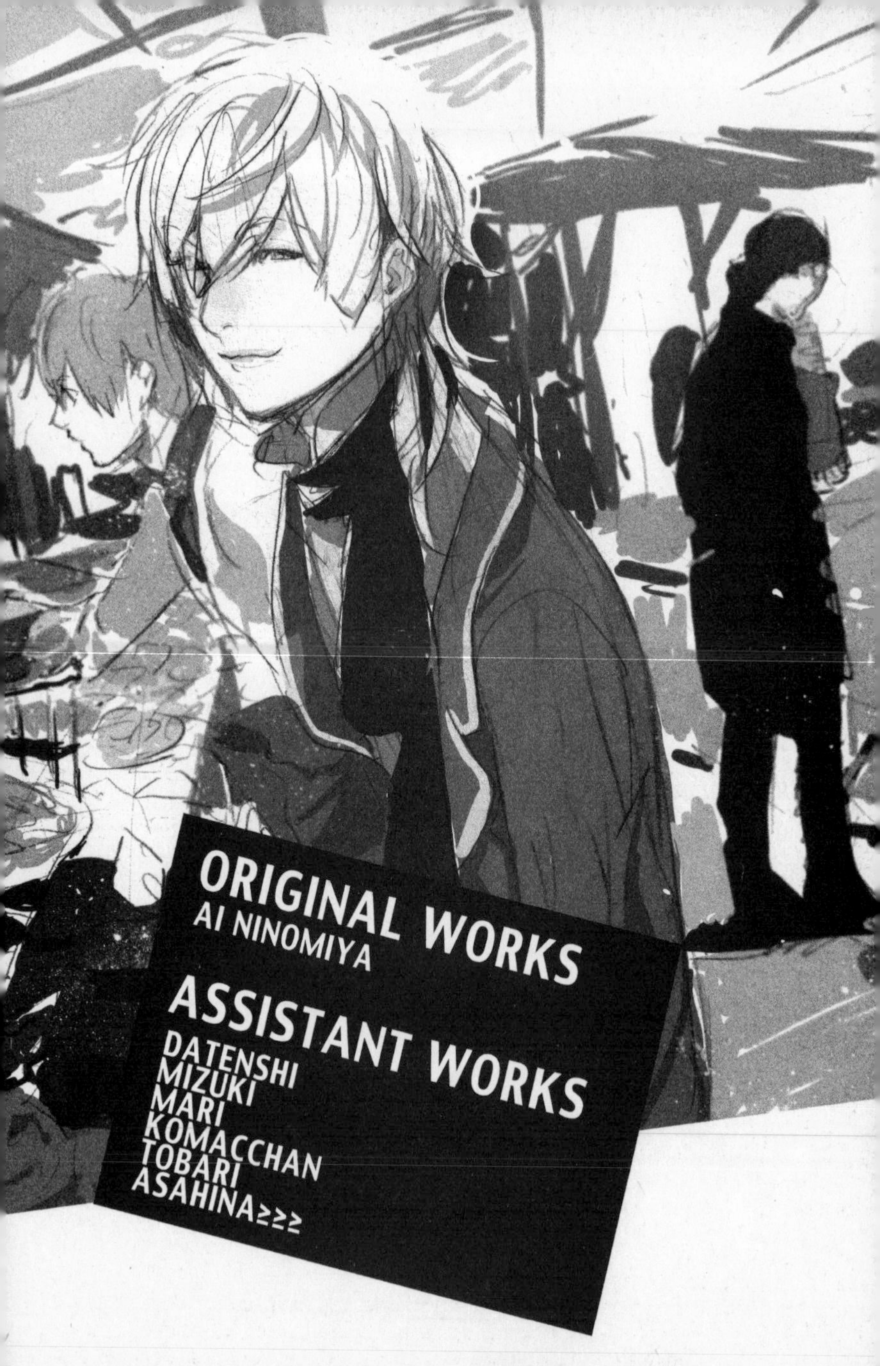
ORIGINAL WORKS
AI NINOMIYA
ASSISTANT WORKS
DATENSHI
MIZUKI
MARI
KOMACCHAN
TOBARI
ASAHINA≥≥≥

In addition to the March Hare and the Jack of Hearts, the mysterious egg man, Humpty Dumpty (a pseudonym), also makes an appearance—providing much comic relief—as a guest character in the extra drama CD *Are You Alice? Alice's Tea Party* series.

I can't believe we've lasted all the way to Volume 11...

These boys with wonderful, comedic soul... or should I say, strong conviction.

I'm always looking forward to your messages of support.

And with that, I hope to see you again in Volume 12!

Ai Ninomiya

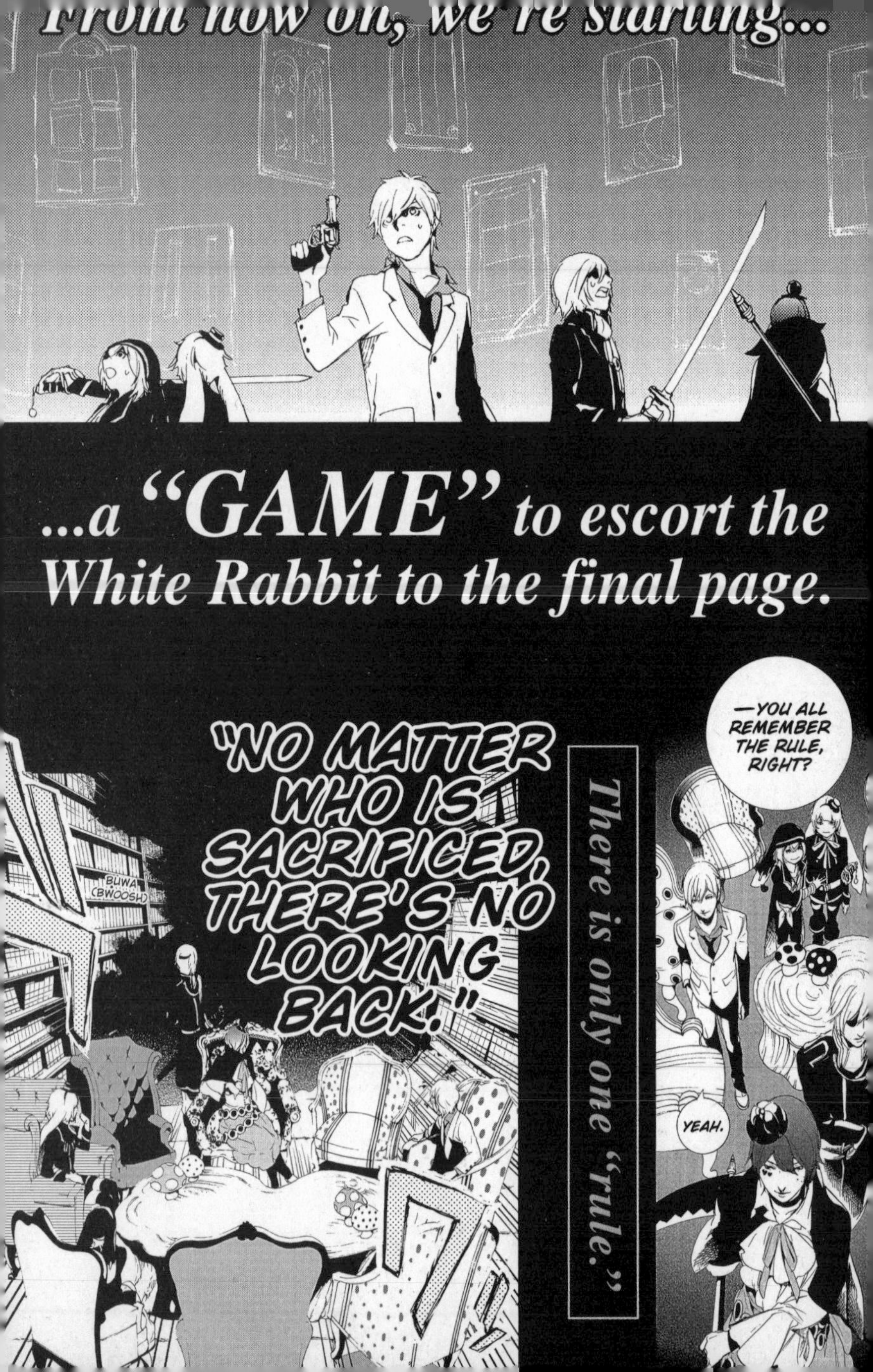
From now on, we're starting...
...a "GAME" to escort the White Rabbit to the final page.
—YOU ALL REMEMBER THE RULE, RIGHT?
YEAH.
There is only one "rule."
"NO MATTER WHO IS SACRIFICED, THERE'S NO LOOKING BACK."
BUWA (BWOOSH)

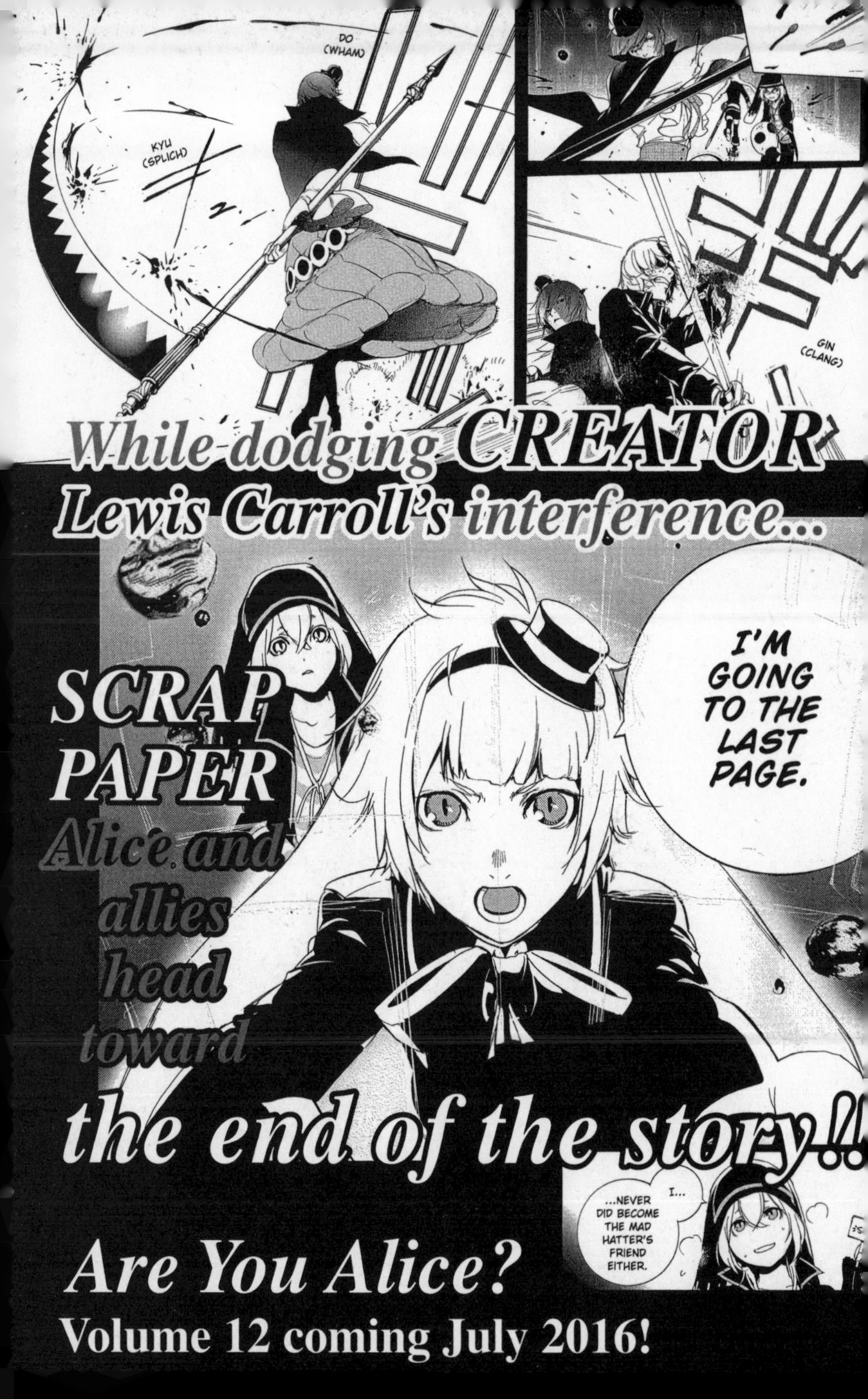
GIN (CLANG)
DO (WHAM)
KYU (SPLICH)
While dodging CREATOR Lewis Carroll's interference...
I'M GOING TO THE LAST PAGE.
SCRAP PAPER
Alice and allies head toward
the end of the story!!
I...
...NEVER DID BECOME THE MAD HATTER'S FRIEND EITHER.
Are You Alice?
Volume 12 coming July 2016!

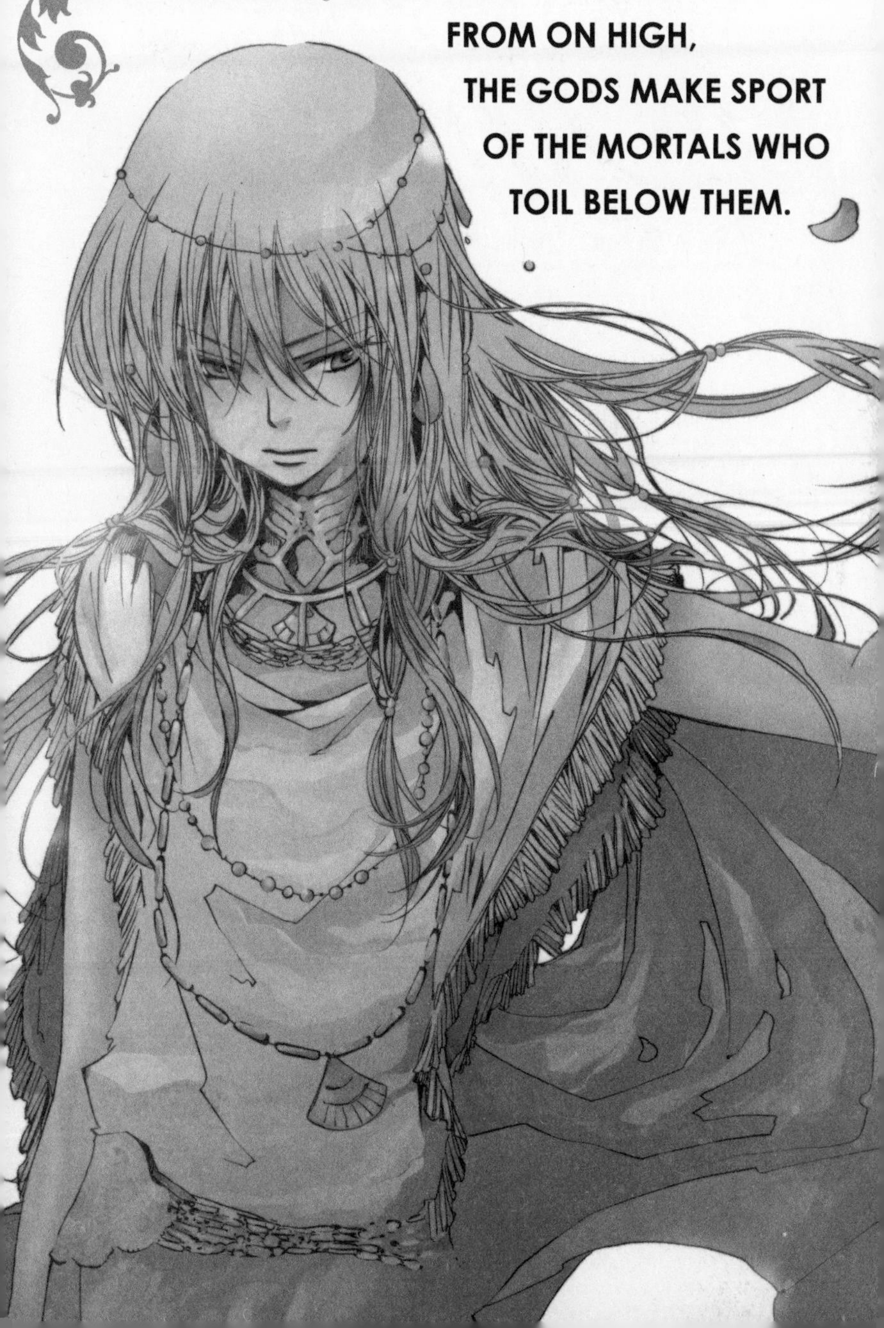
FROM ON HIGH,
THE GODS MAKE SPORT
OF THE MORTALS WHO
TOIL BELOW THEM.

ARE YOU ALICE? 11

IKUMI KATAGIRI
AI NINOMIYA

Translation and Lettering: Alexis Eckerman

Are you Alice? © 2015 by Ai Ninomiya / Ikumi Katagiri. © IM/Re;no, Inc. All rights reserved. First published in Japan in 2015 by ICHIJINSHA. English translation rights arranged with ICHIJINSHA through Tuttle-Mori Agency, Inc., Tokyo.

Translation © 2016 by Hachette Book Group, Inc.

Yen Press
Hachette Book Group
1290 Avenue of the Americas
New York, NY 10104

www.HachetteBookGroup.com
www.YenPress.com

Yen Press is an imprint of Hachette Book Group, Inc. The Yen Press name and logo are trademarks of Hachette Book Group, Inc.

The publisher is not responsible for websites (or their content) that are not owned by the publisher.

Library of Congress Control Number: 2015952600

First Yen Press Edition: February 2016

ISBN: 978-0-316-26908-7

10 9 8 7 6 5 4 3 2 1

BVG

Printed in the United States of America